DEEP HARMONY

by

Grenville Jones

ISBN-13: 978-1517271930
ISBN-10: 1517271932

With fond Memories of Mr Brutus

All the characters in *Deep Harmony* are fictional.

Any resemblance to people alive, dead, or singing in your choir is entirely coincidental.

CONTENTS

The choir website is: www.verlis-singers.org.uk

ACKNOWLEDGMENTS

The hundreds of singers and audiences across the world who I have encouraged to sing and smile and Brian McGee who looked over my shoulder.

Guidance Notes

A mixed voice adult choir normally sings in four parts: **S A T B** – **S**oprano **A**lto **T**enor **B**ass.

There are ladies with high voices who sing soprano or alto (ladies with lower voices) and men with high voices who sing tenor or bass, the men with the deep voices. Some choirs who struggle to attract men may sing in three parts as SAB. Therefore all the men will sing, together, a line written in the bass clef of the music.

Note: A clue to a person's voice usually comes from the speaking voice but there are exceptions. The conductor auditioning a man with a rich low speaking voice may be surprised to discover that he can hit the high notes of the tenor range with ease.

A mezzo-soprano has a range that enables her to sing either soprano or alto. There are however more solos for sopranos, so most mezzos desire to join the soprano section in a choir.

Most men these days fall into the baritone voice category. Sadly there are fewer and fewer true top (high) tenors or deep bass-voiced singers. Conductors therefore have to make the most out of men with baritone voices allocating them into either the tenor or bass sections of the choir.

Sadly, the wearing of tight underpants does not help men hit the high notes. If it did, the wearing of saggy boxer shorts would assist the singing of lower notes and that is also not the case.

Sight-reading is the ability to look at a score of music for the first time and sing it straight off. Most choir members learn to sight read to an acceptable standard but will never say, '*I am a sight reader.*'

Being able to sight-read does not necessarily mean having a good voice. Many professional singers are not particularly good sight-readers.

As with all things, it should never be forgotten that practice makes perfect.

Soprano voices – '*the sops*'. A mixed-voice choir is as good (or bad) as its soprano section. It is the most important section in a choir, usually singing the melody line. A good true soprano section maintains a strong sound that is 'in tune'. This enables the other sections to hear the melody and balance their voices against that clear sound.

Conductors love sopranos, but not all at the same time. Because they are so important to the choir conductor this explains why most, if not all, sopranos are divas.

Choir conductors should beware the charming new soprano who auditions for his or her choir, when she pleads, '*Please* do not ask me to sing a solo,' she actually means the opposite: 'Ask another soprano to sing a solo instead of me and I will stand for election as a choir committee member and make your life a living hell.'

In a boys' choir the soprano (top) line is sung by boys with angelic treble voices. Think here King's College Cambridge and Christmas Eve on the BBC – you've got it!

Some ladies have voices, which have that clear tone of a boy's treble voice. They are to be cosseted, however obnoxious they may be, as they may be needed to sing the solo in the first verse of *Once in Royal David's City* at the annual Christmas carol service, and therefore make the audience weep.

Alto voices are, more often than not, sopranos who read music. Quite often they are married to a man in the choir. This is excellent for recruiting choir members for an away tour as singing couples like to go together.

A good alto section is a bonus for a choir leader. True altos who possess rich, low voices are a godsend but altos do tend to be the choir members who talk all the way through rehearsals. Their commitment to being a choir member can also mean that they are in the front line when tea and cake making is required for a choir social. The chatting, whilst irritating, is therefore worth tolerating.

In some choirs, where men are in short supply, selected (non-tea making) altos will sing the tenor line. This usually means the choir is in decline and will disband imminently.

Some men have alto (falsetto) voices; they are called counter tenors. *Sun* or *Mirror* readers will snigger at the sound of them singing and make remarks such as, 'He sings like a girl.' Knowledgeable musicians will react in a different way but secretly think, *He sings like a girl.*

Note: *never ever tell a counter tenor to his face, 'You sing like a girl.' The chances are that he will be a testosterone-fuelled heterosexual male with a delightful wife and six kids. He will punch you on the nose.*

Tenors (gold dust!) are men with naturally high voices who do not have to sing falsetto to reach the top notes. Good tenors are few and far between and can get away with missing (or arriving at the last minute for) rehearsals, just turning up for concerts and generally being arrogant.

This is bloody annoying if you are a soprano, alto or bass, but a fact of choir life!

Note: *Some tenors are baritone singers who do slip into a falsetto range above a high G. Not ideal, but far better than a lady amongst the tenor section. It should be noted that there are some true lady tenors. They are few and far between, but they do exist.*

Bass singers form the *base* of the choir. Bass singers who join a choir from a brass band background should wear a label around their neck saying '*potential shit stirrer*', as they will use their superior sight-reading skills to humble others who know not a dotted crotchet when they see it. The unsuspecting choir conductor should also be on his or her guard.

As previously explained, many baritones find themselves in the bass section.

One positive point about bass singers is that they are the choir drinkers. They are always first to the bar and eager to purchase the choir conductor a bevvy.

Much modern choir music is written by people who know that voices have changed and therefore do not ask basses to venture below bottom G – all is therefore not lost.

Enjoy your singing! If you are not in a choir – why not join one?

www.verlis-singers.org.uk

Hear them sing on the choir website.

Deep Harmony

These are words written by Isaac Watts (1674-1748), an English hymn-writer, theologian and logician. He wrote over 700 hymns and many are still sung.

The tune came from the pen of a Yorkshire man, Handel Parker in the early 1900s. He was one of a large family of musicians, most of whom were named after composers.

Sweet is the work, my God, my King,
To praise Thy Name, give thanks and sing,
To show Thy love by morning light
And talk of all Thy truth at night.

Quote:

'*I hate that bloody hymn.*'
– Patrick Nicholls QC, a bass in The Verlis Singers.

In Memoriam

1921-2002

Members of the Grenfell family welcome friends to share in a celebration of the life and music of Isaac Kevern Grenfell, OBE at Verlis Cathedral on Wednesday, November 6th 2002 at 2pm.

These words had been printed in the Cornish Leader for two weeks in October, following the death in August, in Verlis General Hospital, of Isaac Grenfell aged 81. He was at home in the council house where he had lived for the past 57 years, playing the cello when he had suffered a massive stroke. Despite the efforts of doctors and nursing staff at the Verlis hospital, little could be done to save him.

***

November 6th 2002

Len Fyfield and his wife Mellyn had arrived at Verlis Cathedral an hour before the memorial service for Isaac Grenfell was due to start.

David Grenfell, Isaac's eldest son, had shown them to their reserved seats in the centre aisle, something of an honour as these seemed to be the only reserved places in the whole Cathedral. Mellyn was reading a newspaper cutting she had in her handbag, taken from the previous week's Cornish Leader. They had produced a whole page spread on the man they called 'Cornwall's Mr Music'. It included a nice quote from her husband Len, with his picture and referring to his

2

singing years in the choir with Isaac.

'Isn't that Isaac's grandson over there, the one who went to Brazil to live?' she whispered to Len.

'It's a Grenfell family show of strength, luv,' Len replied quietly with a wry smile, squeezing her hand.

BBC South West TV News had reported on the passing of Isaac Grenfell, stating that he was the only choir leader in Cornwall to receive an OBE. They even showed an old *Songs of Praise* clip from the days when he was conductor of The Verlis Singers, saying he had made it, 'one of the finest mixed-voice choirs in the whole of the UK.'

Len whispered, 'It's Isaac's last audience, and a full house. He would love that. There must be a thousand people in here. That's Andy Smith from Farmouth Male Voice Choir over there with a few of their boys. They will try to out sing the rest of the congregation, that's for sure!'

Terry Davies and his wife Joan were sat in a side aisle. Postman Terry had got off work early to attend the service, but the traffic into Verlis had been horrendous. By the time they got to the Cathedral the building was almost full.

'There's some of the Cabourne Choral Society sat over there. They always looked down their noses at Isaac. Bloody hypocrites! Nothing like a big service in the Cathedral to bring out the great and good!' said Terry quietly to Joan.

'Terry, don't swear in church,' responded Joan. 'You had great respect for Isaac, he got you singing. Just remember why you are here.'

Terry continued, 'Sorry love. Look, Tom Grenfell's fiancée is playing the Cathedral organ today. She's at Cambridge University on an organ music scholarship. She's supposed to be brilliant, pity we can't get her to play for our Rotary Christmas service here.'

Amongst the mourners gathered in the majestic Cathedral were many former members of The Verlis Singers, the mixed-voice choir founded by Isaac Grenfell all those years ago in 1952. Faces and voices from the past, now also in their later years. Today was a day for memories, for thoughts of rehearsals past and concerts gone, but not forgotten, and the man who led the choir on its path of inception, harmonic glory and, then, discord.

The organ was suddenly silent, the last notes echoing around from pillar to pillar along the length of the majestic building. Joan put her hand on her husband's arm. 'Shush! Here they come.' The massive wooden doors to the Cathedral swung open and a thousand people turned round to see the funeral cortège enter the main doors, led by the very tall Rev. James Grenfell, grandson of one of Isaac's many brothers.

He had flown in from New Zealand to answer the family call that all Grenfell family members should be on parade. The procession was made up of around a hundred people, including family members who had travelled from across the globe to remember a very special man.

He was Cornwall's renowned 'Mr Music'.

The family had made it clear that no specific choir should be asked to lead the singing. Even the offer of the Cathedral Choir had been politely turned down.

The singing would be led by family members themselves. They filed solemnly into the choir stalls as well as the reserved front pews, leaving space for the six tall young Grenfell men who now carried the coffin in through the massive cathedral doors and down the centre aisle.

The wonderfully clear soprano voice of Jayne Roberts, daughter of Isaacs's sister Helen, soared up to the arches of the roof as the cortege moved down the nave, and, unaccompanied, she sang the first verse of Cornish folk song *The White Rose*. A member of the English Opera Chorus and BBC Singers, her superb voice filled the Cathedral, touching every heart.

As the coffin was placed on the bier and the men withdrew to their pews, she sang without any accompaniment:

Now I am alone, my sweet darling,
I walk through the garden and weep,
But spring will return with your presence
Oh lily white rose, mine to keep.

Of the thousand people in the congregation on that rather warm November afternoon, probably ninety per cent were singers. When the organ played the introduction to the first hymn, *Guide Me O Thou Great Redeemer,* and the congregation burst into song, the atmosphere was overpowering. In its many years of history never before had Verlis Cathedral witnessed such singing from all corners of the magnificent building; for everyone present, an overwhelming experience that would live on in their memories for a long time.

Tributes to the great man were read by three family members: they alluded to his many years of music, his love of everything Cornish, and how he had influenced so many people through his natural gift of musicianship and choral interpretation. At no time during the memorial service was any reference made by name to the choir he founded, The Verlis Singers.

Mellyn whispered to Len, 'Not a single mention of The Verlis Singers, that's really so very sad, what a great shame.' The family had certainly not forgotten or forgiven the way Isaac had been unceremoniously kicked out of the choir he had started. On this day of all days there was a point to be made, and made it certainly was.

Jayne sang again, this time the beautiful *Pie Jesu* from the Faure Requiem, with organ accompaniment, and the service proceeded with the lusty singing of more hymns: *How Great Thou Art* (a favourite of Isaac's), *Just as I Am*, and ending with Parry's *The Day thou Gavest Lord is Ended*. Isaac Grenfell had loved the music of Charles Hubert Parry.

Printed at the back of the service sheet were the words of the hymn *Deep Harmony*. This hymn held a very special significance to the life of Isaac Grenfell as well as many in the Cathedral that afternoon. More than one person in the Cathedral that afternoon during the singing of the hymns fancied they could hear a baritone voice above everyone else, the powerful voice of Isaac Grenfell booming out the tenor line, or was it just their imagination?

***

At the end of the service, in a silence broken only by the sounds of sobbing from around the building, the Grenfell men took up their burden again and carried the coffin back down the long centre aisle to the main doors which were now open.

Suddenly, the silence was broken as a lone voice started to sing from the central pews. Len Fyfield had been a staunch member of The Verlis Singers for many years and a great friend to Isaac. His rich baritone voice rang around the building, singing the melody and words of the first verse of the hymn *Deep Harmony*. The family had asked him to bring the service to a close in this way. He even had a reserved central seat so his voice could be heard. This was a rare honour, especially considering that Len was not a member of the Grenfell dynasty.

Immediately, from all corners, voices started to join in, some singing the melody and many more adding the harmonies. Terry Davies had tears flooding down his face, immensely proud to be part of the largest Cornish chorus of all time, joining together in praise of Isaac Kevern Grenfell and his contribution to their individual lives.

Sweet is the work, my God, my King,
To praise Thy Name, give thanks and sing,
To show Thy love by morning light
And talk of all Thy truth at night.

It wasn't that often he got to sing the whole hymn so by the second verse he had composed himself enough to let rip with the tenor line, his voice still quivering as he tried to sing through the tears.

Sweet is the day of sacred rest,
No mortal cares disturb my breast;
O may my heart in tune be found
Like David's harp of solemn sound!

My heart shall triumph in my Lord,
And bless his works, and bless his word:
Thy works of grace, how bright they shine!
How deep thy counsels, how divine!

Then shall I see, and hear, and know
All I desired or wished below;
And every power find sweet employ
In that eternal world of joy.
- Isaac Watts, The Psalms of David, 1719

Joan Davies clung onto husband Terry's arm, crying uncontrollably as they walked out of the Cathedral. She had managed to maintain her composure until the moment that

Len had started to sing *Deep Harmony*. The experience of being surrounded by the beautiful sound of the massed singing of The Verlis Singers 'anthem' all around her had touched emotions she didn't know she had.

'Bloody hell, girl,' whispered Terry in her ear. 'That was something special. Old Isaac would have loved every minute of it.'

Joan replied, 'Such wonderful singing and a lovely tribute to the man himself, but why couldn't there have been just a mention of the choir he started that has touched so many people's lives? Do you remember when he picked you out for your first solo? You were so chuffed. We all know he wasn't a saint, but through the choir over all those years he influenced so many lives and brought a lot of happiness.'

Terry Davies put his arm around the shoulders of his wife as they walked across the Cathedral Square. He said: 'The Grenfell family must really despise The Verlis Singers.'

Chapter 1

8 years later

*Monday October 4*th *2010*

'Bloody hell, it's cold!' Terry Davies stepped out as he pushed his post bike up Richmond Road at 6am as the city was starting to come to life.

It was a bitter cold October morning. Winter had arrived early in the Cornish city of Verlis and Terry (or Taff as he was known) was nearing the end of his round. Gundry Road was long and wound up to the top end of the city, close to the main hospital. He always had to walk the last section as the road was so steep. Heart-attack Hill as it was known in postie circles.

Terry had often mused that if the Good Lord called him to join the great chorus in the sky and his ticker packed up on that hill, Verlis General Hospital was so close by, the chance of life-saving assistance might give him a few more years singing, making love on Thursday afternoons to the lovely Joan, Mrs Davies, and walking Brutus, the daft dog.

On more than one occasion the *Verlis Gazette* had dubbed him 'The Singing Postman', but on a freezing cold Monday morning, approaching the age of 50, Terry wondered if his days of delivering post were coming to an end and perhaps the time had come to apply for a warmer, cushy desk job.

He couldn't feel his fingers even though he had double strength gloves on. Two layers of M&S thermal undergarments also seemed to have no effect. He wondered how the Postmaster General would view a claim for frostbite!

He had been a postie for nearly 33 years. He joined straight from school as his dad had told him it was 'A job for life, a nice pension, and afternoons off to play golf.' He knew every terrace, road, cul-de-sac and twist and turn in the city. Terry also boasted second-to-none knowledge of the dodgy letterboxes across the city that could take your finger-ends off.

More importantly, he knew every crazy psycho dog in Verlis who would lick other human beings with affection, but, faced with a postman's uniform, would go straight for the jugular, or the testicles.

No warnings given, bite on sight.

On more than one occasion he had been forced to kick a dog hard – prior to anticipated teeth contact with his leg or private parts, drop his bag and run like hell for the gate. New recruits to the city postal force who valued their fingers (or their manhood) would be encouraged to take Taff out for a pint at an early stage of employment and note down the no-go areas. Terry's advice to all was if in doubt – kick, then run.

At a fundraising concert for the Cornwall Cats and Dog Welfare charity two years back in Carlingford, he had spotted one of the lady owners of a dog he had laid out with his right boot not so long before sat in the audience. She had complained bitterly at the time to the Verlis Post Office about 'the brutal and totally unacceptable treatment by a dog-hating postman.'

Fortunately, his boss at the time also hated dogs and postie Terry Davies did not resemble tenor Terry Davies, all scrubbed up in his DJ with slicked-back hair and on choir concert duty with The Verlis Singers. In the interval the lady concerned had even tracked down Terry and complimented his tenor solo in the Scottish folk song, *Ca the Yowes*.

'What a lovely solo, you have a very good tenor voice,' she told him. Tempted to tell her that he also did a damn fine version of *Old Shep*, Terry thought better of it and politely thanked her for her charming compliment.

To put the record straight, Terry quite liked dogs. In fact the family Davies had a four-year-old black standard Schnauzer by the name of Brutus. To make him safe to the public (and other dogs) Brutus had his balls removed at an early age and was as daft as a brush. Brutus and Terry were big chums and totally devoted to each other.

***

Final letters stuffed into number 87, and his post round over for the day, Terry turned his bike, swung his muscular leg over the crossbar, and sat on the saddle. He adjusted the thermal gloves and woolly hats and pushed off down the hill to the depot. One thing about being a postie on a bike, it certainly kept you fit. *'Another shift bites the dust,'* he sang out loud in true Freddie Mercury style as he headed back to base.

The tenor line of one the new Bob Chilcott jazzy carols The Verlis Singers were learning for Christmas was also ringing around his brain as he freewheeled down the hill. One particular section which his fellow tenor and smart-ass, Dominic Gordon, had picked up with ease (much to Terry's annoyance) was frustrating him.

But it was choir that evening and he felt sure that Gavin, the choir conductor, would sort it out. He had not been impressed at first when Gavin James had become the new conductor, but over the last couple of years Taff had come to appreciate Gavin's undoubted musical talent. Now he was a big fan and supporter of the choir's charismatic leader.

Monday was choir rehearsal night with The Verlis Singers, and sacrosanct with Terry. He loved his choir. He had even tolerated (just) the years after Isaac when the gorgeous Heather had been the conductor prior to Gavin. Totally useless she was at taking rehearsals with her silly warm-ups, but she was very attractive and had splendid large firm breasts and would wear low-cut dresses at concerts to show them off.

Terry and Joan Davies went through a period early in their early marriage when attendance at Verlis Methodist Chapel in St Clewin on Sundays was an important part of life. One Sunday evening about twenty years ago they had attended an evening service, which promised 'Favourite Hymns from The Valleys'. Terry had enjoyed singing *Bread of Heaven* and many other Welsh hymns with great gusto and at the end of the service a tall, rather distinguished man approached him, holding out his hand to introduce himself to Terry.

He explained that his name was Isaac Grenfell and had noticed that Terry had been singing out with 'a very fine tenor voice', and did he (Terry) sing in a choir?

Terry replied that he didn't think his voice was good enough and he couldn't read music. Mr Grenfell however, was not to be put off and invited Terry to come along to try out his choir, The Verlis Singers. They rehearsed every Monday evening in the centre of Verlis.

'Don't worry about reading music, Mr Davies. God gave you a fine tenor voice and it should not be wasted. Please come along and just see if you enjoy it.'

Terry attended his first rehearsal of The Verlis Singers the next night with the encouragement of his wife Joan. From that day on he hardly missed a Monday rehearsal or a concert performance. All because of a man called Isaac Grenfell, who once heard him singing hymns in Chapel.

Isaac had encouraged Terry to develop his tenor voice and had even given him some lessons in the early months to improve his breathing and technique. Soon after joining, Isaac had asked Terry to sing some solos. When The Verlis Singers were recorded by BBC Radio Cornwall Terry had sung the second verse in the hymn *Deep Harmony*.

Singing in a choir was actually in the Davies DNA. Taff's dad in Wales still sang in the local male voice choir and his granddad had also sung. When Adam had started the Garden of Eden choral society, there would, without doubt, have been a Davies descendant in the tenor section. As the years progressed the Welsh side of the family had even travelled to Cornwall to hear The Verlis Singers with Terry Davies in it.

***

An hour later Terry shot around the corner into Baragwanth Road on his post bike. The central depot was situated close to the city rail station. Patrick Nicholls QC was striding along the road carrying his impressive lawyer's briefcase. Patrick was a prominent barrister in London, who commuted to the capital most days. He was catching the 8.25am to Victoria. Spotting Terry flying past he shouted out to him, 'Hey Taff, no speeding! See you tonight Boyo?'

'You bet Pat and it's your turn to get 'em in after choir at the pub.'

'Give the judge my love,' called back Taff as he sped into the depot, almost doing a wheelie as he turned into the entrance gate.

***

Peggy Trenholm was a Cornish lass through and through, although now, at 74, hardly a lass any more. Peggy and hubby Ron lived outside of Verlis about ten miles west in the village of Hendra. They owned and ran the village store for years. One day, three years ago, the Select Inns suits came knocking on their door with an open chequebook and plans for an 80-bed hotel. Peggy and Ron eventually decided to take the money and bought a smallholding a few miles out of Hendra.

In truth, they were now millionaires, although you would never know it, and they certainly didn't let on! At first they did not want to sell up, but their eldest son David, an airline pilot, had sat them down and reasoned: 'Mum and Dad, with the money you will get by selling up you will never have to bother about paying any bills again. You can do what you like and when you like.'

To Ron, a simple man who did not understand the ways of

the business world, his son was someone he admired greatly for his success in life. David's advice was always adhered to. They were a simple couple, but both their children had gone to university and then on to top jobs. David's sister Helen worked for one of the leading international stockbrokers in London. David had also included Patrick Nicholls from the choir in the discussions. His parents were in awe of the bass-singing QC and Patrick got a colleague from his London practice to advise the family on how to invest their newfound wealth. They were set up for life! So, with guidance from both children and with Patrick agreeing to be a trustee of a sizeable trust fund, selling up it was.

With the village store sold and the cheque banked, Ron and Peggy purchased the smallholding in Hendra and set about enjoying their new life.

'I'm getting the eggs.' It was about 7.30am and Peggy shouted up the stairs to Ron to make sure he heard her.

'Ok my bird,' came the reply.

Pulling on her topcoat, Peggy opened the back door to let herself out.

Monday today, she thought, and choir tonight.

Peggy had been a stalwart of The Verlis Singers soprano section for over 30 years. She loved the choir. Husband Ron did not sing, but he hardly ever missed a concert. Conductor Gavin had once remarked to Ron that he probably knew the pieces better than anyone else in the choir! Peggy was slightly uneasy about the choir, as she knew that there was a committee meeting coming up when the thorny subject of three-yearly re-auditions for all singing members was on the agenda. Her voice was not what it used to be and she had rather blotted her copybook two Christmases ago. This had resulted in the choir secretary Rona Hancock giving her what can only be described as, 'a severe bollocking'.

The Verlis Singers had a very enjoyable annual Christmas

booking at the big Fostors Department Store in the centre of the city. Singing carols was always followed by a free glass of bubbly and mince pies. It was the annual choir Christmas jolly, looked forward to with eager anticipation, and loved by all. The festive fayre was always liberally set out in the store canteen for the choir members after they had sung. Peggy was in the habit of taking a large canvas bag each year and stocking up for the festive season at home from the leftovers. Whilst this was not quite a cardinal sin in itself, last year she had decided to wear her tight-fitting plastic fun Santa outfit to sing in.

One step too far!

It was an invitation-only evening for upmarket VIP customers and the new-to-the-area store manager would be there. It was rumoured that he had joined The Verlis Gilbert and Sullivan Society and had a very good singing voice. This was his big chance to impress the top brass.

However, he was not best pleased at having a shiny plastic-clad Santa grinning at his gold-card clientele from the front row of the choir singing *Joy to the World*. Especially as members of the store-owning Foster family were present, running the rule over their new manager, of whom great things, and improved profits, were expected. A letter had duly been received the following month after the seasonal appearance, informing the choir that it was time to give another local group the chance to perform. Not surprisingly, the G and S group were getting the gig in 2009.

Peggy pushed the shed door open on her morning egg hunt. She didn't keep many hens these days, but the Trenholms were creatures of habit, especially when it came to making love. As she checked through the coops she heard Ron come into the shed. For egg collecting duties Peggy always travelled 'commando', even on bitterly cold Cornish winter mornings!'

'All right my bird?'

She felt his big hands on her thighs as she leaned forward and he gently pulled up her coat and dress underneath. At 76 years Ron's ardour had never wavered and the chicken shed ritual was something they both looked forward to, at least twice each week.

'How is that my bird?' whispered Ron and he made his grand entrance.

'Lovely my Ron, ohhh, just lovely, I do love you.'

***

It had been a sleepless Sunday night for Gavin James. The 42-year-old conductor of The Verlis Singers owned a photographic shop called In Focus, which was in Southcott, an alleyway close to Verlis Cathedral. To say that Gavin owned the shop was not quite the case. The bank in fact owned the shop and Gavin's business was in meltdown. The branch manager Simon Callaway had called a meeting at the Verlis branch of HCB BANK. This was not a 'let's have a friendly chat with your bank manager' meeting, but an instruction by Simon to Gavin to attend at 11am on that morning with the 'guidance' that Gavin should bring his accountant along with him.

Gavin had seen Internet sales destroy his business. He could not compete on price and his once full order book for photographic paper and developing materials had disappeared. His comfy but profitable small business was now in serious financial trouble. He had well and truly missed the boat when it came to jumping on the Internet bandwagon and now it was too late to catch up.

Simon Callaway and Gavin James were both members of Verlis Rotary Club. The club met every Tuesday at the County Hotel for lunch followed by a short talk by some local organisation or other. Simon was Rotary President this year and, as part of his duties, had to preside over the committee that organised the annual Rotary carol service in the Cathedral, which this year would be Wednesday

December 1ˢᵗ. This was the popular service, which always starred The Verlis Singers.

Gavin fancied that Simon had avoided sharing his table these past few weeks on Tuesdays, something to do with the desperate state of his business overdraft, he had pondered.

Mrs Georgina James, on the other hand, had no inclination of the state of husband Gavin's business. She had been married to Gavin for 19 years and the couple had no children. They hardly ever spoke to each other anymore. Both knew that the marriage was dead but their lifestyles rarely crossed and so the question of parting had never really cropped up.

Georgina was head teacher at the Trimanter Primary School, on the outskirts of Verlis. She had been having a highly charged affair with Trevor Scarron, the young sports teacher, for the last two years. Gavin had no idea this was going on, although he was surprised when she joined a local gym and lost a huge amount of weight. He had noticed that her late night working was becoming more frequent and Richard Parish, the smutty bass, had told Gavin that he had seen his wife in town and she was looking 'seriously fit'.

The phone rang in Gavin's small office at the back of the shop. It was 9.15am and a young woman's voice said hello when Gavin answered, introducing herself as Polly Jones. She explained that she had just moved to Verlis to work as a junior accountant and was looking for a choir to join. A friend had seen them on *Songs of Praise* and told her that The Verlis Singers were very good. Polly had decided to call Gavin the conductor and had found his number on the choir website, which said that Mondays were the rehearsal night. Could she pop along tonight, and how did new people join?

The call helped to lift Gavin's Monday morning pre-bank meeting gloom. Yes, she had lots of singing experience with choirs in Edinburgh where she had studied accountancy at university. She considered herself a good sight-reader, and she had a top soprano voice. Gavin invited her to attend the rehearsal that evening and Polly said she would be there. If she liked the choir he would audition her next week before rehearsal. They were working on a concert at Exeter and Christmas music. It was a good time to join.

Putting down the phone Gavin felt pleased, she sounded bright and good new sops, especially young ones, were always welcome. Just perhaps, the question of who would sing the opening verse of *Once in Royal David's City* at the Cathedral carol service in December had been solved. It was always good to ring the changes. Choir life was strange, he thought to himself. Someone new joins and more often than not, someone else departs.

Later today he planned to call in to see Len Fyfield at his house. Len was dying of cancer and Gavin had been watching Len deteriorate these last few months. Gavin had promised to pop in the music for a lovely new carol he had found. He wanted to include it in the Cathedral Christmas carol service this year and to give Len the chance to learn his line at home.

Being a choir conductor was the same as being a teacher. Standing out in front of people, you looked out at a sea of familiar faces week in week out. You saw when they were happy or sad. You really had a privileged insight into people's lives on a regular basis.

Len had a wonderful deep bass voice and had been in The Singers for 42 years. Once a soloist in the choir he had been a faithful servant, happy to help new members learn their parts, he even accepted and encouraged new (younger) singers to perform the solos that he once sang.

He had been one of the members who had welcomed Gavin warmly when he took over as conductor. Gavin and Len had become firm friends, and Gavin had noticed the weight loss at first and, then, as weeks went by and as Len became frail, the times when he had had to sit down increased when the rest of the choir stood to sing.

He had sung under all three conductors. He was a close friend of Isaac Grenfell, the founder, and had even been asked to sing at the memorial service in the Cathedral. In Len's view, however, Gavin now had the choir back to where it was all those years ago before Isaac fell out with the committee.

Len had been diagnosed with progressive pancreatic cancer last January. It had spread through his body and now his fellow basses had a rota to collect him from home and bring him to choir every Monday in his wheelchair. But he was becoming increasingly weak and had missed the last two rehearsals.

Len loved to sing and although his breathing was affected by the cancer that was destroying his body, its richness of tone was still there. He knew that his life was coming to an end but was determined that he would sing this year at the annual Rotary carol service in Verlis Cathedral on the first Wednesday in December. Nothing would stop him.

The Verlis Singers always led the singing. It was part of the tradition of Christmas in Verlis. It would be his swansong and he knew it. He hoped that he would make it to Wednesday December 1st, but he knew that he could die before that date. His time on Earth was coming to its close.

***

It was 11 o'clock and Gavin James pushed opened the main doors to his bank on the corner of Boscraven Street, a short walk from his shop. Anthony Richards, his accountant, was waiting inside for him.

***

In Hendra, Len and Peggy Trenholm pulled up outside the Co-op store. Len was driving the old Land Rover they had owned for 13 years. Attempts by David and Helen Trenholm to persuade Mum and Dad to buy a new vehicle from the substantial proceeds of their smallholding sale to Select Inns had fallen on deaf ears.

'There's still a few hundred miles left in her,' Len had said.

Thankfully, neither David nor Helen knew that the sexual antics in the back of the old Land Rover in summer months out on the moors were part of their parents' long-established ritual of lovemaking. Old habits (in familiar circumstances) were best left unchanged, especially as they were still enjoyed so much by both parties.

Peggy had her empty egg basket with her as she got out of the Land Rover and headed for the Co-op doors. She would be buying her usual two-dozen eggs in readiness for choir practice later that day.

***

ALL IN THE APRIL EVENING

The Verlis Singers sing the Hugh Roberton choral classic in Verlis Methodist Chapel conducted by Isaac Grenfell and recorded in 1972.

www.verlis-singers.org.uk.

Chapter 2

A Cornishman, Isaac Kevern Grenfell, founded the Verlis Singers in 1952. Grenfell was from tin mining stock and part of a family who were pillars of the Wesleyan Chapel of that time. The family lived on the outskirts of Verlis on a council estate.

From working in the mines as a boy, after they had closed down, he had left to train as a draughtsman at evening class, and then joined a local engineering company. He was married to Bronnen and they had three children. From an early age he was perceived as a naturally gifted singer and musician. Even at school and in his teens his choral compositions amazed the school teachers. He also performed as a boy treble at local music festivals across Cornwall, usually singing his own pieces and winning many awards.

Isaac was from working class origins and when aged 31, he started his choir for men and ladies, there was a public outcry. Cornwall was known then as a bastion of Male Voice Choirs, with virtually every town and village boasting its own. The perception was that whilst ladies may be allowed to be part of church or chapel choir on Sundays (with posh ladies belonging to the Choral Society in Verlis) out of church time their role should be restricted to tea and sandwich-making duties at male voice choir socials.

***

The Grenfell family were big so Isaac had numbers on his side. He was a committed Wesleyan and local preacher. A good old-fashioned bible-thumper, he would attack his congregation and roar the gospel from pulpits around the county. Fire and brimstone were his speciality and he loved singing hymns. He possessed a hugely powerful baritone voice that could drown out any congregation, however large.

He was a passionate and striking slim man standing well over six feet. He always wore his hair long and as he aged it turned white. He sported a beard and with his flowing locks it was easy to see how women would throw themselves at him.

In Chapel circles he was known as 'T-P-G, Three Points Grenfell', as his sermons were always based on three clear messages. When he reached point number three the congregation knew it was getting close to the end of the sermon. This was usually followed by a belting good hymn to conclude the worship, Isaac leading the singing from the front, with his booming baritone voice.

The Verlis Singers was a working class choir. In its early days it sang at chapel anniversaries and was made up almost entirely of members of the Grenfell Cornish clan.

Isaac had four married brothers and two sisters. He was the youngest. As they were all singers, including the wives and the numerous teenage children of the elders, that amounted to a pretty useful core for any choir. They were very good for their time. The repertoire was simple, performing with many of Isaac's own arrangements of hymn tunes. In true Von Trapp, *Sound of Music* fashion, they swept the board at the Cornish Festival in the small choir class for a number of years in the 1950s and 60s. Other choirs were heard to murmur, 'Not those bloody Grenfells again!'

No one really knew where the *Deep Harmony* choir anthem came from. It was a good old-fashioned hymn but its association with The Verlis Singers was vague. Perhaps Isaac just loved the simple words and melody and there was also the fact that it was written by another Isaac, Isaac Watts. From the start it was always sung at the beginning of every choir practice and, as the years rolled by, at all other choir occasions, whether happy or sad. It was The Verlis Singers' anthem. And, despite some attempts by brave individuals over the years, it was still sung at the start of every choir practice.

Isaac Grenfell certainly was a gifted musician; it was in his heart and soul and from his interpretation of music came a choir who would be respected across the United Kingdom. In his later years he would also go around Verlis giving piano lessons. He was especially popular with some of the mothers of his pupils and he would often stay on after the lesson for tea (and crumpets) as the child protégé was despatched out to play.

In 1995 he was awarded the OBE for his services to music in Cornwall, a considerable honour bestowed on a man who did not seek such recognition. The announcement caused great consternation amongst many people in the higher echelons of music and the arts across the county.

At some point in time, as the choir grew, a committee was formed to manage its affairs. In the early days this would be a cartel of Grenfells, but as years passed others infiltrated the ranks. These were usually choir members who wanted to take the choir on a different path to that chosen by its founder conductor. In the words of a well-known song, 'there would be trouble ahead', and there was.

Isaac saw it as his right to agree concert venues and would book soloists without referring to the choir committee. When this caused eruptions he would simply claim that The Verlis Singers was HIS choir and HE had the right to do as HE pleased if HE thought it best. He led the choir for 45 years but the cracks started to show in the 1980s. Isaac began to be at odds with the choir committee and would regularly miss the monthly meetings. This was a heaven-sent opportunity for the committee to plot his demise – behind his back.

Ladies loved Isaac and an alleged liaison with a soprano member of the choir had tongues wagging. Within the choir his insistence that his sister Gwen continued to sing all soprano solos when, in all truth, her voice was well past its

sell-by date also started to provoke consternation. Matters
came to a head when he invited a group of former members
back to augment the choir for the annual Christmas Rotary
Carol service in Verlis Cathedral in 1997. Numbers had
dwindled because of the increasing unpleasantness and the
Verlis Singers were not the musical force they once were.

By then Rona Hancock was the choir secretary and Ken
Mitchell was chairman. The choir was losing members as the
bad feelings spread like a disease. Isaac could see his
weakened choir not being any way near up to the usual high
standard for the Christmas Carol service. Without any
reference to the committee he called in 12 additional good
singers from around the area to come in and augment the
choir just for the Carol Service.

Most of them of course, were from the Grenfell family
clan and after the service it was discovered that Isaac had
even organised clandestine rehearsals for his additional
singers in his front room.

At the rehearsal before the carol service they all arrived at
the Cathedral with the music and Isaac placed them at the
front of the choir. There was a huge row after the rehearsal
and only intervention from the chairman, who phoned
around the entire existing choir persuading them to sing, kept
their reputation intact. The Verlis Singers were therefore able
to perform at the Cathedral and maintain their reputation,
with Isaac, his flowing locks on this occasion tied back in a
ponytail, in his most flamboyant conducting mood.

Two other committee members at the time were husband
and wife singing members Tony and Elaine Bridges. Elaine
and secretary Rona were firm friends and they were
determined to bring their conductor to book. After a
thoroughly unpleasant committee meeting at the home of the
chairman Ken Mitchell, Isaac was asked to step down in
January 1998.

The *Verlis Gazette* ran a story with the headline:

Choir out of Tune with Conductor

Radio Cornwall also reported on the bust-up and the departure of the founder conductor under something of a cloud. Isaac himself kept a low profile; his wife was not well and he knew that this time he had gone too far! Later on, when Gavin James became conductor, and with the 55th anniversary approaching, Gavin instigated attempts to build bridges between the choir and its founder. Isaac was offered the position of Vice-Patron (much against the will of Rona Hancock and others) but flatly refused.

***

Isaac Grenfell passed away in 2002, aged 81. A memorial service saw Verlis Cathedral packed to capacity with many weeping mothers of his former piano students present. The choir committee, in their great wisdom, recruited Heather Strong as the new conductor of The Verlis Singers in 1999. She was a complete disaster and rather remarkably lasted for eight years. As a very young Head of Music at the local girls' school she certainly appeared to have everything the choir needed in terms of musicality. Her school choirs were winning awards and whilst she did have an undoubted skill at handling young children, with adults she was totally inept.

From the outset she treated the choir at rehearsals as she would a class of children at school. She insisted on introducing 'warm-ups' at the start of rehearsals, something never ever before known during the reign of Isaac Grenfell. These would be words set to simple phrases to encourage good breathing, the pronunciation of vowels, and to get the choir into the correct frame of mind needed (in her opinion) for singing. The Verlis Singers men (particularly Taff Davies and his cohorts, Eric Stroman and Jim Best in the tenor section) chose to ridicule these warm-ups.

One of Heather's favourites was a simple scale sung to the words:

'GOOD VOWELS AND CONSONANTS… MAKE A CHOIR RIGHT'.

The tenors would blast out:

'OPEN BOWELS AND FLATULENCE… KEEP YOU UP AT NIGHT.'

Her choice of music was strange and rather old-fashioned. The choir had two cupboards stacked with old music from past Isaac years. When she dug out an old four-part song called *She's like the Swallow,* and the tenors changed the words to *She likes to swallow,* the ladies of the choir were in turmoil and the writing was on the wall.

Then, one cold Monday in January, Heather Strong somehow 'forgot' to start the practice with *Deep Harmony.* Rona Hancock immediately called an extraordinary general meeting, where the old guard voted Heather out and that was the end of her relationship with The Verlis Singers.

Chapter 3

Monday October 4th

Polly Jones was settling into her new life, and liking Cornwall. Even Mondays were okay when you had a new job and you actually looked forward to going to work.

Stroman, Maycroft and Associates were thriving accountants with a strong client list across the county. She got the trainee post against opposition from a list of 'hopeful local yokels' she was told after she had arrived and had soon settled in. The work was well within her capabilities, she was something of a shining light at University in Edinburgh and many of her friends had asked, 'Why go to Cornwall?'

She loved her new situation. A proper job, great salary, and the potential of many new male encounters, perhaps even true love, a hubby and kids! She had been brought up in Guildford and preferred the small city existence. Polly had found a well-priced cosy little house just outside Verlis to rent and the 26-year-old was only lacking one thing in her life: a man, or lots of men!

Tonight she was off to try out a new choir called The Verlis Singers. The website was good and the conductor quite cuddly if a bit too old for her. They had done some TV stuff and, who knows, there might just be a young rich bass baritone with pecs to lust after, who was desperate to find the love of his life. More to the point he could pop around to her house, as she chose, for the occasional full-on shag. As she said to her university friend Moira (who stayed on in Scotland to find work) when she phoned last week, 'I have not had a good shag for months Moy, even Roger the Rabbit gets a sodding headache these days!'

***

Gavin had stuck a pizza in the oven for his tea. The decision had been made to confront his wife with the details about his bank meeting earlier that day. If things developed into a row he could always escape to choir early to do auditions. However she had not appeared, no doubt working late at school again.

He didn't know what Georgina's reaction would be to the news that the bank had set him a six-month deadline to clear his £25,000 business overdraft. There was no way he could hope to do this, but now he had to tell his wife. She had a fiery temper when roused and he feared an eruption.

The bank meeting had been difficult, even though the manager, Simon Calloway, had tried his best to be supportive. The Area Director, a young man called Bruce, was tough and obviously did not suffer fools lightly. He laid it on the line to Gavin. His business was not performing, the bank had run out of patience, and the overdraft had to be cleared in six months, whatever that meant for Gavin. He also made it clear to Gavin that he would have preferred a three-month stay of execution but the local manager had argued Gavin's case strongly, so six months it was. 'With some reluctance,' he added.

The bank had given him very little room for manoeuvre; his business had been going downhill for the past two years. This was something that Gavin should have seen coming and taken the appropriate steps. The loan to Gavin's business was unsecured and Gavin thought that his manager was very nervous about the outcome should he choose to go down the bankruptcy route.

He would have to close the business and try to find a buyer for the lease. His days as a shop proprietor were over and he had no idea what he would do next. Georgina's head teacher salary was good, but would she be sympathetic to his situation? They had survived off her salary but Gavin knew that Georgina was close to giving up on the prospect of propping up her husband's business any longer.

He went to the small office he had in the spare room downstairs at their house to see if there were any interesting emails. Gavin James had become an expert at burying his head in the sand and ignoring the realities of life. One email immediately jumped out at him, a round robin to UK choirs inviting them to sing at the Krakow Choral Festival in Poland next June.

It was a few years since The Verlis Singers had competed in a festival and perhaps the time had come to do so again? Poland was an interesting country and there was always Tatania, the young Polish woman who lived in Verlis and now sang in the alto section. She could be very useful if there needed to be any communications in the Polish language.

He quite fancied the idea of preparing the choir for a competition and as the festival was only over four days it might attract many of the members to take part. Choir tours were great for morale as well. He knew it was a tradition that the conductor's place would be paid for from choir funds, so he didn't have to worry about 'affording' to pay for it.

Poland would be an exciting adventure for the choir and he sent back an email asking for more details. Was it a competitive festival? Were there set pieces that all choirs sang or could each choir choose its own repertoire? Whatever the reply from the organisers, Gavin had made up HIS mind that he wanted to do the tour. All he needed to do was get the choir chairman on his side and then it would certainly happen.

***

Mrs Georgina James had not been surprised to hear that her husband's business was going tits up. She had treated him like a naughty 10-year-old who had kicked a football through a school window. After she had come back from school that evening at about 5.15, he had explained that he had something important to discuss with her. Everything had gone downhill from then!

'Gavin you should have seen this coming, why did you ignore all the signs? You must have seen sales dropping. You are a bloody loser, but I suppose we'll work something out.'

With that she had gone for a shower as she had an early evening school meeting to attend. Her husband quickly grabbed his music case and escaped!

***

Gavin drove into the Post Office staff car park. It was 7pm and his weekly parking arrangement was courtesy of postman and tenor Terry Davies who had fixed it with the Post Office Manager, as the reserved spaces were not all used in the evenings. He had not liked hearing his wife call him a 'loser', that evening but she was right, certainly when it came to his business.

Tenor Terry had been in the choir forever, although he was only around 50 years of age. Taff, as he liked to be known, had a really sweet wife called Joan, not a singer but one of those people who would always be helping out at choir socials with a big smile for everyone.

When Gavin took over the choir at first, the relationship with Terry was strained. He had heard tales of how Terry Davies would cause upset at the rehearsals of his predecessors and did not know quite what to expect. Over the months and years Gavin and Taff had become as friendly as a conductor could get with a singer. These days at rehearsals, Taff could have got the gold star for being teacher's pet.

Earlier that day a surprise email had come through to Gavin from Heather Strong, the former conductor of The Verlis Singers.

Hello Gavin,

I hope all is well. I hear great things of the VS, good for you. They are certainly back on track and I can see now that adult choirs are not for me. I will stick to getting the little ones to sing!

You really sounded great on Songs of Praise earlier this year and you have lots of new younger faces in the choir.

Anyway, as the Cornish Festival next year is the 75th anniversary from May 19-21. There are plans to make it a special year. We will still do the competitions as always but we would like to create a special big event on the final Saturday May 21st, probably in the Cathedral.

The committee have suggested a festival massed choir but want to attract lots of people who don't sing in the more 'traditional' choirs, sort of a giant Cornwall community choir if you like.

Anyway, we all agree that you are the man to conduct it – what do you say?

We hope your answer is yes… if so, could you come to a meeting to discuss this with us? There will be some rehearsals, probably on the weekends before, and a bit of money to pay you of course. There will also be budget for music and the accompanist you choose.

I'll be in touch soon with the date and venue for the meeting.

You are our first choice, please say yes.

H

Gavin had been very pleasantly surprised to hear from Heather and even more so by the request. He replied by return:

Hi Heather, you bet – yes of course and thank you for asking me. I would like to hear more – when is the next meeting? I'll be there.

He thought he would keep the invitation to himself until he had attended their meeting to find out more. He had met Heather on a couple of occasions and the girls' choir at her school had an excellent reputation, even if her years with the Verlis Singers had ended in disaster.

After parking next to Verlis Baptist Church Gavin headed down the stairs to the large rehearsal room the choir had used for many years, going back to the Isaac Grenfell era. There were two cupboards stacked high with music. Gavin was entrusted with a key to the cupboards, as were Jane Younger, the choir librarian and Rona Hancock, the choir secretary. It had been quite a day. The face to face with the bank, revealing all to Georgina and calling in to see Len had taken its emotional toll.

Walking in with his music briefcase, Gavin immediately felt at home. This was his domain and he really liked taking choir in the airy, spacious room. He occasionally varied rehearsals by moving the seats around and tonight it would be 'Singing in the Round'. He would put the chairs out in one big circle before people arrived and would conduct from the centre.

Sheila Stirton, the choir accompanist of 27 years, would be positioned inside the singer's circle, sat at the piano, which the men in the choir would move for him, as it was a heavy iron-framed one. Gavin would have to raise his voice to tell her which pieces they would sing. At 69, she was getting deaf and Gavin knew that he would have to 'persuade' her to stand down soon. That was not going to be easy, as Sheila was as thick as thieves with the honorary secretary, Rona Hancock, and some other members of the choir's 'old guard'.

It would be a brave Gavin James that tackled this subject but he knew it had to be faced sooner rather than later. Time soon for a quiet word with the chairman! That was the problem with the old guard of members. They simply hated change.

He was well into setting out the chairs when Peggy Trenholm bustled in. She was wearing a bright yellow pair of what were best described as dungarees, and carrying a large canvas bag, containing eggs, no doubt. Peggy was slightly miffed to find Gavin there before her. Chairs were her job.

'Hi Peggy!' shouted Gavin, seeing her come in. 'You are looking drop-dead gorgeous this evening. I thought you were the new young soprano coming to join the choir.'

Peggy beamed. She loved the choir even more now Gavin was in charge. He didn't even mind her plastic Santa suit!

Practice started at 7.30pm and members began to arrive and chat to each other. There was a friendly atmosphere. Tony and Elaine Bridges had been away in the sun in Tenerife and were showing off their tans. They greeted Gavin as other Verlis members drifted in and looked to their conductor for the evening's seating instructions.

'One big circle folks, sopranos next to tenors – don't all rush girls to sit near Taff Davies. Then the altos and basses, please leave some space for any latecomers.'

***

When Gavin had first moved to Verlis he had gone along to The Verlis Choral Society to see whether he'd like singing with them. That was before he had even heard of a choir called The Verlis Singers. He had to arrive early to audition for the rather pompous conductor and passed with ease. Gavin came from a family where singing was second nature. He had a reasonably good tenor voice and fancied singing again in a choir. Georgina had encouraged him then, she knew he was very musical and thought a new hobby would be good for him.

Good young male singers were few and far between and his sight-reading was exceptional. The audition was very simple for Gavin, he sang the tenor line from a score of an Easter hymn from The Crucifixion, and Dr King recognised a good sight-reader who would be a great addition to his tenor line.

He was asked by the musical director Dr Herbert King to sit at the back and 'observe the rehearsal.' The Choral Society were practising a boring Mass and after half an hour Gavin decided to muscle his way into the tenors, taking an empty chair, only to be told by a rather rude tall man, 'You cannot sit there, it is Bernard so-and-so's seat and he may come later.'

Gavin sneaked out during the interval. In his view choirs where people had their own seats were old-fashioned and going backwards. With The Verlis Singers he regularly moved people around. It kept choir rehearsals interesting and never boring. Encounters with Dr King at music events in the city had since been strained. He obviously remembered the tenor who had dared to pass an audition and then walk out. For most of The Verlis members the moving of seats made choir life varied, except that is for Rona Hancock and her alto cronies. They objected to any form of change.

***

A tall young woman wandered into the rehearsal room at about 7.40pm. Gavin spotted her straight away. He would not describe her as pretty, but she had a nice open face with blonde hair tied back, no makeup. Although she was wearing jeans, her long legs went on and on forever! She walked towards Gavin, held out her hand and introduced herself as Polly Jones who had called him that morning. Gavin welcomed her and took her over to meet Clare Taylor.

He had two Clares in the choir, actually a Clare and a Claire. They both had super soprano voices. Gavin knew that if he sat Polly with Clare Taylor, at the end of the evening she would give him an honest opinion of Polly's singing. If Clare gave Polly the thumbs up, an audition was a formality. Hopefully he could do that before next Monday's rehearsal.

Bank hassle and impending financial doom forgotten for the time being at least, Gavin James now got down to doing what he loved (and what he did best), conducting The Verlis Singers on Monday evenings.

The full choir was now about 60 voices. When he had taken over as conductor, numbers had dropped to around 30 as many had jumped ship in the Heather years. Morale was again low. He had got to know Heather Strong (who seemed to have left the choir suddenly) quite well since as they had met at Cornish Festival performances. She was a very attractive blonde who also worked for the Cornish Education Service. She was in her early 30s and had a (new) dashing young solicitor husband. Her email earlier that day certainly had come out of the blue.

Back then, Gavin had read in the local paper that the choir were looking for a new conductor. He had helped at Georgina's school conducting the parents' choir at Christmas and really enjoyed it. Heather had warned him about 'The Verlis Vendetta' and whilst he knew there were some issues within the choir (and most every other choir come to that), he had taken on the conductor's role with an open mind.

Gavin had applied for the conductor's position and took two rehearsals. There were four other candidates who also took 'tester' rehearsals. The members of The Verlis Singers then voted and Gavin was offered the post. He was told later that 'a high percentage of the choir had voted for him, because he made the rehearsals he took very enjoyable'.

As he had worked to build up the choir, some old members had returned. Gavin had insisted on re-auditioning them, which had caused some rumblings but non-singing choir chairman Brian McNeil (himself fairly new to the choir) was keen that Gavin should do things his way and gave him full support, and that was that.

The re-auditions had been gentle and Gavin had tactfully asked two of the older sopranos to move to the alto section, as their voices could not reach the higher notes. One of the tenors, Geoff Black, a rather unpleasant man with a strident voice, was asked to move down and join the bass section, which did not go down to well. Thankfully after a few weeks he left to join the Farmouth Male Voice Choir.

Not long afterwards Geoff had come into Gavin's shop to look at a few cameras and then, after wasting Gavin's time for 35 minutes said, 'I can get this one a lot cheaper online,' adding (as he left the shop), 'Oh by the way I am now in the Farmouth Male Voice, Andy Smith the conductor said I am a true top tenor.'

Good riddance, thought Gavin.

***

Gavin James also used his publicity skills to get the *Cornish Gazette* to run a big feature on his membership drive when he took over the choir. Letters were sent to all local churches and flyers and posters invited all interested singers – experienced or not – to come along. These were distributed to pubs as well as churches. Radio Cornwall reported on it as well and an open night attracted nearly 40 potential new members, including some very good singers.

He had told his first committee meeting that the choir should have at least 45-50 voices:

12 sopranos, of which 6 should be top voices – the rest mezzos for eight-part pieces

12 altos

8 tenors

12 bass of which at least 6 should be low basses, the rest baritones, again so they could tackle eight-part pieces.

But, as he pointed out, should a very good new singer want to join and membership was close to the 50 mark they would definitely be accepted. After all, if Sir Alex Ferguson got a call from Christiana Ronaldo saying, 'any chance of a game Saturday?' he would hardly be told, 'Sorry we're full mate, go and play for Chelsea!'

***

It was a good night for new faces. Bass Tony Bridges was talking to a smart couple who had just walked in. Gavin went across to say hello, even though Rona and some of the other ladies were huffing and puffing as practice was late in starting.

The new couple were called David and Laura Honey. They explained that following the sale of David's successful business in Norfolk they were house hunting in the area and staying in rented accommodation meanwhile in Verlis. David explained that he had sung bass in a very good (his words) mixed choir in Norwich and his wife also sang. She was an alto, but not as experienced a singer as him.

Gavin invited them to sit in. David eagerly went to find a bass seat, although his wife preferred to sit at the back and listen. By now Rona, Elaine, and Marian Thomas were muttering and looking at their watches.

'OK good people, quiet please!' shouted Gavin, and then briefly explained to the new faces that they would now sing *Deep Harmony*, the choir anthem, which always started a rehearsal. Sheila gave them the opening chord and they sang in harmony, unaccompanied:

Sweet is the work, my God, my King,
To praise Thy Name, give thanks and sing
To show Thy love by morning light
And talk of all Thy truth at night.

As the final phrase ended the door opened. Patrick Nicholls QC walked in with Claire Nesbitt and Tatania Bakowski. Gavin knew that Pat hated singing *Deep Harmony* and always timed his arrival to perfection to miss singing it; he gave Claire and Tatania the benefit of the doubt. Tatania's partner was a policeman so his shift work often meant her arriving late.

Now well past the proper starting time, Gavin got the choir singing through some of their current repertoire. There was one more concert to come before the Rotary Christmas service; this was at Exeter in two Saturdays' time. Gavin had to balance his rehearsal time between items to perform at Exeter and note bashing the Christmas music.

The Verlis Singers had some pieces that audiences almost expected them to sing at concerts. The choir were, generally speaking, bored with *All in the April Evening* and *The Long Day Closes*, turn of the century arrangements by Hugh Roberton and Arthur Sullivan.

Gavin realised that the choir still sang them beautifully and as they were on the Verlis Singers LP of many years ago, and conducted by Isaac Grenfell, they were very popular.

The choir's recordings were still occasionally played on Radio 3 and Classic FM and had picked up in their popularity after they had both been performed on *Songs of Praise* earlier that year.

If Gavin left them off a concert programme, he knew he would be approached at some stage before the concert or during the interval by someone who would enquire: 'Will you be singing *All in the April Evening* in the second half, Mr James?'

Although he had no formal music training, Gavin James had developed into an excellent choir leader. Between the ages of 15 and 20 he had helped care for his father who had Motor Neurone disease. The James family lived in Newbury and university was not an option. His dad had died when he was 18, the same year he met Georgina on holiday in Greece. She lived just outside Verlis and Cornwall seemed a good option as a place to live.

Conducting some church choirs, the parents' choir at his wife's school for Christmas, and singing himself, had given him excellent practical experience and now here he was conducting what was probably one of the best choirs in the West of England. He knew that when he started he lacked some of the necessary ability on notation and general musicality. He had worked hard at home, reading guidance books, but it was the practical experience week in week out that was now paying dividends.

Gavin knew the choir wanted to hear news of Len Fyfield but deliberately held back. He would tell them of his visit before the tea break so people could then share their sadness in a non-singing time. It was impossible to sing when your emotions were charged with sad news.

One of the Christmas pieces he had chosen this year was a lovely carol by Bob Chilcott called *Remember O thou Man*. Gavin liked it as it had a bluesy jazz style and a great piano part. Frustratingly, accompanist Sheila could not do it justice. Ask her to play Mozart or even John Rutter and she would be fine, but anything syncopated or modern and she really could not cope with the style required.

Gavin picked out a section in the middle that he knew the tenors were struggling with, all except Dominic Gordon, that is, who was the star of the tenor section. In his early 20s, he was an excellent sight-reader and singer. He was a deputy with the Cathedral Choir, which meant that he stepped in when one of the vicar's choral (paid tenors) was away.

He was a class act.

Gavin had figured that Dom was probably gay and some of the ladies, especially Peggy, certainly could not work him out at all, except that he was 'such a very pretty boy!'

Apart from Sheila's difficulties keeping up with the Chilcott piece it was, Gavin felt, going to be one of the best yet performances of The Verlis Singers this year in the Cathedral. The choir had developed so much in the last 12 months. Every section now had its strong singers and the overall sound was unique. Gavin encouraged singers to use their natural voices, as he liked to hear the individual accents coming through.

He once told the choir, 'There are so many very good mixed voice choirs who all sound like they are straight out of an Oxbridge University Choir. They all sound the same. The Verlis Singers have warmth of tone and expression that we will always work on. Let's be different to all the rest.'

Gavin himself had also gained confidence and experience. New pieces were being learnt very quickly and as The Verlis Singers performed without music at concerts it did require some of the members working hard at home on memorising their parts.

With the help of Dick Wilson in the bass section, a bit of a whizz on IT technology, Gavin offered learning CDs with the parts. This made it far easier for the choir members to learn their notes away from the rehearsal room. Gavin James had embraced new technology with the choir but somehow ignored it as his business. The Rotary Christmas service in the Cathedral was an exception however. That evening they sang all the pieces from music. This gave Gavin more scope to choose new pieces as it would have been impossible to commit them all to memory in the rehearsal time allowed.

***

Break time was around 8.30pm so at 8.25pm, Gavin gave the encircled group of singers his Len Fyfield update. He started by telling the new people present the background about Len and how he had been a choir stalwart for over 40 years. He was now very ill with terminal cancer. He explained how he had been to see Len and his wife Mellyn that afternoon.

Len had a message for all his friends in the choir. He wanted them all to understand that he knew death was very close but was determined to sing at the Cathedral for the last time. It was his 40th Christmas consecutive service. He would be there with them.

'Len asked me to tell you all that it is like singing the Messiah in full. He has had so many good times singing through all the many pages but now he had to accept that he was on the final Chorus, The Amen. I am saving my last few bars for the Cathedral and I want to share them with all of you.'

Many of the choir members gulped back tears as Gavin's voice faltered, as he also felt the pain.

It was time for the break.

The silence was broken by a cheery voice from the soprano section.

'Does anybody want any eggs?'

Peggy to the rescue!

Chapter 4

Terry Davies was peddling back to the post office HQ at Verlis. It was a Thursday morning and another brisk October day, although thankfully not as cold as the previous week. He was feeling good with the excitement to come of the weekly snuggle-up under the sheets with the lovely Mrs Davies, and a walk with Brutus the daft dog, after lovemaking of course.

In the evening, it was off to the monthly committee meeting of The Verlis Singers at the Cricket Club. They were normally held on Thursday evenings. Taff had avoided the committee for years. Public speaking was not his forte, but as fellow tenor Eric had pointed out in the pub one night after a rehearsal when Taff had been sounding off about choir matters, 'For Christ's sake Taff, if you are going to moan on about the way the choir is run, stand for committee and have the balls to say what you think to those who make the decisions.'

Fair point, Eric.

So that is exactly what he did, being voted in at the March AGM in preference to four other choir members who stood for the solitary place on offer each year to a singing member of the choir. That person was duly elected for two years, hence there being one elected singer from the ranks each year, and two on the committee at any one time.

He had found the 'official' side of the choir a fast learning curve and in many ways it seemed far removed from the real choir. However, the more committee meetings he attended, the more he enjoyed being able to influence decisions that, in the end, set the path for the way the choir would go in the months ahead.

Arise, Terry (Taff) Davies, The Verlis Singers people's champion.

He even found that he got on rather well with Brian McNeil, the choir chairman. Brian was in his early 70s and not a singer, although his wife had once graced the soprano section a few years back. He came from an engineering background and lived in a village outside Verlis.

Brian had joined the choir as chairman just after the Grenfell fallout and the testing years with 'that bossy teacher' (although a fine-looking young woman) who took over and then, thankfully, left. Things now in the Gavin era were somewhat smoother and The Verlis Singers, to his admittedly tuneless ear, were as good these days as he had ever heard them.

Eric was right, moaning on in the pub was one thing – 'getting involved' was different. Taff relished his new role as the man of the people. For example, Taff had never really thought about (or knew) how much the conductor was paid. He coughed up his subs each year and that was that. Committee life soon gave him an insight that the choir was quite wealthy, with around £44,000 in its coffers. This was an amount built up over the years from old record royalties – another fact of choir life he had no idea about.

The Decca LPs from the days of Isaac Grenfell had sold across the world and royalties made up a large part of the surplus sitting in the bank account. Royalties still arrived in the choir's bank account each year. These days a couple of hundred pounds only but 'surprise income' as the choir treasurer called in.

At the AGM in March each year the finance details were given out but at first Terry found them hard to understand. Rather than admit ignorance, like many others, he had kept quiet. He had showed them to his wife, who had helped to explain income and expenditure, assets and other such matters. Mrs Joan Davies had a really good brain when it came to figures and helped out with the bookkeeping at a local builders' merchant three days a week. Choir accounts were a doddle to understand, she explained.

When the review of the conductor's payment had come at the June meeting it was Taff Davies who took on the challenge and flew the flag as Gavin's champion. The dreaded duo of secretary Rona and her cohort, publicity officer Elaine, thought they had the committee in their hands and they had tried to sidestep the annual review of the conductor's gratuity. Terry was having nothing of it. After a fiery discussion he moved, and was successful in putting through an increase so Gavin's rehearsal fee doubled to £50 a night. A revised payment of £150 for each concert was also agreed.

Taff had surprised the rest of the committee by telling them that he had researched what other choir conductors were paid. He had even approached the choral society and a couple of the Cornish Male Voice Choirs. He came to the committee armed with the facts.

'That pompous arse Herbert King is paid £50 a rehearsal to conduct the jumped-up Choral Society and that also compares to what the male voice choirs pay their conductors. Our conductor should get at least the same.'

Mindful of the bursting choir bank account (and also hearing rumours about Gavin's failing business) he felt that they should give all the help they could to a 'sodding good choir conductor'. No reference was made about the rumours to the committee. And to top that he put forward, just to really wind up the wicked witches (his description of Rona and Elaine), and got through, a clothing allowance for Gavin of £150 each year. This would cover the cost of dry cleaning his DJ after hot sweaty concerts. Terry Davies, committee member and the people's champion, was certainly flying.

As the choir conductor Gavin was an ex-officio committee member and left the room when decisions about his remuneration were made. He was delighted to be called back in and told of the increased payments. The Verlis Singers jungle drums however beat out loud and clear, and he soon picked up the news that he had a new and vocal committee supporter in tenor Taff Davies.

***

Rona Hancock took off her coat and hung it on a peg in her immaculate utility room. She lived in the town of Fort Major, 15 miles from Verlis in a smart detached house all bought and paid for. Duffy the rescue dog had been let off the lead after his daily walk and went hurtling into the lounge, barking like crazy.

Now nearing 65, she had sung in The Verlis Singers for 39 years in the alto section. All of her employed life had been spent working her way up to being a very senior admin secretary in the Ministry of Defence, who still employed over 200 staff at their Verlis offices. It was her secretarial skills that led to an invite to take over the role of choir honorary secretary and she had been doing it now for almost 32 years. She had never married, had a good pension and life was comfortable. Her mother had lived with her for many years and died in January – eight months ago. She had lived to a grand old age and died peacefully in her sleep. Rona, however, was still grieving, a fact she kept very much to her herself.

In Rona Hancock's book of life, feelings were not for public display. They were private and should never ever be on show to the world at large. Going into her kitchen, she found the tears welling in her eyes as she remembered that the first job back after dog walking was always to make her mum a cup of tea. Her heart ached and she sat in the lounge. She sobbed uncontrollably, her arms tight around herself. *Why Mum, do you have to go?* As the tears rolled down her cheek she felt the warmth of Duffy as he snuggled up against her, somehow understanding her grief.

Kettle boiled, she poured out a cup of green tea and popped in a spoonful of honey. It was supposed to be good for the voice but Rona actually did not have a voice any more. Many years ago she could just about hold an alto line but not these days. But she was honorary choir secretary of 30 years' standing and The Verlis Singers would be nothing without her.

She settled down in front of her computer as Gavin had asked her to update the concert diary on the choir website, something that irritable Welsh postman had also remarked about at the last meeting. She had confided in chairman Brian that she was finding it hard at home to cope without Mum and he had told her not to worry and do the changes when she felt up to it. It would be done by the time of the meeting later that day and she would make a point of announcing it if only to shut up that annoying Welsh twit!

There was also an email about a Poland Choral Festival, which she chose to ignore.

**

Thursday afternoon October 7th

On his way walking home from the depot, Terry found himself thinking about oral sex. Whilst this was a subject he would regularly talk about with his postie pals in the depot, it was something he actually knew very little about in reality!

The new postie – a 20-something called Daniel Scott or 'Cocky Scotty,' would hold forth to the rest of the boys about his sexual encounters, usually on a Monday morning after a 'rampant' weekend. In his words, all Cornish girls were 'gagging for it' and a Saturday night in Verlis meant the guarantee of a shag or, 'At least, a blowie. Cornish girls just love the dick!' he informed his older postie colleagues.

Taff and the older men had scoffed at first. But it had to be said that Cocky was a good-looking boy and women of all ages seemed to fall at his feet. As Cocky Scotty boasted to his colleagues, 'Panty elastic disintegrates when Scotty walks in the room, boys!'

Terry did wonder if, after so many years of married life to the lovely Joan, the subject of a blowjob could be subtly dropped into the conversation. Perhaps this might be on Sunday night whilst he and Joan were watching the Antiques Road Show on the Beeb.

'Well, fancy that love, that chest of drawers, bought at a car boot sale for a pound is worth two bloody million. Duw Duw, who would have thought it?' Followed by, 'Any chance of a blow job?'

Perhaps not!

***

Back at 31 Rhiandon Terrace, close to the centre of Verlis, it was 12.30 midday and Mrs Joan Davies was in the shower. Aged 47, she was a small attractive woman whose life revolved around three things – daughter Jenny who was studying engineering at Bath University, Brutus the dopey dog, but right at the top of the list, 'Her Terry.'

Prior to showering, Joan had had a lady shave and wax and used her expensive body wash. This was a birthday gift from daughter Jenny and hidden away so Terry could not get his hands on it. It was, after all, Thursday afternoon. When she had started her bookkeeping job to earn some extra cash, she had pointed out that Thursdays would always be a day off for Mrs Joan Davies.

One hour later she was tucked up in bed when she heard Terry come in downstairs shouting abuse at Brutus. There was his usual threat to kick him up the ass, which of course he would never do, and a reference to the fact that Brutus had no balls. Joan knew that Terry loved the daft dog and Brutus in turn worshipped Terry. The master of the house ran up the stairs and straight into the shower. Joan curled up in bed. She was wearing a loose-fitting T-shirt and nothing else.

She laughed out loud as he let rip with *Delilah* and *The Green Grass of Home*. This was in his silly Tom Jones forced voice and Joan reflected on her joy (and pride) when, in amazement, she heard her husband singing a proper tenor solo at a concert with his Verlis Singers for the first time about two years after he joined the choir. He truly did have a lovely voice and she had cried when she heard him that night for the first time.

He shouted out to her from the bathroom, 'Hello gorgeous, Hugh Grant here! Taff Davies told me it was OK to pop around and give you one.'

***

Thirty minutes later he pecked her softly on the cheek.

'Hey Catherine Zeta, how was that for you?'

Lovemaking was usually a 25-minute pleasure on a Thursday afternoon for Mr and Mrs Davies. Terry always climbed on top and Joan loved to feel his body close to her. The actual act of penetration was OK for Joan but the best feeling in the world was to feel Terry all over her – skin to skin, body entwined to body.

Sex had become a little more adventurous in recent months with the introduction of body lotion, which Joan had deliberately left next to the bed. Terry had been encouraged to rub the cream over Joan's firm breasts and when she had reciprocated Terry had found Joan's attention to his nipples 'a bit kinky at first'. However now he was more than OK with it. In truth he bloody liked it and it seemed to have the effect of making him 'really hard'.

Also, as the years had passed Joan had introduced her loving husband to the fact that a climax was to be enjoyed by both partners and after Terry had reached a personal top G he would cuddle her gently and use his magic fingers (guided by Joan) to bring her to a noisy crescendo.

When it came to the Davies' bedroom, Joan had certainly taken control and the marriage had blossomed. She also secretly longed to give her hubby a blowjob, but she wondered if he would be shocked. For all his silly bravado, he was actually a bit of a prude!

***

The October committee meeting was held in the usual venue, Verlis Cricket Club starting at 7.30pm. They were the main cricket centre of excellence for the county with a youth coaching squad, and more teams of all ages than you could shake a bat at.

President of the club was one Phil Harwick, a good baritone and sight-reader, who hardly ever missed a concert with The Verlis Singers. He was single, having departed the family home some five years hence, and some of the available ladies in the choir had him firmly in their sights. Phil was a good choir member. However, if the choir had to go on a coach journey, sitting next to Phil was not advised. Unless that is, you wanted to hear non-stop chatter about cricket, cricket and more bloody cricket.

The choir's monthly meeting was held in the Cricket Club's committee room courtesy of Phil Harwick's contacts. It was a large room adorned with team pictures over all the walls. There was hardly any space left, next they would be attaching the 2010 team pics to the ceiling, or building an extension.

Chairman Brian McNeil and hon. sec. Rona arrived together, closely followed by sun tanned publicity officer, Elaine Bridges, choir (non-singer) treasurer Gerry Head, Taff Davies, in his first year of a singer's two-year stint, and alto

Jenny Dalton who was in her second year, also as a choir-singing elected representative, but Jenny hardly ever spoke at the meetings.

Gavin James arrived at 7.30pm just as the meeting was about to start. Also attending was Patrick Nicholls, as requested by the chairman, as there was a legal matter on the agenda. Gavin looked strained and certainly not his usual self. A letter had arrived that day confirming the Bank's terms for repayment of his debt together with a paragraph suggesting that Gavin should have seen his misfortune on the horizon and contacted the bank earlier. They had not taken much time to follow up on the Monday meeting.

Sheila Stirton, as accompanist to the choir, was also invited to every meeting but was on a family holiday; otherwise it was a full attendance.

Chairman Brian commenced the meeting asking for acceptance of the last minutes, at which point Terry Davies enquired why discussion about replacing the accompanist (which had taken up a big slice of the previous meeting and some pretty heated exchanges) was not minuted. Sheila had also missed that meeting and Gavin had seized on the opportunity to bring the subject of his concerns to the committee's attention.

Rona's hackles visibly rose at this point. The chairman, displaying his customary tact and diplomacy, reminded all present that as choir members could ask to see the minutes he had personally requested to the hon. sec. that this would be a non-recorded discussion. He felt that this should certainly be 'off the record!'

'It is best that Sheila, our choir accompanist, is not aware of this discussion and we should ensure that it is kept that way. She was not at the last meeting and is away on holiday at the moment. This is very sensitive and we do not want to upset someone who has been a great servant of the choir.

'The Verlis Singers have been criticised in the past for the way some people think we treat our musical staff. We do need to be careful about this matter, ladies and gentlemen.' His unusual, somewhat fierce glance around all the room was a point well made. It seemed to placate all those present. Brian was a fair man in all respects if, on occasions, he seemed to vanish for weeks on end, without explanation.

The Chairman then thanked Patrick for attending and all agreed that the matter which needed his attention should be the next item on the agenda, allowing him to then leave the meeting.

'Patrick has been in London all day and came straight here, so we need to be quick so he can go home for his supper.'

Gerry Head had raised a point of order about the choir's status as a charity. He was concerned that when The Verlis Singers went on tours the money collected should not go into the charity account, as there could be tax implications. They could, he suggested, be breaking the rules of their charity commission status.

Taff Davies drowsed off at this point, but Gavin sprang to life. His day had been dominated by being kicked around by bank managers and accountants and therefore to once again be sitting through a discussion on finance was NOT what he wanted at a choir committee meeting. He wanted to get to the nitty gritty of a possible trip to Poland.

The Chairman spotted a Gavin intervention and intervened to coax the meeting forward. A conclusion was reached that Patrick would consult with one of his partners – an expert on such charity matters and report back – and he duly left the meeting with a wink to Taff as he departed.

Taff responded 'Hwyl fawr Pat' – goodbye in Welsh, learnt from a Teach Yourself Welsh phrase book.

Treasurer Gerry Head had a skeleton in his closet. Only the chairman had knowledge of this as they were friends, and fellow Masons! A few years back Gerry had run and owned a successful building company. He had taken on a contract to build 30 homes to the west of Verlis. The property developer went bust and Gerry was left owing builders' merchants, his staff, and the bank. He was declared bankrupt and from that day on (understandably) was ultra-cautious when it came to spending money, any money.

Brian McNeil was a fair man who knew that Gerry was one of life's honest people who had been taken for a ride by a disreputable businessman. He kept The Verlis Singers accounts in a scrupulous way, if on occasions he could be boringly pedantic when it came to spending the choir's money.

After Gerry had reported on the continuing healthy state of the choir funds, it was over to Elaine for her publicity officer's report. Much to the surprise of all present she turned on Gavin and asked why HE had agreed to be interviewed by Radio Cornwall about the choir's forthcoming concert at Exeter.

'I am the publicity officer and the interview should have been with me. I was not even consulted!' she snorted.

Before Gavin had time to gather breath Taff Davies took up the challenge and jumped in. He didn't much like Elaine and had observed since joining the committee that Gavin was a natural when it came to the local media and publicity. About all she could do was organise the printing of a few tickets and the last time she did that there was a stupid spelling mistake on them that 'any intelligent person would have spotted.'

'Why the hell would Radio Cornwall want to talk to you, Elaine? This man here is the choir conductor; he is the face of The Verlis Singers and the person who represents us. Get with the real world and stick to posters and printing tickets. Preferably without spelling mistakes!'

Gavin almost choked. Rona turned pink and Elaine looked as if she was going to self-ignite. Taff Davies was a star, straight in. Go for the jugular. Chairman Brian quickly intervened with his usual tact, giving Rona one of his 'not now' looks. He could also sense that a secretarial catalytic explosion was imminent.

The Verlis Singers, he pointed out, had a great reputation and now, with Gavin as conductor, much of the bad press of recent years had been forgotten. He had heard the interview whilst driving in his car and thought that Gavin had come across extremely well. In fact he felt rather proud to be the chairman of such a well-respected Cornish choir.

'Gavin is a natural when it comes to interviews,' he said. 'And,' he added, 'it's Radio Cornwall who should decide on who they want to speak to, not us.' He also reminded the committee of the very pleasant email from the *Songs of Praise* series producer who had commented on Gavin's musical and his interview skills.

The Verlis Singers had appeared on *Songs of Praise* earlier that year and Gavin's relaxed style had endeared him to the executive producer and the BBC team. They had sung three pieces for Easter including the Stainer version of *God so Loved the World*. The producer had remarked that it was sung, 'quite beautifully, with great feeling'. The other two pieces, *All in the April Evening* and *The Long Day Closes*, had resulted in 'a very high number of letters and phone calls from listeners asking when The Verlis Singers could again be heard on the programme.'

'Hear hear!' piped up Taff. 'Gavin is great with the media,' with a smirk aimed directly at Elaine, who by now had turned from Ambre Solaire bronze to bright scarlet.

There was normally a short break during each meeting and the chairman tactfully suggested that now was the time. 'Back in ten minutes,' he said, heading off out of the door to the club bar, which (thankfully) was always open in the evenings. He needed a pint and some committee members needed to cool down.

Gavin had switched his mobile to silent but noticed that he had a text message from his wife, of all people, a very unusual occurrence these days. She wanted a chat. He responded that he would 'catch up with her later'. Perhaps she was going to ask her wealthy parents to help bail out the business. Not much chance of that as they were so bloody mean and didn't like him much.

When they resumed, Gerry Head gave the treasurer's report verbally. He had not had time to prepare it for them in writing. The Verlis Singers had £41,500 in their reserve a/c and over £9,000 in the day to day business a/c. Cheques to the conductor and the accompanist were due for the final quarter of the year and he had just paid the rehearsal room invoice for the next six months as the church had agreed to hold their charge for 2011 at £38 a night.

The choir finances were 'sound,' but as always Gerry made the point that they needed to be prudent. 'The money belongs to the choir and its members – we are charged to always be prudent about expenditure.' Brian McNeil wondered how many times Gerry Head had used the word 'prudent' at choir meetings.

The rest of the committee meeting passed off relatively peacefully. All was prepared for the Exeter concert that Saturday. Coach booked and choir members' pick-up points established. Rona was chasing some of the members who had still not paid their annual subs and got her monthly dig in at Peggy Trenholm who she said was overdue and claimed she was waiting for her pension credit to come through.

Choir auditions was on the agenda, a very thorny subject, as some of the committee members knew of their vocal imperfections. Gavin suggested that they should be put back to the New Year and everyone agreed (some with sighs of relief). Tempers were allowed to calm, it was then back to business, well Any Other Business in fact. Going round those present Brian asked each person. There was nothing until it came to the conductor.

Gavin explained that he had received details of the Krakow Music Festival next June and wanted The Verlis Singers to enter the competitive mixed voice class and also the own choice of music class. At this point the hon. sec. interrupted and said that such matters should have been sent to her first, NOT the conductor, and she would have brought it forward.

'Or conveniently not bothered if you didn't think it was a good idea!' chipped in Taff, ignorant of the fact that she had actually seen the email!

Time for the Chairman to suggest that this was a matter for Gavin to speak on and that all present should give him the floor. Over to the conductor.

'I think the choir is ready for a tour and a competition. It will focus on new music and Krakow is not far with flights from Bristol airport. I really want to do this,' Gavin told them.

Rona and Elaine kept quiet but, to the amazement of all, Jenny Dalton spoke. This was the first time in 18 months she had ever made a contribution to any committee meeting. She was a good and loyal soprano who had been coerced to committee duty by Rona because she knew that Jenny would never speak or, more importantly, disagree with her!

The time had come however and Jenny spoke out in a quiet voice. She said that if the conductor felt that this was good for the choir (and they could certainly afford to subsidise the trip) then the members should be told that it was going to happen. She wasn't sure that she would be able to get time off from work to go herself but The Verlis Singers should go.

'Well said Jenny!' offered Terry Davies, and Chairman Brian nodded his blessing.

Elaine Bridges, taking care not to catch a glare from Rona, also spoke up in agreement. The one thing that she and husband Tony loved in retirement were cheap holidays. They had not visited Poland and if it was a choir trip, and subsidised, she and Tony were in.

During his business life, Chairman Brian had regularly visited Poland. He had made some very good 'contacts'. He wondered if he could wangle going with the choir and leave his wife at home.

It was agreed that Gavin would tell the choir at the next rehearsal that the committee would like to attend the Krakow Music Festival and that the Chair, Treasurer, Hon. Sec. and Conductor would meet in the next few days to look at costings. It was then 10pm and Brian felt that the choir should be told that the committee would consider subsidising the tour. As time was getting on there would be no further discussion at this point, stopping Gerry Head from speaking.

The first stage was to get an idea on numbers who would be interested in taking part.

'Don't you think the choir secretary should do that?' blurted Rona, and it was agreed that both Rona and Gavin would tell the choir at the next rehearsal.

'Thank you all for attending, and good singing to you all; we can thrash out the finances Gerry when we have a clear idea of numbers.' Meeting over.

The date of the next meeting was set for Thursday November 11th.

Gavin remembered that his wife wanted a chat, but decided to accept the chairman's offer of a drink in the Cricket Club lounge bar next door. He certainly didn't want to go home yet. She would probably again remind him that he was a bloody loser. She was right, but he didn't want to hear it.

Chapter 5

It was around midnight when Gavin eventually arrived home. Taff Davies and Brian the choir chairman had been in no hurry to leave the cricket club bar and the last thing Gavin wanted was a face to face confrontation with Georgina about the desperate state of his business finances.

Taff had driven to the meeting and was drinking shandies. Gavin had walked, so had a couple of large dry white wines and was grateful to Taff for the offer of a lift to the end of his road. Taff did have an ulterior motive though. Gavin was surprised when the Welshman broached the subject of his camera business and was asked by Taff if things were 'Going OK, Boyo?'

He had not been aware up to that point that the members of The Verlis Singers were gossiping about the state of his business, or even if they knew that the shit was about to hit the proverbial fan. Obviously they did. When quizzed about the reason for the question, Taff waffled on and said, 'Well, it must be bloody hard running your own business these days with the economy in such a mess.'

Fact was that Cocky Scotty, the randy postie who covered the city centre and delivered to Gavin's camera shop had made a comment about the amount of letters from 'H M Customs marked urgent' to the lads in the locker room at Postal HQ.

Hearing this, Terry tore Cocky off a strip, giving him short thrift on the rules and regulations on confidentiality that a postie signs up to. But he took note of the remark nevertheless. Gavin had fobbed off the inquisitive Welshman in the car but he actually trusted Taff Davies. Perhaps one day he would tell Taff about his crap business and his crap marriage. He didn't really have anyone else to talk to about it, apart from his brother David who lived in Swindon.

All said and done, Taff was the committee member who had fought the old guard to get his retainer increased by quite a significant amount, not to mention a clothes and dry cleaning allowance. But on the way home from the committee meeting was not the time to take Taff Davies into his confidence.

Some other time perhaps?

***

All the lights were off at his house. Gavin went to the kitchen to make himself a mug of tea. He wondered if Georgina was asleep and crept up the stairs to check. He opened the door quietly. The sound of heavy snoring meant the coast was clear. Whatever had prompted the earlier text, discussion, or a row, would thankfully wait till the morning at least.

He shut the bedroom door quietly and went back downstairs. Mug of tea in hand, he sat on the sofa, kicked off his shoes and put on the TV. He heard the sound of a text close by and realised it was from Georgina's mobile. He wondered where the phone was as she always had it with her. He found it down the back of the sofa, where it had obviously slipped from her bag.

Gavin wondered if it might be important. He knew that her father had been to see the doctor that day for a heart check-up. He was in his 70s and had a couple of strokes so the family was quite concerned about him. The text could be news that she may want to be told, even if it meant waking her. Late night texts were unusual and it could be an important message.

Deciding that he did not want to wake her as that might prompt a confrontation, he concluded it was best to read the message, just in case it was crucial.

Pressing text messages he saw:

Hey G your desk will never be the same again

a whole new meaning to .. what a GOOD HEAD !!!

Trev the pecs !!! xxx's ......all over ..

See you tomorrow at school, can't wait!

When Gavin and Georgina had first met at Portsmouth Station in 1988 it had not really been love at first sight. They were both going to the Isle of Wight on holiday. Georgina was with two girlfriends and Gavin was with four of his pals from the Sunday football team at the local pub in Newbury. It was a holiday romance that eventually led to marriage two years on, in 1990.

Gavin had then moved from Newbury to Verlis where they had bought a small terraced house. Georgina was teaching at a village primary school and Gavin got a job on the photographic team of the Cornwall Leader, transferring from the Hants Leader, as both papers were in the same group.

Life had been pretty good then. They were young and ambitious, especially Georgina. Even the sex was great in those early years. They couldn't keep their hands off each other back then.

As the years rolled by Gavin had discovered that his wife would not contemplate having children, as it was her profession and progression as a teacher that totally dominated her life. When she was appointed head at Trimanter Primary School outside Verlis, Gavin was put finally on the sidelines.

Conversations at home were led always by the politics of

school governor relations, issues with teachers, the parents, Ofsted reports and, a conversation that always began with the words…

'At school today…'

When Gavin was offered redundancy because the newspaper was staff slashing, he took it. All the money went into his new venture, a little camera shop in the centre of Verlis, just behind the Cathedral.

Those were the halcyon days of dark rooms, developing holiday pictures, wedding jobs (although Gavin had lost interest in taking pictures); people bought cameras and photographic equipment from shops.

Then came digital.

***

Gavin recognised that whilst Georgina was ambitious to the point of obsession, she was a thoroughly dedicated head teacher who had worked to make her primary school one of the highest regarded in the county. She was bloody good at her job.

She had never showed any interest in his music making and had only once attended a charity concert of The Verlis Singers for the local hospice. Gavin had learned afterwards that the chair of the school governors was on the board of the St Catherine's Hospice. On this single occasion, being the ambitious school head *and* wife of the choir conductor offered possible brownie points for respect and future promotion.

He had also been useful when the parents had wanted to form a choir for Christmas. They had actually been quite good and she saw her husband in something of a new light.

Gavin had never for one moment stopped to wonder whether his wife would have an affair, let alone with one of her teaching colleagues. Now, sitting on his sofa at home looking at her mobile phone text, that was exactly what he had to face up to. He had met Trevor Scarron, the sports master at her school at the open day in the spring. He had to be the Trev in the text. He was all testosterone and tracksuit and not much else in Gavin's eyes, and he had remarked as such to Georgina at the time. He wondered how long the affair had been going on.

His mind was in turmoil, but fortunately Gavin James had the ability to store his problems away neatly in brain 'compartments'. Nothing could be done now and in the morning he would, for the first time for many years, confront his wife with a list of issues. His failing business, the £25,000 he could not repay and probable bankruptcy had already been discussed. Now on the James agenda was the state of their marriage. The text he had seen surely meant she was having it off with a teacher at her own school. Not really such a clever thing to do, having an affair with a staff member, pondered Gavin. Verlis was a close-knit Cornish community where everybody knew everybody else.

'Shagging your sports teacher is not very smart.'

He went to his office, which was on the ground floor. There was a spare single bunk bed and he took his mug of tea with him. All of a sudden he felt very weary. He got undressed, fell into bed and was soon asleep.

NOT one of the best days of his life!

***

Monday October 11th

It was 7.20am and Polly James was showering and thinking about her weekend spent with friends in Edinburgh. Once best pal Moira had travelled from Glasgow and they had all squeezed into a tiny flat owned by old uni friends Ruth and Alice.

It had all been a massive let down. A fucking disaster actually, and that was an understatement. Polly mused on the fact that they had all changed so much since the heady days at university in Edinburgh and she now didn't really have all that much in common with the other three girls.

How could things change so much in such a short time?

Moira had stayed up north and was still studying for a Masters and bored everyone rigid with how hard she was working. Ruth and Alice had become silly with constant tales of men and failed relationships. Polly wondered bitchily if they were actually lesbians, as they were very cuddly together, and it was, after all, a very small flat!

All hopes of clubbing or even 'pulling' went out of the window when Ruth announced that they had ordered pizzas, had a fridge full of wine, and a night in to 'reflect on old times and look at the old uni photos' was planned.

This was going to be the Saturday evening's entertainment, totally bloody boring.

Polly had drunk too much red wine and enthused about her super well-paid accountancy job to her friends and also her new choir in Cornwall. Whilst they all knew that she had sung in the uni choral society whilst in Scotland, they were all rather disdainful on hearing Polly's singing news.

When Polly bragged that they had sung on *Songs of Praise* they all hooted with derision. It was, Alice said, a programme for bible punchers and 'sad and lonely old gits.'

There was little talk of the new well-paid job, which Polly had in Verlis, which she put down to pure bloody envy. They had all gone to bed grumpy, frustrated, and very pissed.

She told them on Sunday over breakfast that the choir had a concert the coming Saturday in Exeter and was going on the coach with them. She wasn't ready to sing yet but thought it would be good to hear them in a concert. Alice then chipped in with her opinion that she was not the Polly they remembered from the past and that she should find herself a bloke, be pursuing a more 'mature' hobby and was becoming 'a bit sad, singing in a choir.'

This annoyed Polly who completely lost her rag, told all her three (ex) friends to 'Fuck right off.' She had already packed her bag and wanted out. She stormed out of the flat and set off south for Verlis rather earlier than anticipated and in a BIG strop. It was a very long car journey home to Cornwall and she wondered why she had bloody bothered going to meet them. Never again, she decided over coffee and baked beans on toast at a service station near Gloucester.

Today she had a meeting with the finance director and team at the big snooty independent Verlis department store in the centre of town called Fostors. The Partners at Stroman Maycroft Accountants had asked her to work on their account.

This was something of an honour for someone so new to the practice. Fostors were a well-connected and established family business. Polly was looking forward to the meeting. She would be going with one of her senior partners, Mark Richards. He would 'ease her in'.

Mark seemed a decent enough guy, a bit of a gentle giant and one of the practice partners. She quite fancied the idea of 'easing him in'. She was certainly getting ever more desperate for sex.

To get a feeling for the business, she had shopped in Fostors and thought it a very old-fashioned store. Later today she would probably get an insight into just how it was doing! In her view it certainly needed to move into the modern world.

Verlis was a lovely place but fashion-wise it was ten years behind London. Even the big M&S store in the centre of town didn't seem to stock the same fashions as she had seen further north.

This, she concluded as she brushed her teeth, would be a stocking and suspender day. Wearing her tight two-piece business suit and high heels, the young Mr Foster she was meeting was in for a treat. He would be putty in her hands, marriage material even?

She decided that she would leave them on for choir practice that night and flash her long legs at that randy Welshman and the rest of the tenors during the first half. Taff Davies seemed an OK sort of guy who probably had a very sweet little wife back at home, ironing his shirts and Y-fronts for him. She wondered if he wore string vests. Probably, and only ever did sex 'on top'.

The tenor section would find concentration impossible in the second half as Taff would, no doubt, spread the word during the tea break about Polly, 'wearing the tackle'. All tenor section eyes would then be on her, hoping for a glimpse of bare top leg flesh.

'Sorry Gavin for buggering up your tenor section's concentration in the second half,' she said out loud to herself, and she wondered how easy it was to sing with a hard on, and laughed out loud. She also remembered that she had to get to rehearsal early, as Gavin was going to audition her before everyone else turned up. She would pass the audition of course, but didn't think she should flash her stocking tops at him.

***

Monday evening and choir rehearsal – Peggy Trenholm arrived early at 6.45pm and was putting out the chairs when Gavin walked in.

'Good evening Mr Conductor,' she greeted him cheerily.

Gavin mumbled back and Peggy could see that he was not his usual self. Enquiring if he was okay, he mumbled something about it being a bad day and was glad to get to choir to 'get his mind off things'. He also had 'a new soprano' to audition and she was coming in early.

The one thing Peggy Trenholm understood was grown up men and their emotions. She had nursed both her parents until they had passed away. Many times she had cradled her dad in her arms as his life waned. She had cared for hubby Ron through his prostate cancer scare and had helped son David through a bad state of depression that followed the breakup of his marriage to Karen. Sad, distraught males were the one thing in life she knew how to cope with!

Walking towards him, she wasn't really surprised when he started to sob. She had sensed that something was really wrong and knew that if she could get him to talk about it that would help.

Whatever it was, he was bottling up something. The sight of a smiling Peggy obviously released the cork from the bottle.

Persuading him to sit down, Peggy went and shut the doors to the rehearsal room. The last thing she wanted now was any other choir member to walk in and see Gavin so upset. She would not tell anyone and could be discreet. Not so most of the others in the choir, especially the females.

They sat down together and she reached across and held his hand. Gavin told her that he had just had a lousy weekend and his life was in a bit of a mess. He had found out that his wife Georgina was having an affair and the massive row that followed meant that they would certainly be splitting up. To add to the confusion, his camera shop was going down the pan and he had to sort out quite a few 'financial problems' in the days ahead.

He told Peggy, 'It's all gone a bit pear-shaped.'

Talking to Peggy, and telling someone, really helped. She was a good person, if slightly mad, with her plastic Santa suit and wacky dress sense and sometimes equally bizarre behaviour. Gavin didn't go into much detail, but explained that his business was going downhill and to make matters worse his marriage to Georgina was 'on the rocks'.

Gavin's composure had returned. He felt better for telling Peggy his troubles. The door opened and the new prospective soprano Polly Jones walked in for her audition. Polly didn't notice Gavin and Peggy at first sat in the corner until Peggy stood up, said hello to Polly and disappeared into the kitchen. She knew that the conductor liked to do auditions on a one-to-one basis.

Auditioning new singers could be enjoyable or difficult, depending on one simple fact: could the person standing in front of Gavin, as he sat at the piano, hear a note, and sing it back to him? That was the only thing that mattered. Could a new potential member sing in tune? Could he or she listen to a note and then sing it back to him?

Sight-reading was not an issue, totally irrelevant. Even most experienced choir singers would say that they could not read music. That of course was rarely true. If someone had sung before, looking at the music on a page, they knew where their line was, when the note went up and down. They recognised where rests came and had some musical terminology. For a conductor, a new sight-reading choir member was a bonus. But intelligent people who were new to singing soon picked up the science of reading a line.

Gavin himself could see a piece of new music and hear it in his head. He could also sing back the melody of any other part come to that, almost instantaneously. He put that down to the hours spent on Sunday nights as a boy when his Methodist parents would invite back people from the chapel.

This always ended with a hymn-singing session, with sister Hannah playing piano and Gavin singing one of the parts, dependent on who was there. His dad would say, 'We don't have a tenor tonight so you can sing that line, Gavin.' The next time it might be the bass, or even the alto line.

Gavin hit middle C on the piano and asked Polly to sing it to him. Eureka, back came her clear voice singing the note and perfectly in pitch. Next came some scales to see how high or low she could sing. Polly was a true top soprano, and when he pushed her with some arpeggios she could easily hit a top A.

She was very nervous at first, a point Gavin noted. Singers with nerves, however good their voices, had to be coached before they could take on a solo at a concert. Polly could perhaps sing a solo line one day with The Verlis Singers, but not for a while yet. Clare Taylor had already told him that Polly was 'a good singer' after sitting next to her last week but he always needed to hear new potential members.

Sitting at the piano looking up at her, Gavin could not help but notice that she seemed even taller than last week when she had come to choir for the first time. She was wearing very high heels and a very smart business suit and looked as if she had come for a job interview, not a choir audition. She certainly had the most incredible pair of long legs.

Polly explained that she loved singing and that her parents were in a choir in London. She sang with the University Choir and the local choral society whilst at uni but they were 'mostly bald men and little old ladies with grey hair!'

On telling her that she was definitely accepted, she rushed forward excitedly and gave him a hug. Gavin mused that all was not that bad, two hugs in one night. At that point – hug number one – Peggy came in with a cup of tea, which she put on Gavin's table next to his music stand.

There was a new membership form to fill in for Polly, so Gavin walked over to the stand and filled it in. He marked her voice as 8 out of 10 and put the form on his music stand to give to Rona who would sort out the membership payment details, uniform etc. He noticed a piece of writing paper on the stand. Opening it, he read,

Dear mr special Conductor – our Gavin
We would love yu to come to tea
this Sunday – roast chicken and all the triminns

about 12? .

mr and mrs Trenholm – your friends.

***

Good old Peggy – he would go of course, a good excuse to escape the marital home on a Sunday and enter a friendly no-war zone. He must remember to take a bottle of wine though, as Ron Trenholm's homemade brew enjoyed the reputation of being Cornish fire water which could blow the top off your head.

Choir members were now flooding in and a massive cheer went up as the doors burst open and Len Fyfield was pushed into the room in his wheelchair by bass Dick Wilson. Len's wife Mellyn walked in behind him.

Everyone burst into song. 'For he's a jolly good fellow' filled the room and Taff Davies rushed over to Mellyn, picking her up and dancing round the room with her. This was the very best side of the caring family that was The Verlis Singers. All the men were patting Len on the shoulders and shaking his hands whilst the ladies lined up to smother him with kisses and affection. Everyone was shocked at how desperately thin and ill he looked. The big man whose wonderful bass voice could fill a church was now a shell of the Len Fyfield they remembered. Death was very close; everyone could see that!

Encouraging the choir members to take their seats, Sheila Stirton hit the chord for *Deep Harmony*. Richard Parish, the oversized bass, and Dick Wilson had moved a seat to make room for Len's wheelchair. It was one of the most poignant renditions of the choir anthem for a long time.

Gavin had tears in his eyes. He could see that this was probably the last time Len would attend a rehearsal of the choir that had been such a big part of his life. The responsibility of being conductor and leader overwhelmed him. In the front row of the altos even tough (never show your feelings) Rona was shaking and sobbing. Elaine who always sat next to her, had her arm around Rona's shoulders. She knew that seeing Len had brought back all the feelings of despair that Rona had felt after her mother passed away.

Gavin, sensing the sadness (and still feeling it himself), then asked the choir to sing the Flanders and Swan arrangement he had composed for the silly song *In the Bath*. This featured bass Richard Parish, who, in spite of being a pain in the bum most of the time, did actually have a very good singing voice. As they sang it, Richard went and stood behind Len in his wheelchair. Len joined in the solo; his now weakened voice being overshadowed by the booming tones of big Richard.

The choir sang as best they could.

During the interval Claire Nesbitt went up to Gavin and told him about a friend of hers who had just moved to Cornwall. Claire explained that she was a brilliant accompanist and if Sheila was ever not there perhaps Gavin might be looking for someone to fill in?

Knowing that Sheila was going to be away the next Monday at a WI meeting, he suggested that Claire might like to bring her along. 'Would she want to see the music before the rehearsal?' he asked.

'No need,' replied Claire, 'she can sight-read anything. Her name is Becky, Becky Morris; we were at school together at Melksham in Wiltshire. You will like her Gavin, she's a laugh.'

Gavin decided not to tell anyone. If she came it would be a bonus, as he had been going to bang out the notes himself, calling on Norma Bailey from the altos when it got complicated.

Len and his wife left during the interval. Their son came to collect them as he was staying for a few days and Gavin concluded that this would be the last time they would ever see Len Fyfield at the choir's rehearsal room. Surely he would not live long enough to sing at the Cathedral carol service, which was still eight weeks away.

In a way Gavin was glad Len was not there for the second half. He was going to tell the choir about the proposed Poland trip and it would have been difficult to do this in front of Len, who would surely know that when this happened he would not be around.

The choir programme for the Exeter concert was on the board. Most of the pieces had been in the repertoire for a few months. It included a folk song section and some John Rutter favourites.

The choir started the second half rehearsing Stanford's beautiful *Blue Bird*, another item for the Exeter Concert that Saturday. They sang it unaccompanied. This was a lovely piece and The Verlis Singers performed it the way founder Isaac Grenfell had interpreted it. Back in the old days, Isaac's sister Gwen had sung the solo, these days it was Claire Nesbitt. The piece needed concentration as the pitch could drop and Gavin gave the altos a dressing down for singing what he described as 'a lazy line'.

'Just because we have sung it many times before, this will be the first time the people in the audience at Exeter will have heard you sing it. Let's go again from bar nine...'

Once the blue bird had flown, this time perfectly in tune, Gavin told them all about Poland, with Rona called out to stand next to him; a united front was required on this occasion. They explained that the committee had discussed the invitation to sing at a festival in Krakow, Poland next June. Gavin was very keen that they should go, as it was a while since The Verlis Singers had competed in a festival and it would really give them something to work towards next year.

One important point, he told them, was that there had to be a good balance of the singing parts and the final decision of whether or not to go, would have to depend on that. Rona then told the choir that a sub-committee had been formed and the suggestion was that the members should be subsidised from choir funds. That would be a decision made by the full choir committee and it would be Rona who would then report back to them all.

Murmurs of enthusiasm greeted the announcement and Gavin was pleasantly surprised at what seemed to be a consensus of approval. Time would tell though when people had to commit to the dates and pay their deposits. Choir rules were such that conductors and accompanists did not pay to go on choir tours. Chairman Brian had called him earlier that day to remind Gavin of this. Obviously he also knew that the conductor was in dire financial straits!

At this point Norma Bailey (a music teacher at Verlis Girls' School) stood up and said, 'Perhaps Tatania would agree to be on the sub-committee. It would be such a help to have her Polish knowledge. There might be some language problems she could help with.' Rona responded (so all could hear) that as she was not a committee member she could not sit on a sub-committee.

'It's not in the rules,' she said.

At this, Patrick Nicholls QC rose to his feet from the back row of basses, hands on suit lapels, taking up a pose that resembled a mocking court appearance straight from the TV series, Rumpole of the Bailey.

'We certainly would NOT want democracy to stand between this choir and common sense, me'Lud!' he boomed.

Everyone (except Rona and her alto pals) fell about laughing, the perfect antidote to the earlier sadness of Len's visit. Rehearsal over, the usual crowd headed for the pub, just round the corner from the church where they rehearsed.

Chapter 6

Saturday October 16th

It was a wet and miserable Saturday afternoon and the members of The Verlis Singers were starting to turn up at the Exeter coach park in Thames Street to set off for the concert. Peggy and Ron Trenholm were first to arrive with a bag laden down with sandwiches, flasks and other homemade goodies, Land Rover parked in the nearby free car park. Five minutes after finding their seat near the middle of the coach, Ron was tucking into a cheese and pickle wedge.

It was about a three-hour trip, allowing for a piddle stop at the motorway services, and Hon. Sec. Rona Hancock was standing next to the coach door, holding her umbrella and balancing a clipboard in her hand, ready to tick off the singers and some partners who were making the trip.

The concert started at 7.30pm and they were sharing the programme with a Welsh Male Voice Choir from somewhere up 'in the Valleys'.

One fact of choral life was that choir members across the globe 'cherry pick' the concerts they choose to sing at. The Verlis Singers were no exception. Paid up choir membership was now well over the 60 mark with new members such as Polly James taking numbers up to around 65.

The choir would be at around 45 singers for the Exeter concert. Looking ahead to the annual Christmas showcase concert in the cathedral, The Verlis Singers that evening would include everyone. No one would miss the big annual prestige sing. Six weeks before every concert a singers' list would go up on the choir board in the rehearsal room and the faithful regulars would quickly add their names. Gavin then kept his eye on the list and insisted that Rona regularly told him who was going to turn out.

Whilst numbers were obviously important, it was the singers and the balance in each section of the choir that was most relevant to the conductor. Not much use the celebrated Verlis Singers going on stage with a depleted tenor section or with some of the leading sopranos missing. It was not unusual for Gavin to cajole some of the singers to make a special effort to sing at a concert if they had not committed to attending.

More often than not they responded favourably to the popular conductor's pleas, changing plans if necessary and adding their name at the 11th hour, much to the annoyance of the honorary secretary. This meant that her singing lists were changing day by day as the concert date arrived, causing great annoyance, which would no doubt be aired at the next committee meeting.

***

Tenor Eric Stroman had arrived with his trolley of CDs to sell with his wife Karen. She did not sing, but never missed a concert and always sat with Ron Trenholm at the back of the audience. She would look after the choir CD sales during the interval and also as people left after the concerts. There were three different CDs to sell. These had been recorded over the past ten years after the vinyl discs from the Isaac times had gone out of stock, even though occasional radio plays still earned royalties.

The three recent CDs had been recorded by a local company in the Heather Strong days. They were a collection of favourite hymns, one featuring UK folk songs and the other a Christmas CD. On a good night sales could be up around the 30 mark. At £10 for each CD that was another £300 for choir funds. On the return coach she would give the evening's takings to Rona to bank in the choir account.

On Gavin's to do list was another CD in 2011, as he felt that the choir had now reached a good enough standard to undertake another recording. The singing on the Heather CDs was okay, but it would be good to get one of 'proper' recording companies interested. With the *Songs of Praise* appearances this might be possible. Something for Gavin to turn his promotional talents to in the New Year!

The line-up for Exeter and balance of singers was a strong one, however, and Gavin arrived, suit carrier and briefcase crammed with music under his arm, and with his music stand. The church where the concert would take place would certainly have a stand, but Gavin liked to use his own so it always went with him.

He was looking forward to the concert, a chance to get away from the crap and the arguments at home and to do what he did best, charm an audience with his witty stories, and direct his choir. Tonight he would wow the good people of Exeter and show them just how good The Verlis Singers really were.

One by one the singers piled on to the coach. Each one arrived carrying a bag containing their uniform, which was dispatched in the coach hold. The choir always travelled with Decadian Coaches from Verlis and driver Neil was the usual man behind the wheel. He knew most of the choir by name and always attended the concerts, sitting in the back with the CD sales team.

Gavin had sent the list of songs the choir would perform to the concert organisers weeks before, but fancied dropping in another piece in as a finale encore. The choir had sung the John Rutter arrangement of *When the Saints Go Marching In* in past years and Gavin had recently dug it out of the choir cupboard and revived it. It was a good piece to end a concert and with an allocated 30-minute rehearsal before the concert he would have time to brush it up. Sheila Stirton, the choir accompanist, knew it well and Gavin had bought two copies of the score with him so Sheila could not make an excuse for not being able to play it.

The final chorus was written for audience and Gavin would get them to stand and sing it through and join in with the choir. It always went down well and, as it was the final piece, it therefore guaranteed a standing ovation and a great end to a concert.

***

Polly Jones was sat with Clare Taylor on the coach. Claire had volunteered her to help Karen with CD sales. Polly had called Rona the week before to ask if she could come along and help 'behind the scenes!' The hon. secretary had grumpily agreed.

'Go on Polly just flash your long legs at them. CD sales could be at an all-time high tonight,' Claire joked with her new friend.

Taff, Eric, Tony Bridges, Richard Parish, Patrick Nicholls, and some of the other men were at the back of the coach organising a sweepstake on the first song that the Welsh Male Voice Choir would sing to open their programme. Eric had drawn up a list of 40 favourites including many hymns.

Patrick had cut up the song list and had all the slips in a hat so everyone on the coach would part with a pound and enter the sweep. The winner kept the proceeds. Taff Davies (being Welsh) had been consulted on the choices by Eric and as Patrick explained: 'He has inside knowledge, being a bloody Taff, and if he picks the winning song he will go on about it all the way home.'

The hat was passed around the coach on the way to Exeter, together with the sweet tin supplied by Jenny Dalton. Everyone put in a pound in including the coach driver. Favourites were *Mae Hen Wlad Fy Nhadau*, *Tydi A Roddaist*, with *We'll keep a Welcome* way out in front. Everyone agreed that *Myfanwy* was a drop-dead cert for some stage of the evening though. Every Welsh Male choir in the world sang *Myfanwy*, usually as an encore.

Taff Davies kept quiet. He actually didn't speak Welsh and just knew a few phrases plus of course the Welsh National Anthem, *Hen Wlad Fy Nhadau.*

'Wouldn't it be nice to do a concert with a Welsh Male Voice choir that sang some different pieces?' said Gavin. He quickly added so all could hear, 'Sorry Taff, no offence meant.'

Time for a Richard Parish smutty quip from the back seat of the bus!

'I'm looking forward to 'My-fanny', she's my most favourite Welsh song.'

'But worry not Mr Conductor – transfer negotiations are in place to sell Taff Davies to the West Cornwall Male Voice. They have agreed with our legal representative, the 'orrible QC Mr Nicholls that we will pay *them* the princely sum of £10,000 to take him off our hands!'

'Worth every penny!' Cheers all around the bus.

***

Spirits were high on the coach and some of the singers were asking Tatania about Poland. Gavin listened in on this conversation from his seat and was delighted that there seemed such a positive vibe to the proposed trip next year. Peggy announced that she had already purchased her Polish phrase book and Taff cheerily shouted out that all Polish virgins should be warned that the best looking singing Welshman was on his way.

He had obtained permission from 'the lovely Joan' to travel solo as she would be at home organising the celebrations that followed later in June, their wedding anniversary. He didn't mention the 50th birthday party, which was about the same time of the year, as he was trying to avoid working out which of the choir would be invited.

Oversized bass and comedian Richard Parish piped up again from the back seat, now stuffing a cheese and ham super sandwich, scrounged from the Peggy supply bag.

'Soggy soggy soggy… oy-oy-oy…'

Everyone joined in the Cornish anthem, roaring with laughter, even Rona the Hon. Sec. allowed herself a chuckle.

***

The Verlis Singers had arranged to be at the church for 5pm, allowing 45mins to rehearse and acclimatise to the acoustics of the building and also work out their standing positions. The Male Voice Choir would rehearse after them from 5.45pm to 6.30pm. Doors opened at 6.45pm to let in the queuing audience for a 7.30pm concert start.

The host ladies from the Exeter Church had prepared a light tea for both choirs on arrival, thus giving Richard Parish ample opportunity to tell those unfortunate enough to be behind the tea counter his tried and tested range of buffet jokes.

Verlis would sing first to open the concert after the welcome from the Minister. Then the Male Voice group of songs took the concert up to the interval. The order then changed for the second half, which meant that The Verlis Singers ended the concert. This was official recognition from the organisers that they were seen to be the better choir. This pleased Gavin but did not go down well with the frosty lady conductor of the Welsh choir.

Gavin had selected a programme of songs that started with more traditional choral pieces followed by a group of folk songs. The church was packed for the concert with about 350 people in the church and The Verlis Singers were in fine voice. Gavin was a natural in front of an audience and soon had them eating out of the palm of his hand.

For this concert the ladies had been instructed by Rona to wear the crimson uniform with silk scarves. The men always wore dinner jackets with white shirts and a dicky bow in the same red material as the ladies' dresses. Gavin also wore a DJ but usually with a black wing-collar dress shirt he had purchased from Fostors. He always looked presentable and the DJ look suited him as he was slim and 6ft in height. His hair had grown very long and he was long overdue a visit to the barbers.

'Are you all ready?' Gavin turned to ask the audience as he introduced the folk song group.

'We are now going on a whistle-stop coach tour of the British Isles, the coach leaves in five minutes, form an orderly queue please and hold on to your seats.'

They loved his relaxed style and applauded loudly after each song. Some of the pieces, such as Vaughan Williams' *Linden Lea* had been in the repertoire for many years and someday soon would have to go. But audiences liked them and, after all, the customer is always right.

The Welsh Male Voice Choir did indeed sing all the old favourites but the audience equally enjoyed them. A rather frightening, stern middle-aged lady conducted them but Gavin won her over by congratulating the choir on their wonderful singing in front of the audience. She, in turn, made no such comments about The Verlis Singers. Secretly she knew that she was sharing the concert platform with a very good concert choir with a quite beautiful sound and a charismatic conductor who had complete control of the choir from Cornwall. They were all they were cracked up to be!

Gavin finished the final group of the concert with the John Rutter *Saints Go Marching In*, getting the audience and the Welsh choir members to join in. He had rehearsed it earlier even though he knew Sheila was not happy at having it sprung on her. But it brought the house down and earned both choirs a standing ovation.

***

The coach was jumping all the way home. Everyone was singing. Peggy did her party piece – *I'm a Cornish Bird in a Gilded Cage* – and bass Richard let rip with his after-concert solo, *The Marrow Song*, everyone joining in the chorus:

'O what a beauty, we've never seen one as big as that before.'

Eric won the sweepstake with *Tydi a Roddaist* and asked Rona to send his winnings to the St Catherine's Hospices, as he knew Len would be going there soon.

CD purchases on the night were an amazing £480 and Polly was nominated 'super girl' on sales! At half time she had even walked around the hall asking people if they wanted to buy a CD. No one had ever done that before. Selling 48 CDs in one night was a record and sales to men in the audience was particularly high, something to do with the long-legged sexy sales girl, no doubt. Not surprisingly, the majority of sales were to males in the audience as well as the men in the male voice choir.

***

It was good to be in The Verlis Singers and it was a great concert, a standing ovation for both choirs. And tomorrow afternoon, Gavin was going out for lunch. Roast chicken and all the trimmins!

Chapter 7

Sunday lunch was indeed very enjoyable, that was something of an understatement! Peggy and Ron rolled out the culinary red carpet for their special guest. Gavin had driven out to their house, arriving at just before 12 noon. There was a bus option, but he had decided to drive so there was a good excuse not to sample Ron's infamous brain-blasting homemade brew to excess.

Gavin had not realised how seriously ill Ron had been with prostate cancer, but heard of how the past few years had been very difficult for the couple. The treatment had been successful and Ron was now much better.

'Everything is back in full working order,' he whispered to Gavin with a wink whilst Peggy was beavering around in the kitchen.

'Enjoy every day!' Ron beamed at Gavin, and smiled at his beloved wife as she came back in to set the table for Sunday lunch. 'Don't you agree, bird?' Peggy smiled back at her husband. Sunday afternoon lovemaking was certainly a definite in the Trenholm house. They hoped Gavin wouldn't stay too long after lunch as the electric blanket was set to come on at 2pm.

The table groaned under the weight of 'chicken and all the trimmins'– it was the best Sunday lunch ever, a feast. Roasters, sprouts, parsnips and homemade apple pie with custard for afters.

Gavin didn't say much about his personal problems and neither Peggy nor Ron probed. Choir memories from Peggy abounded, talk about Isaac Grenfell's days, trips abroad, concerts, and much more. Gavin had heard many stories about the 'Isaac days' from older members but Peggy had some new ones. Peggy obviously had held the choir founder in high regard.

'You know, Gavin, he could be a cantankerous old so and so, especially towards the end, but he was a very handsome, tall, striking man who the ladies worshipped, and he turned a bunch of people from ordinary backgrounds into a lovely choir. When he got the OBE, a lot of people in Cornwall had their stuck up noses put out of joint.'

As he staggered out of the door to leave, Ron shook Gavin's hand firmly and said, 'Peggy loves the choir now you are in charge, Gavin, don't let the buggers wear you down, will you?'

***

'I really do love Trevor.'

Georgina had been waiting for him in the lounge when he got in and had her script prepared.

'Our relationship only started two years ago and we do intend living together. He is applying for teaching posts at other schools, as we both know that it would be frowned upon if I was head teacher at a school where he worked.'

Gavin, now back at home on Sunday evening, sat listening to his wife's outpourings. Logical, fact-by-fact, with little emotion (certainly not for him to observe) and that was the way it was and Gavin had to accept it. He did not believe the two-year bit but what the hell, what was the point of making an issue of it? She was shagging the sports teacher and it would soon be public knowledge. Certain members of the Verlis Singers would soon be whispering about it, that's for sure.

The subject of money had to be addressed. Georgina knew his business was under the cosh as he had told her. He hadn't received much in the way of sympathy on that front either. When he told her he was £25,000 in debt she just laughed at him.

'Everyone told you to get into digital, but you stuck your head in the sand in true Gavin James fashion, so you only have yourself to blame!'

They had a nice house, but Georgina had paid the mortgage these last four years as Gavin's dwindling income from the shop became more dependent on the bank business overdraft. He knew that he should have acted earlier but then the bank was happy to increase the facility, and he got deeper and deeper into debt. He was living off the overdraft and payments out were fast overtaking payments in! He approached the subject of money. Not surprisingly Georgina had it already worked out.

'Come on Gavin, we both know that our marriage is dead. You are wed to that sodding choir and I wouldn't be surprised if you are in the panties of half of the ladies in it anyway!'

Giving Gavin no time to reply, she continued:

'The house is worth about £150,000 and we owe £60,000 on the mortgage which incidentally I have been paying off these last 48 months. If we'd relied on your earnings we would have been out on the streets long ago! What I am going to do in the future is nothing to do with you, but I am going to put up the house for sale at £156,000. Whatever I get, you will receive 30% after paying the mortgage off and then we'll get a divorce.'

Gavin was staggered at her cold-heartedness and calculated approach. She had been planning this for weeks and, he suspected, and had probably already had the house valued. He knew he could call Pat Nicholls for legal help but really did not want to bother him. This was personal after all, not choir business.

She had it all worked out. Georgina now knew he owed about £25,000 to the bank and he could see that if, and when, the house sold, he would get something close to that amount, clear the bank slate and start afresh. Spluttering that he'd have to think it over, he got up to leave the kitchen.

'Sorry Gavin, but that's the way it is! Please let me know how you want to proceed by the end of the week so I can call the estate agent.'

He, Gavin James, had been well and truly dumped!

***

Monday October 18th

The meeting with the Fostors management had gone very well the previous week and Polly had long forgotten about the weekend with her (ex) uni friends and the horrendous drive back from Scotland to Cornwall.

She had flirted with Guy Williams, the store MD, over lunch. The stockings and high heels had certainly not gone unnoticed. He had told her that he was a singer and a member of the local Gilbert and Sullivan group, but she had not divulged her musical leanings. He was single, she discovered, attractive, but most likely gay, she guessed.

Best not to mix business with pleasure, something an astute lecturer had drilled into her at uni. Said professor had also drilled her regularly in the last year at university, but he was married so it was only a 'friendly fuck', if extremely enjoyable whilst it lasted. Shame he lived so far away.

The Foster family fully owned the business and, most importantly, the asset of the premises, prime space in the centre of Verlis and worth millions. Polly suspected there was more to the meeting than she was allowed to know, as after lunch her boss Mark Richard had stayed on for a 'confidential session' without her. Some of the Foster family had actually come in to attend that meeting. She would, no doubt, pick up some office gossip if there was anything to know. Today she would wear a less sexy outfit to choir. The randy tenors would be disappointed.

***

Gavin was at his shop, sat in the back office, pondering the meaning of life and wondering if he would get any customers in. The phone rang; it was choir chairman Brian.

'Hi Gavin, I have been thinking about the Poland trip. I would love to come if that's okay; I have told Rona to put me on the list. I used to visit Poland on business and would like to go back. It's a great country.' He continued: 'Could I suggest we have a preliminary meeting soon to push things along? Gerry (the treasurer) is away for a couple of weeks and I think we should get together before he gets back. He's a great bloke, but will be nervous about spending the choir funds and will remind us to be 'prudent' – I don't agree with that. What is the point of sitting on all that cash?

'Anyway Gavin, I have called Rona and put her straight that this is a tour committee and it's separate to the main committee. I have suggested that you, Rona, three choir members and I form the group and tonight at rehearsal she will ask for volunteers.

'The Polish girl Tatania is a must and we must also work on Jenny to attend after she spoke up about the tour at the last committee meeting. It might be a good idea to have Patrick on board, as he is a hard man to disagree with. I will send him an email.'

Gavin listened intently. It was brilliant that the chairman wanted to go to Poland, the money could be allocated and even Rona had been persuaded. At least he'd get a holiday break next year. The way things were looking he would not be able to afford a holiday himself. Thanking Brian for his positive call, Gavin hung up.

***

Brian McNeil and his wife Helen lived on the outskirts of Verlis. Aged 72, he was fit and active for his age and retired at 65, after 35 years with a local print company. Helen had ended her career as a Ward Sister in the oncology unit at Verlis General Hospital. They both had good pensions and, with two grown up children and one grandchild, with another due early next year, life was good, apart from Brian's bipolar diagnosis three years back.

He had always suffered from bouts of deep depression and the specialist explained that his lows and erratic highs were typical of the condition. Regular medication now kept Brian on a more even everyday keel.

'I suppose I shouldn't tell you Brian, but with all your pals in the Masons and Rotary, you will hear soon enough,' Helen called to Brian from the kitchen, where she was preparing supper.

'I bet it's the talk that Gavin and Georgina James are splitting up!' responded Brian. He had bumped into Simon Callaway, this year's Rotary president in the town earlier in the day. Simon had asked if the rumours were correct. Brian had not said anything, as this was news to him. Brian could tell from Simon's guarded response that there was, indeed, something amiss.

Helen McNeil's sister Joan was a governor at Trimanter Primary School where Georgina James was head teacher. She was up on all the gossip.

'Joan called me today, Brian,' his wife had told him. 'It's the talk of the school. It seems that she has been having an affair with that arrogant young sports master!'

'Bloody hell!' said Brian. 'That's a bit dangerous. Have the governors been officially told what's going on by Georgina? She seems to be a very good head teacher but I can't see your sister and her governor chums turning a blind eye to her bonking the games teacher!' said Brian.

'Don't be disgusting, that's all you men ever think about. Joan did say that Georgina has already seen the Chair of Governors, as she wanted him to know. Seems the house will be up for sale and by some odd coincidence the sports teacher has said he is applying for a new teaching post elsewhere. Now there's a thing!'

She had bought Brian in a mug of tea and sat down next to her husband.

Brian said, 'I always thought Georgina was bit of a control freak. She's never had time for Gavin and the choir that's for sure. I know Gavin's a bit of a damp squib at times but if the other rumours are correct about his business going bust, I feel sorry for him because he is a really nice guy and he has certainly transformed The Verlis Singers.'

Brian wondered if this was the time to approach the subject of the proposed tour to Poland with his wife and how he wanted to go on his own. Perhaps he should save that for another day.

'One thing I do know, it'll soon be the talk of the Verlis ladies. I'll ring Rona and make sure she eases off Gavin for a while. The bloke's got enough on his plate, without the hon. sec. snapping at his heels over some silly committee rule he has ignored! I'll pop along later and see them all at rehearsal. I hear the Exeter concert went well so it'll be a good atmosphere tonight.'

***

Taff Davies and the tenor section had all the facts. Verlis was an overgrown village and the jungle drums had been beating all day. Joan Davies had a call from a friend whose children attended Trimanter School.

'Everyone at the school knows, Terry. Georgina has told the Governors and the guy who she has been having an affair with is off for pastures new.'

'Or could be pussies new?' said Taff.

'Don't be so dirty, Terry Davies! The two of them could actually be in love, who knows? We should not judge. Anyway, it's sad for poor Gavin, who is a lovely bloke. Pity he can't find someone in the choir to fall in love with.'

Gavin arrived very early for the Monday rehearsal. He was due to audition the newcomers David and Laura Honey at 7.15pm. With Peggy on doorstep duty to keep everyone out of the rehearsal room, he could do it in private. He wondered if Claire Nesbitt would bring her pianist friend and if she would be any good.

He hadn't told anyone about it, but was concerned that if Sheila found out there might be bad feeling. Sheila had not liked Gavin including the Rutter *When the Go Saints Marching In* at the Exeter concert and complained bitterly that she should have been forewarned. With older age had come a fear of the unexpected and Gavin had felt a bit guilty at dropping the surprise piece on her.

'But Sheila,' Gavin had tried to reason with her during the interval, 'we sang it through a couple of weeks back and it really went well. It's a great finale piece and I will get the audience to join in the chorus. It will be a brilliant end to the concert!'

It had worked well, but he was aware of Sheila and Rona and some of the other lady members in a huddle at the concert interval. With so much else going on Gavin wondered if it would be best if Claire's piano playing friend did not turn up tonight.

Gavin sat in his car for a few minutes gathering his thoughts. He'd been pleasantly surprised earlier in the day by a telephone call from Heather Strong, the former Verlis conductor. She had apologised for taking so long to get back to him. There was a festival meeting coming up and she'd soon be back in touch with the date and the venue. It would be good for him to meet the committee. There was great enthusiasm for him to conduct the festival's special choir next year and they had confirmation of a Lottery Arts Grant to pay for the music, the hall hire and a fee for him.

'It's going to be a fantastic finale to the Festival Gavin, and it will be great to work with you.'

***

David Honey was immaculately dressed as usual when the couple walked in. He wore a dark pinstriped suit with an expensive-looking shirt, red tie and red silk handkerchief flopping out of his breast pocket. His wife Laura was looking dowdy as Mr Honey was certainly out to steal the limelight. Gavin auditioned Laura first, which annoyed David no end, as he had to stay outside. Laura had taken some persuading to audition, but Gavin had persevered. Laura Honey actually had a very true alto voice and when encouraged by Gavin to 'really sing out', telling her not to be nervous, 'After all, there is only me in the room,' she had impressed The Verlis conductor. She was a good sight-reader with considerable choir experience and seemed pleased when Gavin suggested that she should sing first alto.

She was solo material. David of course expected to perform a solo piece as part of his audition, and was miffed when Gavin said that he only wanted to hear some scales and arpeggios. Cutting across David's attempts to list his many solo performances whilst living in Norfolk, Gavin sat at the piano and suggested some simple scales to establish his voice range. He was a bottom bass, well able to sing down to a low F but in the upper range, a rather reedy vibrato took over as he tried to force his voice. Not nice.

Gavin accepted both the Honeys but made a mental note to listen out if The Verlis basses were singing above the baritone C. David's voice could come through and he would have to tone down. Laura would certainly be an asset to the alto section and he filled in the forms to give to Rona, who seemed to think that the couple would be a great addition to the choir.

'David Honey is a very highly qualified accountant,' she had told the chairman, who had passed this info on to Gavin.

7.20pm auditions completed and Peggy relieved of her Rottweiler door steward duties, people started to pour in. Spirits were high following the very successful Exeter concert and with the Christmas Carols in the Cathedral and Poland next year to look forward to, only Len's terminal illness cast a dark cloud over The Verlis Singers.

Then of course there was the gossip about Gavin's marriage failure and his business woes!

Jenny had brought along a new friend called Lizz and asked Gavin if she could sit in the back and listen to the rehearsal. Gavin always liked visitors as he put on a show for them. Tonight was certainly going to see the conductor putting aside his worldly worries and getting on with what he did best.

Claire Nesbitt came towards him and introduced Becky Morris. Becky had been studying music at The Guildhall, but for some reason, which was not explained, she was now living in Cornwall. Gavin shook her hand and welcomed her to The Verlis Singer's rehearsal. She was about 20, Gavin thought, a little girl, skinny with greasy hair, who looked as if she hadn't eaten for days. She was wearing jeans that needed a wash and looked a bit scruffy. Gavin suggested that she might like to listen in to the first half and sit with Lizz. At this suggestion a big smile lit her face.

'Oh no Mr James, just let me have the music for each piece. That'll be fine; I'll watch you for the tempo.'

With choir members all seated and strange glances at the skinny young lady behind the piano, Gavin gave the choir the chord for the opening salvo of *Deep Harmony*. Strange, he thought. Even Pat Nichols was here in time to sing it. Gavin had not realised that the faithful were all there early to show support for him and his problems.

'Sheila is away on holiday so I'd like to introduce Becky, who is a friend of Claire's. She has come to play for us tonight, which means you'll not have to put up with my duff piano playing,' he joked.

Personal issues accepted (perhaps) but the hon. sec. Rona and Elaine Bridges were already tut-tutting. 'How dare Gavin bring in another pianist whilst Sheila is on holiday?' Rona whispered to Elaine.

'I'm calling Brian about this tomorrow!' she said loudly.

Gavin handed Becky the music for the Bob Chilcott jazz carol *Remember O Thou Man,* wondering if this was an unkind way to introduce the young girl to the choir, with what was in fact quite a difficult piece. He sensed that the choir also felt the same way. It started with a few bars of piano only. Becky seemed completely unfazed by the complicated score. Gavin gave her an indication of the time by clicking his fingers and, amazingly, Becky played the intro, note perfect in the lazy jazz style required. So surprised were the sopranos, who started the piece on their own, that some of them forgot to come in on the first beat. Stopping Becky and the choir, Gavin said: 'Well folks, with Sheila on holiday you could have had me banging out the notes. I think we are all rather fortunate that Claire brought Becky along tonight.'

'Hear, hear!' shouted Taff Davies, who also started to applaud. Everyone joined in, except the hon. sec. and Elaine Bridges, who sat with arms folded on the front row.

***

Chairman Brian made an unexpected entrance during the first half and sat in the back; even Gavin didn't know he was popping in. Asking Gavin if he could speak to the choir,

Brian (not the greatest of speech makers) addressed almost a full rehearsal of The Verlis Singers.

'Good evening everyone, and hello also to the new young lady who is playing the piano so splendidly. The choir committee has agreed to support Gavin's request to visit Poland next June. I am sure he has told you that he feels a choir tour would be great, and I certainly agree. In fact, my name is on the list to come, but don't worry, I won't be singing.'

'Hooray and cheers!' from the tenor and bass sections and much laughter.

'We want to set up a small tour sub-committee with myself, Rona, and Gavin as members plus perhaps three or four others from the choir. Tatania has agreed to be one, as her knowledge of her home country and the language will be invaluable. I will stay on for the interval so if anyone feels that they would like to be a tour sub-committee member then please come and chat to me.

'Thanks. You sound great tonight. It feels like Christmas already and I'm sure we are in for another wonderful Rotary Carol Service in the Cathedral this December. Well done everyone – Poland here we come!

'Finally, with regard to the finances, the main committee has agreed that members going to Poland will be subsidised. We don't know yet to what extent, but I suggest at this stage you sign up if you are really keen to go. We will then get back to you after talking to the festival organisers in Poland re costs and consulting The Verlis piggy bank.'

'What's the Polish for "Here we go, Here we go!" Tatania?' roared big Richard Parish.

Tatania stood up and uttered some words in Polish. Everyone clapped and Gavin called out over the din that it was the interval. No one heard Peggy shout.

'Anybody want any eggs?'

***

During the break Jenny Dalton introduced Gavin formally to the new potential alto she had brought along that night. Lizz Ozroy had recently moved to Verlis. Her husband was a professor and a surgeon from Cyprus, now working for the Cornish Health Service in a senior management role. A big cheese!

She was well spoken, quite tall, slim and with curly auburn hair and glasses; even Gavin noticed that she was a very stylish lady, wearing clothes that had certainly not been purchased at Fostors in town. Lizz had not sung in choirs for a while, she explained to Gavin, but loved the music they had done in the first half and would like to join if that was possible. She had tried the local light operatic group but found them to be 'very bitchy and unfriendly', even if the music was fun to sing.

Gavin welcomed her with a smile and suggested that she joined the altos for the second half. He explained that she could sit in for a couple of weeks and then perhaps arrive early for an audition. 'It's painless,' he told her, adding, 'if you like the choir then you could sing at the Cathedral. We do sing from copies that night so it's not quite the same as learning everything by heart.'

During the second half Becky continued to show her considerable skills as an accompanist. Gavin couldn't help but wonder how he could move Sheila out from the pianist stool without too much wailing and gnashing of teeth. It was not going to be easy. He didn't want to upset Sheila, who had given fantastic service to the choir for many years. But, if The Verlis Singers were going to become the choir he wanted them to be, a younger accompanist was required.

Becky Morris, without any doubt, was the person for the job. She was brilliant but might need some considerable 'scrubbing up' for a concert.

Gavin also knew that if he didn't snap up Becky Morris to

play for The Verlis Singers, some other choir would find out about her and that would be that.

Chapter 8

Tuesday October 18th

The choir chairman was on the phone at home, at the receiving end of a real dressing down from the Hon. Secretary.

'Now come on Rona!' he spluttered, starting to get annoyed. 'I'm sure Gavin was not planning the demise of Sheila by asking that young girl to play at the rehearsal last night. Whatever you may say, The Verlis Singers has become a really good choir again with Gavin as conductor and you must realise this. Look at the BBC comments after you did the *Songs of Praise* recording. I am sure they don't write to every choir that takes part, praising the conductor, and they said The Verlis Singers would definitely be used again next year.

'As I understand it, the girl is a friend of Claire in the sopranos, and Rona, at the end of the day, even though I am not a singer or musician, even I could tell that she was very, very accomplished.'

Not to be deterred, Rona continued on the attack: 'That is all well and good Brian but Gavin has to understand that it is the committee that govern the day-to-day decisions of the choir and its members. We cannot have another Isaac situation developing, you know.'

Brian replied, still on the defensive, 'We will of course discuss it at the next committee, but I suggest that we do so ONLY if Gavin brings it up. He has enough on his plate at the moment without having to cope with a committee row. I really don't like the reference to the founder conductor, Rona. It was different back then even if before my time. Isaac was the founder of the choir and that does put a much different slant on things, you know. We should for now be giving all the support we can at present to Gavin, don't you think?'

Rona tactfully agreed with the choir chairman but she was still seething. Gavin had no right asking a newcomer to play at rehearsal. He should have consulted the committee before. That's what committees were for.

Brian had also checked with Rona on the Poland Tour group; Pat Nicholls had offered to attend when he could, and Tatania Bakowski. Terry Davies had volunteered as well, a fact that also annoyed Rona. Emily Thomas from the soprano section had also put her name forward and Brian wanted to include the new bass David Honey, which pleased Rona as she felt it would be better to have someone else with financial skills looking after the money side of things. Treasurer Gerry Head could get into a bit of a flap over the choir finances at times, when there really was no need.

One thing's for sure, she thought, Chairman Brian McNeil certainly had the bit between his teeth regarding the Poland Tour. She had seen him like this before on occasions, really full of enthusiasm, calling everyone and sometimes even making some occasional controversial decisions. Quite often, though, after one of these slightly crazy spells of enthusiasm, he would 'disappear' and miss a committee meeting. There would be little or no communication from him as his wife would always answer the phone.

Rona had also come around to rather like the idea of the choir trip to Poland. It was something she could really get her teeth into and she could easily afford it, subsidy or no subsidy. It was the only chance she would have for a holiday. She had few friends outside of the choir and hated holidays on her own.

Going on choir trips was very relaxing for a single woman. She felt safe with people she knew around her and the men always helped with the cases and lifting duties. She hoped Jenny would go as they could room share, as they usually did on choir trips past. Time would tell, something else to discuss quietly with Brian.

She sat down at her desk at home to check emails. There was one from the BBC and *Songs of Praise*. Rather annoyingly, she saw that it had been copied to Gavin. 'Choir matters should go to the secretary NOT the conductor,' she said out loud. Duffy the dog barked at hearing her voice. The email said that *Songs of Praise* were going to do a special programme in the spring, featuring the top 20 hymn tunes as selected by viewers. Different choirs from around the UK would sing two each, and would The Verlis Singers like to be one of the ten choirs? They would represent the South West of England.

Even Rona in her most crotchety mood knew that was a great compliment for the choir and immediately responded with a polite, 'Yes of course.' She cc'd her reply to Gavin and to all of the other committee members so they could share the good news. She then sent a personal email to Gavin saying that she would tell the choir at the next rehearsal, but that it would have to be agreed at the next committee meeting, adding: 'I am sure this will be just a formality.'

***

The relationship between Gavin and Georgina Jones was now a mutually established no-speaking zone. Gavin had reluctantly agreed to the financial arrangements put to him by his wife, as he really did not have a leg to stand on. The house was on the market and, in many ways, he felt more settled. At least now he knew where he stood. Ok, his finances were knackered but if the house was sold he could pay off the bank debt, wipe the slate clean and embark on a new life – the 'next chapter', was how Peggy had referred to it. Whatever 'new life' meant, he had no idea, but the choir was his *strength and stay*, to quote the words from a well-loved hymn.

Georgina had left Gavin a note suggesting that he should list the household items he considered to be his. She had written a P.S. suggesting that if he wanted to leave all the furniture and just take his clothes and personal things, she would pay him an inclusive additional amount of £2,500. Not much to show for 19 years of marriage, but an offer he would probably take up. The extra money would come in handy after all as he would soon have to find somewhere to live.

***

Lizz Ozroy was preparing dinner for her husband Olag and their daughter Emma, who was home from university for a few days. They had moved back to England when he had been offered the top job with the Health Service based at their South West head offices in Verlis. Lizz was English and they had met at university in Oxford. He had swept her off her feet and before she realised it, the marriage was planned, date set, relations galore from Cyprus invited, and a coach booked to take them from London Heathrow to Leamington Spa for the wedding, where the couple first lived.

They had then moved to Italy as Olag had a senior teaching post in one of the top universities. Lizz had worked hard to build up a successful garden design business. Two children later and back in England, in a large detached five-bed house, to outside observers all seemed to be perfect. Her parents lived in London and whilst Verlis was a four-hour drive from their home, the job had come up in Cornwall for Olag, and Lizz was desperate to move back from Italy.

Lizz had always loved singing and had discovered The Verlis Singers through Jenny Dalton, a friend of a friend and wife of a Rotarian who worked with her husband. Olag had insisted on signing up to join the Rotary Club in Verlis when they first arrived in Cornwall.

'It is the way to meet important people and, because I have a very influential job, they will welcome me with open arms.'

He was correct, and they did.

***

Wednesday October 20th

The choir chairman, Brian McNeil, called the first meeting of the Poland sub-committee to order.

Those present at the Cricket Club were choir secretary Rona Hancock, Taff Davies, Tatania Bakowski, Patrick Nicholls, Emily Thomas, and David Honey. Accompanist Sheila Sterton had offered to be on the committee, but was absent, still on holiday. Gerry Head could not attend as he had a Masonic Lodge meeting.

Rona read out the syllabus that had come from the Krakow Festival Committee. It appeared that choirs from across the world were regular attendees. Only 12 were selected to attend on CDs or performance videos that had to be submitted. It was a five-day festival, Rona pointed out smugly, not four days as Gavin had said. The Festival were responsible for booking accommodation, with the choice of three, four or five star hotels.

The choirs arrived on the first day and all attended a 'welcome party'. Rehearsal rooms were available for the second morning and there were various concerts organised in and around churches in Krakow. Each choir performed a 20-minute programme at the concerts. There seemed to be some performance awards as well which she would find out more about.

Tourist excursions were offered on the third morning to the

choirs at additional prices and a similar round of concerts took place on the third evening, with choirs performing at different venues to the previous night, alongside different choirs.

Only 12 choirs were chosen to participate and, reading in between the lines of an email from the festival committee and following a call to them from Tatania, they appeared delighted to have an English choir taking part. The Verlis Singers certainly would get one of the 12 places and were known in Poland. Rona had spoken to a choir from Bath called The Circle of Song who had attended the previous year.

'It is a very well organised event but the adjudicators tend to favour choirs from Poland,' she had been told by the very helpful choir secretary.

Rona told the sub-committee that the Bath choir had struggled to send a balanced choir. They were getting over what Rona described as a 'conductor bust-up' and had lost many of their best singers, who had left to join a new choir formed by the ex-conductor who was quite a charismatic character. 'It seems that many of the stronger singers went to join his new choir. That could have had a bearing on their performances at the festival,' said Rona.

Tatania told the committee that she had been on the phone to her sister in Rzeszon. This was in another part of Poland and was where she originated from. There was an airport and internal flights from Krakow. It seemed that Tatania had sung in a very good ladies' choir in the city and they wondered if The Verlis Singers could fit in an additional day to go there. The visit could include a concert in a local church with Tatania's old choir. Everyone agreed that this would be an excellent idea and that the additional days could be added on to the Festival visit making the choir tour five or six days in total.

David Honey had researched the flight costs already. He had a great knowledge of travelling abroad and suggested that the group would get better prices if they divided them into two and booked into different EasyJet flights from Bristol. Whilst this would involve two coach fees, everyone agreed that this was probably the most economic way to get to Krakow. Everything, ultimately, was dependent on numbers going on the tour.

Gavin had obvious questions on repertoire and, at Patrick's suggestion, Tatania was asked to contact the organisers for the answers.

'It is a great help to have you in the choir and on the committee, Tatania,' said the chairman, beaming at the hon. sec.

Although not entirely happy with this arrangement, Rona did not dispute that communicating with Poland through Tatania was entirely sensible.

Finances were then discussed. It appeared that around 30-35 people from the choir were already keen to go. Discussion took place over whether partners should be allowed to join. Rona was dead against this idea as was Chairman, Brian. After considerable debate it was agreed that only singers should be allowed to go to perform at the festival, as that would make things more manageable. Partners could not be subsidised and it would be very complicated establishing the additional charge.

Gavin was pleased that the balance of the parts seemed OK although he would like to see some of the younger members, the two Cla(i)res for instance, signing up. Brian suggested that he attend the next choir rehearsal to pass on this information, secretly acknowledging that the person unhappiest about this decision might be his wife, Helen.

The additional visit to Rzeszon was agreed by everyone and Tatania added that her ex-choir members could probably offer some overnight hosting, thus keeping costs down. It was enthusiastically agreed that this seemed a splendid suggestion. Tatania would get in touch with her sister and report back and David agreed to look into the additional flight, timings and the costs.

Brian had taken views from other committee members, as well as treasurer, Gerry, and it had been agreed that £20,000 could be allocated from the choir funds. This could be a subsidy of as much as £500 per person if 40 singers went. This amount could be transferred to a new tour account at the bank. All payments from the members would go into this account which he would open the following day. As Chairman he was a signatory on the bank account, as was the treasurer. Only two signatures were needed and he gave Rona the form which he had signed. She would also get Gerry to sign.

'After the tour we will distribute the full details of expenditure and income to the choir. Any surplus will be transferred back to the normal fund,' said the chairman.

Truth was that Gerry was dead against any subsidy. Brian and Gerry had almost fallen out over the matter. Gerry felt that the choir funds should not be frittered away on 'jolly outings for people who could well afford to pay the full amount'.

'We have a responsibility to be prudent with the choir funds,' he had told Brian.

Brian was dead set on the trip and chose not to tell those present of the choir treasurer's strong objection to the subsidy. It was therefore recommended, and minuted, that the £20,000 would be moved to the tour fund. The Poland group would meet every month until the tour itself which started on June 15th 2011. On this occasion, Treasurer Gerry Head would have to do as the committee chose. The meeting ended with great enthusiasm from all present, Brian announcing, 'Well everybody, that's the meeting over. Poland here we come!'

***

Later in the week, Gavin got a text from Heather Strong telling him that the meeting for the Festival Committee was

planned for the following Wednesday, November 3rd at 7pm
in the Grand Hotel, close to the town centre. Gavin thanked
her for the info and, of course, he would be there.

Another call had come from the bank and the secretary to
the manager, Simon Calloway. 'Could you pop in Mr James
early next week as Mr Calloway has some documents he
would like you to sign?'

The formal use of 'Mr' really annoyed Gavin. She normally
called him by his first name but now he was being put firmly
in his place by the bank. Gavin did not use the 'F' word very
often but on this particular occasion he said out loud in his
shop office to himself.

'Fuck you Simon and double fuck your fucking bank!'

***

Polly Jones had a new chum. Since joining the choir she
had got to know tenor Dominic Gordon. He was, she first
observed, ridiculously pretty and just had to be gay. She was
correct, but Polly loved the company of gay men. Dominic
was very camp and naughty and always 'on the hunt'.

The friendship had started in the pub after choir rehearsal
and blossomed. Dominic had even been around to Polly's
house for supper and they really enjoyed each other's
company. One day, Polly had decided she was going to get
him very drunk and see if a person of the opposite sex, who
was determined to get into his Calvin Klein boxers, could
seduce him! Whatever happened, it would not spoil their
friendship but she knew he would be a wonderful kisser.

Dominic worked in the Waterlines bookshop and had
opted out of university somewhere in the East of England
where his parents still lived. They were very wealthy and he
had gone to Eton where his beautiful voice had led him
straight to the boys' choirs, tours abroad, and the attention of
one or two of the Masters. Dominic had a preference for
older men, especially wealthy ones. Polly had discovered that

Dominic's current 'special friend' was a big noise at the Cathedral, probably a Trustee or something similar. Although he was cagey about revealing names, Polly had gleaned that the older man was very well connected and scared shitless of being discovered, but loved to 'play with me and spank my bottom!' as Dominic described it.

On the subject of Poland, Polly had immediately put her name down and was delighted that Dominic was also going. He was being 'subsidised' by one of his rich benefactors. Polly suggested that they should room share. Dominic thought this an outrageous suggestion.

'Christ Poll.' She loved him calling her Poll. 'That dragon Rona will have a seizure if we say we want to share a room.'

They both agreed that it was something that should be done, although she pointed out to Dominic that he would certainly not be getting his leg over in Poland, however drunk he got her!

Chapter 9

Dear Hon Secretary,

I hereby hand in my immediate resignation to The Verlis Singers as honorary treasurer. I have enjoyed my time with the choir, which I believe to be as strong now musically as they were in the halcyon days of Isaac Grenfell.

*However, I believe that funds raised should be kept in reserve away from subsidising choir tours, which do **not** benefit all of the membership.*

Whilst the choir does have a very strong bank account, I cannot be part of the decision made behind my back to subsidise the Poland tour from tour reserves, without consideration of my views as the elected choir treasurer.

I wish the choir well in the future and would be grateful if you could contact me to collect the choir financial records etc.

*G Head, **ACCA***

***

The letter arrived at Rona's house. All correspondence came to the honorary secretary. As she read it she allowed herself a wry smile. Brian was definitely going for the Poland trip big time and with enthusiasm, and she didn't think he would worry too much about losing a very good treasurer, even if he could be hard going and also downright mean at times.

She decided not to call Brian that day but to hold fire. The new bass David Honey would make an excellent choir treasurer, she thought. There were no other obvious candidates in her view. She would suggest that to Brian when they spoke.

***

Mellyn Fyfield had been making arrangements to take her husband Len into the local St Catherine's Hospice for the first time. He would attend three days a week, spending that time in the day care unit. The hospice had volunteer drivers who would collect Len and bring him home at the end of the day and Len had agreed with his wife that this was a good idea. He realised the huge stress that his illness had put on his loving wife and, if he was to spend some of his final days sat in the garden room at the Hospice, looking out at the scenic and peaceful Cornish landscape, that was not such a bad thing.

'I will call Gavin for you darling,' she called to Len, who was dozing in their lounge in his favourite chair. 'Perhaps he'll pop in and see you as he has some Christmas music he wants you to look at.'

'That would be nice,' murmured Len. His voice was very weak and Mellyn didn't catch what he said.

Len wondered if his tired, deteriorating body would indeed make it to the Christmas Carol service. Five weeks to go. If he was a betting man he wondered whether he would actually have wasted any money on a wager. He whispered a prayer to a God that he had not entirely been close to these past years. Now it was different, he was on his way to meet whoever his maker was, and he dearly wanted to be at Verlis Cathedral for that one last time.

'Isaac Grenfell, if you are up there, I'll bet you and God are singing together. Put a word in for your old friend Len Fyfield from Cornwall, then I'll join you and we can make it a trio, but please not until after the Cathedral carols.

'If it is possible, please fix for me, just five more weeks!'

***

Gavin was walking to the bank for his Friday morning meeting with Simon Calloway. It was another cold Cornwall morning and people were rushing about everywhere. The Christmas lights were up and the City of Verlis was preparing for the season of goodwill. Gavin wondered if his bank manager was also in the festive spirit of goodwill to all men. He doubted it.

He had given his notice to the owners of the lease and his shop would close in six weeks. They didn't seem too concerned, as there was a waiting list for small shops close to the city centre. He owned all the stock and winced at the thought of putting up the CLOSING DOWN notices on the windows. Later on that day he would do a final stock check and then mark up all the sale prices. It had to be done, so he might as well get on with it.

The landlord had allowed him four additional weeks to pay his overdue rent and, from the sale of some reasonable cameras and other stock, he should be able to cover that amount and clear one debt, at least. As for the future, and earning a living, Gavin really had no idea.

When he arrived at the bank he was kept waiting in the reception area. He was told, 'Mr Calloway is on a call at the moment. He won't be long. Please take a seat.'

Fuck the bank! thought Gavin. *Double fuck them!*

Unbeknownst to Gavin James, Simon Calloway was taking a call from Patrick Nicholls QC.

***

Simon Calloway actually seemed in good spirits when he eventually welcomed Gavin into his office.

'We'll be seeing each other later in the week Gavin at the Carol Service meeting in the Cathedral on Thursday at 12 noon.' The meeting had actually slipped Gavin's mind, so he was grateful for the reminder and polite discussion then took place on the great importance of the annual Lessons and Carol service to the City of Verlis and the Rotary Club members in particular.

Gavin owed the bank £25,000. This was made up of loans accruing over recent years as trade had diminished. He had managed to pay the monthly repayments up to six months ago but then had started to miss the fixed date. His application for a further £5,000 had been refused and the debt was 'under scrutiny' by the bank. Then had come the call to attend the 'meeting'.

Simon Calloway knew about Gavin's marriage breakdown from local gossip, but put on his official bank manager's voice to ask Gavin how his finances were looking and how he planned to earn a living after the shop closed. More important, of course, was the unsecured £25,000 overdraft, which was increasing month on month. How did Gavin intend clearing that debt?

Simon Calloway had received a serious reprimand and a call from his local HSB director asking why this particular small business client had been given an unsecured loan in the first instance. Simon had tried to placate him with an explanation of how the business owner, Gavin James, had a small but profitable camera shop and a wife who earned a good salary as a head teacher. In the 15 years of doing business, Mr James had been a good client to the bank and he had never seen fit to ask for security against the loans. Yes, they owned a property, and yes, he should have insisted on this as security. Simon Calloway was under the spotlight from on high. He had not told his director that Mr James was a fellow Rotarian, and happened to conduct a very good mixed-voice choir in Verlis.

Gavin responded: 'The house is on the market and I hope to receive about £24,000 from the sale, Simon. There are rent debts as well, but I am sure the final closing sale will cover these. I am up to date on VAT and National Insurance payments, so hope to avoid having to declare myself bankrupt. When the house is sold I will pay off the bank debt. I won't have a job or anywhere to live, but hope I can find a flat that is affordable. I do have a small income from the choir, of course, but that's not enough to live on. I will have to look around and see if there are any jobs I could apply for.'

Gavin was flabbergasted when Simon Calloway interrupted him and offered to hold the debt for four months without any additional interest payments.

'I think we can help you,' he said. 'I am sure the house will sell, Gavin. The market is strong and if it is still not sold we can meet again to review the situation. 'I will keep the debt at £25,000 and take off the interest payments for the last three months. That's what you owe the bank, Gavin, and I hope the house sale goes through so you can start to plan that new chapter in your life.'

As Gavin left the bank, he felt rather guilty at having used the 'F' word so often. He had been offered a lifeline by the bank. He could not believe it.

***

Simon Calloway put the Gavin James file back in his client tray on his desk. He was off the hook with his local director. He wondered if Gavin appreciated how certain wealthy people who lived in Verlis were watching out for him. He was a very fortunate man. But it was not his place to tell Gavin!

***

Lizz Ozroy was sitting in the coffee section of the restaurant at the Fostors department store in the centre of Verlis. Looking around, she pondered that this really was a funny old-fashioned place. It was like going back 20 years in time. It reminded her of the store in Staines where she had grown up. She expected old Mr Grace from *Are You Being Served* to totter into view at any time.

On the way to her coffee meeting with Jenny Dalton she called into the big bookshop in the centre of Verlis. A handsome extremely camp young boy had noticed her and flounced across to her to say hello. 'Hi, I saw you at choir didn't I? 'I observed you from afar in the tenor section,' he joked. 'Did you enjoy it, are you going to come back?'

Lizz assured the twinkly young man that she had loved the music and hoped the conductor would allow her to join and that she was terrified of doing the audition.

'Oh don't worry, just give him that lovely smile and Gavin won't be able to say no. See you next Monday,' said the young man, mincing off in the direction of Historical Novels.

'I do love that coat!' he twinkled. 'You will certainly be the choir's style icon. Vogue has come to Verlis, at last, oh, by the way, I am Dominic.'

***

Jenny Dalton sat down opposite Lizz in the Fostors Coffee Shop and they chatted about life, families, boring husbands, gay handsome bookshop tenors, and singing. Lizz explained that she worked at home as a garden designer. They had lived just outside Rome for many years, where her husband had been a senior administrator at the very large hospital.

Lizz had been introduced to Jenny by one of her friends, Carol Bookman, whose husband Richard was a Rotarian. Richard and Olag Ozroy had met when Olag had joined Verlis Rotary. Soon after, his wife Lizz had been roped in by her husband to join the ladies' section, the Inner Wheel, which is how Carol and Lizz had met.

Jenny had already noticed that Lizz had some fabulous clothes and realised that they had probably all been purchased when she lived in Italy. Jenny Dalton knew she was dowdy, but sitting here with the elegantly dressed Lizz Ozroy in a gorgeous black high-neck winter coat (Dolce and Gabbana) and flowing silk scarf, dark stockings and wonderful high heels, she felt out of place. Yes, she certainly made Jenny and every other woman 'doing lunch' at the Fostors restaurant that lunchtime look pretty ordinary.

Lizz, Jenny had soon discovered, was a really lovely person and they chatted and laughed until Lizz, looking at her expensive watch (a gift from her husband) realised that she had to fly as she had an optician's appointment. She was considering laser treatment. Assuring Jenny that she would be at rehearsal next week and would not fret over the audition, they said goodbye. Jenny watched her go and was aware of the glances of many of the ladies sat in the restaurant 'doing lunch', obviously working out the cost of the outfit she was wearing. She had not bought those clothes from the Fostors ladies' department, that was obvious!

***

Sunday October 24th

'I thought he was a really good friend of yours, a fellow Mason and all that,' Brian McNeil's wife Helen said. 'You don't seem a bit concerned about him resigning from the treasurer's job. Shouldn't you call him and pile on the McNeil charm and beg him to reconsider?'

Brian shrugged his shoulders and buried his face in the Sunday newspapers.

'Ah well, perhaps it's for the best, poor old Gerry can't get over going bust with his business and is frightened of spending any money. We'll find another treasurer and Rona already has someone in mind – a new bass with a posh accent that wears expensive suits and seems pretty business savvy.

'I would prefer a treasurer who is not a choir member but it's difficult to find people to commit the time to an organisation they don't really understand.'

Bringing a mug of tea for Brian, she sat opposite him.

'You *are* taking your tablets every day Brian McNeil, aren't you?'

Brian put off the question of going to Poland on his own for another day. He would call Gerry later on that day. Masons were supposed to stick together after all, and he had fought Gerry's corner when he went bust as some in the Lodge felt he should stand down and, yes, he was taking his tablets.

***

It was Sunday afternoon and Rona was working on the minutes of the Poland sub-committee. She had just taken a call from Sheila the choir accompanist, asking if it was true that Gavin had brought in a young girl to play whilst she was on holiday. Rona had, on this occasion, put Sheila fully in the picture without any malice. She explained that the young girl Becky was a friend of Claire Nesbitt and had come to the rehearsal by chance. She had offered to play and Gavin had said yes. It was not pre-planned as far as she knew, it just happened and Sheila should not get in a state about it. Rona could not answer the question from Sheila, 'Was she very good?'

'She seemed to be able to play all the pieces and it was a better rehearsal than having Gavin plonking out the notes for us.'

Rona was not sure that Sheila was entirely happy at the explanation and switched the conversation to Sheila's holiday, which had been very relaxing. They would see each other tomorrow evening at rehearsal.

Sheila had been visiting her daughter and husband in Wales. A surprise dinner was arranged at a nice Italian restaurant on the Cardiff Docks when the couple announced that Sheila was going to be a grandmother for the first time. The baby was due in June but Sheila had not (yet) put two and two together. Fact was that this coincided with the planned tour to Poland she had already committed to. Putting the phone down, Rona DID put two and two together and wondered if Sheila would still be able to do the Poland trip as the dates could clash.

***

Pat Nicholls pulled up outside the house of Peggy and Ron in his flash new BMW. He had promised to call in on Sunday afternoon between 1pm and 2pm, although for the life of him he couldn't understand why the time was so specific. Pat's wife, Eunice Nicholls, was not impressed at his disappearance at midday Sunday on 'choir business', but he did earn a huge salary, was away four days most weeks, and her gold card account was never queried.

Pat reported to Peggy and Ron: 'The bank are more than happy for you to underwrite Gavin's business loan and Simon Calloway will treat the arrangement as entirely private.

'I am sure Gavin will sell his business and you may have to send the bank a cheque for around £5,000 at the most. I can organise that for you when the time comes. This covers the interest payments that, through your generosity, Peggy and Ron, he will not now have to find! The Bank Manager has already told Gavin about this with absolutely no mention of your involvement of course.'

Peggy and Ron were sat on the sofa holding hands and Patrick Nicholls QC wondered, and felt very envious, at being in the company of two elderly people who were obviously still entirely devoted to each other. He couldn't remember the last time he held hands with Eunice.

'But Patrick, where is our Gavin going to live when that woman sells the house?' Peggy asked.

'I guess he'll have to find a flat, Peggy. Why, have you something else in mind?' asked Patrick, already guessing the answer.

'Well,' spoke up Ron. 'You know Patrick that we have those three little cottages in Morladen Street in Verlis. The ones our David bought from the hotel money as an investment. Well, one of them has been empty for a while, so Peggy and I would like you to tell Gavin that we would like to make it available for him to live in. It has been redecorated and there are some things in there, bed and kitchen things, so he won't need to spend out much. It's a nice house for Gavin.'

After further discussion, Patrick agreed to call Gavin. He would have to know Peggy and Len owned the house, although he would not be told of the bank arrangement. The house rent would be for six months at no charge to Gavin, and then they would look at it again, although Ron had pointed out that they weren't putting any time restriction on the arrangement.

'Gavin James is a very blessed man, Peggy and Ron,' said Patrick, aware that Ron was fiddling with his watch. It was time to go.

'I'll call him tomorrow morning. I must be off.'

Peggy and Ron Trenholm watched their financial advisor and trusted friend walk down the drive and get into his big shiny car.

'Two o'clock my bird; time for bed!'

Chapter 10

'What's for breakfast?' David (a.k.a. Sebastian, Huw or Laurence, in most recent years) called out to his dutiful partner in the kitchen.

'Eggs, how would you like them?' Laura (her real name since baptism) called back.

David said, 'If they are the ones that dotty woman sold you in the choir, they are probably fresh and from her own chickens. She probably laid them herself! I would like them lightly boiled my dear, a bit like her,' he replied in a Cornish accent. The man with whom she had shared her life these past nine years was actually not her husband, even though he told people differently. He was also totally brilliant at imitating accents, any part of the UK, any foreign country. He could mimic them all convincingly.

'Don't be unkind,' responded Laura. 'She is rather sweet and the fact is, Laurence, oh sorry, I mean David, she is very similar to the many generous big-hearted people who have given you help in the past when you needed it.'

Choosing to ignore the reference to his past life, David sat down at the kitchen table to await the arrival of his boiled eggs and toast.

Laura Harvey had been a staunch member of the Salvation Army in Suffolk. The Sally Army was in her blood. Her father and his father before him had been pillars of the movement. She wore the uniform with pride, and gave up her evenings for the homeless shelter, cooking meals for those who lived on the streets. She helped out at the soup kitchen on Friday evenings in Norwich and sang in the Citadel Choir every Sunday, and even banged a tambourine when required.

There had been a 'sort-of' love affair with Andrew, another Salvationist, whilst in her 20s. A marriage was certainly on the cards. However, he had turned out to have a preference for the uniformed young boys in the Boys' Brigade. This fact came to light when, after a summer camp, one of the 11-year-olds, whose father was a policeman, enquired of his father if it was 'usual' for the Brigade Captain to sneak into his tent (and his sleeping bag) in the dead of night with no clothes on and want to kiss him. Andrew disappeared soon after. Rumours abounded that he had converted to Catholicism, but no one really knew.

When in 1998 a letter had come into the office at the local Citadel where Laura volunteered two days a week to do the secretarial work, she had opened it. It was from the governor of the local Highpoint West Category C prison enquiring if there were any members of the Salvation Army who could help with their need for new prison visitors.

Category C prisons, the letter explained, were for men who couldn't be trusted in open conditions but who were unlikely to try to escape. Anyone showing interest would undergo a tried and tested training programme before actually entering and meeting some of the selected prisoners who, it was felt, would benefit from social interaction with the outside world.

The letter explained that there had been many successful and trusting friendships forged and the opportunity for offenders to talk with visitors had changed the lives of many when they had been released into the community. Careful screening and monitoring always took place before introducing offenders to the visitors, the letter explained. Laura replied, saying that she would like to be considered.

The first visit was on a fine summer day. Laura was met at the car park at the main entrance and walked with a prison officer and four others down a long path with the high barbed fence on their left. They were told that the site was divided into six different areas, each for the various categories of offenders. There were many 'lifers' in the prison, they were told, but at no time would visitors be told the crimes of the offenders.

At the entrance gate the visitors had to produce passports as proof of identity and were then shown into the prison area itself. Laura felt very intimidated at first. The officers were pleasant, but the routine of opening and locking every gate by the escorting officer underlined the strict security routine.

It was on her third visit to Highpoint West, with three other visitors, and after the induction process, that the Governor himself welcomed the four people on the current befriending programme into his office. This was a short walk from the entrance and he told them that they were going to meet and hear the new choir that had been started by one of the prisoners. This had the full support of the Prison Board and the added enthusiasm of the Prison Chaplain, who was a keen singer.

'I think this is a first for our Prison and we have about 30 men who attend each week. Of course I accept that this is a chance to get out of their cells and, whilst some might not take it at all seriously, it seems to be going well. We do have an offender who is a fine pianist and also John who is in fact a Professor of Music and was in charge of choral music at a very well respected public school.'

The one thing consistently told to visitors during the training sessions was that staff would never disclose the reasons why the men were serving time. In the months that followed when Laura listened to the choir, she had wondered if John the Professor also had a preference for young boys, although, in this instance, not in the Boys' Brigade, more likely the boy trebles in the church or school choir.

Laura, with the other three new prospective prison

visitors, walked to the chapel where the choir rehearsed, all gates on the short walk unlocked and then relocked by the Governor himself. They eventually entered the medium-sized chapel led in by the Governor. They were greeted by a chorus of about 20 men singing the spiritual *Steal Away*, a rather odd choice, Laura reflected, for a group of men locked away for 'goodness knows what' misdemeanours against society.

Later, she was to discover, all the music came from local choirs, 'hand-me-downs', and discarded old music scores. Some of the repertoire was a gift from the widow of a former choir conductor. She had come across piles of old mostly Edwardian male choir music after his death and donated it to the prison on hearing that they were starting a choir.

The men were making a reasonable sound; singing in parts and the pianist was thumping out the harmony notes. Laura immediately noticed a man in the second row. He was tall, dark haired and extremely distinguished-looking. He, in turn, noticed Laura looking at him and smiled. He had spotted her as she walked in with the Old Man, the Guvnor. She was rather plain and mousy-looking, he thought. Here was a sweet bible-punching Christian woman to whom prisoners would certainly turn for help and support in their search for a better life of honesty in the world at large. Spotting people who helped 'lost causes' was part of his professional armoury. He was an expert, without equal. To Sebastian Locking-Thomas, a convicted fraudster and con man of considerable experience. She stuck out like a sore thumb. Today was his (and her) lucky day.

He decided there and then that he was certainly going to get to know this lady. As the choir sang the final section of the song Sebastian turned up the volume on his deep bass voice and sang directly to the lady now sat in the front row.

I ain't got far to go home…

He could see that she was blushing. Even in prison the old charm still worked.

The friendship had blossomed whilst he was incarcerated. She visited him as often as she could and, when he came before the parole board, her unquestioning belief and faith in him had a great influence on the decision that released him back into the community. When he eventually left prison, Sebastian Carter told Laura that he would use the Christian name David in future and moved into a Salvation Army Hostel in Norwich. He would also use her surname; it would be easier for her that way.

Their relationship developed, David claiming that Jesus had entered his life and all his past misdemeanours were all behind him. Laura was financially sound, as her grandmother had left a nice house to her favourite granddaughter. David made promises about finding work, but nothing ever materialised. Eighteen months after being released from prison, and now a free man, he suggested that they should move to a new area of the UK.

'We need to make a fresh start, a new life Laura,' he said.

They had arrived in West Wales and the 'new life' commenced. Laura soon noticed that Huw (his new name for Wales) had a totally convincing soft Welsh accent. When she plucked up the courage to enquire where it came from, he had replied: 'Ah yes, it was one of the things we were taught at drama school. The Welsh like to think that you are one of their own and it will help us to get accepted.'

As always, the dutiful Laura agreed with the answer from her new partner with the Welsh accent.

***

Monday Evening, October 26ᵗʰ

Lizz Ozroy had successfully passed her audition with

Gavin. She had arrived early as planned and, after a brief singing session, they had chatted about her past life living in Italy. Gavin had felt quite inferior talking to someone who was so widely travelled, was fluent in many languages, and who seemed so comfortable with her life.

Peggy had busied herself in the kitchen. She seemed more pleased to see Gavin than usual and gave him a big cuddle when he walked in to find her putting out the chairs. Gavin wondered what he had done to deserve it.

Lizz arrived wearing a bright red winter coat. It was a cold evening and as always she looked like she had just walked out of a fashion magazine. She had a rich, low alto voice and, whilst she claimed not to be a sight-reader, Gavin knew that this was something that she would easily overcome. Lizz had told Gavin that she was a garden designer, building up a new business in Cornwall. She spoke French, Italian, Spanish, and German fluently. She would work hard to learn the pieces for Christmas, if he would allow her to sing, and would certainly be putting her name down for Poland, a country she had never visited. Her two children were both at university in London so getting away, and affording it, was not a problem.

***

'I have some good news for the choir.'

Fifteen minutes into the rehearsal, *Deep Harmony* (the choir anthem) duly sung and all latecomers in place, Gavin spoke:

'We have been invited by *Songs of Praise* to take part in a special programme next year. One choir from each BBC region will sing two hymns that have local links and reflect their part of the UK. We have been chosen from the South West, which is brilliant, and I am sure The Verlis Singers will be the envy of lots of other choirs. The programme will be recorded sometime in the spring, probably in the Cathedral, and will go out before we set out for Poland, which is also excellent publicity for the choir.

'I should hear in the next few weeks which hymns we will sing and the BBC may also make a CD of all the hymns. We will receive a small fee for choir funds but it's the fact that we have been chosen that is so good for our choir. The researcher for the programme told me that they want traditional four part harmonies, no descants or key changes, so it should be quite straightforward for us, although I would like The Verlis Singers to sing our two hymns without music and words.'

Gavin paused and took a deep breath.

'I should also tell you that Len is going into St Catherine's Hospice this week as an in-patient. I know that many of you will want to visit him. Rona has kindly offered to keep in touch with Mellyn, so I suggest that you contact Rona, who will know about the visiting times. We are all thinking about Len and Mellyn of course, and you know how determined he still is to be in the choir at the Rotary carols. We must do all we can to make this happen.'

The rehearsal continued, with emphasis on the Christmas pieces that the choir would sing at the Rotary Carol Service. The Monday rehearsal on November 22nd would probably be in the Cathedral, Gavin announced, and there would not be a rehearsal on Monday 29th as that was the week of the Wednesday evening Rotary Carols on Wednesday December 1st.

'I want you all bright and fresh for the night of the service,' Gavin told the choir.

Gavin had the running order already worked out for the service, but had to show it to the Rotary people, at a meeting on Thursday. He knew that the fuddy-duddy old-fashioned men of Verlis Rotary Club didn't like the choir to sing anything too modern, but he was going to slip in the jazzy Chilcott arrangement without actually telling them too much about it!

He had sent his suggestions across to the Rotary

committee in charge, a couple of weeks ago. They had to approve everything but it was a formality really. The Verlis Singers would contribute seven pieces and the choir was well advanced on preparing them for the big night when over 1,000 people would be packed into the Cathedral. Gavin was not sure yet who would play the organ.

The Verlis Singers would sing:

Love Came Down at Christmas, arr. by John Rutter with organ.

Stille, Stille, Stille, arr. Mack Wilberg with piano/Sheila.

Remember oh Thou Man, arr. Bob Chilcott with piano/Sheila.

Possibly – *Gabriel's Message* – unaccompanied.

Stille Nacht, sung every year! – Unaccompanied.

In the Bleak Midwinter, arr. Harold Darke (another Rotary favourite) with organ.

Lullay my Liking, Gustav Holst – unaccompanied.

Dominic was to sing the solo in the first verse of the carol *Stllle, Stille, Stille,* which he did rather beautifully. He certainly had a quality tenor voice and, after the choir had sung it through for the first time with Dominic singing the solo faultlessly, there was spontaneous applause led by his fellow tenors, with whooping from Polly and some of the younger sopranos.

The carols for the audience to sing would be the old favourites taken from the green *Carols for Choirs* book, all well-loved Willcocks arrangements with familiar descants. Gavin secretly longed to introduce more contemporary pieces, but the Rotary Club always made the point that this was their service and that it should follow the 'usual traditions that people loved year on year'.

Next year perhaps he would try to slip in a couple more new pieces.

The well-loved Harold Darke arrangement of *In the Bleak Midwinter* would again be included, a hardy annual at the service as requested by the Rotarians. All the sopranos would sing the first verse and Terry Davies would sing the tenor solo to verse three. Clare Taylor would sing the first verse of the opening carol *Once in Royal David's City*. Gavin had told Taff and Clare at the start of the rehearsal that they were going to sing solos in two of the choir pieces. They were both very happy to hear the news from their conductor.

Rona spoke to the choir after the interval and reported that numbers were growing for the Poland trip and now stood at nearly 40 singers. She asked that members should consult their diaries as room reservations and flight bookings would have to be made before Christmas to get the best rates, so there was some urgency.

Sheila Stirton had been particularly off with Gavin that evening, no doubt her reaction to hearing that another pianist had occupied her accompanist seat the previous Monday without informing her. Gavin had wondered at the start of the rehearsal whether or not to speak to her directly about it but decided it was best just to carry on as if nothing had happened.

At the end of the rehearsal Taff Davies asked Gavin if he was going to the pub, Gavin said he thought he would, as there was no one to go back to at home.

'I must owe you a pint for the solo spot,' Taff joked, secretly over the moon at being given a solo in the Cathedral and had sent a text to the lovely Joan:

Hold the front page – stop press sexy – Tom Jones gets
Bleak Mid Winter solo again this year in Cathedral. YES!!!

The Royal Hotel bar was the regular after-rehearsal drinking venue. It was just around the corner from the rehearsal room and there were usually about 30 choir members there laughing, chatting and enjoying a drink together. Gavin noticed that Jenny was with Lizz, who was buying her a drink at the bar. Seeing Gavin walk in, Lizz asked him if he would like a drink.

'It was part of the bribe to allow me into the choir,' she joked. Gavin laughed and asked for a gin and tonic.

The choir members pulled up chairs to form a massive 'together' area. The hotel owners were always pleased to see the choir, as they were regular customers. One of the highlights of the year was the evening of the carol service in the Cathedral. Many of the choir and audience would head for the hotel bar after the concert and the choir would always sing carols until closing time. The regulars loved it. It was always a great night, and, always produced record pre-Christmas bar takings.

Bass Richard Parish arrived late, a deliberate ruse to guarantee that he would not have to buy anyone a drink and also in the hope that some sucker might offer to buy him one.

'It's your round Richard!' shouted Taff Davies as he walked in, to everyone's amusement.

Gavin sat down next to Polly and Dominic, who were giggling together. Half an hour later it was Polly and Dominic who left the party first with excuses about having a busy day tomorrow. After they had gone Richard Parish boomed forth.

'Was Polly looking for a lift home… or is Dominic giving her one?' Everyone collapsed into laughter.

Richard Parish could be a pain but he certainly was a witty man when he wanted to be.

***

It was time to go. Everyone headed off to their cars. Gavin was the last to leave for once. It had been a good rehearsal but now his mind was filled with thoughts of closing down signs and a wife that had fallen out of love with him, and what the hell he would do next to earn a living!

Chapter 11

It was almost 8 o'clock in the morning and Gavin had received a call on his mobile at home. Since his marriage break-up he was sleeping in the office downstairs on a bunk bed. All communication with Georgina was by notes, usually left on the kitchen table.

This morning's said:

G – Home late tonight, Estate Agents showing people around today so leave your office tidy – no smelly socks please.

They have Keys – G

It was Pat Nicholls QC on the phone. He wanted to know if Gavin's wife was in earshot of the conversation as the subject was a private one.

'No it's okay Patrick, she's gone to school and anyway there's not a great deal of communication these days. It's like sharing a house with a stranger. Talk about ships passing in the night!'

Pat explained that he thought he had some very good news for Gavin. He explained that had been 'summoned' to see Peggy and Ron the previous Sunday. They didn't want him to talk to Gavin at rehearsal, but told Pat to wait until today, as there were some 'arrangements' to make.

'Anyway Gavin, straight to the point, I don't know if you are aware, but Ron and Peggy are extremely wealthy. I know you wouldn't think so sometimes when you see her flogging eggs and pinching sandwiches, but they are. They obviously think a great deal of you and are concerned about your personal predicament, they certainly don't want to be nosey but do want to help and I have to tell you that one of the cottages they own in Morladen Street in the centre of town is yours, rent free if you would like it. It's one of three they own in that road. It came empty a few weeks back and has been tidied up with some new double-glazing and central heating I think.

'Anyway it's yours for six months, although they see it as a fairly permanent arrangement. I am sure that you will want to pay something to them when you get sorted, but I suggest Gavin that you take the six months, and then we'll see how things stand.'

He continued:

'There are some furnishings and Peggy has called me early this morning to say that she'll bring the keys next Monday to choir so you can move in as soon as you like. It's a nice little cottage, two or three beds I think, and there's a small garden and garage around the back. It's been redecorated, new carpets and all that. That mad Welsh tenor would probably refer to it as the 'dog's bollocks!'

'We haven't talked about rates or electric and they are not very well up with those sorts of things, but we can sort that out later on. Perhaps I should explain that I advise them on legal matters and do what I can to help them both. This of course is entirely between us, but they really are a unique couple and, as you know, Peggy loves the choir and, my friend, she loves you for all you have done to rescue it these past years.'

Gavin didn't know what to say. The offer had come as a complete surprise. Taff Davies and Richard Parish often joked about Ron and Peggy as Lord and Lady Verlis and he had heard the talk about them selling up their post office and its land for millions to a hotel chain. Obviously the rumours were true.

'Anyway Gavin, it's a bit out of the blue I'm sure, and I expect you are lost for words? Are you still there?'

'Yes,' he gulped. 'Thanks Patrick, that's just brilliant news, I really don't know what to say.'

'Don't say anything, Mr Conductor. Fact is that they really do care about you and they want to help in your hour of need. Think yourself bloody lucky Peggy didn't insist on a Christmas solo in the Cathedral in return, wearing that fucking absurd plastic Santa suit! That would have put you on the spot, old thing.'

Both Gavin and Patrick chuckled at the thought.

'Anyway Gavin you'll get the keys on Monday from Peggy and this will not be anyone else's business. Very few people even know they own those cottages as an agent deals with rent from the other tenants and the actual landlord's name is not divulged.'

'OK Pat,' said Gavin. 'I'll certainly pick up the key Monday; this is such brilliant news, thanks, thanks! Should I call them to say how grateful I am?'

'They would prefer you not to Gavin. They will be a bit embarrassed; they are very modest folk. Just give Peggy a big cuddle when you see her – that's all you have to do. There is one thing though which you need to sort out. Peggy wants Ron to go to Poland with her. I'm afraid we are going to have to wangle that. Obviously they can afford the extra, I'll have a quiet chat with Brian. Where there's a will and all that. Anyway they know how grateful you will be and you deserve it, Gavin. A new chapter waits, onwards and upwards. See you on Monday. I am very pleased for you.'

Patrick wondered how Gavin would react to the fact that

the Trenholms were also underwriting at least £5,000 towards his bank overdraft, but he was sworn to silence on that one.

Professional etiquette as a leading QC meant that this would indeed be a secret, as requested by Peggy and Ron.

***

'Are you OK?'

Joan Davies was propped up in bed on Thursday afternoon. It was that quiet 'after sex' time when Terry was usually very noisy and made silly jokes, but not today. He had woken up after a short nap and was laid down, head on pillow, looking up at the ceiling, eyes open. Joan had been to the loo and had put her nightie back on. She snuggled up next to him and gave him a little nudge.

'Hey, Colin Firth, my sexy Welsh Mr Darcy. Why so quiet?'

'Bloody hell Joan Davies you are certainly full of surprises these days. I don't know what to say, that was...' his voice trailed off.

'That's a first, Terry Davies.' She giggled and kissed the back of his neck. Oral sex had been introduced extremely successfully to the Davies marital bed.

Later that afternoon, Taff Davies and Mr Brutus the daft dog were out for their regular Thursday five-mile walk. The route was always the same, taking in the long path around the outskirts of Verlis with a steep climb up to the top of the hill and the park, with a panoramic view of the city.

Brutus was on a long lead. Terry had come to learn that it was dangerous to let him run free. The dog was so daft that it would chase off after a cat or a squirrel and not come back. On one occasion Brutus had run straight out in front of a lorry on the main road and almost caused a massive crash. As always they sat on the bench next to the park gate for some reward biscuits Terry had in his trouser pocket.

Taff Davies had a secret. He just had to tell someone and Brutus was his best pal after all. He put his arm round the dog's neck and dragged him close, whispering in the dog's floppy ear: 'Well Mr Brutus, even though you've got no balls, I feel I should let you into a little secret that no one else knows about, but bloody hell, I gotta tell someone. So this is just between you and me and do NOT go telling any of your doggy friends.'

He looked round just in case there was anyone human in earshot. It was okay, the coast was clear.

'This afternoon, your mummy, my wife, the lovely Joan Davies gave her husband, the Welsh tenor and postie, me... a bloody wonderful blowjob! Duw fucking Duw!'

***

Earlier that morning during respective lunch breaks, Gavin James, together with Rona Hancock and Elaine Bridges, the choir publicity person had met at the Cathedral with the officials of Verlis Rotary Club, including Rotary President Mr Simon Calloway. They were there to discuss proceedings for the annual service of lessons and carols at the Cathedral. Alison Moyes, the Cathedral events manager, was present. She was a super-efficient young woman and Gavin had met her on a number of occasions at past concerts in the Cathedral.

Even though the Cathedral Choir performed a similar service on Christmas Eve and the Choral Society filled the building for the annual performance of Handel's Messiah every December, The Verlis Singers Christmas concert never failed to pack the building to capacity. For many people who attended year on year, it was the start of their Christmas.

By tradition, it always took place on the first Wednesday evening in December and one of the Cathedral organ staff played for the audience carols. The grand piano was used for the pieces performed by The Verlis Singers, six or seven especially learnt items. Alison reported that the Cathedral had a talented new deputy organist who would be playing for the service. She would forward the contact details to Simon and Gavin so they could discuss the running order.

The choir always sang *Stille Nacht*, unaccompanied and in German, at the close of the service. No one really knew why, but it was a tradition from the old Grenfell days. Gavin confirmed to the Rotary team that they would of course sing the carol this year, as usual. Admission was free and Rotary bucket shakers enticed donations at the end of the service. The total last year had been over £1,850, a record. This money was distributed to the needy of Cornwall by the Rotary organisation over the Christmas period and helped to pay for an annual Christmas day lunch for the elderly.

Many years ago, in the Isaac Grenfell reign, Decca Records had made an LP from the service. It was a live recording, coughs and all. The LP had sold worldwide and the proceeds from that LP were now contributing to the current members' tour to Poland, an interesting twist in the life of The Verlis Singers.

***

The meeting at the Cathedral had gone well. The Rotary men had already organised the readers of the lessons and were delighted that not only the Mayor would be reading this year, but also the new vice-chancellor of Verlis University. She was a dynamic Canadian who was making big changes and dragging the university into the 21st century.

Another tradition was that one of the readers would be the lady chairperson of the Inner Wheel. This is the female equivalent of the Rotary and made up mostly of Rotary wives. Simon informed Gavin that this year's President had only just been elected, and had recently moved to the city. She was quite keen to join the choir and was trying to pluck up the courage to attend a rehearsal. She was therefore very new to Inner Wheel and Verlis, but was making her presence felt.

'They certainly are overdue a move into the modern world

Gavin, but don't tell my wife I said that. She was President last year.'

The service schedule was pretty well set in stone. Gavin did discuss the fact that one of the Verlis members would be in a wheelchair, so space should be left for him at the front. He, Gavin, would push Len Fyfield in and, so as long as he knew where the space was, all would be fine.

Gavin seemed chirpy at the meeting and was keen to accommodate the requests of the Rotary members present, including Simon Calloway, who was wearing his year president hat. He would read a lesson and Gavin suggested that as Simon's was the reading relating to the Angel Gabriel seeking out the Virgin Mary, the delightful little carol *Gabriel's Message* would be the ideal piece to follow Simon's reading. This would be an additional piece to the six but as it was very short, the Rotary team agreed it should be included.

Mr President in particular thought it was a splendid choice. Being Bank Manager to The Verlis Singers' conductor was not so bad after all, especially when well-heeled local people bailed out customers who were in the shit with their finances.

***

Putting on his most matter-of-fact voice, Brian McNeil said, 'I am thinking of going on the choir tour to Poland next year.'

Brian and his wife were sitting at the table after dinner on Thursday evening. She responded.

'Well, you used to go out there a lot when you were working, so your local knowledge could be quite a help, I suppose. You can speak a bit of Polish, but then you do have that policeman's wife in the choir who is Polish. She will certainly come in handy translating the menus in the burger bars!'

'You don't think I should go do you? I am sure your number one fan Rona would prefer me not to be there so she can fuss all over you.'

Brian had chosen his moment well. He had a good marriage and Helen had supported him in his depressive periods when the bipolar thing took over his head. She had always managed to keep people at bay to give him time to get back on an even keel on many occasions.

'I don't think there are partners going. The committee has stipulated singers only, but we really need to keep it that way. Non-singers of course would not get the choir subsidy so it's more manageable without partners.'

'Looks like you are heading for Poland, Brian McNeil; I am sure you will have a great time. You will have to take your tablets and you must use them. Just make sure Gavin does not ask you to sing, as everyone knows that whilst you may be the chairman of Cornwall's famous Verlis Singers you have a ruddy awful voice.'

The chairman of The Verlis Singers allowed himself a quiet sigh of relief and wondered how he could make contact with a certain Polish widow whom he had met during the later years of his job.

'Can I get you a glass of wine darling?'

Chapter 12

Sunday October 31ˢᵗ

Mellyn Fyfield was busying herself packing a case for her husband. The previous day they had a visit from the Macmillan Nurse who had suggested that Len should go into the St Catherine's Hospice for a few days to give her a rest. The nurse had explained to the couple:

'Our doctor is a specialist in palliative care and he feels that your husband's pain relief could be better managed if he stayed at the hospice for a few days. You can come and see him every day, Mrs Fyfield, and we have a room with a bed next to Len's room which you are very welcome to use, if you want to stay overnight?'

It had been agreed that this was the best course of action and now Mellyn was carefully putting a set of clean, warm pyjamas in the case. She started to cry quietly and sat on the bed, holding the pyjamas close to her face, but being careful not to get her tears on them. She remembered the man whose rich voice had led the singing all those years ago at the memorial service of Isaac. How proud she had been of him that day. She thought back on their happy family life, the children growing up, the laughter of the grandkids, the many concerts with her husband enjoying his choir so much.

It was all about to end – her husband was dying. She would soon be alone.

Downstairs, Len Fyfield was sat in his corner chair also dreaming of past times, and memories of the choir, his devoted wife, his family, friends and his life, which was now slipping away.

He sang to himself in his mind:

Sweet is the work my God my King, to praise thy name, give thanks...

... And sing.

Tears were falling from his eyes as his frail voice sang the bass line.

***

Terry Davies was lounging the on the sofa watching *Songs of Praise*.

The day had been a lazy one and Joan had insisted that they start planning, 'The BIG event for next year,' as Joan had called it. This was their 25th wedding anniversary and Terry's 50th birthday. It would be a big family occasion and the one problem would be keeping Terry and her mum apart!

'Hey Joan, come here gorgeous one,' he shouted to his wife who was in the utility room doing some Sunday evening ironing.

'Come and listen to this, it's bloody ridiculous, a kids' choir singing Mozart's *Ave Verum* on *Songs of Praise*; some choir conductors are such snobs. This is a piece for an adult choir, not little children, stupid, and to make matters worse, their top line is flat. The esteemed conductor of The Verlis Singers would agree with me I'm bloody sure.'

Joan looked round the door at him.

'I am sure you are right, Terry, of course. With your superior knowledge, you should be on the panel of judges for the Choir of the Year competition. You'd tell 'em that's for sure!'

She smiled and bent down next to Brutus the daft dog, stroking his ear. He was dead to the world, spread-eagled all over his round comfy doggy bed, somehow filling every available inch. The bed was a Brutus gift from her mother Audrey, not so fondly referred to by her loving husband Terry as 'The Queen Mum'.

Audrey was a big dog lover but not particularly keen on sons-in-law, especially crass Welsh ones. Even if loved dearly by one's daughter. They had both taken Brutus out for a long walk that afternoon, held hands, and Joan had laughed at some rude jokes Terry had told her; the latest output from the coffee break room at the postie depot. Kneeling down in front of Terry, Joan forced his legs apart so she could snuggle between them.

'Terry Davies.' Her voice was soft and she looked at him. 'You do know that whilst you are the most infuriating man at times, I would not run off with Colin Firth or Hugh Grant even if they begged me to. I might seriously consider Tom Jones though, as I do rather like the older man.' She paused. 'We don't just have to do sexy things in bed you know Terry, and only on a Thursday afternoon.'

She was undoing the belt on his trousers and pushing her hair back behind her ears. Reaching for the zip on his trousers, she giggled.

'I do think we need to do something about your choice of underwear though Mr Davies, the next time I am in M&S I am buying you some new sexy boxer shorts AND you will wear them. Bloody hell Terry, turn the TV down I am not doing this to the background of a school choir singing *Rock of Ages...*'

In the corner Mr Brutus lifted his head, very slightly, glanced across and went back to sleep. Terry wondered if, on the next programme – *The Antiques Road Show* – some bloke would bring on a wardrobe he had found in a skip.

***

Monday November 1ˢᵗ

Gavin was lying in bed. It was 6.45am and another cold morning. His half-drunk cup of tea was on the chair next to the bunk bed. Tonight at rehearsal he would get the keys to the cottage and his new life, thanks to a rather special couple. He had gone into town and walked round to see it the previous day. It really did look very cosy through the windows. It was in a terrace of about six, probably all former tin miners' cottages. Each had a tiny front garden and a lane led around to the back, where there seemed to be long gardens and a garage for each house.

He had heard Georgina up and about upstairs, probably in the shower, and he seized the opportunity while the coast was clear to make his cup of tea. He did not want their paths to cross. He was going to leave her a note to find when she got home from school. It would tell her that he was moving out very soon and he had somewhere to live.

Cup of tea made and drank, Gavin was dozing in bed. It had gone very quiet in the house so he assumed she had gone to work early. He was surprised to get a tap on the door of his room.

'Are you there Gavin?'

Gosh, he thought, *it's the head teacher wanting to bollock me off about something.*

'Yes Miss, you can come in of you like. I am decent.'

Georgina James entered. Gavin sat up in bed and observed that the woman in front of him was now almost a stranger. Once she had been his wife and, in the early years of marriage, they had actually been in love with each other, or so they thought. He had to admit to himself, she looked great. God knows how much weight she had actually lost but she DID look different. Richard Parish was right; she certainly was, 'seriously fit these days'.

Georgina spoke:

'Gavin, I have agreed to sell the house to a family and everything is going through. I accepted an offer of £148,500 after some haggling. The solicitors are pushing everything along as they have already sold their place and want to move in ASAP. I think you will eventually get about £26,500 from the sale plus the £2,500 I said I would pay for the furniture and other stuff here. You didn't respond to my note about buying everything here so I presume that you agreed?'

'That's fine, Gina.' He had not called her that for a long time. 'I will let you know where I am living, the address and all that,' adding: 'Oh, by the way, I have found a cottage in town and will probably move out next weekend so you won't have me around cluttering up the place anymore. If you're not here I will leave the keys on the kitchen table when I go. I am going to ask Dave to come down from Swindon with his van to lend a hand!'

Georgina was certainly taken aback at the news that he had already found somewhere to live and seemed to have accepted that he was moving out.

'Um,' she spluttered, 'that's good Gavin, you will soon have the ladies from your choir lining up outside the front door with Cornish pasties for your supper!'

Changing the subject, Gavin said, 'You look super smart today, something special on at school?'

Georgina frowned.

'It's the first full Governors meeting since...' She stopped. 'So I expect there could be some personal questions to answer. I am not looking forward to it but it has to be done. I think most of them understand the way things are and that my private life will not interrupt school business. Anyway you will know all about that, your choir members and their pals have no doubt been having a field day gossiping about you and your unfaithful wife these last couple of weeks.'

'Probably, but the dust will settle soon and they find someone else to talk about,' Gavin replied.

'Anyway, better get off to school.' She turned then looked around at her husband. 'I was sorry to hear that your friend Len is so poorly. He has been a good supporter of yours hasn't he, since you took over that choir?'

It was Gavin's turn to be knocked off guard, all of a sudden Georgina was speaking to him in the way she used to, long before their marriage had spluttered to an end.

'Yes, yes, he won't be around for Christmas that's for sure, but he is a lovely man and, you know Georgina, he has accepted that he will soon die and really is ready to meet his maker. He is determined to sing for the last time at the Rotary Carols in the Cathedral but I am not sure if he will make it.'

She turned to leave. 'I hope he does and that your new house works out for you.'

'And I hope your meeting goes OK,' Gavin replied.

Hearing the front door slam, Gavin James snuggled down in bed and his thoughts went back to the early days of being married to Gina. He remembered the times together, the smell of her scent, the laughing, kissing the nape of her sexy neck in the mornings. Loving each other and just happy to be together.

***

Claire Nesbitt was standing in the queue inside the Tasty Pasty Coffee Shop in Low Cross in the centre of Verlis, famous for its Cornish pasties to die for. She was meeting Becky Morris, her piano-playing chum of many years. They had known each other a long time. Both girls grew up in a Wiltshire town and attended the same secondary school. People had always thought that they made an odd couple as they grew up together. Claire was a regular churchgoer, sang in the church choir and then went off to do a catering course in Plymouth. Becky was always in trouble at school. Homework was never done; if it was not for her musical aptitude, she would probably have been thrown out on a number of occasions. When she moved up to secondary school (with Claire, who was the model pupil), Becky flatly refused to wear the school uniform, swore at the teachers and generally disrupted the classes.

However, at music she was quite brilliant. By 12 years of age she had achieved top grades in violin and trumpet, but her outstanding talent was as a pianist, gaining her grade 8 with distinction at the remarkable age of 11 years. Encouraged by her music teacher at secondary school, she had won a scholarship to the Guildhall in London but had only lasted there for one term.

Becky had returned home a deeply disturbed young lady. She had found it very hard to be surrounded by so many other talented young people. She was housed in uni accommodation with two girls and one boy, who all came from public school backgrounds. Becky had gone in with an 'anti-everyone' attitude from the start, making it impossible for the others to accept her, let alone like her. This was the first time she had lived away from home and she was dreadfully homesick. After a few weeks staying in her room, attending very few lectures, and numerous calls to her mum, she went back home to Melksham in Wiltshire one weekend and didn't return.

Becky, eventually, and not surprisingly, turned up 15 minutes late to find Claire was sat in the corner of the coffee shop tucking into a Cornish pasty. She had bought a Diet Coke for Becky and the bottle and a glass were waiting, even though Claire knew that her rebel friend would drink it out of the bottle. Becky was wearing the same tired old jeans and scruffy furry coat that she had on when she came to play the piano at The Verlis rehearsal last week. She really did look as if she needed a hot bath. Claire wondered when the last time was that Becky had actually washed her hair. Becky had finally moved into Claire's flat the previous weekend from Wiltshire and the two were enjoying each other's company, even if the flat was starting to look untidy.

'Hi sod face, how are things at the restaurant? Thanks for getting me the Coke, I might have a pasty too in a minute, it smells good. I haven't had any breakfast as I didn't wake up very early.'

All the years that they had been friends Becky had never been an early riser. The teachers at their secondary school breathed a sigh of relief if they were taking the first lesson of the day as, more often than not (unless it was music), the disruptive Becky *the* Menace (as she was called by the teaching staff) would not have arrived yet.

'Work is good Becks,' said Claire. 'I like the restaurant, it's a hotel as well and the family that run it are really sweet. Good thing is that they don't open on Mondays so getting to choir is no problem. They also let me have a weekend off each month so I can get back to Melksham to see the family. Grandad's not too well so I always go and spend some time with him.'

Becky had moved down to stay with her friend to see if she could settle in the Cornwall town. The next day she had an interview for a support job in a nursery school and Claire was going to suggest that a good soak in the bath, hair wash and 'scrub up' was a must in the morning. The jeans had to be left behind, a chance to put them in the wash if Claire had her way.

'What did you think of the rehearsal Claire?' asked Becky.

'Everyone was knocked out that you were so good, especially Gavin. I bet he would love you to play for the choir full time but of course Sheila has been there for an age.'

'Yeh, it was good. You sing some nice stuff and they seem like fun. I did get frosty looks from some of the altos but I can cope with that. The conductor seemed nice, what's his name, Gareth?' Claire put her right.

'That's it, Gavin, yes nice bloke; he knows what he wants and the choir sound very good. He is lucky to have such a good soprano line even if you are in it! Just joking Claire, you have always had a brilliant voice. Do you remember when we entered that snooty music festival in Bath and we won the piano and voice class by a bloody mile?'

'Yes I do,' said Claire, 'even if the adjudicator made a snide remark about your skimpy dress not being 'suitable for a music festival."

'Dirty old sod couldn't keep his eyes off my legs.' Becky sniggered. 'I bet he went round the back for a wank after! Anyway we had top marks. Do you still have the cup on your sideboard at home Claire?'

They were interrupted as Polly Jones came across to speak. She was also on lunch break and had come in for a takeaway cappuccino.

'Hi Claire, and friend. Hey, didn't you come and play the piano at choir last week?' Polly leaned over and whispered to Becky, who nodded and grinned.

'You were fucking awesome.' And then louder, 'Are you going to be our new accompanist? I bet the lovely Gavin would like that. The old lady is good but, shit, you were amazing, had you really not seen the music before, did you just sight-read it?'

'She is a genius,' said Claire. 'Trouble is she doesn't realise it and always wants to be the rebel. I went to school with her.' She gave her untidy friend a look.

'Well ladies, I have to shoot off, work calls,' said Polly. Turning to the two girls as she left, she said: 'Have you seen Gavin's little camera shop? It's got closing down posters all over the front window. I heard someone saying that his shop has gone bust. I'll have to pop in and buy something to help him out. It's hard running a small business.'

'And his wife has dumped him for a hunky sports teacher at the school where she teaches,' said Claire.

'That's a double bummer then,' replied Polly.

'Tell you what ladies, he is a bit of a dish, he has that thing that makes you want you cuddle and look after him. If he was ten years younger he would be fighting yours truly off!'

Stepping out for the door, Polly said: 'See you tonight Claire and hopefully we'll soon have you as the choir accompanist, Becky, then you can come to Poland and we will all go out on the town and find ourselves some hot Polish guys (whispering) to shag!'

Claire and Becky watched her go. There was something about Polly Jones that you couldn't help but like. She was feisty and full of confidence but had that ability to get on well with most people. Claire had not really thought much about Poland but decided that afternoon to ask her boss if she could have the holiday time off next June so she could put her name down. It could be a lot of fun although she would certainly not be shagging any hot Polish boys.

***

Gavin's music stand was out at the front with an envelope on it. His name was written on the front and he recognised Peggy's writing. He opened it and read the note:

Dear Gavin,

Here are the keys to number 3 Morladen Street it is all redy for you – we want you to be happy and are glad to help.

Ron says get all those ladies round and have a good time.

Lots of luv Peggy and Ron x

Gavin found Peggy busying herself in the rehearsal room kitchen. Walking up to her, he put his arms round her giving her a massive cuddle, and managed to say: 'Peggy I just don't what to say to you and Ron, you…'

Cutting him off mid-sentence Peggy said: 'Well Gavin my dear, there is nothing to say then. Let's get the chairs out, people will soon start turning up. Ron sends his love.'

The rehearsal went well, with all the time now spent on the Christmas pieces. The choir knew *Gabriel's Message*. It would be sung unaccompanied and Gavin asked four of the choir to sing the middle verse as a quartet. The chosen four would be:

Soprano, Jenny Dalton, alto Laura Honey, tenor Jim Best, and bass Richard Parish.

It was not the strongest four voices from each section but Gavin knew they were each more than capable of singing the verse unaccompanied and very well. He noticed that his choice of Laura for the alto part caused some eyebrows in that section to be raised in the front row. It did not concern him. The Cathedral offered the chance to give people a solo and Laura did have a very good voice. She had told Gavin that singing in the Salvation Army had been a big part of her life and Gavin knew that with more confidence she could even sing a solo on her own one day.

As already explained, and now confirmed to the Rotary top brass, Clare Taylor would sing the opening verse of *Once in Royal,* at the start of the service, Dominic would solo on the carol, *Stille, Stille, Stille* and (at the request of the Rotary club) they would again include the Harold Darke arrangement of *In the Bleak Midwinter,* a favourite of Gavin's. The first verse would be sung by all of the sopranos and Taff Davies would indeed sing the third tenor solo verse.

Gavin also spent a considerable amount of time on the Christmas piece *Lullay My Liking* by Holst, and performed without accompaniment. Maintaining pitch was vital and Gavin went over the individual sections carefully.

'There is no way that the Verlis Singers are going to lose pitch on one of our unaccompanied pieces,' he told them.

Rehearsal continued with some time spent on the descants for the audience, which would be accompanied on the organ, Gavin telling the choir that he expected to hear from the allocated organist in the next few days.

Claire Nesbitt came up to him at half time with the news that her hotel owners would certainly let her have the time off for the Poland trip. They had even offered to pay half of her costs. She also gave Gavin an update on her accompanist friend.

'Becky is going for a job tomorrow and if she gets it she will be staying in Verlis for the time being. I am going to tidy her up for the interview.'

Gavin asked Claire to wish her all the best for the interview. A permanent job in the town was one step nearer to being the choir's accompanist.

Claire joining the Poland tour was great news for Gavin and he told her so. Numbers were now creeping up nearer to 40 and he would have a word with Clare Taylor, his other leading soprano. She lived with her boyfriend, who was a carpenter, and they had very little money. Gavin would chat with the chairman to see if some sort of extra subsidy could be arranged. She had a beautiful voice and was a great asset to the choir.

For this Monday's rehearsal, Gavin had split the four sections of the choir into a square format. The piano was in the middle of the room from where he also conducted that night. This meant that the singers were looking across at each other, giving Gavin the chance to stress one of his personal niggles that 'faces are very important in a choir'.

'Have you been to a concert and looked at the choir and thought how miserable they look?' he asked the Verlis Singers around him.

'Faces are very important, look as if you are enjoying yourself. If there is one miserable face you can bet the audience will spot it!'

Thankfully he did not see the tenors pulling their faces into weird contortions and making the sopranos opposite them giggle.

At the end of the rehearsal Rona gave out to all the committee members the agenda for the next full meeting. Glancing through, Gavin spotted that item three was the resignation of the Choir Treasurer Gerry Head. It was the first time that he had heard of this. 'It would make for an interesting meeting,' he thought.

***

Parking in a road near to Morladen Street, with his scarf wrapped tightly around his neck to keep out the cold November wind, Gavin stepped out along the row of cottages, finding the gate with number 3 on it. Walking up the short drive he took the keys out of his pocket, opened the blue front door and stepped into a small hallway. He had not gone to the pub after rehearsal and was dead keen to see inside his new home.

It was a really cosy terraced cottage; the hall led into a medium-sized room, which had an open log-burning fireplace. There was a comfy sofa that looked fairly new and another chair. Glass doors led into a good-sized kitchen. The cottage also had a small downstairs loo. Upstairs there were three bedrooms, and a decent-sized bathroom with a new shower, which was still wrapped in cellophane. The smallest bedroom, Gavin thought, would make a great office.

Climbing back down the stairs, Gavin slumped onto the sofa. Speaking out loud to himself: 'This is your new home Gavin James and it's free. Bloody hell, you really are a lucky sod. Thanks Ron and Peggy.'

His feelings of relief were overwhelming, without any

146

knowledge that the couple were also underwriting his bank loan. He walked into the little kitchen, there was a nice wooden table and chairs, on it a plate with fruit cake covered with a cloth and next to it, a hand written note:

Just for you Gavin, homemade, Ron sends his luv, there's a bottle of Ron's brew in the cubberd.

Chapter 13

Gavin walked into the meeting room on the first floor of the County Hotel, answering Heather's call to attend the Festival Committee she chaired. It had been a busy day at the shop with lots of customers, something he was not used to. Amongst the shop visitors had been a number of loyal members of The Verlis Singers. The bright dayglow posters were now all over the windows so the world at large all knew that this was a closing down sale.

Knock down unbeatable prices – buy now for Christmas!

Business had actually been exceptional over the last few days. Gavin had sold four cameras that morning alone and over £300 worth of equipment, tripods, lenses and the like. Prices were low, but as Gavin had already paid for the stock and he kept above the recommended retail sale prices, as far as he was concerned, everything was legal and above board.

Eric Stroman from the choir bought a £200 camera, telling Gavin that it was for his wife Karen, who had a birthday coming up. Gavin fancied he was buying it just to help him out which was really rather humbling on a cold November morning in Cornwall. People were 'rallying round', that was obvious.

Lizz Ozroy, the new alto, had come in (looking dead classy as always) and bought a £450 camera, paying by a Gold card. The sale of the day! She had spent a long time choosing and after leaving the shop with her new camera she had popped back twenty minutes later with some M&S sandwiches and a takeaway coffee for Gavin. He had told her that his lunch was not organised, so her thoughtful delivery (not to mention the camera purchase) was very welcome and she flatly refused any payment for the snack.

'I love the choir and Jenny is becoming a good friend. She is a super lady and such a fan of yours.' Lizz added, 'Oh by the way Gavin, I didn't realise when I agreed to be chair of the Inner Wheel, but I have been told that part of my duties is to read a lesson at the Carol Service. It seems that it's a tradition. If that makes it difficult for you Gavin, I will ask someone else. Singing in the choir is more important, especially as I am actually an atheist! But keep that to yourself, if Audrey Arnold, the dreadful Inner Wheel secretary, finds out, I will be burnt at the stake!'

Gavin assured her that it would be fine as members of the choir had read in the past and thanked her again for the sarnies and coffee, adding: 'If you need any help with the camera, just ask.'

***

Heather Strong stood up to welcome him to the Cornish Festival Committee meeting with a smile, and gave him a kiss on the cheek. There were six other people in the room. Gavin recognised some of the faces. Verlis may be a city but on the musical scene it was just an overgrown village and those who were involved in the vibrant arts and music all either knew each other, or had fallen out at some time in the past!

Heather invited Gavin to pull up a seat and proceeded to introduce everyone. One of the committee members was Andy Smith, the conductor of the Farmouth Male Choir, and Gavin, knowing that SOME choir conductors could be very envious, even resentful of the achievements of others, wondered if Andy was happy about Gavin being there.

Heather seemed to be in charge. She was an extremely attractive woman and well connected with the music education department at the county council. As head of music at the Verlis Girls' School where she had a number of excellent choirs, she clearly had the male members of the committee eating out of her hand. Whether the two rather stern ladies in the room felt the same remained to be seen.

She explained that the festival committee had won a Lottery Arts grant to support the 2011 75th Festival Celebration next May 19-21. The festival would run its regular programme of competitions for choirs of all ages and sizes, but, as a special event on the final Saturday, it would promote an open workshop event called *Sing out for Cornwall.* The day would be targeted at people across Cornwall who probably did not sing in a choir, but hopefully would introduce them to the experience. During the day, rehearsals would take place at her school and the choir would take part in a celebration at the Cathedral that evening, singing the songs they had learned at the workshop. Some of the top winning choirs from the choral classes would also be invited to take part.

She told those present that all of the Cornwall choirs would also be invited to the workshop day to put on a display about their own group. This would give everyone attending a chance to perhaps 'find a choir for them to join'.

'I hope you will want to take a stand for The Verlis Singers, although you are probably not looking for new members,' she said with a smile.

Gavin said that he was sure they would be interested and that the choir were singing again on *Songs of Praise* in the spring and would be taking part in a competition in Krakow in June so the timings were just right.

'That's fantastic,' said Heather. 'You certainly seem to have the touch when it comes to publicity.'

'And that's one of the reasons we hope that you will lead the festival community choir,' chipped in Andy Smith, with what Gavin hoped was a friendly comment.

A rather fierce-looking gentleman then spoke up. He had been introduced to Gavin as David and explained that he lived in Penzance and was a retired music teacher. He was a trustee of the festival and they would announce the three-day programme at the start of December at a special launch party, when everyone involved in the local music scene would be invited. The festival Patron, Lord David Williton, would host the reception and the final Saturday's event would be a major announcement.

'Whilst we have been running the festival successfully for many years, the local press generally take no interest. Perhaps this new project might encourage them to wake up and give us some coverage,' he said.

Heather then butted in, sensing the prejudices of some people present could steer the meeting in a negative way. One of the elderly ladies, Joyce Everitt, had complained bitterly about Gavin's invitation. Her husband Peter was the accompanist to the West Cornwall Male Choir and, in their view, Gavin James did not have the necessary musical knowledge to be endorsed by the Cornwall Festival.

She had told Heather:

'Peter was a music teacher in London for many years and thinks that Gavin James is not professionally trained. I believe that he never even went to university?'

Heather had pointed out that Gavin's success with The Verlis Singers could not be questioned and the respect he was getting from people such as the BBC was more important than academic qualifications.

'He has a natural gift and it is great pity that some people choose to ignore that fact!'

Heather was having none of the prejudices aired at the meeting, and continued:

'Gavin, it will be great to have you conducting the Saturday choir. We can liaise about the logistics of the day after Christmas but, if you are in agreement, we will announce in a press release that you have accepted our invitation. You will be paid £500 as an inclusive fee for your participation as there will be a need for you to spend time on the planning in the run-up to the day. There is additional budget for purchasing the music and paying an accompanist of your choice. We are thinking of three or four pieces to learn, but that's really for you to decide.'

She explained that her school hall would be ideal for the workshop during the day and coaches would take the singers into the Cathedral, where Gavin would be allocated a 45-minute slot to rehearse the workshop choir pieces. Gavin fancied that Andy Smith took a sharp intake of breath when the £500 fee was mentioned.

'That is very generous,' he said. 'I would love to do it. Thank you for asking me and I will do all I can to make it a success. I also have a very good young accompanist in mind who could play on the day.'

Sensing that there were other matters to be discussed, he took his leave. Heather would be in touch soon when the launch date was confirmed. As he left, David stood up to shake Gavin's hand. He was in fact a very tall man, well over six feet.

'Thanks for coming, I am sure you are the right man for the job. My name is David Grenfell by the way.'

Gavin left the room and then it suddenly hit him. Of course, he was a Grenfell; bloody hell, that man is related to Isaac, The Verlis Singers' founder. Gavin had seen pictures of Isaac, who was an imposing tall man; David had to be his son. Gavin had no contact of course with 'The Isaac Days' but knew of the bad feeling that still existed. Perhaps it was time again to build bridges? Time would tell.

***

*Thursday November 4th*

Richard Parish parked his car in the St Catherine's hospice car park. There was some form of conference on and an extended car park ran into the nearby field. He was a big man at around 20 stone plus. The diet would start next week. At the entrance reception, Richard asked the silver-haired lady behind the desk to direct him to the day room, where he hoped to find his friend Len Fyfield. She pointed down the corridor to the area where he would indeed find his friend.

Len was sat in a high-backed chair in the large bay window of the hospice day care room that looked out at the November Cornish landscape. He had a rug over his legs, although the room was very warm. There was a youngish woman sat reading by the door and Richard beamed at her and said hello. Richard Parish was not used to being inside a hospice, a place where he thought people went to die. He walked over to Len and touched his frail shoulder.

'Hey up Len, you old sod, the number one bass from The Verlis Singers has a visitor.'

Len smiled. 'Richard Parish, my dear boy it's lovely to see you, pull up a chair and sit down. Tell me how things are with you. Is there a lady yet? Bloody hell Rich you've been trying for long enough to find someone to keep you warm at night.'

The two friends chatted together. Richard and Len had sat next to each other at choir in the bass section for the past eight years since Richard had joined. For all his size and his ever flowing banter and stack of jokes, Richard was a very vulnerable man and Len seemed to recognise this and they had forged a firm friendship. This was not entirely blessed by Mellyn his wife, who found Richard at times somewhat overbearing.

After 15 minutes Richard could see that Len was tiring. Even simple conversation now obviously wore him out. Len had told Richard that he would be singing in the Cathedral and Richard would have to sit next to him.

'I need to lean on those big shoulders, Richard, for the last time, if that's okay? We'd better be on top form my friend.' Len reached over and touched the hand of his younger overweight pal.

Big Richard Parish had to look away and hurriedly pulled out a grubby hanky, blowing his nose to hide his tears.

'I had better go Len and let you have a snooze...'

Len's voice was now very weak. 'OK Richard, off you go, take care of yourself you big ugly sod, and give my regards to the boys in the bass section. Find yourself a girlfriend, you need looking after when I will not be around to keep an eye on you. I hope to be there for the Rotary Carols in the Cathedral.'

***

Joan had cooked homemade lasagne for Terry's supper, his favourite. The regulatory afternoon of Thursday lovemaking had gone extremely well and her husband had performed his duties admirably. He had worn his new boxer shorts from M&S, although they had not stayed on for long! Terry had taken the dog out for the usual walk after the bedroom activities; although Brutus was not over keen, as it was a bitterly cold day. Whilst Terry was out she had texted her daughter Jenny:

Hi Luv – hope u are ok – 2night your dad is DEF going to discuss the celebrations next year – I will not let him off the hook this time! PS he is singing a solo in the Cathedral they might have to enlarge the doors to get his head in !!!!!!!!!!!!!! – any chance u could be there – he would love that. xxx mum

She confronted her husband:

'Ok Terry Davies you *have* to concentrate on next year.'

Joan had turned off the TV and had plonked herself down on the sofa alongside her hubby.

'Next year, 2011, is your fiftieth birthday and it's also our 25 year Silver Wedding Anniversary and we need to start making plans or at least DISCUSS it,' she said, giving Terry a big push as he had picked up the *Cornish Leader* newspaper from the coffee table.

'Put that bloody paper down you infuriating man, I tell you what Terry Davies, if you do not give me you undivided attention, today will have been the last time that I... Well, you know what...'

As if by magic Terry sat up.

'What do you have in mind Mrs Davies?' he asked, putting on his serious Welsh voice.

'Well we have to fix the date and I think it should be a double celebration. That way you and Mum don't have to tolerate each other for too long.'

The somewhat fractious relationship between Terry and his mother-in-law had not improved with the years. From early niceties had come toleration, now replaced by obvious dislike at being in each other's company. Terry found her bossy and a snob. A 'bloody pain in the arse'. Joan naturally loved her mother but did realise that there were faults on both sides. Her mother would not have agreed, however. She thought her son-in-law was rude and brash. He was, most certainly, not good enough to be the husband to her lovely daughter Joan. After all he was just a postman, for goodness' sake.

Audrey Taylor had admitted to friends in the past that whilst her daughter was married to a rude Welshman, surprisingly they did seem very happy together and had a lovely daughter. This was a fact she simply could not comprehend.

Things had come to a head two Christmases ago. Audrey

and second husband Bill had hosted the annual Christmas bash attended by all the immediate family. Joan's sister Sally and brother, Declan, with partners and children various, had been there and, over Christmas pudding and brandy butter, Declan had made a very snide remark about the Trade Union movement. This had struck a nerve with Terry and the resulting discussion turned into a rather unpleasant political argument, which was only stopped by Joan standing up and shrieking at the two men to stop. Audrey, who thought that the sun shone out brightly from the Conservative rear of her lawyer son, and anxious that all the family should be ready and in position for the Queen's speech, was appalled (but not surprised) by the views expressed by her Welsh working-class son-in-law.

At Joan's insistence, the family then dispersed to the lounge for the 3pm broadcast. To make matter worse Terry then announced: 'Well, you can all watch the Queen patronising the great British viewing audience from the comfort of her Palace, which WE pay for... I am taking Brutus, the dog with no balls, for a walk.'

Not exactly the sort of behaviour one expects of one's son-in-law at a true blue middle-class family Christmas Day get-together.

***

Joan had a 2011 diary on her lap and Terry seemed ready for a serious planning discussion. The wedding anniversary and Terry's birthday fell in mid-June, but as Terry would be in Poland with the choir from June 15th to 21st it was decided that the celebration would take place on Saturday June 26th, the weekend after Terry came back.

'I can get on with all the last minute plans whilst you are away, Terry. You just go and enjoy yourself safe in the understanding that your dutiful wife is doing all the preparation. I will tell Mum and Bill that she must stay at a hotel in town. That way the two of you will be kept apart. I will talk to Bill. He actually likes you a lot but is frightened to death to admit this to Mum! Hopefully both of you might just make an effort to get on for this weekend, perhaps for mine and Jenny's sake?'

Terry smiled and reached across to give his wife a big wet sloppy kiss on the cheek.

'Mrs Davies, my very sexy wife, I shall be on my very best behaviour and will even pile on the charm with the Tory dick Declan, that opinionated brother of yours.'

There would be a lunch on the Saturday at a hotel and in the evening a party with invites to about 100 people. Joan would get some costs worked out but they had to make it a special occasion. Whilst they were not wealthy, they could afford to make it a good do.

'We can't invite the entire choir Terry, but nearer the time we will have to make up a list. Do you think many of your family will come?'

Terry said he didn't know, as he had not mentioned the celebration year to any of them.

'But... you know what they say Joan; the Welsh love a party. Especially if it's a bloody freebie!'

Chapter 14

The note on the kitchen table was waiting for Georgina when she got back at about 7pm. She had spent the day with her lover at the flat where Trevor lived.

Hello and goodbye I suppose to the former Mrs James (well almost)

Here are the keys as I have moved out today to the house in Morladen Street, Number 3 to be exact.

I think I have taken everything but should you happen upon a dead sock or stained pants tucked away somewhere then please put in in a sack and pop it round.

I was not sure what to do with the photos of us around the house so I have left them. I think that's something for the future to sort out.

Let me know when all the money is sorted please and how the future will unfold – presume you will want one day to go down the D------ road – sorry can't bring myself to write that word.

Also G not sure how to end this message to you so, I won't.

Reading the note in Gavin's handwriting, she suddenly felt very sad and lonely. Her life had turned upside down, something that she had completely orchestrated herself. It was entirely of her own making. Georgina James now wondered what she had done, and how she had changed the lives of so many people around her. It was her turn to cry.

***

Monday November 8th

The facts were that a very high proportion of the statements made by David Honey in the past were total lies, designed to impress, gain the confidence of gullible people, and to make money.

However, when David told folk that he had a Business Degree, it was the truth. When asked where he obtained it, the reply was always a lie. Truth was that it had taken him five years of study whilst in prison. He was a highly intelligent man and had signed up to the course and had been a model pupil, the shining star, without doubt. The prison had an education wing and David (Sebastian Locking-Thomas as was) had seized the chance it gave to gain every advantage of the system and every opportunity it offered.

In addition to the Business Degree he also had an IT accreditation. For obvious reasons access to the Internet was very carefully scrutinised at the prison but David had (not surprisingly) convinced the education team that he could be entrusted to pursue such knowledge as part of his learning programme and as part of: 'My rehabilitation to the outside world, with the good Lord and Laura at his side.'

***

'Have you received the financial projections for the tour from David the bass?'

Chairman Brian was on the phone to Rona. He always called her on the week of the choir committee meeting to establish if there were any moans and groans that could cause conflict at the Thursday evening meeting. David had sent out his proposals by email attachment to the choir committee and also to the tour group.

'Tell you what, Rona, it must have taken him ages to do the plan but it's brilliant to have someone who can do this. I see he has based it on a party of 45, which I think is about right. I know dear old Gerry was against spending the choir's historical funds and subsidising the members, but this way I am sure many of the younger ones will now be able to come. The future of the choir is with the young people; we do have to accept that.'

With no reply to this comment from the honorary secretary of The Verlis Singers, Brian ploughed on: 'I suppose Gerry's resignation could prompt some debate but I intend taking this as an early item on the agenda to get it over with. We will send him a letter of thanks, say lots of nice things, and then move on. Do we have to advertise for a new treasurer Rona?'

Rona assured him that within the articles of memorandum of the choir that was indeed the case. A notice would have to be put on the choir notice board inviting nominations. These had to be supported by at least two current choir members. If there were more than one it would then be a closed vote, probably at a Monday rehearsal. When asked if Rona thought that David Honey would be a possible choice she replied: 'Well the information just sent out for the tour is something we have never had before, Gerry certainly would not have spent the time preparing such a helpful document. Even in the days of John Liveak (the choir treasurer for over 20 years in the Isaac days) we never had such well-prepared financial information to work on. His wife Laura told me that he has a Business Degree and that certainly shows in the tour figures we have all just received.'

***

Polly Jones was sat in front of her computer at work. The weekend had been quiet by her standards. In the absence of sex these days she had flung her energies into decorating her house and had enlisted the help of Dominic, her new (gay and safe) best chum and buddy. He had spent the biggest part of Sunday with her slopping paint on walls, or holding the ladder whilst Polly did the ceilings. There was also endless drinking coffee, a bottle or two of wine, and pizza. Whilst peering up at Polly perched on the top of a ladder he had commented: 'Fucking hell Poll, your legs do go on for ever, gazing up at them from below I almost wish I was straight. I suppose you also know that you have a great ass! I can see why you drive the tenors and basses to distraction when they are standing behind you in the sops. I bet they all fantasise about getting into your panties.'

'Don't be disgusting Dom, I cannot help it if I'm *just a girl who can't say NO.*'

Cue for a song led by tenor Dominic joined in by Polly who started laughing so much she nearly fell off the ladder.

A big smile crept across Polly's face as she remembered the ladder moment. Much needed light relief as she prepared the draft end of year accounts of a small electrical business in Verlis. They were one of the hundreds of small business accounts managed by SMA, Stroman Maycroft and Associates, Cornwall's leading accountancy practice. Choir tonight, lovely carols, cuddly Gavin, that randy Welshman and his pals and a fun drinking session with Dominic and the gang after in the pub.

***

Gavin was settling into his new house. The place was a bit of a tip, but over the weekend his younger brother Dave had visited to help out with the move. David lived in Swindon and had driven down in response to a desperate call for help from his big brother. Dave was a builder by trade so had all the practical skills, plus a van, which was used to hump the little furniture and sacks of clothes that needed to be taken to the new Gavin cottage.

Gavin decided not to tell his brother about the good fortune that had bought his new home, instead fobbing off all his inquisitive questions. Dave was single as his second marriage had fizzled out. Aged 38 with two ex-wives and two kids, the brothers were quite different, although they did get on very well. Gavin had even persuaded his brother to stay on for a day and come to the rehearsal of the choir he took on Monday nights. David would now drive back home on Tuesday morning.

Gavin had decided to attend his Rotary Club that week. He had taken a leave of absence these last few weeks but felt okay now to return even if some of the old stagers would probably give him the cold shoulder. At least he would not now be going bankrupt. Sales in the shop were over target to pay off his debts and, thanks to Peggy and Len, he had a nice temporary home.

Whilst also coming from the same Methodist background, brother David was not musical but could do a seriously good Robbie Williams on a karaoke night out, if pushed, or if there were attractive ladies to impress. He had been staggered to discover that his organised straight-down-the-line older brother had got himself into such a financial mess. He had always been rather scared of Gavin's dominating head teacher wife, generally giving her a wide berth. He did have first-hand experience of screwing up a marriage (well, two in fact) but just didn't expect it to happen to Gavin.

***

With only two more rehearsals to go before the Rotary Carol service The Verlis Singers were now polishing the pieces they would perform on their own as well as spending some time on the carols that would also be sung by the congregation. Brother David was sat in the back. A few of the choir members had met him before.

Deep Harmony sung, and latecomers settled, Gavin introduced the stranger in the room.

'You may have noticed that the young-*ISH* man sat at the back is rather handsome and debonair. This is due to that fact that he is my younger brother David.'

A round of applause and wolf whistle from Polly followed

by laugher all round.

'David has been allowed out for the weekend to help me to move. He does not sing, so he will be sitting at the back keeping quiet, something he is not good at.'

Gavin then reported that Anthony Sheppard would play the organ this year in the Cathedral. He was fairly new to the Cathedral staff but he had been assured that he was extremely good. Gavin had spoken to Anthony, who had asked if there could be a special rehearsal for the choir with him. Such requests for rehearsal time had been turned down in the past, as the Cathedral had such a busy December schedule with daily communions, evening prayer and the like.

'I will have the keys to open up, it is all sorted and in the Cathedral diary,' Anthony Sheppard had informed Gavin, and also that he was looking forward to playing the organ at what he understood was 'one of the highlights of the musical year for the people of the city'. Gavin was delighted that Anthony could fix a rehearsal.

'It's all sorted,' he told Gavin. 'If your choir can make it we can rehearse between 2.30 and 5pm on the Sunday afternoon November 28th. We are all booked in.'

This meant that the rehearsal on Monday 22nd would now be at the choir's usual venue. Rona scowled at hearing this, as it was the first she knew of such arrangements, she would have to call the church office to re-book the choir in that Monday.

But this was great news for Gavin. Conducting in the Cathedral was far more complex than might seem. The massive building has something like an eight-second reverb and to add to that the organ was set way up high. A rehearsal there on the Sunday afternoon was just what he wanted. The acoustic was wonderful but the singers had to be confident with all the pieces. Many of The Verlis Singers had sung there before, but total concentration on the conductor was required even for the audience carols. Gavin remembered the first time he had performed there with the then director of music at the Cathedral playing the organ. At the end of the service Gavin had asked him if there was something on the TV that night he particularly wanted to see. The rather perplexed and arrogant Richard Stigford-Evans had enquired, 'Why?'

'Well, the pace you took all the audience carols at, I thought you must be in a rush to get home!'

The following year Gavin asked the Rotary to insist that a different organist was on duty. Fortunately, Mr Stigford-Evans had left for pastures new, somewhere in the Midlands.

***

The rehearsal was going well. At half time Claire Nesbitt told Gavin that her friend Becky had got the job at the nursery school and would be staying in Verlis for the foreseeable future.

'Anytime you need a deputy she would love to help out, Gavin. I am hoping that she will really settle down now she is Verlis.' Gavin wanted to find out more about Becky but could see his brother bursting to speak to him. David rushed forward and slapped his brother on the shoulders.

'Bloody hell big brother, you are fantastic. I saw you waving your arms about and posing on that TV hymn programme last year, but just didn't realise.

'Tell you what Gavin, I have seen you in such a different light in this room. You have a real talent; you are a genius, what an amazing sound. I want to join a choir!'

Next in the queue to speak to him was Lizz:

'I have already been out today with the camera, it's brilliant but I think I need to sign up to a course to understand how to get the best out of it, don't you think Gavin?'

Agreeing with her, he again offered any help he could give. The years taking pics on the staff of the newspaper had given him a good insight into most things that needed to be known about photography.

'I will pop into your shop later in the week to pick your brains, and bring you a coffee.'

Rona spoke to the choir at the end of the rehearsal. Len was now in St Catherine's Hospice and she knew that several choir members had visited him already.

'Mellyn has asked please if the visits could be short. Len gets very tired and he will never ask you to leave. Please everyone remember that if you do go and see him. We do need him to have as much time as he can with his wife and family.'

***

'Brother dear, don't wait up for me, I may be late returning home. Leave the back door on the latch and I will let myself in.'

Gavin had noticed that David was paying a great deal of attention to Polly Jones in the pub after the rehearsal. They were stood by the bar with Dominic and Richard who was reeling off the latest round of jokes. Gavin didn't see his brother sneak out with Polly Jones.

'I don't suppose you want to come in for a coffee Mr James junior?' asked Polly to the handsome man who had kindly offered to give her a lift home from the pub. David had fancied the girl with the everlasting legs the minute he set eyes on her at Gavin's choir practice. For some reason, he thought all ladies in choirs were straight laced and virginal. He soon discovered that Polly Jones was the exception.

Nearly tripping over a pot of paint as he entered her house in the dark, they had hardly got inside the front door of her house when she turned to David and wrapped her arms around his neck, kissing him violently, her tongue exploring the inside of his mouth. One of her hands then reached down to undo the top of her jeans so they slipped to the floor. Pushing his hands down her flimsy pants to grab her buttocks, she could feel his dick hardening against her. Biting his ear she whispered, 'David James, I am going to fuck you like never before. Take me to bed and eat me!'

Chapter 15

Tuesday November 9th

When Gavin came downstairs early on Tuesday morning, he found his younger brother fast asleep on the sofa with the duvet pulled over his head. For reasons he didn't really understand, he was angry. He should know better, after all Dave had been picking up girls and doing his overnight disappearing act ever since he became a teenager. It had been a really good rehearsal last night and he had especially liked the adulation from his brother at half time, but then he had to spoil it by picking up Polly James and going off to have sex with her, or so he presumed.

Going through to the kitchen, he noisily put the kettle on and started busying himself doing scrambled eggs and toast for breakfast. A voice from beneath the duvet spoke... 'Whatever you are having, do some for me, Gavin.'

Without turning round, Gavin snapped at his brother, 'It's scrambled eggs, orange juice, toast and coffee and I am NOT going to ask what *you* had last night, you randy sod; you don't bloody change do you?'

Sitting up, Dave responded: 'Tell you what brother dear. I do think you are jealous. Do you fancy Polly with the everlasting legs? Have I trod on your baton? I tell you what that girl is seriously hot, I thought she was...'

Cutting off his brother mid-sentence, Gavin snapped back, 'I do NOT want – a blow by blow account of your shagging antics,' which earned a snigger from his brother. 'And as for me and Polly, that's fucking stupid, she is far too young for

167

me and I don't think I want to get tangled up and hurt by any woman in the near future. Don't forget I am the sad ass bloke whose business went tits up and his wife buggered off with the sports teacher.'

Realising he had touched a sensitive nerve, and not wanting to upset his big brother any more, David quickly changed the subject.

'Tell you what, though, Gavin, you really are brilliant with that choir; I saw my big brother in a totally different light last night, can't you earn a living doing music? I am also going to give you a bit of advice, Gavin, which you may not like, but you need to listen to. You need to get out and get some more modern clothes, get your hair cut and tidy yourself up. You say you are a sad ass; your words not mine. I don't know the state of your finances, and I guess they are shit, but you have a lovely little cottage here, although I don't know how you are paying for it. Do the charity shops; throw away that bloody old grey jacket and those scruffy jeans. You were always the brother the birds fancied, it used to fucking piss me right off. Come on, Gavin, get yourself tidied up and the next time I visit I want to see some notches on your bedpost! I am your little brother and I want you to get happy, and by the way hurry up with those bloody scrambled eggs, you sad ass. That Polly wore me out last night.'

***

A momentous decision had been made in the Davies household. After many years pushing his bike around the highways and byways of Verlis delivering letters and parcels, Taff Davies was going to apply for an office job. Joan had been keen on the idea for a few months and had worked on her husband to the point where the penny had eventually dropped into place. Terry had come home last week to say that one of the old stagers in the planning office was retiring and the chief had suggested that he might like to apply.

'Well Terry, that's fate taking a hand,' said Joan when he

told her. 'You are always moaning about the early shifts, so now is your chance to work sensible hours at last with more holiday time and a slightly better salary. We will just have to rearrange our Thursday afternoons!'

The CV had been worked on over the weekend with the help of Joan and, after his Tuesday morning round, Postie Davies would pop his official application into the internal mail at HQ. He would not say anything to his colleagues yet, just in case he didn't get it. He knew Cockie Scottie was also applying, but as he had only been in the job for a few months Terry didn't see him as a threat.

'Nothing ventured luv,' said Joan, and she was right. She was always right, which was why Terry was devoted to her.

***

Lizz and Jenny were having a ladies' lunch at the trendy Lannings Hotel bar on Orange Street. It was not the sort of place that Jenny would have gone before meeting Lizz but a new world seemed to be opening up now she had a sophisticated friend. Jenny had confided with Lizz that she was very nervous about singing in the quartet at the Cathedral. Lizz assured her that she had nothing to be concerned about.

'You have a lovely soprano voice Jenny. Gavin wouldn't have asked you unless he knew you could do it. If I can read about Jesse's rod you can sing about gentle Mary meekly bowing her head.'

They both giggled.

Jenny's husband Brian was a solicitor who specialised in family law so he could be on call from the police some weekends. They had met at a tennis club, fell in love, married and had two teenage children. Jenny was a trained midwife and still did shifts at the Royal Cornwall Hospital in Verlis. Brian was a keen golfer and would be captain at Verlis Golf Club next year. When Lizz asked how many babies she had delivered Jenny didn't have the faintest idea.

'It will be quite a few that's for sure, probably hundreds. Just imagine,' she said, looking around at the packed bar and restaurant, 'I might have seem some of these pop out in their birthday suits!'

The conversation then changed to the Rotary Carols in the Cathedral in three weeks. Jenny knew that Lizz was going to read a lesson in her role as Inner Wheel President, even though she had only been in the post for a few months.

'I feel a bit of a cheat really Jenny. I am not religious at all and most things about church services, except the singing, make me cringe, but I shall grit my teeth and do my duty to the dear ladies of Verlis Inner Wheel. I am doing the reading about the Rod of Jesse; I hope I don't snigger – I will be struck off by the dear ladies of the committee!'

Main salad courses arrived and conversation turned to the subject of lonely discarded choir conductors.

***

'Come on, Rona, if Sheila had opted out of the Poland tour and we did not have a potential replacement then we might have a problem.'

Choir chairman Brian was trying to smooth over the honorary secretary who had rung him at home to say that she had a call from accompanist Sheila, whose pregnant daughter was due to give birth during the time the choir was in Poland. That meant the choir's accompanist would be taking her name off the list. Trying to be firm but tactful, Brian continued.

'Why is it such a problem Rona? You must know after all your years in the choir, the upsets and rows, the fallouts with conductors that we now have a very good choir and a committed younger man who really does care about The Verlis Singers. I have not got a musical ear but I do hear what people say to me, the choir is as good now as it has ever been, don't you agree?'

Forced by the charming choir chairman to see reason she replied, 'Yes, Gavin is very good but I don't want him to get too big for his boots and try to take over the choir in the way Isaac did.'

Starting to lose his cool, Brian barked back: 'Why don't you give him a call and tell him about Sheila not being available for the tour. Why don't you suggest that YOU get in touch with that brilliant young accompanist who played the other night and invite her to join the tour?'

Leaving Rona to make up her own mind, Brian said cheerio and hung up. Rona could drive him up the wall on occasions.

***

Thursday November 11th – Verlis Cricket Club

Committee Meeting of The Verlis Singers dated Thursday Nov 11th.

Agenda

Apologies

Minutes of last meeting

Matters arising

Requests for concerts

Choir treasurer – vacancy

Conductor's report

Financial report

Forthcoming concerts

Poland Tour

Any other business

Choir Chairman Brian McNeil looked at his watch.

'Good evening all, I think we have a very full meeting and it is nice to see Sheila back from her holidays. It is now 7.30pm so let's see if we can finish by 9.30 and keep all discussions short and to the point or we could still be here after closing time at the bar. We don't want that do we?

'I am not sure where Gavin is as he is always very punctual, but he will be on his way and probably trying to find a parking space.'

The meeting room at the Verlis Cricket Club was full to capacity and the atmosphere was relaxed. It had been a cold but frosty day and everyone had discarded winter coats on the coat hanger, plus hats and scarves, to find a seat around the table. The door opened and Gavin walked in looking very flustered and shaken.

'I am sorry Mr Chairman, but I'm afraid that I have some very sad news for everyone. I had a call from Mellyn just as I was about to leave. I am so very sorry to have to tell you that Len passed away this afternoon at the Hospice. Mellyn and all the family were with him when he…' Gavin stopped to try to control his tears.

The bombshell caused everyone present to gasp. Rona started to sob and Jenny stood up and turned her back, standing up and walking towards the door. Brian, in a quiet voice, said: 'Oh dear, dear, this is very sad news for us all. I think we should just take a short break before we continue. Let's have a time to gather our thoughts and convene in ten minutes ladies and gentlemen. Perhaps some of you may feel better if you went out to take a short walk in the fresh air?'

Taff Davies quickly stood up and left the room followed by Jenny and Sheila. Brian moved across and sat next to Rona, putting his arm around her shoulders. Elaine stayed in her seat, head in hands.

Ten minutes later the committee meeting of The Verlis Singers continued under a very dark cloud of sadness.

Brian spoke. 'It is my view that we should continue the meeting, as I know this would be the wish of Len. We all know how close he was to the end of his life and it is such a tragic shame that he didn't see his wish come true to sing at the Rotary carols for the final time. How sad this is for his wife and his family. We must do everything we can to support them. Are we all agreed that we should carry on with this meeting?' asked the Chairman. 'We do have a lot of business to discuss but you might feel unable to carry on. I will obviously take your advice and you must all decide.'

Elaine proposed that they should continue, as there was so much to go through. Taff spoke up: 'We all knew Len very well Brian, and because of that we all know that he would want us to carry on so I agree with Elaine.'

'I also agree,' said Rona in a soft voice. 'I was with Len and Mellyn last week and the one thing that he wanted me to understand was that the choir should not be affected by his passing. I really do think we should carry on. I think he knew deep down that he would not live long enough to sing at the Cathedral.'

All heads nodded and then Rona, as choir and minutes secretary, took the lead:

'There are no apologies Mr Chairman. Does anyone have any comments on the minutes of the last meeting?'

With no interruptions, the Chairman continued. 'I am sure we will all agree that flowers and a card should be sent to Mellyn and I know we can rely on Rona to take care of that on behalf of the choir in her usual ultra-organised way. Does anyone have any matters arising?' No response. 'In that case we should continue with the next item. Rona do we have requests for concerts?'

Rona then read out emails from various organisations, enquiring if The Verlis Singers would perform at concerts in 2011. Rather surprisingly, she reported that she had received a call from the PA to the manager of Fostors Store, asking if the choir could sing at their Christmas open night on Thursday December 16th. Seemingly one of the Directors knew Dominic from the tenor section and had seen The Verlis Singers on TV.

'The lady told me that all the tra-laa-laas from the G&S Society last year were not very seasonal and if, with apologies for such short notice, The Verlis Singers *would* consider returning, then perhaps they could wear their choir uniforms this year? There would be a donation of £500 to choir funds, which is very generous.' This brought much needed light relief to the meeting.

Gavin spoke up. 'I will talk to the choir and ensure all reindeer head gear and plastic Santa suits are left behind.' It was agreed that Rona would confirm the booking. Another request was from the Methodist Church in the centre of Verlis who held a Spring Music Festival each year.

There had also been a communication from *Songs of Praise*, who were negotiating with the Cathedral for a recording date for the hymn-singing programme. Rona reported that it would probably be in early February as the programme was planned to go out in late May.

Gavin said that he felt that it would be good to have a concert in March at the Methodist Church to aim for after Christmas, but wondered if the committee might like to consider organising a concert themselves dedicated to the memory of Len's service to the choir with all proceeds going to the Hospice who had cared for him in his last weeks.

'I think that is an excellent suggestion from our

conductor.' Nods of approval from everyone. 'Are you suggesting that we should not do the Methodist Spring concert Gavin?' asked the chairman.

'We can't do two Verlis concerts close to each other, as it would be the same people to a great extent buying tickets for both.'

Sheila spoke. 'I know Paul Leaver very well at the Methodist Church. He is the organist and the man behind their event. I could contact him and explain the situation with Len, I know he would understand and we could always sing for them some other time.'

Everyone agreed and Taff chipped in that perhaps the choir members could be asked for their views on how Len's contribution to the choir for so many years could be marked. He also suggested that the choir did not take the fee for the Christmas sing but instead ask Fostors to sponsor the memorial service for the Hospice.

The Welshman continued: 'Why do we not do the concert at the Methodist Church for Len and combine the two? We could sing for nothing and ask that the proceeds are split between the hospice and the church charity – whoever it is?'

At 8.03pm on Thursday November 11th at the Verlis Cricket Club, a momentous situation took place. It was the first time that the Welsh tenor and the honorary secretary had ever agreed on a point of discussion.

'I think that is a very good idea Terry,' said Rona. It was then minuted that she would contact the Methodist Church and see if they would agree to the idea.

Discussion then took place on the next item – finance – and replacing Gerry, the choir treasurer.

Rona reported that a letter had been sent to Gerry from the committee thanking him for his contribution to the choir. He had dropped in the accounts disc to Rona's house, as well as all the record books.

'There is already interest from three members within the choir even before we advertise,' Rona reported.

Hearing this, Elaine Bridges interrupted. 'THREE? I knew that David Honey and Richard were keen, who is the third person?'

With a frosty voice Rona replied, 'Polly Jones has asked me about the vacancy, although I personally do not think we should consider her as she has only been in Verlis a few months and we know that career young women tend to flit in and out of the choir.'

'Hang on Rona.' Taff Davies, the people's champion, was fired up. Anyone present thinking that the new bond between Rona and Terry was going to last more than six minutes was wrong. Normal bad tempered service had been promptly resumed!

Terry continued, 'David Honey is as new to the city as Polly, so how come he is being considered? A bit of sexism here, Mr Chairman, I think. I don't know much about Polly, but she is a fully qualified accountant and she would not have got a job with that poncy accountants in Orange Street if she was not very good at her job. I was told they had over 100 applicants for the place she got.'

Rona snapped back, 'I am NOT against her because she is a female, but David Honey is doing some excellent work on the tour finances, so we have seen first-hand that he has considerable accountancy experience. I understand that he also has a list of qualifications.'

Jenny Dalton spoke up. Her new friendship with Lizz Ozroy was certainly bringing out a 'new Jenny', something that did not best please the honorary secretary.

'We should not forget that Richard is also a qualified accountant; I know that he is treasurer to the Masonic Lodge in Verlis. He may not be the most popular member of the choir but we have to be fair to everyone who applies,' she said.

Sensing that things could get out of hand, the chairman took control.

'Let's post the notification on the choir board and see who applies, but we should make it clear that nominations have to be supported by at least two current choir members.'

It was agreed that an email or letter would be sent to all choir singers, informing them of Gerry's resignation and inviting applications for the position of treasurer.

'When we have seen who applies, that is the time to discuss the applicants, not now! Next item on the agenda please Madam Secretary?'

Rona reported that as Gerry had passed over all the choir financial records to her, she would do all banking for the time being.

'We need to make a quick decision, as this is an important role with the governance of the choir. I would be happy to come to choir early one evening if we needed a short special meeting to discuss this before you start,' said Brian. 'But please, let's move on.'

Next item was the conductor's report, normally the most interesting part of the meeting. Gavin said that he was very happy with preparations for the Rotary Carols although Len's passing would certainly have an effect on the choir that evening and would touch emotions. He felt sure the choir would rise to the occasion and it would be another memorable Christmas concert.

'I went to the Rotary lunch last Tuesday and the members are all geared up. It is a very important part of their fundraising calendar and they know it will be a full house; they are hoping this year to hit a record £2,000 on the bucket collection at the end of the night. It will be a difficult for the choir and of course Len's funeral will be the next few days and will be attended by many of the members.'

He then reported on an email he had received from *Songs*

of Praise giving him the hymns and tunes the choir would sing.

'The hymn tunes are not difficult and all have a Cornish link. We will start working on them straight after Christmas, when we come back in January. I would like the choir to learn them without the music. It does mean that with the Poland tour in June and now the possible memorial concert for Len we are going to have a busy start to 2011. I should also tell you that I have been invited by the Cornish Festival to conduct a workshop on the final day of the Festival next year in April. On a personal note you all know that I have split up with Georgina and I moved into a cottage in town last week. I am not sure what the future will bring but it won't be selling cameras that's for sure. Heather Strong is very involved with the Festival and I actually met David, the son of Isaac Grenfell, last week, as he is also on the Festival Management Board.'

The mention of Isaac and Heather, the founder of the choir *and* his successor all in one sentence at a committee meeting of The Verlis Singers was not received too well by certain people present, but Gavin persevered:

'It has been a difficult few weeks for me but the choir members have been brilliant, lots of them have been coming into the shop to buy stuff I don't think they really need.'

Taff Davies chipped in: 'Well done Gavin, we all wish you well. I might even buy the lovely Mrs Davies a new camera for Christmas. Got any special offers?'

'Everything in the shop is on offer Terry,' replied Gavin with a smile.

The Poland tour then came under the spotlight. Rona told the group that 36 singers had already put their names down and would be asked for a £100 deposit by the middle of December. This would go into the new tour account and she knew that several other members were still looking at their diaries to see if they could join the tour.

Sheila then spoke up, telling the committee that she had taken her name off the list as her daughter in Belfast was pregnant and the baby would be born at the same time in the middle of June.

'I am very disappointed to miss the tour. I am sure our conductor has someone in mind to accompany the choir in Poland.'

The sarcasm in the final remark from Sheila was such that Gavin could almost reach out and touch it.

Interrupting, Brian spoke:

'Well the musical side of the choir is the responsibility of our conductor, so we must leave that to him. I am sure Gavin will find someone and that person's tour costs will of course be paid for by the choir, as is the tradition for tours. Perhaps that young lady I heard the other night might be available, but it's up to you Gavin, of course.'

Brian glanced across at Rona in frustration. Why oh why could she not have done what he suggested and contacted the Becky girl before the meeting? She certainly could be totally infuriating at times. Rona (ignoring the look from Brian) reported that the Poland Tour Committee was going to meet again soon and had costings and excellent travel proposals from David Honey. She was awaiting some further details from the Polish organisers and hoped to get out a newsletter to the choir before Christmas.

The chairman had a note to bring up whether partners could also come as he had received a call from Pat Nicholls earlier in the week making a case for Ron Trenholm. However, he thought it best to leave this matter on hold, sensing that it would cause controversy. He would speak to Rona direct and try to win her over. Knowing what she felt about Peggy and Ron, it was not going to easy to get her support, an additional issue being that other partners might just want to go. And that might include his wife!

Brian then brought the December meeting to a close.

'It has been a difficult time tonight but we must all reflect on Mellyn and Len's family, who will be grieving the passing of a very special friend of The Verlis Singers. Len, like so many before him, gave much to this choir and we never forget those who are not with us anymore, but whose contribution made this choir what it now is.'

Wise words indeed, from the chairman.

Driving home after the meeting, Gavin pondered what a strange day it had been. Sales had again been terrific and when he got home there was a large box on the floor of his cottage in the living room. It had been delivered earlier that day, inside was a brand new big-screen TV. On it was a note:

A practical house warming pressy from your randy brother – sorry I pulled your fave lady in the choir. Invite her round to watch yer new TV !!! GO ON.

And get yourself sorted and looking f…. smart,

Dave the shagger x

P.S. If Polly does comes round; tell her that you aren't as good as your brother!

Gavin smiled, he was still reeling from the news of his friend's death. He knew that Len was so close to dying but the call from Mellyn earlier that evening has really shaken him. He had to look ahead and was planning a phone call the next day to see if Becky Morris would like to join the Poland tour as choir accompanist. He would never ever get used to the twists and turns of life in a choir.

Chapter 16

Wednesday November 17th

Polly had been surprised to get an email out of blue from her friend Moira in Scotland. The parting of the ways had been pretty bloody acrimonious after all, when Polly stormed out of her flat a few weeks back. Moira was contrite. She had been very rude to her friend and wondered if she could be forgiven. She had broken the contact with Alice and Ruth since then as they could be 'pretty venomous and dead fucking bitchy'. Moy had some holiday due and was coming down to Cornwall to see an aunt just before Christmas. Would Polly meet up for a drink or supper perhaps? Could her friend forgive her? And she promised she would NOT say rude things about Polly's singing hobby and her new choir in Verlis.

Polly emailed her straight back:

Fuk off, bitch face...

And then, sent straight after, another email:

PS – Of course Moy, you dozy cow, all forgotten... I wanna see you – WHEN are you coming ????? Pxx

Polly and Moira had been very good chums through uni. Although they studied different subjects, it had started with a house share in year one and they had hit if off straight away. At one time they even shared a boyfriend called Adam and the three of them eventually went on crazy backpacking holidays together. She had missed contact since the fallout and was really pleased to get the email from her old friend.

She thought that she would get Dominic over for supper with Moira. He would make sure that things did not get nasty again and this time and it would be on HER territory. He was becoming a good friend, even if some of his texts after she had screwed Gavin's brother Dave last Monday were bloody outrageous. How was it that HE could go out at night and pick up a gay man for grubby sex in a park, but she was not allowed to take a horny bloke back to her house for a friendly fuck! Anyway, it would be great to have a catch up and the two of them, Dom and Moira would get on like a house on fire.

Gavin had found a letter on his mat the previous evening when he got back in from the shop. It had been delivered during the day; he presumed by Mellyn. At the top it said, 'Gavin dear, please read this out at the next rehearsal of The Verlis Singers.'

The letter read:

Dear members of the choir that meant so much to my husband Len,

Len asked me the week before he died to write to you all, as he knew that his time was getting very close. He wanted you all to know that your support over the last few months has given him such joy. He remembered with great happiness the lifts to choir from the boys in the bass section, the cuddles from all the ladies, and the wonderful friendship of your very talented conductor Gavin.

The one thing Len wanted you all to know that he really didn't want you to be sad at his leaving. He told me on several occasions that the choir must NOT sing at his funeral. He said that he had struggled on some many occasions to find his voice at funerals and to this day never knew how he had managed to start up the Deep Harmony at Isaac's memorial service all those years ago. Please, he asked, tell members of The Verlis Singers and my friends, no sadness, no black ties, happy memories only at my going.

Len said, let's remember the special times together, that is his wish — he loved The Verlis Singers very much. There will be a get together after the funeral and I do hope many of the choir members who knew Len will be able to come. I will be in touch with Rona with the funeral details.

With much love and thanks,

Mellyn Fyfield

Gavin scanned the letter and sent it to Rona and to Brian by email. He didn't want any bad feeling over who did what, after Len's death. If Rona wanted to read the letter next Monday at choir that was fine by him.

The call to Becky had been made early that morning with the invite to play for the tour. Claire had given him her mobile number. She was over the moon on hearing from Gavin and would *definitely* be up for it. She now had her new job and wanted to settle in Verlis. Gavin also explained that the choir would pay for her to go on the tour and, after Christmas, they could meet up to discuss what the repertoire would be and some dates when she could come and play at rehearsals.

He knew that this would be a difficult one to manoeuvre around with Sheila, but Gavin also knew that whilst the choir's accompanist could be awkward at times, she was very dedicated to The Verlis Singers. He hoped that when she heard Becky play, she would see and hear for herself how good Becky was and her opinion might soften.

Gavin also mentioned a day he was leading for the Cornwall Music Festival next April, which he would also like her to play for. There would be a small fee. 'You bet,' was her reply.

***

The trouble about being married (well almost married) to a former criminal and fraudster was that you could never be in company with other people for more than about ten minutes. David told so many lies and had so many secrets that there was always the chance that an untruth could catch him out. He had impressed the Poland committee and other members of the choir with his accountancy knowledge and business talents. He was a very clever man with brilliant organisational skills and the ability to research, plan, and deliver a project, however complex. Everything had to be done at arm's length so personal conversations were avoided.

They had received an invitation to a supper party at the home of Lizz that Saturday evening, from the stylish new alto in the choir. Deep down Laura would have loved to accept. The Verlis Singers were one of the best things that had happened to her for a long time. Nice, genuine people and a conductor who had even asked HER to sing a solo part. Dinner parties would always be a no-go area though, whilst David continued to live his double life.

Sometimes, in quiet moments, she dreamed of the day when she would be somewhere in company with David around a dinner table. With a group of friends perhaps? He would be asked a question about his past and would reply: 'Yes, I did my degree whilst in prison. I was sentenced for ten years for fraud when I conned the investment bank I worked for out of £15 million, but I had to give it all back. It was a major national story at the time and during my sentence I used all the time I had to study and get a degree in Management Studies and also to study IT. Then I met Laura who was a prison visitor. She walked into the choir practice at prison and we got to know each other after that. Meeting Laura showed me that I could look forward to a new life with her, being honest and telling the truth. Because of Laura I was released on parole after seven years. Meeting her changed my life.'

This was Laura's dream. She had told Lizz that they had another commitment that evening. Next time perhaps, or sometime in the future? There was no harm in hoping.

***

Monday November 22nd

Terry had his interview date the following week and thought the job was his. Another family issue had caused some heated discussion over the weekend.

Terry had always considered himself a good dad. His daughter, Jenny, was his little angel; the minute Joan had given birth to a pink little bundle Terry had been totally devoted to her. His postie job had meant that he could do school afternoon collection runs when Joan had been working at Verlis College doing a bookkeeping course, and they had enjoyed so many special times together as a family. In the early days both Joan and Terry had wanted a second child, but try as they might, nothing happened.

Jenny was now 20 and studying Engineering at Bath University. From recent phone calls, Mum and Dad had been told about Daniel, a new young man, who now seemed to be a very important part of their daughter's life. Jenny wanted to bring Daniel home for Christmas. There was nothing wrong with that, as Terry and Joan couldn't wait to meet him.

Jenny had always had boyfriends but this seemed more serious. Daniel had moved into the house that Jenny shared and had confided in her mum that they were now a couple and sleeping in the same room. Joan had not yet told Terry about this, as she knew what his reaction would be!

Jenny wanted to share a room with Daniel when they came for Christmas. She had called her mum to tell her. This revelation had caused more than a little anguish at the Davies' home, when Joan had plucked up the courage to tell Jenny's doting sad that his 'Little Angel' expected to sleep with her new boyfriend in her room when they visited for Christmas.

'For Christ's sake Joan, she is my little girl. How am I supposed to lie in bed knowing she is in her bedroom with... doing...?'

Joan had argued with her hubby. Of course she knew that he was devoted to his daughter but he had to accept that she was now a young woman with a boyfriend who she obviously really cared for. They were probably sleeping together in their lodgings, so if they came to the house for Christmas, surely they should allow it?

A decision had not been reached. Terry simply refused to consider the fact and insisted that the boyfriend should sleep in the spare room. In a fit of pique, he had taken a very disgruntled Brutus out for another Sunday walk to get out of the house. On his return he had buried his head in the Sunday colour magazines and flatly refused to discuss the matter further. Joan Davies decided to bide her time, she would eventually get him to see sense and Jenny would share the same room with Daniel when they came to stay at Christmas. She always got her way in the end.

***

Chairman Brian had phoned Gavin that morning to tell him that the funeral of Len Fyfield would take place on Thursday November 25th at Verlis Methodist Church, and Rona had undertaken to contact all choir members. She would read the letter that Gavin had sent over by email from Mellyn that night at the rehearsal.

Gavin had also received a text from Heather Strong on Monday morning in the shop. The Festival launch was on Wednesday December 8th at the Cornwall Guildhall in Verlis. BBC Radio Cornwall would be contacting him, as they wanted to do an interview with him about the special choir idea. They liked the story about encouraging new people to sing. Heather said that the Festival website for 2011 would soon be launched with all the details of the special choir. She asked Gavin to send a picture of him and some background info for the press release.

'I will pop into your shop soon Gavin, as my big sister has a birthday coming up. I want to buy her a new camera so perhaps you can help me out?'

He had also had a surprise text from his randy brother Dave that afternoon:

Hey Brother – got in touch with a male voice choir here in Swindon and am going along to try them out. The conductor is Welsh and seems a bit of a prick but hey no harm in trying them out. They might have a hot pianist or I may have to turn over and go gay !!

Have you booked your hair cut yet ??? keep smiling – tell sexy Polly with the everlasting legs I miss her bottom. Haha

D

Gavin had not yet booked his haircut, but was going to. He had looked at himself in the mirror that morning and realised that the bloke looking back at him was a bit of a shambles. He was going to tidy himself up, his brother David was right.

This coming Sunday afternoon The Verlis Singers would rehearse in the Cathedral for the Rotary carols, so he expected a good attendance that evening, even though the death of Len would overshadow the rehearsal. Gavin would ask Rona to read out Mellyn's letter at the start so the choir could then get on with the work of tidying up some of the pieces and the solo parts.

***

The evening rehearsal went well, all things considered,

concentrating on the Christmas pieces and congregational carols. Rona announced that the Fostors Christmas sing was back on and that the choir, with a glare in the direction of Peggy, HAD to wear uniform this year. She would put up a list of choir members on the notice board, so people could tick their names if they were available.

Rona read out the letter from Mellyn to a hushed choir at the start of the rehearsal, after the singing of *Deep Harmony*. Everyone in the choir knew that Len was so close to death, but he was a very special man and Richard stood up to say a few bumbled words about his 'dear friend'.

After the interval Rona told the choir that as Gerry Head had resigned she had posted on the notice board a list for names and nominations for those who may like to be the choir treasurer. Any member could put their name forward but nominations had to be supported by two current members who should also sign the notice. The choir committee would hope to appoint someone as soon as possible after Christmas, but in the meantime she would hold the fort and undertake the treasurer duties.

Gavin also told the choir that the committee was planning a concert to support the hospice, in memory of Len. This was received with applause from all the choir.

'2011 is going to be another special year for The Verlis Singers; we will remember Len at the concert and record for *Songs of Praise*, probably in April. Then of course we will work on our repertoire for Poland in June. Meanwhile, I will see you all at the Cathedral at 2.30pm this Sunday. For our full rehearsal with the organist, Anthony Sheppard, please try to be there on time, as we have a lot to go through. Entry to the Cathedral is by the rear passage.'

Polly turned round and gave Dominic a big thumbs up and a dirty smirk. Fortunately, the ladies in the front row of the altos did not see.

Chapter 17

Thursday November 25th

'What the choir needs is a social committee.'

Lizz was on the phone to Jenny and was fired up at the thought of organising a social event in the New Year for the choir members and their partners. Lizz Ozroy was one of the world's natural organisers and she had the time, and the necessary enthusiasm, to put into getting a more active social life going for the choir.

She had just finished a big garden redesign project for a stately home in Staffordshire and had some time on her hands.

'I have been thinking, Jenny. Could we organise a dance early in January or February? Perhaps your husband would enquire if we could hire the golf club? I went to an Inner Wheel meeting the other day there and it's ideal. A nice bar area, room for dancing and, of course, a massive car park, what do you think Jenny?'

Jenny Dalton caught the enthusiasm bug straight away from her new friend.

'Fantastic Lizz, shall I call Brian and ask him to get some dates and costs? He is captain of the golf club next year so he can pull a few strings. The new club manager is a nice young lady with an eye for attracting more outside events so should we ask her for some catering costs per head, a finger buffet perhaps?'

'You will meet Brian when we come to your house for dinner on Saturday, what a lovely invitation. We don't get many chances to go out together these days.'

Both agreed that the social event could be a winner. The costs needed to be kept low and it would be a great start to the New Year for The Verlis Singers.

'Let's call it The Verlis Singers Glitter Ball,' said Lizz.

'Brilliant idea Lizz,' replied Jenny. 'Let's do it, I will call Brian later today. Are you going to Len's funeral?'

Lizz replied that as a new member she had not known Len so would not be attending.

'I do think that a funeral is such a sad occasion that people who knew and loved him best should attend. I will see you at the choir rehearsal on Sunday afternoon, though, in the Cathedral, we can discuss the Glitter Ball then and perhaps have a coffee after!'

'Or a glass of wine?'

***

The funeral of Len Fyfield took place at Verlis Methodist Church at 1pm that afternoon. The church was filled with many current and past members of The Verlis Singers as well as a number of representatives of the Grenfell family who had come to pay their respects.

When Gavin arrived at the church he spotted the tall figure of David Grenfell standing outside the church with a lady he assumed to be his wife. After making his acquaintance at the recent festival committee meeting, Gavin walked over to the tall, rather austere man and held out his hand.

'Hello Gavin,' David replied.

'This is my wife Jeannette. It's a very sad day for all of Len's family and friends. As I am sure you know Len was a close friend of my father's. They worked together when they were young men and the friendship lasted for many years, until Dad passed away.'

Gavin couldn't help but note that David Grenfell could not bring himself to mention the three words, The Verlis Singers. He wondered if ever the day would come when the resentment of the Grenfell family would subside towards the choir that Isaac Grenfell, his father, had started back in 1952.

It was a simple funeral service, as Len had wanted. The Methodist Minister, Debbie Nott, led it, and, at the start of the service, unbeknown to the members of The Verlis Singers present, a recording of the choir, made by Radio Cornwall earlier in the year was played. In it they sang all of the four verses of *Deep Harmony* with Terry Davies singing a solo in the second verse.

'The family have asked for this to be played today,' the Rev. Nott told them. 'The Verlis Singers, the friendship of its founder Isaac Grenfell and the conductor today, Gavin James, meant so very much to Len.'

Gavin was proud to hear the choir recording being played. It had actually been done in The Methodist Church when the radio station were featuring Cornish choirs in their Sunday morning show. It was a good recording though, and Gavin looked down wondering what David Grenfell's reaction would be.

There were just two hymns, *Onward Christian Soldiers* and *When Morning Guilds the Skies*. Len's grandson Paul read a simple poem. At the start of the service the Minister had asked, on behalf of Mellyn and the family, that this should not be a sad occasion but one of celebration and all those present did their best to comply with the wish.

At the end of the service the Minister told the congregation that they would play Len's own choice of a final piece of music. The voice of Louis Armstrong singing *What a Wonderful World* boomed out from the sound system as everyone filed out of the church.

'Wasn't that nice, Mellyn? And the family asking for the recording to be played at the start and with you singing the solo as well. I am so proud of you Terry Davies. But why do the lovely people have to die before their time?'

Joan Davies snuggled up to her husband, remembering the day a few years back when Len's singing of *Deep Harmony* had brought 1,000 people to tears at Isaacs's funeral.

'That's too hard a question for a simple Welsh tenor to answer,' gulped Terry Davies.

On the way out, Gavin again caught the eye of David Grenfell, who was leaving the church from the opposite door. A smile and a nod seemed a good way to part company on such a sad day.

***

Sunday November 28th

Perhaps a cathedral is not the place for a wolf whistle, but that's what happened at 2.15pm. Quite a few of the Verlis Singers had arrived early as requested for the special Christmas rehearsal, when Gavin appeared at the back of the building and walked through the centre aisle towards the choir stalls carrying his music stand and briefcase. The whistle came from the tenor row, but as Polly Jones was standing chatting to Dominic, she might have been the responsible adult, however, the Gavin James that made his appearance was somewhat different to the one previously seen by all in the choir!

The day before Gavin had set out on a shopping spree and had his hair styled. Gone were the long scruffy locks and here was the new look, as prescribed by his brother Dave. It was a chilly November Sunday afternoon in the cathedral and Gavin wore a new long black overcoat and bright red scarf. His hair had been cut very short and the grey streaks of late

40s were only just starting to show through. He was wearing blue cord jeans and a new dark red denim shirt.

'Crumpet or what!' said Dominic to Polly, as Gavin smiled at the welcoming whistle from somewhere around the tenor section.

A young man was standing at the back of the Cathedral and came forward to introduce himself as Anthony Sheppard, the deputy organist who would be playing for the Rotary service. Gavin and Anthony shook hands warmly and Gavin introduced Shirley, The Verlis Singers' accompanist. Anthony asked if the grand piano was in the right position for Gavin. It was in the centre aisle in between the choir stalls, which was perfect. Anthony set off to climb the steps up to the organ loft where he could look down and see Gavin in his central conducting position.

The rehearsal went very well, taking the order exactly as it would be on the following Wednesday. All the soloists were nervous and Gavin allowed them the required time to go through their individual contributions. The quartet for *Gabriel's Message*, Jenny, Laura, Jim and Richard were very shaky at their first attempts, so Gavin encouraged them to come out from the choir stalls to stand together to sing the third solo verse, going through it twice and then praising them.

'That was beautiful,' he told them, and the rest of the choir who were on either side in the choir stalls, 'Well done!'

Dominic sang his opening verse of *Stille Stille* with supreme confidence, as a deputy Cathedral choir member he was well used to singing in the building and it showed. As he was singing, he turned to Polly in the soprano section and winked at her. Taff Davies also rose to the challenge and sang his third solo verse In the *Bleak Midwinter* after a false start. As the organ played the opening bars of the solo verse Taff suddenly thought of Len Fyfield and his voice just gave out. This was one of the pieces that required organ accompaniment.

'Sorry Gavin,' he spluttered. 'Blame poor old Len for that!'

'Don't worry Terry,' called Gavin from his conductor's podium in front of the choir, guessing the reason for the Welshman's nerves.

'Let's do it again from verse one, Terry, just try and collect your thoughts whilst the rest of the choir sing the second verse and you'll be fine.'

The piece *Lullay My Liking* had been sung by the choir before. It was unaccompanied and needed full concentration from all sections. Gavin had divided the haunting soprano line, so both Claire and Clare had their solo moments. The male section, which started with the words *Herod the King* was not right, with some uncertainty from the basses on their entry, and Gavin suggested that the ladies should take a break whilst he worked on that section with the men only.

When the ladies returned to singing positions the choir sang it through. A voice from above – the organ loft – shouted out: 'That was brilliant!'

Everyone beamed and Gavin felt very proud.

Shirley had obviously been working hard on the Chilcott piece, *Remember O Thou Man,* and the choir sang it through three times. That was the definite advantage of having access to the Cathedral for a two-hour practice, and ample time to polish up the items they would sing.

At the end Gavin called up to Anthony, who was in the organ loft, and the choir gave him a round of applause. He was indeed a very competent organist, who insisted that Gavin should conduct the audience carols, something he had not been asked to do before. The organ loft had a small TV screen, so the organist could clearly see the choir conductor beneath him and follow the beat he set. It was a magnificent and historic building for a choir to perform in and Gavin loved every minute of the rehearsal, encouraging the entire choir to enjoy the pieces they sang but always to watch his beat.

At the end of the rehearsal, Gavin reminded the choir that there was no rehearsal the next day, Monday and that they should all arrive by 7pm at the latest the following Wednesday, for the Rotary Carol Service.

'Let's make it a very special evening in memory of Len,' he told them all.

To his surprise, Jenny Dalton then raised her hand and asked if she could speak to the choir before they left. Coming out to the front she told everyone in a very loud voice that, together with Lizz, they were going to organise a 'Glitter Ball' for all members of The Verlis Singers and partners in January. It would take place at Verlis Golf Club on Friday 28th January and she hoped everyone would come. Anyone in the choir who would like to help was welcome to contact her on her mobile or by email. Tickets would soon be on sale at prices everyone could afford, she said. She was organising it with Lizz, who would also have tickets to sell.

'Bloody hell,' Taff Davies whispered to his tenor cohorts in the back pew. We've got a new trendy-looking conductor and lovely Jenny has actually found her voice at last, Praise the Lord!'

Later that evening Gavin phoned his brother in Swindon:

'You'll be pleased to know that I have done the makeover, David. Hair chopped off and new clothes purchased. I wore them to the Cathedral this afternoon as we had a rehearsal for the Carol Service this coming Wednesday night. It went well and I even got a wolf whistle from your girlfriend Penny.'

'Well done bruv, not before time either. You have got to get on with your new life; you know that. Tell you what, I am going to try to come down on Wednesday to see you in action and cheer you on at the Christmas service, would that be ok? I'll leave Swindon in the morning and you might have to put me up overnight. But if I bring a friend I will book into a B&B.'

Gavin replied that it would be fine if he wanted to stay over, although secretly he didn't really want his brother doing a repeat performance with Polly Jones. David said that he would probably stay at a B&B as he had a new girlfriend. Gavin would have to wait to see who it was. She would be his Christmas surprise!

'She is rather special, brother. I might be falling in love, but properly this time.'

On leaving the Cathedral that afternoon, Polly had given Gavin a card inviting him to a dinner party at her house the following Saturday, 'with some friends'. Gavin chose not to mention that to his randy brother!

***

'You should have seen our Gavin!' Peggy was relating the successful afternoon rehearsal to husband Ron on the way home, after he had picked her up outside the Cathedral at 5.45pm in the Land Rover as requested.

'He's had his hair cut short and was wearing some trendy new clothes, Ron. He looked lovely. Tell you what, when that wife of his sees him next she won't recognise him and she'll kick herself for letting him go. Mind you, I reckon he's best off without her. Let's hope a nice new lady comes into his life next year.'

In the knowledge that the usual Sunday afternoon cuddle session had not taken place, Ron cheerily said from his driver's seat as they sped out of Verlis, 'Glad to hear it love, let's have an early night tonight?'

***

That evening at more than one home in the Verlis area, female thoughts pondered on how handsome and masterful Gavin James had been that afternoon in the Cathedral.

Chapter 18

Wednesday December 1ˢᵗ

Posters and leaflets promoting the 2010 Verlis Rotary Club annual Carol Service had been distributed throughout the city and surrounding villages in the county for several weeks. The service was attended by Rotarians from across Cornwall so it always attracted a large number of people. Community transport brought in elderly people from local residential homes and reserved seats were allocated for them at the front of the Cathedral.

Radio Cornwall interviewed the conductor Gavin James on their Monday morning drive-time programme and the *Cornish Leader* ran a big article the previous weekend referring to the choir as 'The Verlis Singers, the choir founded by the late, great Isaac Grenfell and now reaching new heights under the leadership of Gavin James'.

Radio Cornwall had played the track *Stille Nacht* from the LP recorded at the Rotary Carol Service all those years ago on their Sunday morning show. In his Radio Cornwall interview Gavin had mentioned the very recent passing of one of the choir's stalwarts, Len Fyfield. The Verlis Singers, he said, would be singing for their friend and former member Len at the Cathedral on Wednesday evening.

It would be another special Christmas occasion; there was no admission charge and the doors to the Cathedral opened at 6.45pm. The Rotary club did a wonderful job organising the transport for many older people to attend and there was a retiring collection at the end, he told Radio Cornwall listeners.

'Please come along and sing your favourite carols with The Verlis Singers,' said Gavin to the morning show audience.

Gavin certainly came over very well on the radio.

***

The queues started to form outside the Cathedral from 5pm. As it was a free entry Carol Service, it was first come to get the best seats. The Cathedral could hold 1,000 people and at 6.45pm when the Rotary stewards opened the doors wearing their yellow Rotary tabards, the audience poured in. By 7.15pm the place was packed to capacity as Anthony Sheppard played suitable Christmas music to the enthusiastic gathering.

Unbeknown to Gavin, his brother David had arrived with his new girlfriend from Swindon earlier in the day. They had met a few weeks back and the relationship was developing nicely. David had booked into a Verlis B&B and sent his brother a text earlier that day to say that he wouldn't be needing a bed for the night, but would be in the Cathedral to cheer on his brother and meet him afterwards for a drink.

Gavin was used to his brother's wild ways so presumed that he had contacted Polly and sorted out a sleepover, or a shagover!

He didn't believe the story about a new girlfriend. David just wanted an excuse to sleep with Polly again.

The choir members started to arrive at the Cathedral, entering through the north door so they did not have to do battle with the hundreds queuing to get in.

'Tell you what Taff,' said fellow tenor Alan Younger as they walked in. Alan had picked up Taff on the way in so Joan could drive in a bit closer to the starting time. 'I have never seen so many people queuing this early to get in, we'd better be good tonight. I actually feel quite nervous.'

***

The ladies of the choir were changing in the Cathedral

choir rehearsal room, whilst the men were allocated the building next door, which housed the Cathedral's offices. Most men came wearing their DJs but the ladies carried their dark blue choir uniform and changed when they arrived. Gavin was always careful to avoid the ladies' changing rooms, as he had once walked in to see an arrangement of half-naked altos and sopranos, not to mention the unforgettable sight of the honorary secretary in just her tights and bra!

At 7.30pm Gavin found Clare Taylor, who was anxiously hidden away in the corner, singing through her solo verse of *Once in Royal*. Gavin asked Rona to muster the ladies, as it was almost time to get things underway.

With nervous expectation, the members of The Verlis Singers then filed to the back of the Cathedral, the ladies resplendent in their royal blue dresses and silver scarves and the men in their black and white DJs. The men wore a dark blue bow tie, made from the same material as the ladies' dresses. Gavin then led them into position with Clare at his side. This had been rehearsed thoroughly the previous Sunday, as it was very important to get the standing positions correct, otherwise the walk into the Cathedral singing *Once in Royal David's City* could resemble a rugby scrum. Gavin had agreed with Anthony that his final piece, whilst people took their seats, would be in the key of F. This made it easier for Clare to pitch the D she needed as her first solo verse from the back of the Cathedral.

At 7.28pm the packed Cathedral was silent. The choir was standing ready to walk in and Gavin walked a few paces in front of Clare who stood on her own in the centre aisle at the main entrance to Verlis Cathedral. Smiling at Clare, Gavin walked to her side and hummed the opening note, just in case she was in any doubt, using his tuning fork. He whispered in her ear.

'Over to you, Clare.'

Many people in the audience probably thought that they

were listening to the clear voice of a boy treble as Clare Taylor sang, quite beautifully, the opening verse.

Once in Royal David's City, stood a lowly cattle shed.

It was just the start Gavin wanted, her voice rang around the majestic building, and, as the organ came to start the second verse, she was perfectly in tune.

The choir then processed down the centre aisle in predetermined pairs, all carefully worked out, and arriving at the choir stalls to take their singing positions by the end of verse four. The descant came from the sopranos in the last verse – '*And our eyes at last shall see him*' – with organ at full throttle, a brilliant start.

Walking down the centre aisle in front of the choir, Gavin had recognised quite a few familiar faces as many in the audience turned to look at them as they processed in singing. He spotted his brother David, who gave him a big grin, and wondered who the pretty blonde standing next to him was. David's delight at seeing first hand his brother's new short hairstyle was obvious and Gavin looked forward to meeting him after the service was over. There actually was a new girlfriend and she looked really nice.

After the welcome from the Dean of the Cathedral, and a short prayer, it was time for the service to progress. The Rotary men had called in all the readers earlier in the day to rehearse readings and to organise walking to and from the readers' pulpit.

Gavin sat on the side of the choir pews in the Chancel and thought how different it would have been if Len had attended the service. All the fuss of getting him there in his very fragile state on a cold winter night would have been so difficult. Perhaps death had come at the right time for his friend.

The first choir individual piece was *Love Came Down at Christmas*; there were no introductions, as the audience all had programmes with the carols printed that they would sing. The service followed the programme to the letter.

As the choir sat down after their first piece, Lizz Ozroy walked gracefully to the reader's podium in her official capacity as President of The Verlis Inner Wheel. As she finished her reading from Isiah, she retraced her steps down from the pulpit and walked past where Gavin was sitting, to find her place amongst the altos in the choir pews. She gave Gavin a subtle wink as she passed him, not noticed by many members of The Verlis Singers, but certainly by Jenny Dalton and Polly Jones.

The Cathedral Carol service proceeded with The Verlis Singers in wonderful form, all the note bashing and rehearsal effort of previous weeks was certainly paying off. Sheila's playing of the Chilcott piece was a little nervous at the opening, if truth be told, but once the choir came in and Gavin had full control, all was well.

The singing in German of the carol *Stille Nacht* towards the end of the service was always a very special moment. The Verlis Singers had performed this carol at the Christmas Rotary service since way back to the Isaac Grenfell days and it was almost as familiar as the choir's anthem, *Deep Harmony*. They sang it beautifully, Gavin keeping it very soft throughout, the last verse sung so quietly it was almost as if only four voices were singing.

Dominic's rendition of the first verse of *Stille Stille* was moving, as was the clear tenor voice of Terry Davies in the solo verse of In the *Bleak Midwinter*, holding the final top of the word 'adore' with great effect to the accompaniment of the organ.

After the final audience hymn, *O Come All Ye Faithful*, with the well-loved Wilcox descant, the choir filed out again down the centre aisle and returned to the changing areas. The organ was still booming out with the final seasonal voluntary as people flocked out into the Cornish winter's night. Simon Calloway beamed with joy as he approached Gavin at the back of the Cathedral. It was, he said, 'an absolute triumph, his choir were wonderful' and he hoped the packed Cathedral would show *their* pleasure by giving generously to the bucket shake.

Gavin made his way to the ladies' changing room, where the entire choir had filed after the final hymn. The atmosphere was heady as people left their seats to queue and leave the Cathedral. Many were family members and friends of the choir members who whooped and rushed forward to embrace them as they came out.

'You were all wonderful, thank you, thank you,' Gavin shouted, and shook hands with all the men, got a bear-like cuddle from Dominic, and then proceeded to kiss all of the ladies in The Verlis Singers on the cheek, something which delighted everyone, especially Peggy.

When it came to Lizz, Gavin's kiss lasted slightly longer as his lips touched her cheek. He wondered if anyone had noticed, but he didn't care. He had been waiting for the chance to kiss her for quite a while, so why not make the most of the opportunity – seize the day!

Polly made the most of her kiss, throwing her arms around Gavin's neck and jumping up and down, earning a fierce glare from the Hon. Secretary.

As the singers left the room, many to find their relatives and families who were in the audience, Jenny and Lizz were handing out pieces of paper with details of the Glitter Ball they were organising.

***

One notable absence at the Cathedral was chairman Brian. His wife Helen had called Gavin that day:

'I'm really sorry Gavin, but Brian's not well today. He won't be able to attend the Rotary Service, but he hopes it will go well. I was going to come myself with my sister but, if it's okay, I think I will stay at home with him tonight to keep him company.'

Gavin wondered what it was that had kept Brian away from the most important concert of the year for the choir in their home city. Brian always loved the party afterwards at the pub and would go around hugging all the ladies. *He must be quite poorly*, thought Gavin. He would give Brian a call tomorrow.

***

The Royal Hotel was bursting at the seams. On this occasion every year they opened up the downstairs ballroom and put out a buffet, which was meant to entice all the members of The Verlis Singers to all come back after the service, eat their fill and spend, spend, spend lots across the bar.

Becky Morris was cheering and jumping up and down and hugging her friend Claire as Gavin walked in. He was the last to arrive as he wanted to find Anthony Sheppard to thank him for his organ playing and make sure he knew that he would be very welcome at the party. He also had to do his duty to the members of the Rotary Club Cathedral officials, readers and the many members of the audience who wanted to tell him what a wonderful time they had had and how brilliant were his choir.

One elderly couple waited at the back of the Cathedral and Gavin spotted that they seemed keen to say something to him. He was still wearing his conductor's DJ as he had not had any time after the end of the service to change amid the frantic hustle and bustle as over a thousand people spilled out through the main Cathedral doors. The couple told Gavin that they had been members in the early days of The Verlis Singers and were anxious that Gavin should know that. The rather grumpy old gentleman explained that he had been in the tenor section and that Isaac Grenfell was a genius.

'We were of course a very, *very* good choir back in those days, Mr James,' he emphasised.

Gavin felt that a point had been made, but it didn't matter. He wished them both a very happy Christmas and thanked them for coming to support The Verlis Singers of 2010. Gavin wondered if the bad blood between the past members and the choir would ever stop. He felt very weary and would be glad to get to the party.

***

David James was at the very busy bar in the Royal Hotel when he saw his brother come in the door and shouted at him to get him a drink. It was chaos, there was hardly space to move in the place as the choir and others packed in, trying to buy drinks and locate where their friends were.

Gavin shouted back as Polly James threw her arms around him again and Dominic, together with Polly, enveloped the conductor in a mass hug. Gavin eventually prised himself free and found his brother, who introduced the pretty blonde lady who had been standing with him in the Cathedral. This, he was told, was Suzy, David's new lady. She seemed to be very nice and far, far too good for his randy brother, thought Gavin.

'You look bloody fantastic Gav,' said David. 'You are my hero and now, sod it, you are a bloody handsome hero. I wish you hadn't listened to my advice and stayed scruffy and ugly! What do you think of my brilliant brother Suzy?'

Suzy Taylor leaned forward and kissed her new boyfriend's brother on both cheeks.

'It's lovely to meet you!' she shouted. 'The singing was just amazing, you must be so proud of your choir.'

Gavin smiled as an arm came over his shoulder and Taff and Joan Davies accosted him with more kisses and hugs. Joan shouted in Gavin's ear so no one else could hear:

'Thanks for asking him to do the solo, he won't tell you himself of course, but he loves the choir and he loves you.'

Richard Parish was in the buffet room filling a plate with more food than was normally needed for an entire bass section, let alone one man. The place was seething; laughter filled the room as people shouted out to each other across the din.

'QUIET PLEASE!' It was Gavin who had taken his pitch pipe out of his DJ top pocket, the bow tie had been discarded but Gavin was still in his conductor's uniform. He wanted to get out of the Cathedral to be with the choir so had thrown his other clothes in a carrier bag.

As people stopped talking Gavin gave the sopranos the B flat and hummed the opening chord to *Ding Dong Merrily on High*. From around the rooms – bar and buffet – The Verlis Singers belted it out, all three verses with all eyes on Gavin as he set a fast time with arms raised above the throng of people.

Hosanna in Excelsis.

Everyone cheered.

'I need to go and mingle, David, but I'll catch you later, so don't leave without saying goodbye.'

'Of course not,' replied David, with his arm around the delightful Suzy Taylor from Swindon.

Gavin made his way to the buffet room. He was starving and as he got close Rona came towards him with a plate of food.

'I got you this as I knew it would be impossible for you to get to eat before Richard devoured the lot!' she shouted.

'Oh thanks Rona, that's very kind of you.' Rona was standing with a group of people he didn't know and she introduced her sister, husband and daughter who had come to Verlis especially for the service that evening.

'What a shame Brian couldn't be here Rona.' She smiled back at Gavin. Helen McNeil had also called her earlier to say that Brian was having 'one of his turns'. Rona was one of the few people in the choir we knew about Brian's bipolar condition.

The chaos ensued with more carols, lots of jollity, and masses of alcohol being consumed. The manager of the Royal Hotel was ecstatic and insisted on buying a free glass of wine for the conductor.

Lizz Ozroy pushed her way through the crowd to introduce her husband and daughter to Gavin. The husband was quite a short man with dark hair and a strong accent Gavin couldn't work out. He certainly wasn't German or Italian and Lizz explained that he had been born in Greece but attended university in Italy where they had met. The daughter Emma seemed about 18 or 19, Gavin thought, obviously a very bright and nice girl who admitted to Gavin, 'I can't sing in tune, my mum has told me that on several occasions but you were awesome tonight.'

***

'I hope it all went well for the choir tonight in the Cathedral Brian. It's such a shame we couldn't have gone to hear them. Joan was very disappointed as she was going to come with us.'

Brian wasn't paying any attention, he was busy going through a file of financial papers, studying figures and acting rather oddly. Looking at him, Helen knew that tomorrow she'd have to call the specialist consultant at the Psychiatry Unit who Brian had been referred to earlier in the year. She dreaded the thought that one of his obsessive bouts was coming on. With Christmas approaching it would be so difficult to isolate him from people through December. He had obviously not been taking his tablets.

'Was it tonight? What concert?' Brian asked his wife.

***

On the insistence of his wife Joan, Terry Davies had a

shower when they eventually returned home at around midnight.

'Would you like to tell me again Mrs Davies how bloody brilliant your husband sang this evening in Verlis Cathedral?'

Cuddling up to her hubby in bed, Joan sighed.

'You were awful! Now that gay young handsome man, Dominic, he was simply WONDERFUL. When he sang that verse on his own, ladies and men were in tears around me.' Stifling his reaction she said, 'However, it should also be said Mr Davies that for me, there was only one special moment this evening.'

Not allowing Terry to reply she gently put her hand over his mouth. 'Now I want you to be very quiet. No Welsh jokes, no words at all. Just lie back whilst I remove those boxer shorts.'

Climbing on top of her husband and pulling her top over her shoulders, Joan whispered. 'Now I am going to give you your deserved reward for being my very special man. Then you will be ready for your job interview tomorrow morning.'

Chapter 19

Heather Strong had called into Gavin's camera shop early that morning. She looked at the few remaining cameras still left in stock and purchased an expensive Canon for £340. It was for the school's use, she explained, and was grateful to Gavin for letting her buy it at such a fantastic discount. She told Gavin that he looked like 'a different man', with his hair cut short.

'Very trendy, you'll have to watch out, all the single ladies will be lining up in Verlis, you really do look ten years younger.'

Many people had also told her that The Verlis Singers had been outstanding at the Rotary Carol Service on Wednesday night. Praise indeed! Gavin blushed. Heather Strong was a very attractive woman, late 30s, perhaps, blonde hair and extremely curvaceous. The Verlis tenors had all lusted after her. Taff Davies once told Gavin that she had 'the finest and firmest breasts in all of Cornwall, if not the world!'

She had also called into his shop to discuss the festival launch the following Wednesday. Could Gavin arrive at about 6.30pm to meet the top brass, including Lord Williton, the patron of the festival?

'He is in his early 70s, very distinguished, loaded, and loves his music even if he is a bit of a classical snob. He will take to you, I'm sure. We'd like you to give a short speech about the choral day. If you would like to drop me an email with your words, I could look through it before the night?'

This was the schoolteacher Heather that the choir members had told him about. She was speaking to him now as if he were one of the naughty boys in a class at school, submitting his essay.

'Of course Heather, I'll put some words down and send them over for you to check. I'll try and do it later today if I can.' He added, 'Thanks for buying the camera, you didn't have to.'

'Rubbish Gavin,' she replied. 'It's a bargain and we need a new one at school. I'd better get back as I have a class at midday – more Christmas carols to rehearse with my girls' choir. Anyway,' as the door of the shop opened, 'it looks as if another of your lady admirers has come to visit and worship at your feet!'

It was Lizz Ozroy on her own and loaded down with shopping bags; Gavin introduced them to each other and explained that Heather was the former conductor of The Verlis Singers, before him. After Heather had left the shop, Lizz said, 'Gosh she is a stunner, she must have been quite young when she conducted the choir.'

Gavin explained that it was soon after she had moved to Verlis as a music teacher and had taken the choir for a few years. From what he had been told she eventually fell out with the committee when she refused to sing *Deep Harmony* at the start of rehearsals. Lizz told him how much her husband and daughter had enjoyed the carol service. They hadn't realised how good the choir was but were very impressed. Her husband had particularly liked the Holst Carol, *Lully Lullay*.

'He actually said it was singing to perfection and, believe you me Gavin, my dear husband is NOT prone to giveaway musical plaudits!'

Lizz stayed for a while and chatted about her new camera. In one of her shopping bags, she explained, she had bought him a small Christmas present.

'I hope you like it. I was in the shop and saw it hanging up and thought how it would suit you and your new look.' She chuckled and reached out to ruffle Gavin's hair. It was a dark green denim shirt that had obviously been purchased at a designer shop. 'I hope it is the right size.'

'Wow Lizz are you sure? You really shouldn't have!'

He took it out and held it up against his chest. It really was a colour he liked.

'Gosh thanks very much, I am invited to Polly Jones's house tomorrow evening with some of her crazy crowd, I'll wear it then.'

Lizz then enquired how the closing down sale was going and Gavin told her that he had to be out by January end but the way things were selling so well, he might close just after Christmas.

'Tell you what, if you have a free lunch time, Gavin, the week before Christmas, perhaps we could meet up in town for a Christmas celebration lunch. Shall we fix a date now?'

Taken aback slightly by the invitation, he replied, 'Yes of course Lizz, that would be really nice.'

They agreed that Tuesday December 21st was a good day for both of them and that Lizz would book a table somewhere in the city as it would be busy that week. She was going to bring her camera so Gavin could explain some of the technical extras. As she left Gavin told her that her reading was excellent at the start of the service.

'Thanks Gavin, always good to get the rod of Jesse out in the open at the start of a Christmas Carol Service, don't you think?'

She was laughing as she left the shop. Gavin wondered if mentioning supper at Polly's prompted a lunch invite from a rather attractive yet married alto in the choir. He should have had his hair cut short months ago. His randy brother had been right.

***

Helen McNeil had called the hospital first thing to book an urgent appointment for Brian to see the consultant. She also called Rona Hancock, the choir secretary, to explain that Brian was unwell and perhaps it was best not to consult him for the time being on choir matters.

'I am sure he will be on the mend by Christmas and he is so sorry (she lied) that he missed the Rotary carols this year. My sister Joan went with a friend and said it was simply wonderful, the best yet! She couldn't wait to get to school next day for some parents meeting to tell the head teacher Georgina James how gorgeous her ex looks with his new short haircut. A bit naughty perhaps but there's a lot of bad feeling at the school I am told, and the fact that the head teacher is having an affair with another member of staff. The Governors are revolting in more ways than one.'

The consultant had slotted in an emergency appointment that afternoon for Brian at 5pm and Helen drove them both in her car. Brian had been very quiet all day. Gone was the exuberance of past weeks and the almost obsessive wish to get the choir visit to Poland sorted out with phone calls here, there and everywhere. In the consultant's room Brian had admitted that he was having some problems with passing water and the doctor had examined him and taken a urine sample. He explained to Helen and Brian that he suspected a bladder infection was the cause of the problem and was having an adverse effect on the strong antidepressants Brian took each day for his bipolar condition.

'I will get the urine test done very quickly, Mr McNeil, so we can get you back up and firing on all four cylinders again for Christmas. I want to increase the dose of your tablets slightly. This could make your husband very drowsy, Mrs McNeil, so it is best that he does not drive for the time being. Try not to over exert yourself for the next couple of weeks, Brian. Find a good book to read and if you are anxious, Mrs

McNeil, call me whenever you want to!'

***

Terry Davies thought that his interview had gone quite well on Thursday morning. He had followed Cockie Scotty in at 11am and the panel comprised his current boss, Tony Shaw, and one of the Regional Directors who had travelled down from Bristol for the interview. There were four candidates, Terry was told.

The job was in the planning office, still based in Verlis, and one thing that Terry had not realised was that a good IT knowledge was required, as the postal service was becoming more reliant on the internet for its communication and service delivery. Parcels were the new area of expansion in the postal service as people relied more on email as opposed to old-fashioned letter post. Terry had chatted with Joan recently about how Gavin had been affected by Internet sales destroying his retail camera business. For the first time he considered how the communication revolution would have an adverse effect on his own lifestyle and his job as a postie in the coming years.

Terry and Tony Shaw had worked together for many years and, when he got home that evening, he had felt personally okay and reasonably confident about the interview. Joan, as always, was understanding and reassured him: 'You had a go, Terry, that's all you could do. Your CV was very good and you have been a good employee. I can't remember you ever taking a day off sick for years. That has to stand you in good stead. You just have to wait now and see what they decide and who is offered the position.'

***

Mellyn Fyfield was writing her letters to friends and the family who had sent her such warm messages after Len's death, although she had known that his life was ending. Together they had talked at great length about his illness, but she was desolate with grief. The house seemed empty; she missed his smile, his smell, his everything. Attending the Rotary Carol Service was something she had both dreaded and looked forward to. At home last Wednesday evening, knowing what was happening in the Cathedral not so many miles away, had been almost too difficult to bear. How could she look forward to a life without him?

***

Saturday December 4th

Polly James drove to the station to meet Moira who was due to arrive in Verlis at midday. She was looking forward to catching up with her friend and the dinner party she had planned for later that evening. Dominic was coming of course and it had taken some courage to invite Gavin. Conductors were somehow different, the person you looked at and listened to. Like a teacher in school, somehow on a pedestal. He seemed quite sad and almost a reclusive man at times and she wondered if she had done the right thing in seducing his brother. Anyway, David was only a one night stand and now obviously had a rather lovely blonde in tow as he was with her last week in the Cathedral and after at the pub.

One thing was for sure, Gavin had taken the split with his wife hard, all of the ladies in the choir could all see that. Rejection was hard enough but to have your business fall apart at the same time was extra hard. Polly was a very bright young woman who knew first hand through her work as an accountant how some business owners could be badly affected by losing their livelihood. The stories of suicide brought on by business failure were well documented in accountancy circles. She hoped that Gavin would enjoy the company of her slightly crazy friends and she had been working all morning preparing the meal for the dinner party later.

***

Gavin had written and sent his proposed festival reception speech to Heather to allow her to mark it with her red teacher's pencil! He had also had a meeting on Friday afternoon with his accountant Anthony Richards. Shop sales in the past three weeks had hit all-time records as people came in to grab the bargains, whether they wanted them or not. He had paid several hundred pounds into the shop business account. He told Anthony about the bank's decision not to add any interest charges, which his accountant quite simply did not believe.

'Banks don't do that sort of thing, Gavin, they are bloodsuckers, especially in the current economic climate. Something is rather odd about Simon Calloway telling you that.'

This slightly worried Gavin, although he knew that was the way Simon had explained things, and agreed that Anthony should call the bank to confirm matters on Monday of next week. Anthony suggested that it would be good to clarify the situation exactly. Gavin agreed.

***

Gavin opened his shop earlier on Saturdays, especially as Christmas was coming and he was offering some crazy camera deals. It had been another busy day, with a surprise visit from Mrs Georgina James in the afternoon.

'Hello Mr James,' she said as she walked into the tiny shop coming round the counter to give her husband a kiss on the lips. I have heard about my new look husband, so I had to come and see for myself,' she said. 'It is true, the new hair cut suits you and also it looks as if you have bought new clothes. I have not seen that shirt before have I? The colour really suits you.' Gavin avoided answering.

The conversation was pleasant enough. Georgina did not appear to be in a hurry to leave, she told Gavin that the house sale was going through and he should receive his settlement by the end of February. His mobile rang and Georgina said goodbye so he could answer it. She would give him a call if that was okay next week. Not sure why she should would want to speak to him, he replied that she could call him at any time she liked.

It was the manager of the Grand Hotel on the phone, probably the most exclusive hotel in Verlis, on the outskirts of town. Jane McPhael, the manager, explained that they had a five star dinner for guests the Thursday before Christmas on December 23rd and could Gavin bring a small choir of about ten singers to sing carols to the guests between 6.45 and 7.30pm? This would be before they went in for their Michelin two-star dinner.

Jane said that the group they had booked had dropped out and she realised it was short notice.

'Our owner's wife is a friend of the Vice-Chancellor of the university and she went to your carol service at the Cathedral on Wednesday. She thought your choir were absolutely amazing and asked me to contact you in the hope that we might be able to book you. We will pay you a fee of £550 if that is OK and the cheque will be ready for you on the night.'

Gavin agreed to do it in the hope that he could get a good small group together. He would take this on himself, so it was not a choir booking and he would start by asking Dominic and Polly on Saturday if they were up for it. If he paid the singers £25 each he would have over £300 left for himself. Not bad for 45 minutes' work doing what he did best, and he could always sing the bass line if necessary.

***

As anticipated, Moira and Dominic hit it off straight away. Dom was in his most flamboyant mood and arrived at Polly's house at 6.30pm. By 7.30pm when Gavin was due to arrive, the first bottle of Prosecco plus martini cocktails had been consumed by the cheerful threesome! Polly had explained to

Moira a bit of background on Gavin and Dominic had teased Polly, telling Moira that Polly had the hots for the lonely conductor and had shagged his brother recently and probably by mistake.

'Polly actually wanted to bed Mr James senior, but made the mistake of taking the wrong one home, she's such a tart but I'm glad she brought those lovely legs and great ass to Verlis. Moira if I didn't like the dick so much, I would marry her myself and pump out loads of babies.'

The three of them fell about laughing as the doorbell rang.

Dominic sniggered.

'Oh bugger, this must be the man himself, tongues away team and Moira don't you go flirting with him or Polly will get very jealous.'

***

Monday December 6th

Monday December 6th

David and Laura Honey were discussing Christmas. When she had befriended David in prison, her family had warned her about getting close to a man whose background as a convicted fraud and conman could bring problems. When David, or Lawrence as he was then, had moved in with Laura, the family, her father and sister had lost touch.

'Leopards do *not* change their spots!' her father had said rather angrily.

Coming from the brigadier of the local Salvation Army corps and one of the leading figures in the movement in East Anglia, Laura had pondered on her father's true Christmas beliefs, and the fact that he would not bring himself to share the trust that she had in this loving man who she had met in prison. Laura had been busy and discovered that one of the churches in Verlis put on a Christmas lunch every year for older lonely people who had nowhere else to go. A phone call had introduced her to the organiser and the couple's Christmas Day was fixed.

'We will go at 9am in the morning and help in the kitchen, serving the meals and doing whatever is needed,' she told David. 'You can spend your time entertaining and charming the old ladies, you might be able to find a wealthy one. You are good at that!'

Chapter 20

Monday December 6th

Gavin was starting to think about pieces for the choir to sing on their Polish tour. Whilst they had more than enough in the existing repertoire, he wanted to set them the target of learning new songs. He had asked Rona to order in copies of a new Bob Chilcott book of eight folk songs and if he liked enough of them he would then get Rona to order the 70 copies needed for the choir. There would have to be rehearsals in May with Becky playing the piano, as she would be the accompanist on the tour – an issue to address after Christmas.

Gavin had enjoyed his evening at the home of Polly James. He had worn the new dark green shirt purchased by Lizz with jeans and his Oxfam dark brown jacket. He had not realised just how friendly Polly was with Dominic, and they had flirted and giggled together all evening. Polly certainly pulled Dominic's leg about his gay lifestyle and Dominic in turn quipped how she was desperate to get him between the sheets when the couple shared a room in Poland. Gavin was not aware that any rooming plans had yet been made and thought it best not to get involved, although he could imagine the discussion at the Committee meeting when Rona Hancock told the committee members that a single soprano and a young man wanted to room share.

Polly's university friends, Moira, had also been there. She was very nice, very Scottish, and the four dinner guests had a really fun evening together. Polly, Gavin thought, was careful not to let the choir feature too heavily in the conversation and, with Moira, had kept the guests amused with stories of their somewhat wild days at university. Dominic had got progressively more camp as the evening ensued, helped by the bottles of wine consumed. He knew all about Gavin's role with the Cornish festival and that there was a launch coming up the following Wednesday. At first Dominic would not reveal how he knew so much but was constantly pressed for info by the inquisitive Polly.

As the drunken dinner party guests left, Polly asked again, 'Come on Dom, how do you know so much about the festival and the festival choir Gavin is going to conduct next year?'

The, by now, very inebriated camp tenor giggled back, 'I am close to the Patron, Lord David Williton, he likes to towel me down after a shower. In fact he has invited me to Christmas lunch at his palatial mansion.'

During the evening Gavin had asked Polly and Dominic if they were available to sing at the Grand Hotel on December 23rd and they both replied that they would love to do it. Polly had planned to drive home that day to her parents in Essex but said she would rearrange and probably go the following day, Christmas Eve.

On his list of things to do that Monday, Gavin had to see if he could recruit five or six more singers. He suspected that Clare would either be working or with her family in Wiltshire, but hoped that the other Clare might be available. Two good sopranos was an important feature for the small group and he would send emails to bass Phil Harwick, tenor Taff Davies and altos Marian Thomas and Emma West. Emma was an excellent sight-reader who sang in the soprano section but on this occasion she would sing alto.

Gavin would conduct and also sing bass and he hoped that his first choice of singers for the prestige sing at one of Cornwall's top hotels would all be available, even if it was so close to Christmas. He pondered on asking Lizz Ozroy but, as she was a new member to the choir, he was not sure if she knew the alto lines to all the carols, so decided against it.

Christmas plans were being made at the Trenholm family home. Ron had some new homemade wine he would open for the Christmas meal and they were hoping that both Helen and David would be spending Christmas with their parents, although neither had definitely said yes. It was agreed that an invite would also be sent to Gavin, as they did not want him to be alone, particularly on Christmas day.

'I'm sure he'll have lots of invitations love,' said Ron. 'But when you see him tonight ask him anyway. He might even have a lady friend he wants to bring along?'

Assuring her husband that there was no sign of any love interest females in the life of her special conductor, she said she would ask him anyway.

***

Gavin's accountant Antony Richards called him that afternoon to report that he had spoken to Simon Calloway, who had assured him that the bank was indeed waiving all interest payments. The repaying of the outstanding £25,000 would stay on the bank's books, without increasing, until the end of March.

'Well, Gavin, I really do not understand it; it is unheard of for a bank to do something like that. Simon Calloway was very cagey about divulging any information, but he did say that there was a letter in the post confirming it and asked me to convey his apologies to you for the delay.

'He also told me how your brilliant choir had performed so magnificently at his Rotary Club's carol service in the Cathedral, raising a record of £2,400. But that still doesn't explain your very special treatment as one of his business clients. All I can say is that you seem to be getting exclusive attention, Gavin!'

***

Terry Davies waited until he got home to tell Joan his news. The minute he walked into the house, Joan could tell he was despondent and that he had not got the job. She was right.

'They gave it to Cocky fucking Scotty! Sorry love, I know you don't like that word in the house, but I am really gutted as Tony Shaw had almost told me the job was mine. It seems that Cocky has all sorts of computer degrees and that's what swayed it for him. Basically Joan, your husband's a loser and will always be a boring postman cycling the streets of Verlis on his post bike!'

Joan put her arms around her husband and Brutus the daft dog snuggled up to his master's legs.

'There you go Taff Davies, we all love you for what you are, don't we Brutus? Now can we make Thursday afternoons a bit more special in future can't we?'

Terry smiled. Ah well, life could be a lot worse. He wondered just what the lovely Joan meant by '*more* special'.

***

It was a tradition with The Verlis Singers that at the rehearsal after the Cathedral carols, members could put their names forward to perform at the choir's so-called gala night, which always took place on the final rehearsal Monday before Christmas. This was in the usual rehearsal room but members each had to bring seasonal fayre.

The sopranos and altos were charged with quiches and nibbles, Jenny Dalton was the organiser of soprano offerings and Rona Hancock supervised her alto section. Tenors and basses, or their prospective spouses, did sweets, trifles, cheese and biscuits. Partners, on this occasion, were welcome to attend.

The church where they rehearsed did not allow alcohol, so it was soft drinks, teas and coffee normally, under the watchful eye of Peggy Trenholm and Karen Stroman, wife of tenor Eric and from the CD sales concert team. Entertainment would be provided by anyone who put their name forward and there were always plenty of take-ups to perform. Choir chairman Brian McNeil was usually the MC although Rona had called Gavin to ask if he could be prepared to stand in. She wasn't sure if Gavin knew about Brian's illness and certainly would not say anything.

'Brian's wife has been in touch, Gavin, to say that he is not very well, which explains why none of us have heard from him for a few days.

'I'm not sure how serious it is but he has been to the hospital to see a specialist. After all the pain we've had recently with Len's illness and death, I really do hope that whatever is wrong with Brian, it is not serious. Helen did say that he would be back in tow after Christmas, but I think you should be ready to MC the gala night next Monday if that's OK?'

Gavin agreed. He had received a call himself from Helen McNeil that day to say that Brian was suffering from one of his depressive attacks. She had confided in Gavin. It was time that he knew the reason for Brian's sometimes strange behaviour.

'Not many people known about Brian's bipolar condition Gavin, but I wanted to tell you. At the moment he has retracted into a world where everything is very black, but his consultant has increased the tablets he takes and he says he will be better within a few days. I will keep you posted, Gavin, but as I have told Rona, it's best not to contact him at the moment about choir matters. You will just not get a rational answer from him.'

***

Following the success of the Rotary Carol Service it was virtually a full turnout of choir members that Monday evening. A notable exception was Pat Nicholls, who was attending some highbrow dinner in London, and Tatania

Bakowski, who was suffering from a heavy cold.

The choir notice board, decorated with balloons, carried a note announcing that rehearsals for 2011 would start back on Monday January 10th and that there were, to date, two nominations for the role of choir treasurer. Fellow basses Dick Wilson and Pat Nicholls had nominated Richard Parish, and Rona Hancock and Elaine Bridges had put forward David Honey. Under the nominations, choir members were reminded that they still had up to the end of December to put forward names, but that this should be done by email to the secretary. The names of the two nominees (paid-up choir members) must be clearly shown.

A brightly coloured poster also informed all members that tickets for the Glitter Ball on January 28th were now on sale priced 'only £8 for choir members – partners welcome'. Jenny and Lizz had tickets that evening for all to purchase. A list was also attached for names of those who could attend the Fostors Christmas sing on Thursday December 16th with a large note: 'Choir uniform *must* be worn – red for the ladies'. Some wag had written next to it, 'Does that include plastic Santa suits?'

The rehearsal was light-hearted and Gavin seemed in high spirits. He read out an email from the Verlis Rotary Club, full of praise for the choir's contribution to the Cathedral carol service last Wednesday and a record collection at the door of £2,400.23. Members wanting to perform at the annual gala rehearsal were signing up for their slots, which were to a set maximum of five minutes per person. This included 'a seasonal duet' from Mr Dominic Gordon (bachelor gay) and Miss Polly Jones (spinster of this parish).

Gavin spent some time rehearsing the carols that the choir would sing at the Fostors Christmas party for staff and customers. These included old favourites such as *Ding Dong Merrily on High, We Wish You a Merry Christmas* and *Jingle Bells,* as well as all the traditional carols. There would be a keyboard available, so Sheila would be accompanying most of the pieces, and Gavin would introduce the carols. Choir members were asked to arrive at 6pm, as they would sing from 6.45pm to 7.30pm, this giving a short time for a warm-up in the downstairs area of the store, before going to the canteen where the party took place.

During the interval, Taff Davies had confided to his fellow tenors that he would not be given the position of chief of IT communications at Verlis Post Office, as he was over-qualified for the role. Eric Stroman summed it up:

'If it's not meant to be then take it on the chin Taff! Just think of poor old Len and be grateful for all you have, including that lovely wife of yours, although we all wonder what she sees in you, you daft Welsh bugger!'

Rehearsal over, many members headed for the pub, including Lizz who was disappointed that Gavin had not joined them. The conductor went straight home; alcohol was out for tonight, as he was still suffering from the hangover induced by attending the dinner party of Polly James and friends.

***

Wednesday December 8ᵗʰ

The launch of the Cornwall Festival 2011 was well attended at the Guildhall. Gavin arrived to be met by Heather Strong wearing a dark blue velvet dress. It was extremely low cut and guaranteed to catch the eye of every heterosexual male in the assembled throng of Cornwall dignitaries and hangers on. Lord David Williton, the Patron of the Festival, seemed oblivious of the attractions on display and warmly shook Gavin's hand on being introduced to him. The

Cornish press was well represented and two photographers took numerous group pictures. There was going to be a glossy feature in the monthly *Social Cornwall* magazine.

Radio Cornwall had sent a young reporter to cover the launch and there was even a TV camera crew from BBC South West in attendance. Lord Williton, it seemed, had made a significant donation to the homeless charity in Verlis and, as it was Christmas time, when support of those who were homeless was newsworthy, this provided a double story and therefore it was well worth sending a TV news crew.

The TV reporter picked up the fact that a massed choir of new Cornish singers would be taking part in the festival on the last day, and liked the 'human interest' angle, recording a piece with Gavin. This was watched enviously by some of the other festival committee members, who would have loved to have got their faces on TV South West.

Details of the choral classes for 2011 were distributed and Lord Williton spoke to the 100-plus guests crammed into the ballroom, talking at length about the history of the festival. He then introduced Mrs Heather Strong as chair of the development group, which had been established to introduce new ideas to the festival. Gavin watched her as she stepped forward, she was certainly a very glamorous lady and, as Taff Davies had noted on a number of occasions, her breasts were indeed, truly magnificent.

Heather gave the background to the initiative to 'get all Cornwall singing' and then it was Gavin's turn to come forward and speak. Following the eloquent Lord David Williton and the beautiful Heather Strong, stepping onto the small rostrum did not faze Gavin James. Keeping, almost, to the script he had agreed with Heather, he told how this was indeed a chance for anyone who loved singing in the shower, or the car to come along and find their voice.

'If you have always wondered what it is like to sing in a choir, then, whatever your age, please sign up and we will all have a wonderful day together, culminating in the chance to experience singing at Verlis Cathedral on the evening of our 'Come and Sing' workshop. It will be a fitting end to the 75th Cornish Festival and I would like to thank the Festival for their invitation to conduct the workshop choir.'

At the end of the reception, David Grenfell congratulated Gavin on his words: 'I am sure we will get lots of people involved and I know you are the right man for the job.'

Praise indeed from the son of Isaac Grenfell, founder of The Verlis Singers.

Shaking Gavin's hand as he left, Lord Williton said, 'Please Gavin, call me David.'

He smiled and said, 'I hear from a certain young man that you are a very accomplished conductor?'

Gavin was reminded about the 'spanking bottom' comment of an inebriated Dominic a few nights before at Polly's place, and smiled as he wished Lord Williton goodnight.

Chapter 21

Tuesday December 14th

'Mr Davies,' the elderly lady called out to Terry from across the street as he cycled along Pengwyn Lane. It was about 7.15am and the postman was about his morning round reflecting on what might have been. The warm cosy office job that was not to be.

'Hello Mrs Ellis, and how can this 'umble Welsh postman be of service this chilly morn?' Terry knew the elderly lady well and had delivered letters to her house for many years at number 17. Sometimes he would even pop into the local Co-op store around the corner to get a bag of shopping for her. A mug of tea was always waiting for him when he called back in with the goods. This of course was not officially permitted, but rules were meant to be stretched, especially if frail old ladies needed a friendly soul to sometimes do a bit of shopping for them if they were not feeling well and could not venture out.

'You are a very kind man Mr Davies,' she told Terry. 'I wanted you to know that my friend Alison's daughter took the three of us to the Cathedral the other Wednesday. Oh my, what a wonderful service it was, your choir is so very good. I want you to tell your conductor that Cornwall is very proud to have such a special choir here in Verlis. I have been trying to catch you these past few days to tell you, but keep missing you. You looked so smart in your suit and was that you singing a solo in one of the carols, I thought it might have been?'

Terry, feeling rather chuffed, and in his best Welsh modest voice, told her that it was indeed him singing the tenor solo in the carol, *In the Bleak Midwinter*.

'Then last week I saw your lovely conductor on TV talking about another choir he is conducting. He is becoming rather famous isn't he?' Mrs Ellis glowed.

Yes he was, replied Terry. Gavin's appearance on BBC South West News last Friday in the Arts spotlight section of the programme had caused quite a stir. Many of the lads back at Postal HQ had remarked on seeing it. Last night at choir Gavin had received many similar compliments from some, but not all, members of The Verlis Singers.

'Do you want any shopping getting today Mrs E?' he asked.

'Not today dear, I just wanted to stop you to tell you that I think you are a wonderful man. Now you must get on with your work and not let this old lady hold you up. A very Happy Christmas to you, Mr Davies, you are our singing postman.'

Terry said goodbye and reminded Mrs E to look out for The Verlis Singers on *Songs of Praise* next year.

'I'll let you know when we are on.' He set off on his bike reflecting that IF he had been given the office job, who would collect her shopping for her when she was feeling poorly and unable to get out?

***

Polly Jones was sat at her computer in the office when Dominic sent her a text.

Is that the tart who can't say no LOL x

***

The Christmas party last night at choir rehearsal had been a hoot. Polly and Dominic had performed their special number, with a slight raunchy twist! Dominic had dressed up as a girl in a very tight mini skirt, black stockings and suspenders, blonde wig and outrageous make up. Polly had dressed as a man in pinstripe suit, shirt and tie and bowler hat. Her hair was greased back and she had a false moustache.

To describe their duet, *I'm Just a Girl Who Can't Say No* as high camp would be a considerable understatement. The assembled members of The Verlis Singers and partners greeted the performance with a range of reactions ranging from surprise to outright shock!

Polly sent a text back to her special friend:

I think we might be banned from TVS after last night Dom – anyway sod the frumps in the front row, G loved it and the tenors were all drooling over your arse in the mini skirt – you are the tart xx pol xx

PS will you still sleep with me in Poland – pack the sussies …
PPS Santa Baby will never be the same again xx
PPS I love you – but not like that !!!!!!!!!!!!!
PPPS fuk orf

Stock in the shop was now running very low and Gavin was forcing himself to concentrate on retail responsibilities whilst reflecting on the past few days. On Friday evening the BBC had really gone to town on the Festival launch. The Arts section of the regional TV News programme had included a big piece on, the 'people's choir', that Gavin would lead next May. They had also included a short interview with Lord David Williton but far more time had been allocated to the one with himself. The programme had described Gavin as 'one of the West of England's leading choral directors'. The reporter included details of how anyone interested in taking part in the workshop could get details from the Festival Office. They had shown a short clip of Gavin on *Songs of Praise* last year conducting The Verlis Singers.

Heather had phoned Gavin on Saturday morning. She was ecstatic at the coverage.

'We have never ever had that sort of publicity before, Gavin, and BBC South West have already said that they would like to follow up on the workshop choir as people put their names forward.

'They want to be told about the people who sign up, I think the idea is to interview some before and then follow their progress with you on the day. What fantastic publicity, you came over so well in the interview, well done Gavin.'

Another call had come through on Saturday from Neil Farmer at BBC Radio Cornwall. Neil presented the Sunday morning show and asked Gavin if he could be available the next day to talk about, the Festival, the Cathedral service and, 'all his other current choir activities'.

'It's difficult to keep up with you Gavin, there's so much going on in your musical life.'

There was something else that Neil wanted to ask Gavin after they had agreed that Neil would call Gavin at 11am the next day on his mobile for a live chat on air.

'I don't know if you are aware Gavin, but I am being promoted to Station Manager in February as Jenny Woodall is leaving to go to Radio 4. I won't then have time to do the Sunday show anymore. 'Would you be interested in presenting our Sunday morning music show? We have all noticed here at Radio Cornwall that you are a natural when it comes to broadcasting. We would have to get you in for some lessons on the technical stuff, but I'm sure you would soon pick it up. There is a small weekly retainer of course, but being the BBC, and Local Radio, budgets are small. You could do the programme from the Verlis Studio and your knowledge of the Cornwall choir scene would really be invaluable.'

Gavin was staggered at the invitation. Presenting a local radio programme was something he had never dreamed of doing.

'Brilliant, Neil, yes I would really love to do the show and thanks for asking me.'

It was agreed that the radio station would be in touch with Gavin after Christmas to arrange a 'crash course' and that Gavin would sit in with Neil for January, with a view to taking over in February.

A rush of customers to the shop looking for Christmas camera bargains took Gavin back to the reality of Tuesday mornings in Verlis and flogging off photographic equipment.

***

Rona was getting ready to go into Verlis with her teenage niece Ruthie who had stayed on for a few days after coming to the Cathedral Carol Service with her parents who lived in Bristol. Ruthie was very fond of her Auntie Rona and when she was around, Rona's life brightened up considerably. She had taken Ruthie to the choir's Christmas gala night on the previous evening. Ruthie was 16 and loved every minute of the frantic evening, especially the duet by the couple, described by her niece as, 'That crazy duet, they were sooooooo over the top!'

Rona had not known what to think when Dominic and Polly Jones had made their entrance at the end of the first half. She knew that the handsome young tenor was gay but dressed up in a tight mini skirt with high heels, a wig and proper stockings, well. The duet of *A Girl Who Can't Say No*, followed by a saucy version of *Santa Baby* certainly caused a stir and howls of laughter and cheers from everyone present.

Peggy Trenholm had appeared in that ridiculous red plastic Santa suit to perform *I Saw Daddy Kissing Santa*, four of the basses had dressed as ballerinas and danced to a CD playing *The Sugarplum Fairy*. Phil Harwick dressed in a tutu was certainly a sight to behold! All in all it was an exceptional Verlis Singers Christmas gala – even Rona had to admit that.

She was not entirely happy that Jenny and Lizz had come to the evening dressed in sparkly glitter gowns with large posters around their necks promoting the ball they were organising without coming first to the committee to ask for permission. Social events should be sanctioned officially and Rona would be saying so at the next committee meeting. She liked Jenny Dalton a lot but felt that the arrival of Lizz Ozroy on the choir scene had affected their closeness. Jenny was even speaking out at committee meetings these days, whatever next?

Gavin had acted as Master of Ceremonies in Brian's absence and insisted on a final standing ovation for everyone who had taken part. He had then produced a tray of mini chocolate eggs and shouted out, 'Anyone want any eggs?' to massive applause and laughter.

All things considered it had been an excellent evening with so many people really making a big effort to dress up and make complete fools of themselves. It was such a shame that Brian could not be there as he always threw himself into the choir social events with such enthusiasm. Rona hoped that he would soon be back to his old self.

***

Helen McNeil's sister, Joan, had called in to see how her brother-in-law was. She was one of the few people in the tight family circle who knew of Brian's bipolar condition. They were sat in the kitchen with the door closed as Brian was in the living room doing a giant jigsaw puzzle on the table. Helen reported that her husband was very sleepy, as the specialist had increased the dose of lithium because Brian had a kidney infection, which seemed to be getting better.

'Brian has to go back tomorrow for another blood test,

but he seems to be calmer and the obsessions have almost stopped. I do hope he will be okay by Christmas, as the family all arrive on Christmas Eve. They don't really know the extent of their dad's illness but we'll have to see how things are next week.'

Conversation then changed to The Verlis Singers as Joan had heard Gavin being interviewed on Radio Cornwall on Sunday morning.

'He was very, very good Helen, he chatted away to Neil Farmer about this Festival choir he has been asked to conduct next year, and then talked about the Cathedral carols and the choir's tour to Poland in 2011. Tell you what, Mrs Georgina James must be wondering what has happened to her husband since she upped sticks and walked out on him. She might even come to regret that decision, one day in the future. The Verlis Singers were simply wonderful in the Cathedral, it's such a shame you and Brian weren't there.'

Joan hadn't seen the TV interview on Friday, but Helen had. She had hardly recognised the new look with a much tidier, shorter hairstyle.

'Gavin has had all his hair cut off, Joan, I hardly recognised him. They spoke to that posh Lord Williton but really went to town on talking to Gavin. I thought I saw Heather Strong, the previous choir conductor in the background; I guess she was something to do with the Cornish Festival, she seems to have her nose in most of Cornwall's music events.'

Helen did not have a good opinion to share about Heather Strong. As conductor of the choir she had fluttered her pretty eyelids and displayed her ample cleavage to the chairman, her husband Brian, once too often. Brian in turn, had not objected. He had been totally captivated by her. He had been putty in her hands!

'Let's go and take Brian a cup of tea Joan, he's absorbed in a giant jigsaw on the lounge table. It keeps his mind off other silly obsessions. I am sure that next June he'll be getting out with the choir in Poland and enjoying himself. I hate it when he is like this and so want the old Brian back. I think the kidney infection threw his normal drugs out of kilter. I do hope he will be back to normal for Christmas.'

***

Peggy was relating the goings-on of the previous evening to her husband Ron. He had planned to go along with his wife to the annual Christmas celebration but a heavy cold meant he stayed home in front of a roaring log fire watching TV with a bottle of brandy. Peggy had gone off in her shiny red Santa suit, which Ron loved to see her wearing, even if some people in The Verlis Singers were not quite so keen. The couple were regular Radio Cornwall listeners and had glowed with pride on hearing Gavin being interviewed on the Sunday morning show.

'That's our Gavin, TV one minute and Radio Cornwall the next. I am going to join his festival choir, that's for sure. I wouldn't miss it for the world. He sounds so relaxed Ron. We've helped him to get over his problems, you know, I'm so glad we could do something to make a difference. All he needs now is to find himself a nice new lady friend.'

Changing the subject, she said: 'I was chatting to Pat last night; it seems that young Clare is desperate to go to Poland but just has no money. She is such a sweet girl and I do like standing next to her in choir as she has such a beautiful voice. I'm sure Gavin would love to include her in the tour so I whispered to Patrick last night that we would pay for her, but she must not know it was from us, is that OK dear?'

Ron smiled. 'Of course my bird, if we can't help people we care about to have the little things they want, it's a pretty miserable life isn't it? I'll get a box of vegetables up together from the garden for you and we'll pop into town and drop them off at her house.'

***

Thursday December 16th

The choir members were starting to arrive at the Fostors department store in plenty of time for their Christmas performance. Taff Davies spotted Gavin and walked over to him.

'Well done for taking over on Monday in Brian's absence, I hope the old sod's better soon, whatever is wrong with him. I suppose now you are a TV and radio star Gavin, we'll have to increase your appearance fees.'

Gavin laughed.

'Don't worry Taff Davies, I shall not let the stardom go to my head and, if I can't do all the media appearances I might need a handsome Welsh tenor to stand in. Oh, by the way, did you get my message about singing in the small group on the 23rd?'

'You bet Gavin; I'll be there and mum's the word. If I tell the other tenors they will be green with envy. Is Dominic doing it?'

Gavin knew that whilst Terry was a good singer, a small group with him and Dominic on the tenor line would be fine. Dominic was such an exceptional singer and sight-reader; Terry would lean on him if required.

'We've got a nice little group Terry, but best not to mention it to the choir at this stage. I don't want to get people's backs up but it seemed too good a chance to miss out on.'

'Don't worry Boyo what people say. You do your own thing; Joan and I are very pleased about all these good things that are happening in your life. We now just need to find you some love interest!'

***

When the choir was all gathered in the store canteen, Gavin did some simple warm-ups. The store manager walked in and immediately, on seeing Dominic, went across and gave him a hug. They obviously knew each other very well.

Later that evening, Polly asked her chum how he deserved an embrace from Guy Williams who she had once met at a business meeting but who had obviously forgotten her.

'Oh he's a friend of a friend, Poll. By the way, did you know that you are coming with me on Christmas Day to a very posh lunch at the biggest mansion in Verlis, are you home for Christmas?'

Polly did not know this but as she had already decided that she would sing in Gavin's exclusive group and not go home until after the New Year, a 'posh' Christmas Day invite was just what the doctor ordered. The thought of spending the day with Dominic was just what she wanted.

'Ah well Dom, as you know… I AM just a gal who can't say no!'

***

The performance went well in front of about 200 invited guests, the highlight of the evening without doubt being the penultimate number, a performance of *The Twelve Days of Christmas*. Gavin allocated different groups to sing each of the verses, asking all the Foster Gold Card customers to all stand up and sing 'FIVE GOLD RINGS' each time through. This went down a storm.

At the end of the night Guy Williams, the Fostors general manager, presented Gavin with a cheque for £500 and Gavin told everyone present that they would put this towards a memorial concert they would be organising for the local hospice in the New Year.

'This will be in memory of Len Fyfield, a wonderful servant to this choir who sadly passed away a few days ago. I do hope you will be able to support the concert in the spring, it will be widely advertised around Verlis when the date is set.'

During the evening he had been introduced to the wife of one of the Fostors Directors, a very charming elderly German lady called Anna Huffmann.

Gavin announced, 'We will sing as our final item, *Stille Nacht*, in German. This is for you Anna, to remind you of home.'

Frau Huffman cried as The Verlis Singers sang for her and another name was added to the growing list of Gavin James supporters.

***

Friday December 17th

Phone calls between Patrick Nicholls QC to the honorary secretary of The Verlis Singers were rare. However, on occasions, mutual dislike had to be put to one side in the interests of The Verlis Singers and Rona had called Mr Nicholls.

'It's about Brian's absence through illness.' Rona asked Pat if he would be able to take the chair for the main choir and the Poland Committee for the foreseeable future.

'Of course, my dear.' She loathed his ingratiating tone. 'I would be pleased to hold the fort. How long will Brian be out of action? I hope it's nothing serious?'

She assured Patrick that Brian would be absent for a while and there was a Poland meeting the following Monday. He had no knowledge of Brian's bipolar condition as far as Rona was aware. There were some urgent matters that needed attending to before Christmas, would he be free? There was no choir rehearsal that night and the meeting was at the Cricket Club, starting at 7.30pm.

Pat assured her he would be at the Cricket Club, adding: 'I am glad you called Rona, I meant to speak to you last night at the Fostors jolly, but didn't get the chance. I know that Gavin wants young Clare Taylor to go on the tour, as she has such a lovely voice. Of course she and her boyfriend are skint so there's no way she could afford it. She sang the opening verse of *Once in Royal* so beautifully in the Cathedral. Anyway, a supporter of the choir has offered to pay her costs so she can go. She'll just have to find some spending money but as long as it remains a secret I will put in £200 myself so she has some cash to cover meals etc. Would you like to call her and tell her? I am sure she'll be pleased to get a call from the honorary secretary.' He paused. 'There is one other thing, Rona.'

The hon. sec. sensed that she would not like the 'other thing'.

Patrick continued: 'It's quite simple; Peggy will only go if her husband can be with her. I know you have mixed views about Peggy, Rona, but she loves the choir and won't go anywhere without her Ron.'

Rona rose to the bait. 'But we have agreed no partners and there may be others who also want to take theirs. We cannot make exceptions Patrick, the committee has agreed it, and so we cannot change the rules just to suit the Trenholms.'

Patrick was not letting up on this one. 'Well, Rona, I am sure Gavin will support Ron coming and I'm pretty sure that Brian would go with it. Tell you what, have a ponder, and see if you can come up with a compromise before the meeting. Where there's a will there's a way, Rona.'

Rona said goodbye and wondered if in fact she did have the will to make it possible for Ron Trenholm to go to Poland with The Verlis Singers. She looked in her choir file for Clare Taylor's mobile number and called her. It was good that a choir supporter was anonymously paying her costs. Little did she know that Peggy and Ron were the couple making it possible.

***

Monday December 20th

The honorary secretary had called a special meeting of the Poland committee in the absence of the indisposed chairman at the Cricket Club. There was no choir that evening as the Christmas break had started. The Verlis Singers would not meet again until Monday January 10th 2011. Those present were Patrick Nicholls, Terry Davies, Emily Thomas, David Honey, the hon. secretary, and Tatania Bakowski.

Rona started the meeting and explained that, as Brian was not well, one of the members should take the chair. She pointed out that Patrick had agreed to do so but needed a proposer and a seconder, who should both be full committee members. She was happy to propose Patrick. Taff Davies spoke up, 'I will second that, Rona.'

Patrick was an experience committee chairman and got straight to the first point, asking Rona for the latest situation on numbers. Rona then read out a list, which, to the surprise of Gavin, included Clare Taylor. She pointed out that a supporter of the choir was paying her costs and another (different) individual was contributing £200 so she would have spending money. She had spoken to Clare who was going to book time away from her job and was overwhelmed by the generosity of whoever it was that was paying for her to go.

'That's brilliant!' said Emily Thomas. 'That means both Clare and Claire are going, the sopranos all know how they add so much to the choir, you must be delighted Gavin.'

He certainly was, as no one had told him about the support for Clare. He wondered if this was another example of the Trenholms' generosity, as he knew that Peggy had a soft spot for Clare. She was always giving her eggs for nothing and regularly brought to choir bags of Ron's home-grown vegetables for her to take home.

Rona distributed the list. Becky Morris would be accompanist and there were 8 basses, 6 tenors, 11 sopranos and 13 altos. With Gavin as conductor, this totalled 41 in the party, including Chairman Brian. Gavin noticed that Lizz Ozroy and Jenny Dalton were new names to the latest list. David and Laura Honey had also been added as well as cricket-crazy Phil Harwick, one of his strong basses. It was a very good choir with excellent balance across the parts. One more bass might have made it even better, but there was still time for people to sign up.

Richard Parish was not on the list yet, but Gavin was pretty sure he would eventually commit and pay up at the last possible moment. Gavin thought he would call Dick Wilson to see if he would consider coming. A teacher, he would find it difficult to get time off, but Gavin would ask anyway.

'We do have one slight issue to address,' said Chairman Patrick. 'Alan Younger is down to come in the tenor section. As you all know, his wife June is our librarian who does not sing in the choir. Alan would like June to come and Peggy would only come if her husband is with her.' Looking directly at David Honey, Patrick said: 'If we take non-singers David, and they pay the full non-subsidised fee, is that a problem do you think?'

Gavin smiled, it was pretty obvious to him that Pat Nicholls and David Honey had already got their heads together over the matter.

'Well, Mr Chairman,' replied David, 'we have to book a 56-seater coach to take us to Bristol Airport, so therefore we do have plenty of room for more people. If they pay the full amount I see no reason at all why they should not come. We also have to consider that if we do say no we could lose Alan and Peggy.'

Taff chipped in, safe in the knowledge that Joan would prefer to stay home in Verlis, organising the Davies wedding anniversary and birthday celebrations.

'Come on, everyone, June and Ron are both great supporters of the choir, and always there at concerts. It would be cruel to stop them coming if we have the space for more people.'

David interjected. 'I have also spoken to our travel people and, at the moment, they are holding 46 seats for the flight until December 29th so we do have the places. The answer to your question Pat, is yes. There is no reason why we could not add more names, especially when you consider that if we do not let them come, Peggy and Alan will probably drop out and reduce the numbers.'

Tatania spoke; Rona was obviously not going to be allowed to throw a spanner in the works.

'What do you think Gavin?' she asked. 'You are our conductor after all.'

'If we can fit them in, and they pay the full amount, I see no reason why we shouldn't.' Looking at Rona he said: 'I know we agreed this at committee, but perhaps Rona you should send out a note to everyone who is going to say that we have some additional spaces for partners, just in case others want to come? I am pretty sure Eric Stroman will want Karen to join us.'

It was Rona's turn to get involved.

'What if everyone wants to bring a partner Mr Chairman? We will have a party of 80 and that's ridiculous.'

Chairman Pat by now had had enough of the discussion on this thorny subject.

'OK, Rona, please contact everyone who is going and explain that there may be some additional places for non-singers, but they will be at the full cost and not subsidised. What do you think they will have to pay David?' he asked David Honey.

'We should say £1,550 to cover any extras,' David responded. 'We can always repay any monies to people if it works out less than that.'

'Thanks David, £1,550 it is, Rona. If anyone else adds their name we are all on email and can communicate and make a decision. What's next Rona?'

Reluctantly, as she wanted to continue the argument, Rona handed out copies of the proposed schedule saying that she was preparing room places, but could not yet if the numbers were now going to change. Gavin as conductor and Becky as accompanist would have individual rooms and Brian would also have a single room. He would pay the additional supplement and had also insisted to Rona and David that his costs would not be subsidised. Rona explained that Polly Jones had asked to share with Dominic Gordon; something she felt should not be condoned.

'Oh come on Rona!' Taff exploded. 'It's 2010 not 1810! If they want to share a room that's up to them. He's a brilliant tenor and I'm sure Gavin is delighted they are both on the tour. That crazy couple will go down a storm in Poland!' Everyone laughed.

Gavin agreed.

'Any tenor section with Dominic and Terry, plus of course Eric and Alan, Jim and Peter, would be a great asset to any touring choir. Polly and Dominic have become very good chums. I don't think we need to worry too much about them. It's really good that we have many of the younger members going to Poland.'

'Dominic's cheque for the full fee has already been paid from a London branch of Coutts Bank. I have a feeling he is being sponsored by someone who is very wealthy,' added David.

'This choir seems to have some very rich, supportive individuals, we should feel grateful,' added Chairman Patrick. 'What is the next agenda item Rona?'

Rona then referred to the draft tour schedules she had handed round.

Coach from Verlis early morning tbc – June 16 Thursday arrive Bristol Airport for flight midday June 17. Arrive Krakow Airport (flight time 2 ½ hours) mid-afternoon June 16.

Coach pick up Krakow Airport to hotel midday?

3-star hotel option tbc by festival organisers when final numbers confirmed.

Festival schedule to be confirmed first night welcome party (all choir) June 16.

Rehearsals in afternoon and first evening concert on Thursday.

Friday morning June 17 free time – possible coach tour Salt Mines? Would there be time for this? Afternoon rehearsal and second evening concert in different venue.

June 18 Saturday – competitive classes during day and evening third concert

June 19 Sunday am fly Krakow to Rzeszon/Jasionka Airport – arrive midday

Hosted by Rzeszon Ladies Choir members/some in hotel? – Evening concert with ladies choir in a central church.

.........Return to Krakow flight from Rzeszon Monday morning tbc – early??

Flight from Krakow midday to Bristol anticipated arrival mid-afternoon.

Coach from Bristol to Verlis anticipated arrival in Verlis 11 pm Monday, June 20.

Costs to be met by Verlis Singers a/c.

Patrick congratulated Rona on the schedule and also thanked Tatania for her help. She then told everyone that her ladies' choir was busy organising a concert at a big town centre church. It would be the first time her former choir had sung there.

'They are really excited about hosting the famous Verlis Singers from England, Gavin. I think they will be able to offer overnight accommodation to at least 30 of the choir members.'

David said that he would allow for this in the costings he was currently preparing. The tour account had the £20,000 subsidy plus an additional £10,250 as all of the choir members had paid a small deposit.

'The first payment to the Festival is due early in February and we will ask everyone to pay the balance of £650 in March.'

Patrick then gave David a cheque for £950, payable to the tour account; this was to cover the costs for Clare. David noticed that it was payable on Patrick's own bank account. Patrick said, 'It's a cheque from me as the person supporting Clare wants to remain completely anonymous.'

Gavin reported that he was still considering the choir's repertoire for the tour concerts but was delighted that they would sing a longer programme at Rzeszon with Tatania's choir.

He had ordered a new folk song book of Bob Chilcott arrangements, which would be given out when the choir started back after Christmas. 'There are some really beautiful arrangements in it and we will learn some of these for Poland. The Verlis Singers are in exceptional form at the moment. The Cathedral showed off the choir to a packed audience and at the Fostors sing I thought the choir was also very entertaining. The people from Fostors seemed to enjoy everything we did.'

Patrick added: 'And you, Mr Conductor, were also in sparkling form at Fostors. Many of them had obviously seen your TV appearance last week and thought they were in the presence of a celebrity. You were brilliant, they loved all the chances you gave them to join in and the *Twelve Days of Christmas* finale went down a storm.'

'Hear, hear!' chipped in Taff Davies. 'One of those posh ladies was laughing so much singing '*five gold rings*' and enjoying herself. I thought she was going to have an accident!'

It was agreed that they would meet again on Thursday January 13th when, hopefully, Brian would be back with them. At that time, Rona hoped, final numbers would be confirmed. She asked if David could set out the actual costs and send them to her to distribute.

The chairman spoke up: 'Thanks everyone for your contributions and if I do not see you all again before Christmas, the very heartiest of season's greetings to you all.'

Everyone left, exchanging Christmas greetings; Gavin James was thinking about his lunch date the next day with Lizz Ozroy.

***

Tuesday December 21st

Verlis was bustling with Christmas shoppers. The schools had broken up and the city was jam packed with people. The Christmas market was in full swing and coaches lined Gundry Road. It was normally a dual carriageway but during the seven days up to Christmas, one lane was reserved for coaches to park after dropping off Christmas visitors in the centre from across the county and Devon. Fostors store was a mass of sparkle, with lights in the Cathedral churchyard where the traditional giant tree provided by the Verlis Rotary Club stood.

Lizz Ozroy was sitting in the corner of the trendy restaurant in Lannings Hotel in the centre of Verlis. She had booked a table for two and was drinking a glass of white wine to steady her nerves. She did not really know why she was meeting Gavin James, the conductor of the choir she joined after arriving in Verlis six short months ago. Lunching with men, other than her husband, was not something she did. This was a first for Mrs Ozroy and, as she had reminded herself quite a few times these past weeks, she was indeed *Mrs Ozroy*, married and with two lovely teenage children.

She had told her husband Olag that she was meeting Gavin. His response had been typical and he had met Gavin after the Cathedral carols, a few days back. He was a man engrossed in work, the advancement of his career and making money. Romance was a thing of the past.

'Have a lovely time,' he had said in his hard English accent. 'Why don't you have an affair with him? He seems very nice, but don't go falling in love whatever you do.' He had laughed out loud at this comment.

Lizz was wearing a dark green fitted velvet dress and had sat so she could see across the whole room and spot Gavin when he arrived. She looked at her wristwatch, a very expensive silver designer make, purchased for her last birthday by Olag. Why was she here? The place was packed and in the corner a noisy group of office (suited) types were obviously enjoying some sort of Christmas lunch together.

The glasses were gone after the recent laser surgery and Lizz had also been to the hairdresser that morning and her hair was now styled a lot shorter.

Oh hell! she thought. The long legged Polly from the choir had just walked in and the waiter was taking her coat. She had not spotted Lizz and joined the rowdy party table. One thing was for sure, Polly would see Gavin when he arrived AND would certainly see who his lunch date was. Why *was* she here?

Gavin appeared at the entrance and, seeing Lizz in the corner, waved to her. Leaving his coat on the hangers near the door he weaved his way through the tables of lunchtime diners, stopping at a table where two ladies were sitting. One of them, a tallish auburn-haired pretty woman of about 40 put her arms around Gavin and kissed him, quite passionately, Lizz observed. Gavin was obviously then introduced to the other women whom he didn't seem to know and left them to join Lizz. The woman who had kissed Gavin seemed to be very interested in who he was meeting, making quite a point of turning to scrutinise Lizz, with no hint of a smile.

'Hi Lizz, it's great to see you, as always you look spectacular. All the ladies in the choir envy the clothes you wear and Dominic even calls you Miss Verlis Vogue,' he spluttered.

Lizz was not sure which of the two of them was the most unsettled. Gavin explained that he had not expected to bump into his wife here lunching with a friend called Yvonne, who he had never met before. It was school holidays now of course so she would be on school leave this week. She was his ex-wife of course, as their marriage had just broken down; she had a new boyfriend, and he didn't know when they would discuss divorce.

Bloody hell, thought Gavin. *Stop blubbering like a fucking imbecile.* Lizz had started to giggle.

'Hello Gavin, its lovely to see you, shall we stop and start again?' She leaned forward and kissed him gently on the cheek, aware that two sets of eyes were firmly fixed on them from the aforementioned Mrs James as well as Polly Jones, who had spotted them from her table and was now wearing a Christmas cracker party hat. Lizz now knew exactly why she was meeting this tall, dark-haired, rather vulnerable man with the brown eyes, gentle hands and lovely smile. She had fallen for Gavin James, completely and utterly.

Choir conversation followed, with Lizz updating him on the Glitter Ball in January. Thirty-five choir members had brought their tickets, so with partners etc. there would be at least 70 people, probably more. Gavin said that he would certainly be going, but on his own of course. He had paid Jenny for his ticket. They both ordered a light lunch and Gavin also had a glass of white wine. Lizz had reverted to sparkling water and the conversation turned to Christmas plans in the Ozroy household.

'Well fancy meeting you two here; Gavin and Lizz together. You DO make a lovely couple.'

The tall slightly tipsy Polly Jones with silly Christmas party hat tilted on her head had glided through the bustling tables to say hello. Polly draped her arms around Gavin and kissed him on the cheek, the three of them chatting and laughing about the Fostors night, Christmas parties and Polly's outrageous duet with Dominic.

Lizz could see that Mrs James, whose eyes had constantly been on their table, seemed even more confused by the appearance of another young woman who seemed to be very friendly with her ex-hubby. Polly asked Lizz to reserve two glitter tickets for herself and Dom.

'You ain't seen glitter until you see the two of us show up!' she said. 'I'd better go back and entertain those boring accountants, are you singing for Gavin this Thursday Lizz? I think you should.'

Lizz looked confused and Gavin butted in. 'Well, actually I was going to ask you today Lizz, I am taking a small choir to the ritzy Grand Hotel on Thursday to sing some carols from 8.30 to 9pm for their exclusive wealthy dinner guests. Would you be able to join us?'

Lizz said that she was free and, if Gavin thought she was good enough, she would love to be a part of it. 'I can't get enough of Christmas carols now I am back in England; it was one of the things I missed most of all when we lived abroad.'

Gavin's wife and lunch friend had left without Gavin

noticing. He told Lizz that he ought to get back to his shop to open up for the afternoon. Standing up to leave he said, 'I am paying today Lizz, no objections, all those coffees and sandwiches, not to mention the shirt. This is my treat.'

Lizz watched him leave, as did Polly Jones, who caught Lizz's eye and gave her a wave as well as a very saucy smile and a wink.

**

David Honey had called into Lloyds Bank to pay in a number of cheques for the Poland tour that Rona had passed over to him the previous evening. After the meeting, she had told him that Richard Parish had withdrawn his name from the treasurer selection so he, David, was the only candidate and, in Rona's opinion was: 'The best person by far to take over as treasurer of The Verlis Singers.' This would no doubt be agreed by the choir in January, which meant she could then hand over all the files and account details to him.

'I will be glad to hand it all over. I have enough to do with the secretarial duties, as well as the Polish tour to organise and all that involves. I know Brian will be pleased that you have become our treasurer!'

Former prisoner, highly experienced embezzler and conman, yet reformed partner of Laura, David Honey was about to become entrusted with managing the funds of The Verlis Singers.

**

The 'select' group to sing at the Grand Hotel was made up of sopranos Clare Taylor and Polly Jones, altos Marian Thomas, Emma West and Lizz Ozroy, tenors Dominic Gordon and Terry Davies, and basses Phil Harwick and Gavin.

Gavin had told them it was black tie for the men and glamorous black for the ladies, cocktail dresses or long gowns. It was a posh do!

The hotel had set aside a large unused guest room for them to rehearse for 40 minutes before their 8.30am slot. Gavin had put together a list of Christmas pieces they could sing unaccompanied, including some carols for the VIP guests to join in with. He had even printed out sheets with the words, and he would give these out to the guests.

The performance went very well. The group were introduced as 'our guest choir' led by the famous conductor of The Verlis Singers, Mr Gavin James, 'Who you may have seen on your TV screens recently.'

Gavin was pleased, the small choir blended perfectly, every man's eyes in the audience were glued on Polly's very short black cocktail dress and everlasting legs and Dominic seemed to know a number of the rich male diners who were present. It was a triumph and the hotel manager promised she would contact Gavin well in advance next year and, would the choir please return? She gave Gavin an envelope with a cheque inside it for £500 and, as they got changed afterwards back in the allocated room, he told them that he would send them their individual cheques after Christmas. Pat Hardwick told Gavin to donate his £25 to the Hospice fund in memory of Len, as did all of the others except Clare. Gavin knew that she was there because she needed the £25.

Phil Harwick had noticed that it was £450 a head for the Christmas Day lunch. 'I think I will stick to the Cricket Club and their annual turkey feast for £18-50,' he said.

***

'Can I scrounge a lift back?' Lizz asked Gavin as they walked out of the hotel. 'My husband dropped me off but he's gone to a Hospital Board Christmas shindig so I need a lift. That's if you are going my way?'

Lizz had really enjoyed singing that night and was very happy that Gavin had asked her. They chatted about their Christmas plans on the way home in the car, and Gavin told Lizz that he was going to Swindon by train to stay with this brother David for Christmas Day. He had been invited to Peggy and Ron's but had said no as he had already promised to go to Swindon. David's new and rather nice lady friend was going to cook the lunch for the three of them. Wedding plans were in the offing, he told Lizz.

As Gavin's car approached her house in the expensive area of Upper Oldland Park, Lizz said: 'I live over there so pull up here Gavin. I'll walk up to the house, the fresh air will do me good.'

Doing as he was told, Gavin pulled into the side of the quiet dark road; it was 10.25pm on Thursday December 23rd 2010, two days before Christmas.

'Happy Christmas Mr Conductor, and thanks for a lovely evening.'

Lizz turned to Gavin and holding his face with both hands gently kissed him fully on the mouth. Gavin's arms reached out for her as her mouth opened and their kiss became something more longing and lingering.

'I can't believe I am kissing you in your car like this,' whispered Lizz.

Gavin's right hand had dropped and moved down to her waist. Lizz in turn was kissing Gavin softly and her left hand strayed to his thigh.

'God, Gavin, I want you; I think I had better go!' Still holding his face in her hands she kissed him again.

'I really don't know if I should be doing this.'

Chapter 22

Christmas Day 2010, Saturday December 25th

Georgina James got up early and was sat at the kitchen table in Trevor's flat. He was still in bed snoring loudly and stinking of stale beer. They had gone out the previous evening to the Verlis Rugby Club. It was a regular event at this time of year, irreverently referred to by Trevor and his boozy rugby pals as the annual Midnight Mess.

All of the men present had got themselves very, very drunk and way before the end of the evening Georgina had interrupted Trevor who was at the bar with his cronies. She told him that she was leaving and would he come home with her? She was taking the car and he would have to find alternative transport home if he wasn't leaving then. Trevor had declined the lift, saying he would be home sometime soon, belching and saying, so all his pals could hear: 'You get off home to bed, sexy, but don't start without me.'

Today they were at home on their own. Three months ago, sitting in the pub holding hands and all loved up, a romantic Christmas Day spent together seemed to be the idyllic prospect. Now, in the kitchen of Trevor Scarron's scruffy flat, with him in bed sleeping off God knows how many pints of Ruck and Roll, she realised that she had done a very stupid thing. She wondered how her husband was spending his Christmas morning. Seeing him on Wednesday with a very classy lady having lunch and that other girl with the amazing long legs making a fuss of him had hit home. She wished that she was still with him. Georgina James had made the most terrible mistake. She wanted her husband back.

***

The hall at St Andrew's Baptist Church was bursting with people. Trestle tables had been set out across the room with festive table decorations, crackers and everything you would anticipate from a good old-fashioned Christmas lunch. Laura and David Honey had arrived at 9am as instructed by the ladies of the WRVS Verlis branch and set to work in the kitchens with the spud, parsnips, carrots and sprout preparation team.

More volunteers started delivering the old folk from all points north, south east and west of Verlis. Many were in wheelchairs and used walking frames. A minor altercation between two very crotchety old ladies had to be calmed by the chief WRVS lady early in the proceedings.

Many of them expected to sit in the same place each year. This was something to do with being close to the kitchens, therefore avoiding not getting your meal half warm. However peace was restored by tact and an extra seat slotted in at the end of the table, close to the serving hatch!

By 11am the hall was bulging as glasses of sparkling wine raised the atmosphere ready for the grand appearance of MC Harold Turner. He, it seemed, was celebrating his 30th consecutive appearance at this annual event in the city. Supported by a grey-haired elderly lady, his wife, playing a badly out-of-tune piano, everyone was soon cheerily singing out *Rudolph, Winter Wonderland, White Christmas*, and other seasonal favourites.

David Honey, it had to be said, was somewhat overdressed, in blue blazer, cravat and flannels. He was rather hoping for a more central role in the proceedings. It soon became obvious that 'newcomers' were dispatched to kitchen duties, served as waiters, and afterwards had to clear up the debris, fill up black sacks and put out the refuse. All of the menial smelly jobs, in fact. But, as Laura, in true Salvation Army sprit, pointed out to her somewhat dejected partner over a hastily drunk mug of tea during sprout duties. 'David, these people have been giving up their Christmas Days for years and we are new to Verlis and just have to muck in and do as we're told. The same old folk obviously come year after year, I heard one old gent having a real gripe about the uncooked carrots last year, there's gratitude for you!'

David whispered back, aware that WRVS ladies had exceptional hearing: 'Well Laura we shall earn our place in Heaven by being here, that's for sure, even if we will stink of sprouts for the next six months. That old sod should try Christmas prison carrots, he certainly wouldn't be moaning then.'

All efforts to get involved in matters of a more high profile role were quickly rejected by the WRVS ladies who, it seemed, had been organising the event for decades, and to the exact same format.

The president of Verlis Rotary Club, Simon Calloway then arrived to do the official welcome. Much of the costs for the day were met by donations from Rotary fundraising events during the year. He recognised David and Laura as members of the Verlis Singers and made great emphasis on the wonderful carol service this year that had raised a record amount at the retiring collection.

'We are very proud of the choir and it is nice to see two members in the kitchens with their choir uniforms replaced by WRVS pinnies.'

Laura and David were standing at the back as kitchen helpers had been permitted to come into the hall to hear the welcome speech. Laura smiled sweetly at the President on being recognised and David winced and wished he was not wearing a WRVS pinny.

After the turkey dinner, the mince pies had been devoured and it was singalong time again. MC Harold went across to speak to Laura and David, not in the most friendly of fashions:

'Mm, so you are in the Verlis Singers,' he said curtly. 'I was a member of the tenor section for 18 years when Isaac was there. He was the founder, you know, a wonderful talented man. There are people in Verlis who still think that the choir should have ended when he left, but that committee had other ideas of glory.'

Laura responded tactfully before David could get involved: 'Well that is long before our time Mr Turner, as we only arrived here a few months ago. The old people certainly seem to enjoy the singalongs you are leading.'

David and Laura finally left at around 6pm. The turkey was in the oven cooking on the timer at home and thankfully the vegetables had already been prepared. As the couple pulled out of the car park David said: 'I don't think I could face another sprout Laura, can we have beans on toast instead for our Christmas dinner?'

He had not yet told Laura that he was going to be the Treasurer of The Verlis Singers. He was unsure as to what her response would be.

***

Polly Jones had decided not to go home to her parents' for Christmas. There was a family celebration coming up in January, which she was going to be at. Mum and Dad were holding a big 'do' to celebrate their 30th Wedding Anniversary and Polly obviously wanted to be there for that. The invite to sing from Gavin had given her an excuse to not go and Christmas at home was actually a bit boring as she had few friends in the Ipswich area where they now lived.

She had loved getting the invite from Dominic to an extremely posh Christmas lunch with his rich gay chums, and one who just happened to be a Lord! This proved to be at the rather stately house of Lord David Williton, a charming host. Polly couldn't work out what the relationship was with Dom and would ask him later on the way home. Polly was surprised to be introduced to the other guest, who seemed to be his Lordship's current partner.

It was none other than Guy Williams, the MD of Fostors. He instantly recognised her, kissing Polly on the cheek after embracing Dominic.

'Ah ha, the delightful Miss Jones from Stromans the Accountants, we meet again in more informal surroundings. It's lovely to see you, you didn't tell me you sang in a choir when you came to that meeting in your very classy business suit. Didn't your choir sing well for our gold-top rather tedious customers the other evening?'

For Polly it was certainly going to be a different Christmas lunch than the ones spent at home with Mum and Dad in East Anglia. On Christmas Day 2010, as the housekeeper for his Lordship called out that Christmas lunch was prepared, Lord David Williton held out his arm.

'May I escort you, Miss Polly Jones, to lunch?'

Walking from the library into the main hall on the arm of Lord Williton with Dominic behind, snuggling up to Guy Williams, she realised she was a very lucky girl. Polly Jones was so glad she had moved to Verlis.

***

Rona and Peggy Trenholm were lunching at the extremely exclusive Grand Hotel. They had arrived in their beat up Land Rover coughing smoke out of the exhaust and parked amongst the BMWs, Mercedes, Ferraris and at least two Bentleys. Daughter Helen had suggested to Mum and Dad that they should treat themselves to a special Christmas lunch this year.

'Go on, spoil yourselves for once and spend some of that money you keep stashed away. Wear your best suit Dad and Mum, don't go over the top with anything too loud; remember it's the Grand Hotel!'

Their daughter was in New Zealand for Christmas, pursuing a new love whilst chief pilot David was in Dubai on

British Airways long-haul flight duties. The original plan was that they would both be with their parents for Christmas Day, but a Verlis family get-together on New Year's Eve now seemed more likely.

The dining room was full and Peggy and Len were seated at one of the corner tables. Peggy had pulled out all the stops and was wearing a dazzling off-the-shoulder red dress purchased from the Fostors pre-Christmas sale rack. Her long grey hair was tied up in a bun and even at 70 plus, she turned the heads of the men in the room as they were shown to their tables. Lord and Lady Verlis were, indeed, lunching out at The Royal today. Over entrees they had chatted about the state of the hens and concern that egg production was somehow failing and how choir sales of eggs also seemed to be dropping off.

'Perhaps it's time to stop taking eggs to the choir my bird,' Ron suggested. Peggy said that she would see how things went in January when they started back after Christmas.

'Lovely Gavin told me that there have been quite a few applications from new members after the Carols in the Cathedral. New members always seem to buy eggs, so we'll wait and see, my dear.'

Christmas lunch at the Royal Hotel was everything you would expect it to be at £450 per head. Ron, however, was not fazed and called the waiter across to enquire, 'Excuse me young man, any chance of some more roast spuds?'

The charming young waiter smiled sweetly. There was something rather special about this homely Cornish couple.

'Of course sir, and would madam also like some more?'

'Oh yes please, my dear,' Peggy replied, adding, 'I don't suppose you have any more carrots do you, I love carrots, and some sprouts?'

Over dessert they discussed money and the fact that they had so much of it. Len had enjoyed very much the welcome glass of Dom Perignon and the delicious red wine that accompanied the meal. He was glowing.

'Perhaps dear we ought to be a bit more generous with that money in the bank. I don't know about you but I like the fact that we helped out young Gavin with the house and are paying that lovely young girl who sits next to you to go to Poland.'

Peggy agreed: 'You are right dear, I saw on the news that the donkey home in Tremor is having to close down because they have no money. Perhaps we could help out. I do love donkeys.'

'Would sir or madam care to take coffee in the lounge? I have a place reserved for you in the arm chairs by the log fire.' The charming young waiter smiled.

'Thanks love, lead the way,' replied Lady Verlis with a glowing smile.

Before they left she thought she would ask him if he was a singer, and next week they would contact Pat Nicholls and tell him all about the donkeys.

***

Gavin had caught the train to Swindon on Christmas Eve, as suggested by his brother David. He was spending Christmas Day with him and new love Suzy Taylor, who was cooking Christmas lunch for the two brothers. His car was not really up for the long drive from Verlis to Wiltshire and he had enjoyed the relaxing four and a half hour train journey.

He had taken a copy of the Bob Chilcott folk songs book and also some new music from Paul Stipforth, a new arranger with Cornish links whose music Gavin wanted to explore in 2011. He had also heard on Radio Cornwall (as he was waiting to be interviewed last week) an extract from a piece called Sunrise Mass, which was stunning. He had asked June the choir librarian to send off for the music; it was by a composer called Ola Gjeilo. The Verlis Singers would certainly be performing this next year, after Poland.

Foremost in Gavin's mind was Lizz Ozroy, as he sat looking out of the window. As the train sped through the Cornish winter countryside he could feel her lips on his, the scent of her perfume, the warmth of her body. The world seemed to have a very special glow today.

***

'And so, Mr Gavin James, when are you going to introduce us to the new lady in your life?'

Suzy Taylor had cooked a delicious Christmas lunch at David's house. The wine had flowed and it was pretty obvious to Gavin that if his randy brother could keep his dick and wandering hands under control, this was probably going to be a long-term relationship.

'I do believe you are blushing, is there someone already?'

David was in the kitchen where he had been instructed to make his contribution to the Christmas lunch by washing up. Gavin found himself telling Suzy about the new stylish lady who had joined his choir. He had found himself really attracted to her and admitted to Suzy how he had concocted an excuse to kiss her on the cheek after the Carols in the Cathedral. He chose not to tell his brother's girlfriend about the romantic interlude in his car after the carol sing!

'There's only one thing.' He paused and looked at Suzy. 'She is married.'

***

Later that evening Gavin was getting ready for bed in the spare room at David's house. His mobile phoned pinged. A text from a certain married lady, he hoped?

Hi Gavin,

Thinking of you today and feeling very guilty for the last few months.
Gosh you looked so good on Wednesday surrounded by your lovely lunch
ladies.

Could I please pop around and see you later this week, are you in
Verlis? Please get back to me – Happy Christmas!

Gina x

Yes, it was a text from a married woman, but not the one
he really wanted to hear from on Christmas Day.

***

Helen McNeil had always tried to hide away the reality of
Brian's bipolar condition from their two daughters. At one
stage in their early marriage, when Brian was diagnosed with
severe depression, she had been so frightened that he was so
low he might even try to kill himself. He had been admitted
to a psychiatric unit and kept in for almost two weeks. That
was when they lived in Taunton and after the correct
medication had been agreed, he had slowly returned to
something like his old self. There were occasional lapses after
his work took them to Verlis, but the recent one was by far
the worst for many years.

Katy and Emma, with husbands John and Francis, were
home for Christmas, with the addition of first granddaughter
Maisey, Katy, and John's four-month-old baby daughter.

The two daughters were shocked to see their father in
such a confused state of mind. Brian had greeted them all on
arrival with big hugs, but had then disappeared into the
lounge to sit on his own. Ten minutes later when Katy took
her baby daughter so Granddad could 'have a cuddle', he was
fast asleep in his chair.

After Christmas lunch, around the dining table, with Brian dispatched to the TV room and the new Christmas crossword, Helen told her daughters and their husbands the truth about Brian McNeil's depressions and his bipolar condition.

***

Later that evening Brian was sat in bed reading a Christmas present book as Helen took off her make-up, sat at the dressing table.

'Tell you what dear, I shall have to contact Rona next week and pay my deposit for the choir trip to Poland.'

At 11.30pm on Christmas Day 2010, Helen McNeil said a small prayer of thanks; Brian was on his way back!

***

Terry Davies and (potential) future son-in-law were taking Brutus the daft dog for a post-Christmas lunch walk across the park. It was a cold but bright sunny day and Taff rather liked this lanky young man who was sleeping with his beloved daughter. Behind them, a few hundred yards back, were Mrs Joan Davies and Jenny, arm in arm, laughing at something Joan had obviously said to her daughter.

'I told you, Jen, the silly old sod would come round and let Daniel sleep in your room. He can't help it you know, he's a dad, he still wants you to be the little girl who he met from primary school all those years ago. He wants you to be a virgin forever!'

Over Christmas lunch Joan had explained the complicated plans for June next year, and how she was doing her best to keep husband Terry and mum Audrey in separate corners, thus avoiding confrontation at the joint wedding anniversary celebration and Terry's special birthday.

Jenny had turned on her father:

'Dad, why are you so difficult with Nan? OK she can be a

bit of a snob but she has always been special to me. Do you remember when I used to go and spend weeks with her during the summer holidays? We'd go swimming and have such fun. She really is not as bad as you paint her out to be. Take no notice of my dad's comments about 'The Queen Mum' Dan, she is lovely really and she will love you.'

'Yes,' thought Terry, 'especially as he is studying at university and is obviously one day going to have a job the Queen Mum can boast about to her snobby pals.'

After lunch Joan had telephoned her mother with Christmas greetings. The next day, Terry and Joan were driving up to Surrey to spend a couple of days with them. They would be back in plenty of time for the annual post office New Year's Eve dinner and dance, a must in the Davies diary. Terry had faithfully sworn under threat of a one-month lovemaking red card to be pleasant to his mother-in-law for two days. They would certainly not discuss his failure to get promotion.

Brutus the dog was pulling at the lead as another dog had appeared at the other side of the park.

'Mr Davies,' said Daniel, 'do you think it would be OK for me to ask Jenny to marry me? I love her very much and want us to be together for the rest our lives.'

'Duw Duw... UH... (splutter) Of course, Daniel, but you'd better ask her mum as nothing happens in this household without Joan's blessing.'

On Christmas Day 2010 Terry Davies held out his hand to shake the hand of his future son-in-law. Behind them Joan and Jenny Davies, seeing the handshake, cuddled and jumped up and down with glee.

***

Christmas Day at Altarnew House in Upper Oldland Park, Verlis, the Ozroy family home, had been almost perfect. Son William had arrived home on Christmas Eve and had been kicked out of bed on Christmas morning by his sister Emma so all the family could attend the morning service at 11.30 in Verlis Cathedral. Lizz and Olag had prepared Christmas lunch together, followed by long telephone conversations with Olag's parents who now lived in Alkmaar, Holland. Games of scrabble followed, with Olag winning consistently and then evening TV before going off to bed after watching a Christmas present DVD.

From the kitchen fondling of her husband during lunch preparation, Lizz knew that Olag was in an amorous mood, the first time for many, many months. The afternoon she had returned from meeting Gavin for lunch he had wanted to know about their liaison. She had not told him that Gavin had given her a lift home on Thursday evening after the small choir performance. She certainly did not give any details of how they parted.

Throughout Christmas Day, she had desperately wanted to send a text to Gavin James who had told her that he was spending Christmas with his brother in Swindon. Surely it was OK just to wish him a Happy Christmas?

She had gone to bed first and was in her black lace nightdress, plucking up the courage to press send on her mobile phone when Olag came in. They usually slept in separate bedrooms but tonight was different. On Christmas Eve 2010 Lizz Ozroy turned off her mobile phone, the message she so desperately wanted to send, had not gone. After all, she was a married woman and Olag was her husband.

Chapter 23

Five months later...
Wednesday May 18th 2011

Brian McNeil was close to blowing a fuse; he was shouting down the phone.

'I bloody well knew that there was something too good to be true about that man. He has fucking cleaned out the choir accounts and taken over £70,000, every penny the choir has – or had! The police have all the details. I have spoken to Tatania's husband, who is a detective sergeant. He is going to ask his wife not to tell the rest of the choir, yet! What the hell are we going to do about Poland, Gavin? It seems he was in prison for fraud, why didn't we check him out? Fucking hell, we should have seen this coming. What are we to do?'

'Brian, Brian, just hold on a minute, take a breath please. Has Laura gone with him?' Gavin asked.

'I don't think so, he has done a midnight flit, and seemingly she has nothing to do with it and wants you to call her as soon as possible. By all accounts she is devastated!'

Brian explained that whilst he was ill in January, David (if that was his real name) had forged Brian's signature to enable him to access the choir accounts. 'That smarmy fucking shit came to my house, I don't remember much about those weeks before Christmas but I do vaguely remember him telling me that it would be easier for me if I signed some simple bank forms.

'Over the last three weeks, he has obviously and

deliberately moved the money out and disappeared the week before the choir payments were due to the Festival. Air Fares and Hotels in Poland also have to be paid next week.

'The bastard even phoned choir members last week to chase in their final payments, Rona told me. She is traumatised because she was so keen for him to take over the accounts. She feels that she is to blame for this fucking mess because she fell for all the bullshit he gave us.

'He even changed the choir tour account to a different bank, as he knew he could be discovered. The man is a fucking professional and he has conned The Verlis Singers out of every penny we have. I had to call Rona and tell her to check the bank accounts, as you can imagine, she feels totally humiliated.'

***

Brian had called Gavin very early that morning in a highly agitated state and had driven to his cottage at 8.45am. Brian was still highly charged and very angry when he arrived and Gavin had persuaded him to sit down and explain slowly just what was going on.

On hearing the news and taking in the facts, Gavin had immediately called Pat Nicholls, at this time a level legal head was required. He left a message on Pat's mobile.

'Hi Pat, sorry to trouble you, it's really very urgent. Please call me as soon as you can. It IS really urgent.'

Brian was getting angrier as he tried to explain what he knew, as Gavin attempted to calm him.

'We've lost everyone's money; it's my fault for not being more careful. Gerry Head was right, fucking prudent, fucking sodding prudent; we have let everyone down, that bastard, that slimy fucking cunt in his blazers and cravats. He has taken us for complete fools.'

To Brian's astonishment, Georgina James then appeared from upstairs wearing a dressing gown. She had obviously

265

been an overnight guest of her ex-husband and had heard the commotion downstairs. Brian McNeil could only take so much confusion and surprises in one day.

'Brian, you go home and try to relax,' said Gavin. I will call Rona and we'll call an emergency meeting tonight. I think we need to try to keep this quiet for now. I'll get back to you later after I have spoken to Pat and Rona and we have a venue for the meeting.

Gavin's mobile rang. A very hysterical Laura Honey was on the phone; Gavin immediately interrupted her.

'Laura, whatever has happened, it is not your fault. I have things to do and will call you later, are you at home this afternoon?'

Gavin agreed to call in to see her at around 3.30pm that afternoon, making a note of her address, as he no idea where they lived in Verlis.

***

'It's simple Pat, David Honey has buggered off with all the Verlis money, he's a professional conman with a prison record. I don't think Laura is involved.' Pat Nicholls had responded as soon as he saw Gavin's text.

'Yes the police are after him. The total? It's about £70,000 we think, according to Rona, £19,000 pounds from the reserve account, £8,000 from the general account plus £51,000 from the tour account. It seems we have paid the £250 deposits for the flights but the rest of the flights, the hotel and festival monies are due next week. We've been stitched up, Pat. Brian is beside himself and Rona thinks it's her fault for wanting him to do the accounts.'

Pat's voice was calm, his response controlled. 'OK Gavin, leave it with me. I will call the police as I have good contacts. I would be very surprised if he gets away with this and am confident we will get some, if not all of the money back. We need a loan to cover the payments due now. That slimy

bastard is not going to stop The Verlis Singers going to
Poland, you can rest assured of that point. I should have seen
this coming.'

Georgina James was standing behind Gavin with her arms
around his waist.

'Christ Gavin, what the bloody hell is going on?'

***

Georgina left to go to school for a meeting and Gavin
pondered the situation; Georgina James, Brian McNeil, Helen
McNeil, Rona Hancock, Pat Nicholls, Tatania Bakowski, and
Laura Honey of course all knew about the crisis. It wouldn't
be long before all Cornwall found out. Gavin wondered at
what point Radio Cornwall would call him, or perhaps he
should tell them?

If the story broke this weekend with the Come and Sing
Festival Workshop on Saturday, his Radio Cornwall Sunday
morning show and to cap it all The Verlis Singers were on
Songs of Praise this Sunday evening it would raise quite a stir.
Gavin suddenly had a thought. Of course *that* was why David
Honey had not turned up for the BBC *Songs of Praise*
recording back in February. He obviously did not want to be
seen on National TV and be recognised.

Another thought hit him; the £6,500 the choir had raised
for the hospice in memory of Len Fyfield was in the bank
account cleaned out by that scheming fucking bastard. Next
week it was all set up for the cheque to be presented to the
Hospice.

***

Lizz and Jenny were meeting for coffee at the Cathedral
Coffee Shop. Jenny had come from the library next to the
churchyard and was carrying a bag of books. Lizz had missed
some choir rehearsals recently and Jenny wondered if she was
OK. Lizz had arrived at the coffee shop looking as classy as
ever.

'Hi Jenny, how are things with you?'

Jenny reported that all in the Dalton household were fine but she had missed Lizz at choir. She was surprised that Lizz had not sung at the big memorial concert for Len the Saturday after Easter. It had been a fabulous evening with Heather Strong's beautiful senior school choir also taking part. Did Lizz know that Heather once conducted the choir? Lizz replied that she did, and had once met the lovely Heather Strong when she popped into Gavin's camera shop before Christmas when he was closing down.

'She's a beauty, isn't she? A VERY curvaceous lady.' Making her hands to show large breasts, she broke into Italian: 'Tutta curve.'

They both laughed. It was time to be honest with her friend.

'I have been away Jenny... because of Gavin. I wasn't going to tell you but you and I are friends and we will be sharing a room in Poland so I want you to know. I really can't keep it to myself as it is really troubling me. The truth is that I have fallen for him. I think of him constantly. I want to call him, kiss him and, well, you know!'

Jenny didn't seem at all surprised at the declaration by Lizz of being infatuated with Gavin.

'Lizz, has it gone any further? Does he know? Um, does your husband suspect?' Jenny had seen the way they were when they were together, you could almost reach out and touch the frisson between them.

Lizz replied, blushing slightly. 'Olag knows that I like Gavin but that's all. We had a very passionate moment just before Christmas when we were alone together. That's what has made me so restless, since then he has seemed to avoid me and that's why I decided to stay away from choir for the last couple of weeks. If I went I would have probably jumped on him! As for Olag, he just jokes about Gavin, he even said last Monday – why are you not going to your choir to see your lover Mr James?'

Jenny held out her hand and patted Lizz on her arm fondly; she could see that her friend was close to tears.

'I don't want to upset you Lizz, but I think you ought to know something... it might be painful but it seems that Gavin's ex-wife Georgina may be back on the scene. Nosey Elaine Bridges saw her leaving Gavin's cottage early one morning. She was also at Len's memorial concert and certainly seemed to be with Gavin at the wake afterwards.'

Tears were now welling up in Lizz Ozroy's eyes.

'Oh dear,' said Jenny. 'I'm so sorry, I should not have told you that. I am sure it will work out one way or another Lizz, best we change the subject I think. Will you be watching us do our stuff on *Songs of Praise* this Sunday?'

Lizz said she certainly would and the two talked about the enjoyable recording day in February in the Cathedral when the BBC people had filmed The Verlis Singers perform two hymns for the programme.

'All those repeats and close-up camera shots, the young handsome cameraman with the ponytail certainly seemed to go over the top with Miss Polly Jones. I bet we'll see a lot of her on Sunday evening. She certainly seems to attract the men.'

***

Gavin's call to Rona had established just how much Honey had taken. It was far worse than he expected.

'Rona, take a deep breath; this is nobody's fault. Seemingly the man is a professional conman who has been to prison. I am going round to see Laura this afternoon. It won't make any difference but at least I will see what she says and will report to you all tonight.'

Rona had successfully booked the Cricket Club at short notice for the meeting. She called Brian and was going to contact all the other tour committee members plus the full committee.

'We need everyone at the meeting Gavin, this really is a crisis for the choir.' Gavin agreed. Everyone connected to the management of The Verlis Singers had to be told the news. Rona paused and gulped. 'Gavin, it's a huge amount of money he has taken – everything.'

'I have spoken to Simon Calloway at our bank and he called the other bank David used for the tour. Bank managers speak together seemingly when fraud and the police are involved. The total he has taken is... £88,850.'

'Shit, Rona! Christ! Sorry, sorry!'

'I said a lot worse when I was told Gavin,' she said. 'The money is made up of £21,250 from the choir's reserve account, that's all the royalties and CD sales of previous years. The general account had £15,500 in it, as the money from Len's memorial service is included, plus the £850 raised by Lizz and Jenny at the Glitter Ball, and the tour account had £51,250 in it. It looks as if he has taken everything, a total of (taking a deep breath) £88,850! We have paid the £250 deposits to the airline for the 44 people back in March, £11,000. I know that as I saw the email from the travel agent acknowledging receipt. The balance, plus the festival fees is now due. God only knows what we are going to tell the choir members. We need to find around £53,000 if the tour is to go ahead.'

It was silent for a while, then Gavin told Rona that Pat Nicholls had contacts and they should wait for the meeting later that day. He suggested that Brian called the police so he could report to the committee later that evening on what they were doing.

'£88,850 is a lot of money by any standard, but Rona, surely the police will be able to trace it, although I suppose if Honey is a professional he will know exactly how to hide it away. We have to try to be hopeful and do all we can to get the money back.'

***

Terry Davies got the call at 12.30 as he finished his morning round. He had never heard Brian so angry, and he had explained to Terry that there was an emergency meeting at the Cricket Club at 7.30.

'It's fucking desperate Taff! That bastard Honey has fucked off, cleaning out over £80,000 from the choir accounts. All the tour money is gone, that scheming cunt has taken the lot! You must please keep it to yourself for now, Terry, don't even tell Joan.'

***

Gavin didn't think he ever had seen anyone so distraught. Laura Honey was beside herself and was screaming with anger.

'How could he do this? He told me he would never again steal money. We went to bed and the next morning he had gone, all his clothes. He has been planning this for weeks, he is really evil, everything, everything, was a lie and he used me as part of his plan. I have checked my bank account this morning and he has also taken all the money we had, about £62,000. He has left me with nothing... Nothing!'

Gavin had sat Laura down and went to the kitchen to make them both a mug of tea. Laura explained that she had met David in prison, singing in the prison choir, the so-called rehabilitation, then came the months in Wales and the decision to move to Verlis.

'I wasn't happy when he took over as choir treasurer, but I honestly thought he had turned a new leaf. How wrong could I be?'

Gavin explained that the choir committee was holding an emergency meeting later that evening.

'If he had not taken all my money I would give it to the

choir, but I have nothing!' Laura broke down again.

Gavin asked Laura what she was going to do.

'My dad is a Salvation Army officer in Norfolk. Mum and Dad never trusted David. Anyway I called them early this morning and Dad is driving to Verlis now. I can't stay here in Verlis, how can I go out and bump into choir people after what he has done? I'll be leaving later this evening, as soon as possible. I want my dad to drive me straight back home. I know it's a long journey, but he said he would do it. My sister is coming with him so she can share the driving. Verlis will be glad to see the back of me Gavin. I'm so sorry. I loved the choir, you are so very good you know, I've been listening to you on Radio Cornwall on Sundays. You are such a natural on the radio, I shall miss you all so much, please say sorry to everyone. They won't understand will they? But I really thought David was a different man from the person I met in prison. How wrong could I have been?'

***

Wednesday May 18th – 7.30pm Verlis Cricket Club

'This is an emergency meeting of the full management committee of The Verlis Singers and the Poland tour committee. Welcome everyone,' said Chairman Brian in a quiet, shaky voice. 'I must get straight to the point ladies and gentlemen. Our treasurer David Honey has disappeared, taking all the money the choir has in its various accounts... a total of £88,850!'

Gasps from around the room as the tour and choir committee members took in the news.

Brian continued: 'It seems he has also taken all of Laura's money as well, as Gavin went to see her this afternoon. We now know that he was an ex-prisoner, described to me today by the senior police officer in Verlis as "A highly professional conman and fraudster who had served a long sentence in Norfolk Prison for corruption, taking millions from an investment bank." This includes all the tour money. Although we have paid £11,000 for the original air flight deposits,' Brian took a deep breath, 'we need to find about £53,000, which is now due to the Krakow Festival organisers, the remaining flight balances, coach fares etc. It has to be paid, in full by next week. In the general account Honey cleaned out, there was also the £6,000 raised for the Hospice at the concert, which we were going to present next week. I can see how why he was so anxious to get this paid into the choir account.'

'The bastard,' muttered Taff Davies.

'I agree Taff, but we'll get nowhere if we spend our time calling him all the names under the sun. We really do have to focus our minds and discussions to the practicalities, ladies and gentlemen.'

Brian then explained how he had gone to Gavin's cottage early that morning after getting a call from the police. They had called Patrick straight away to see if he could help. Pat Nicholls then spoke up: 'Since Gavin and Brian called me this morning I have asked my contacts in the police and talked to the chairman of the county police committee Lord Williton, earlier today. One of their senior fraud officers then called me back and said that, in these instances, money was normally recovered.

'He did add however, that as Honey is a professional fraudster he would know all the tricks and ways of laundering money out of sight of the police. He would, without doubt, have been planning this for months.'

Elaine Bridges then said: 'As the choir publicity officer I think we should make an immediate announcement to the media…'

'No!' Gavin interrupted sharply and quite angrily. He continued: 'We should NOT do that, Elaine. My suggestion, well my proposal to the committee, is that NO announcement should be made until after the choir meet on Monday. You may think this is selfish of me, but I have the festival choir event on Saturday and we are on *Songs of Praise* this Sunday. It would be a disaster if this got out before then. I certainly won't be saying anything of course on Radio Cornwall this Sunday morning.'

Jenny Dalton spoke: 'I support and agree with Gavin. That gives us till Monday to try and find the money. Would the bank loan it to us?'

It was Pat Nicholl's turn to interject again. 'Gavin is spot on. NO announcements please and we have to try to keep this under wraps until Monday. Can you all manage to do that ladies and gentlemen? NO phone calls to choir friends, NO conversations with partners, whether or not choir members. We MUST ALL keep this quiet until Monday! This will give us all the chance to try and raise the money. Jenny, that's a nice suggestion, but no self-respecting bank would give an unsecured loan to the choir in these circumstances.'

What Pat Nicholls wanted to say was that any bank would want to know why a choir had been so stupid as to let an ex-convict and fraudster take over as its treasurer with access to many thousands of pounds. That point was best not made at this time as it would expose the health condition and vulnerability of the choir chairman, something Honey had obviously picked up on, and exploited to his advantage.

Rona spoke: 'I feel responsible for suggesting David as choir treasurer. I am so very sorry everyone.' She started to sob.

'Now, now, Rona, we were all responsible,' said Brian.

Pat spoke: 'That's right Rona, tears don't help nor do recriminations. We have to look forward. I would like to try to see what I can do between now and Monday, if you all agree?'

'But what can you do?' asked Elaine Bridges sharply.

Brian chipped in: 'Let's leave it to Pat and be thankful we have someone like him in our choir with legal knowledge and contacts.'

'I agree,' said Rona humbly, adding quietly, 'thank you Pat.'

Brian asked if there were any other matters to discuss before closing the meeting. Terry Davies spoke. He recommended that if any of the monies were recovered the first payment should be the £6,000, which was the surplus from the Len memorial concert for the Hospice. This caused lengthy discussion with Brian eventually suggesting that everyone present should be allowed to vote, including the tour members who were not full committee members. Rona was vehemently against this, as in her view only elected committee members should be allowed a vote. After more heated exchanges there were then two proposals to be considered and voted on.

Brian first asked the full committee to vote on the proposal by Jenny that non full-committee (tour) members should be allowed to vote on Terry's suggestion. As the result was a tie, Brian took the decision to use his casting vote in favour of the proposal.

The second proposal was to ring fence the first £6,000 for the hospice IF the money was recovered with everyone present able to vote. Seven people voted in favour with one against and three people abstaining. If any money was recovered, the first priority therefore would be to pay the St Catherine's Hospice the £6,000 raised from the memorial concert.

No one present was in the mood for social drinking, so everyone departed to their various homes. Taff Davies had been silent throughout most of the meeting. He needed to text Joan as he had told her why the emergency meeting was taking place. It was important she kept quiet about 'that bastard Honey.'

Chapter 24

*Saturday May 21*st

Gavin woke up early. He had made a mug of tea and was sitting up in bed with music scores scattered around the bedroom. It was the day of the Cornwall Festival BIG SING workshop, which had attracted over 200 people from across Cornwall as well as some who were travelling down from Devon. There was even a coachload of 50 from a new community choir in Plymouth.

He had decided to try and put the chaos of the Poland tour out of his mind for the day and concentrate on the job in hand. He was also going to record some interviews for his Radio Show the next morning and Dick Scott, from the technical team on the station, had kindly offered to get in early to edit the recordings and help him input them during the programme.

Gavin had struggled with the technical demands at first of presenting the Sunday music show when he first took over in February, but Neil Farmer, the station manager, had been brilliant with his support and had paid one of the keen young trainees to do extra Sunday morning shifts to help Gavin. This made sure that the jingles, traffic reports and news on the hour were on cue, the vital techy stuff!

Gavin loved doing it and, as Neil had said to him last week: 'We are all really pleased with the way you have put your stamp on the Sunday Morning Music Show, Gavin. The choice of music is excellent, especially with some of the new choir music you are introducing. People love your little insights into the history of hymns and the interviews with people from the Cornwall music scene go down really well. Everyone thought the chat with the 80-year-old man from the Four Lakes Male Voice choir, and his grandson who he persuaded to join, was very touching last Sunday. Great human interest stuff, that's what the listeners love. May audience figures clearly show that the Sunday Morning Show with Gavin James is becoming very popular across the county. Well done!'

Seeing a Poland brochure on his bedside table brought Gavin back to earth with a bump. Fifty-five thousand was a lot of money to find in four days. Of course there was always the possibility of getting it back but that shit Honey was a professional fraudster. He would certainly know how to hive off money so it could not be traced.

More and more info on his devious background was coming to light. Brian had called him yesterday to say that the police had told him that Honey had conned an old lady out of £125,000 in Wales. Seemingly, they had lived in Haverfordwest, before 'doing another disappearing act' and arriving in Verlis. Thank goodness Honey had missed the *Songs of Praise* recording, thought Gavin. It would have been very embarrassing to see him in the choir on TV. Laura had been there but that was different. Gavin wondered if the BBC might have withdrawn the programme if David the fraudster was shown on TV singing hymns of praise.

He could tell now why David Honey had missed the recording. He had planned precisely when he would make his move and knew the choir would be shown on national TV after he had gone. Being on a TV screen across the nation was like saying, 'Here I am AND I stole the money!'

Gavin knew that Pat would go to Peggy and Ron Trenholm for a loan. The trouble with that was that Rona made such a fuss about Ron joining the tour and said some unpleasant things to Peggy at choir; Ron had been very upset by the bad feeling. This had been back in January while Brian was still out of circulation. His illness had gone on far longer that everyone expected and he didn't attend a committee meeting until March. By that time the damage had been done. Although Ron and Peggy were on the tour list, with six other partners, Ron was still angry and upset with Rona.

Brian had tried smoothing things over on his return but Gavin was not sure whether Pat had brought Brian into the loop over the Trenholms fortunes, and he wondered if Rona had any idea of the influence the homely couple were having on the wellbeing of the choir, as well as its conductor. And even Gavin James did not know the full story of their support

**

It was 10am and Heather Strong was waiting in the entrance of Verlis Girls' School, a massive campus with the reputation of being one of the finest in the West of England. Giving him a huge hug, the head of music at the school said: 'Hey, Mr Cornwall, radio and TV star, it's lovely to see you. We are over the moon with the numbers of people coming today; the TV interviews on BBC South West and all your Sunday morning mentions have really made ALL the difference. David Wilson is really pleased. Your little pianist Becky is already here. She is very sweet and tells me that she is looking forward to the tour to Poland. You must be SOO disappointed that the Verlis Singers accompanist cannot make the tour?'

She giggled and squeezed Gavin's arm. 'Sorry Gavin, but you will have been told that I didn't exactly hit it off with Sheila Stirton when I was with the choir. And, to cap it all, Gavin James, you will be on *Songs of Praise* tomorrow night. No wonder you are the envy of all the choirs in Cornwall.'

He wondered how long it would be before the Poland fiasco went public.

They walked through the corridors to the main hall where the workshop would take place. The schedule for the day was:

12 noon – *workshop singers sign in (6ᵗʰ form students would help with this)*

12.30 – *Welcome from Heather Strong from Cornwall Festival Committee*

12.45/1.30 – *Gavin takes workshop*

2.15 – *break with soft drinks and sandwiches provides (Festival Committee helpers to supply)*

2.15/4.15 – *workshop continues*

4.30 – *coaches take singers to Cathedral*

5.00 to 5.45 *(prompt as other choirs were also rehearsing)* – *Workshop choir rehearse with Gavin in the Cathedral.*

5.45 – *free time for workshop choir*

7.15 – *in reserved places for start of concert at 7.30pm*

Heather had a number of her senior students on duty as helpers and asked one of them to go and get Becky the pianist and bring her to Heather's office for a coffee.

'It is a busy day for the Festival Gavin, as you know. I have to shoot off in a minute and make sure the choral classes go smoothly at the Guildhall. There is usually some bickering between the various conductors and last year one of the men from a Dublin Male Voice Choir almost got into fisticuffs with a fiery young tenor in the Farmouth Male Voice. Seemingly, Farmouth had gone touring the pubs during the lunch break and this lad was drunk, and looking for someone to punch. I had to use all my charm to keep them apart! Thankfully Farmouth are not entering this year although of course their esteemed conductor IS a member of our committee.' Heather smiled sweetly at Gavin.

'I hear on the grapevine that the Verlis Male Choir is in turmoil again. Another committee bust up I think. They withdrew from the male voice class a month ago. Time to start your own new Cornwall Male Choir Gavin perhaps? That's the trouble with committees isn't it? The people you want to be on them are too nice and can't be fussed, so you end up with the obnoxious people who just want to spout off and cause trouble.'

Heather told Gavin that the adjudicator for the male choir choral classes was coming over from Cardiff.

'Hywel Lloyd is lovely, a real charmer; he is retired now but still conducts the big Welsh Male Voice 1,000 voices bash at the Royal Albert Hall every year. He will be at the concert this evening in the VIP seats. I will introduce you to him. You will get on really well, I know that. He is a bit of a ladies' man and has a beautiful young wife, I'm told!'

Gavin made a mental note that a famous conductor of Welsh Male Choirs would be a great addition to his interviews for the next morning on his radio show. Heather's senior girls' school choir had won their class the previous afternoon and would also be singing in the Cathedral concert.

'You and I together, conducting our choirs in the Cathedral. How's that? To make things even more interesting, David Grenfell will present my girls with the Grenfell Cup during the concert. It is being awarded to the winning senior girls' choir tonight because he could not be there yesterday to do it. All that silly business of his father years ago being kicked out by the Verlis Vendetta still wrangles on, Gavin. Do you know he actually phoned me and said that he did NOT want The Verlis Singers mentioned by name if he was being introduced to the audience in the Cathedral? It's pathetic. Why can't they just all grow up?'

Becky had joined them for coffee and looked really nice. Claire Nesbitt had obviously made sure that her friend looked the part as accompanist for Gavin's big day.

'For once, Becky Morris, you will go looking all prim and proper.' Claire had laid down the law. 'No skimpy skirts showing everything you've got. It's Gavin's special day. He has been really good to you since you came to Verlis so now's your chance to show him. Wear that nice long black dress for the concert as well with your hair tied back. You look pretty stunning in that. I am working during the day but have a ticket for the concert. I am coming with Polly so we can all go for a drink after. I am not going to that sleazy Verlis nightclub after though. Polly said that we should get ourselves in the mood for man hunting in Poland.'

The very thought had made Claire have a hot flush.

***

People were starting to arrive. Gavin had sent Becky the music a few weeks back. He knew that he didn't have to worry about her. The pieces were all very straightforward and Becky had been playing for Monday night rehearsals the past few weeks in preparation for Poland. They had built up a very good rapport. What was the chance of Becky taking over as choir accompanist after Poland? That was not going to be easy to achieve. Heather's suggestion about starting a new male voice choir had also been stored away for future consideration. Becky could be the accompanist.

A film crew from BBC South West was setting up in the main hall with the popular presenter Imogen Voden. Just after the launch they had picked out a family from Ronsea in North Cornwall and had filmed them talking about how they would all be heading south for Verlis to attend the workshop. Gavin had met the couple and their daughter as the TV people had brought them to a Verlis Singers rehearsal last month. Simon and Heather Cole were in their early 40s and daughter Linda and son Harry would be at the workshop. Heather had also persuaded her mum and dad to attend. None of the adults had sung in a choir before, although Heather thought that Simon did have a nice voice.

'Hey brother dear, surprise, surprise, we have come to sing with your workshop.' Suzy Taylor ran forward and threw her arms around Gavin, whispering in his ear, 'And how is the sex life of my future brother-in-law? Still fighting off a stylish Cornish lady?'

David had not told his brother that they had signed up for the workshop but Suzy had managed to get the Monday off so they could have a weekend away.

'We have been looking forward to it Gav, Suzy sings well in the shower and I am now a fully-fledged baritone member of the Wyvern Male Choir in Swindon, even though the conductor is a dick! Anyway you are busy now,' said David. 'We will leave you to it and catch up with you later, perhaps for a drink after the concert? We will look out for you at the end but let's definitely meet up tomorrow. Perhaps in the afternoon, when you have finished charming the old ladies of Cornwall on your radio show, you big diva.'

Gavin was delighted to see them amongst the crowds now noisily flocking in, it would be great to have some friendly faces in the workshop choir and tomorrow he could spend time with them and hear more of their wedding plans. Suzy was a really lovely girl, and far too good for his unreliable randy brother. Perhaps David would, at last, settle down with Miss Suzy James. Third time lucky perhaps?

Peggy was in the back of the room wearing a bright yellow T-shirt. She waved at Gavin. Did she know yet about the Poland disaster? Gavin wondered, and waved back at her.

'Hello Gavin.'

Lizz Ozroy was another Saturday workshop surprise for Gavin.

'Oh hi Lizz, um, what are you doing here? I didn't expect to see you.'

'I am with Jenny and her daughter; we thought it would be fun but didn't expect to see so many people. It's manic! What sort of music are we going to sing?'

Gavin explained that it would all be fairly basic three-part songs from the Voiceworks books, although he had a couple of surprises up his sleeve dependent on the singing experience of the people attending. Heather Strong had walked in with festival patron Lord David Williton. They fought their way through the crowds of people to join Gavin and Lizz at the front.

'Hello Gavin, what a fantastic turnout,' said His Lordship. 'I bumped into Heather at the Guildhall. I was on pot-presenting duties to the cherubic ladies' choirs and wasn't needed for a while so scrounged a lift from the delightful Festival chair who is so good at getting things done… And whom, may I ask, is this delightful lady? Your wife, Gavin?'

Heather saw the obvious effect of David Wilson's remark on the embarrassed faces of both Lizz and Gavin.

She laughed to break the silence. 'No David, this is Lizz. I think we met back before Christmas didn't we? You sing with the Verlis Singers, don't you?'

Lizz replied that she did and was there with friends and was looking forward to the day, saying that she had better go and find them and bag a seat before they were all taken up.

Heather then walked onto the stage, picked up the microphone and asked everyone to find a place to sit, anywhere they could. The workshop would commence in five minutes, she told everyone. Lord David Williton and Gavin were stood together on the side of the stage.

'Gavin, Pat Nicholls has told me about your plight with the choir trip to Poland. That man will be caught I am sure; unscrupulous people with records like him should not be allowed into communities where they can con innocent organisations. I have told Pat that I will help. I cannot offer the full amount but will start your fighting fund off with a loan of £10,000. I know that the delectable Polly and young Dominic are really looking forward to being let loose in Poland and don't want to deprive the young men or older men,' smiling sweetly at Gavin, 'of their obvious charms. I hope you will be able to find the rest of the money you need.'

Heather beckoned Gavin onto the stage, giving him no time to reply.

***

During the interval two jolly ladies had approached Gavin. They were part of the Plymouth community choir who had travelled by coach to the workshop.

'We are having a wonderful day, Mr James, quite a few of our choir members were very shy and reluctant about taking part. They thought they would feel inferior if there were proper singers here. But you have made it so welcoming for everyone. We have something to ask you please? Would you consider coming to Plymouth to take a similar workshop for us? We would do it in August when the schools are on holiday and as you are getting famous we thought we should ask you today before you put your charges up!'

Gavin smiled and told them he would love to take a workshop and if they would email him he would get back to them. 'I am sure you will be able to afford me,' he joked. 'Perhaps we could use it as a recruitment day for your choir,' suggested Gavin.

The ladies had introduced themselves as Babs and Lyn and agreed that this was a fantastic idea and they would get back with dates in the next few days.

'We are all looking forward so much to singing in the Cathedral this evening.'

***

The TV crew were filming an interview with the Cole family and wanted Gavin to be included. They were having a great time and wanted Gavin to start a choir where they lived, they told presenter Imogen.

***

David and Suzy had saved a corner table in the White Hart

pub after the concert, just around the corner from the Cathedral. The place was buzzing with people, many from the workshop with friends or from the other choirs. When Gavin was spotted walking into the pub, everyone started to clap and cheer.

'You are a bloody marvel, Gavin, that's celebrity status for you, what a day!' said David. 'Suzy now also wants to join a choir, you have converted her.' Suzy was bubbling with enthusiasm.

'Gavin you are just SO good,' she said. 'We knew that our workshop choir would have to play second fiddle in the concert to those winning Festival choirs. That girls' school choir was just amazing. David was transfixed by the blonde lady conducting them. Something to do with her unbelievable bust and low-cut dress no doubt. But you actually stole the show, did you know that Gavin? Everyone was talking about you at the end. The way you got the youngsters at the workshop to sing that verse in *Streets of London*, everyone was in tears, then getting all the men to sing *Swing Low Sweet Chariot* and to end up with everyone in the Cathedral, even the Bishop and his Lordship the patron singing along to *When the Saints Come Marching In*, absolutely brilliant. We are so proud of you, aren't we David?'

'We bloody well are but hey brother, enough of all that choir stuff, what's this about you shacking up again with your ex, is that true?' In a packed pub full on local people Gavin did not want to talk about his revived sex life.

'Can we leave that till tomorrow brother?' he whispered. 'Too many flapping ears in here I think.'

Suzy punched her fiancée on the arm. 'You are so insensitive David, you can't ask Gavin that sort of question now.' Turning to Gavin, she said, 'I met a very classy lady in the workshop choir who told me she sings in your Verlis Singers. She had the most beautiful designer dress and a wrist watch that I think was a Regent Silver Dial, they cost about

£600. She was really lovely and told me her name was Lizz.'

She leaned forward to ask Gavin, 'I don't suppose that was the married lady you told me about on Christmas Day Gavin, was it? Is she going on your Poland trip, on her own?'

Gavin couldn't reply as Becky and Claire had pushed their way through to say hello. Polly had stayed at the bar, sensibly avoiding David and his new lady. Gavin wished that his brother had not mentioned the 'P for Poland' word; it had been a fantastic day up to that point!

At that present moment in time he wished that David Honey was standing in front of him and that he had a shotgun in his hand. Without question he would shoot the conniving, scheming, devious bastard.

Chapter 25

Sunday May 22nd 2011

6am – it had been quite a crazy weekend and Gavin was boiling two eggs with toast, his early breakfast before setting out for the Radio Cornwall studio, which was in a room next to the library in the centre of Verlis. It was open during the week for the public to pop in with programme requests and a steady flow of post was coming in specifically for Gavin from Sunday morning listeners.

He always tried to read each one before he went on air and responded to people's questions if he could. He had the interviews from the workshop, including one with the charming Welshman Dr Hywel Lloyd. Heather had introduced him at the Cathedral in between rehearsals. He was quite a character and had been awarded an MBE, recognising his contribution to the Welsh choral music scene.

The interview was based on Hywel's concerns that so many male choirs seemed to be having in attracting new younger men to join choirs. Gavin still had Heather's comment very much in his mind about whether he should set up a new choir for men in Verlis. If he did, an open recruitment day for men to come and find out about choir singing could get quite a lot of interest, especially as he could mention it on his radio show. Perhaps the famous Welsh conductor would come and take the workshop with him? He also had the contact details for the 50 men who had attended the workshop.

Gavin had also recorded a chat during the concert interval

with Heather Strong about the success of her girls' choir in the Festival and how she had become involved as a committee member. She had mentioned her time with The Verlis Singers but Gavin would probably edit this out. When he took over the programme in February, he had decided that plugs for the choir he conducted should not be included as being a bit too close to home. His show went out from 10am to 12-30 and he loved doing it. He spent quite a lot of time at home each week researching the music and tried to include at least two interviews each Sunday. The Festival workshop had gone really well and he seemed to be the blue-eyed boy of most of the Festival committee. Even Andy Smith from the Farmouth male voice choir had given him a begrudging 'well done' at the end of the concert. David Wilson was full of compliments and his generous £10,000 loan to the choir would make a big difference. Gavin was astounded when David Grenfell approached him as he left the Cathedral thanking him for 'dragging the Festival, kicking and screaming, into the 21ˢᵗ century'. Praise indeed.

Later that day Gavin would meet up with his brother and Suzy. They were coming round to his house for supper and also to watch The Verlis Singers on *Songs of Praise*. After Suzy had asked about his 'new lady' he had been pondering on recent months and the increasing visits of Mrs Georgina James and quite a few sleepovers!

***

The phone lines had been sizzling between choir chairman Brian, hon. sec. Rona, and Pat Nicholls throughout Saturday, but they had deliberately left Gavin alone to concentrate on his Festival workshop. After Gavin had been told by Lord Williton that he was loaning the choir £10,000, he had grabbed the chance and called Pat during the afternoon tea break. Pat told Gavin that the fighting fund stood at around £20,500 and said he would call Gavin on Sunday after he had visited Peggy and Ron.

'They are very generous as you well know, Gavin, but Ron is still smarting about Rona's comments to Peggy how choir partners should be left at home and not allowed to go to Poland. She and Elaine were pretty unpleasant to Peggy, you know. He was very upset by the things she said and he told me that the choir secretary should be put out to grass with the other old cows! I really don't know that their reaction will be. All I can do is ask them and see what they say.'

When Gavin enquired where the money pledged was coming from, Pat said that he was at home and would explain more to him on Sunday.

Gavin had decided to call Georgina that afternoon before his brother and Suzy arrived at his cottage. He planned to tell her that he thought their relationship should be put on hold. He had his speech already prepared.

'Since you started coming round after Christmas it's been nice being with you. But I'm sorry that I can't just put the last few months behind us. The deceit and lies and the affair; well I still wonder if one day it might happen again. I would prefer that we don't meet for a few weeks and perhaps we can see what our feelings are after I get back from the choir's Poland trip in June?'

He hoped that he would have the balls to tell her.

He wanted to spend time with Lizz and had missed her at choir recently. She had not sung at the memorial service for Len. That evening Georgina had been in the audience, this was the 'new me', she had explained to Gavin. Gavin wanted Lizz to be there, but he did not want her to see him with Georgina. Thankfully Georgina was away at a school head teacher conference so could not be at the Cathedral evening festival concert.

***

Pat Nicholls turned and waved to Peggy who was standing in the doorway of her house. Ron had not joined her, but he had eventually agreed with his wife that they would put £25,000 towards making the Poland tour happen. The couple had been very shocked to hear about David Honey and his disappearing act with all the choir's funds. Peggy had quite liked him as he regularly bought eggs, but had really taken to Laura.

'She was very sweet and a caring person, I think a lot of people in the choir wondered how they had got together, him being so smart in his blazers and cravats and a wife who looked like a church mouse. We were all surprised to hear what a lovely voice she had when she sung at Christmas in the Cathedral. Our Gavin had her spotted, what a shame it was that she felt she had to leave Verlis.'

Pat had explained the situation and asked Ron and Peggy not to tell anyone as it would be revealed to the full choir at the rehearsal the next evening. He told them that the choir had to find just over £50,000 to pay the remaining airfares and the tour costs to the organisers in Poland next week.

Ron had pitched in about Rona, but Pat had pointed out to them that out of the £23,500 raised so far £5,000 had come from Rona herself.

'I know she has upset you, Ron, but she does feel very guilty about being so taken in by David Honey and pushing for him to be the choir treasurer.'

Pat also explained that the police were after David Honey and there was a good chance of getting some if not all of the money back. Peggy had been keen to help.

'Oh come on, Ron, Gavin has put so much effort into the tour and we have worked so hard on those new pieces. Yes Pat, we will let you have £25,000. We have to go, how we can let so many people down because of that nasty man?'

Ron butted in. 'That's providing it does not go to the secretary or her chums. They can find their own money. I'm buggered if I will help them out after the things they said to Peggy.'

Pat got into his car and turned to wave again to Peggy. He remembered the last time he had been summoned to visit on Boxing Day when the couple had told him to contact the Donkey Sanctuary and send them £350,000. Pat had hoped that Peggy and Ron would allow him to tell the choir of the help they were giving, but they were adamant that their donation had to be anonymous.

'It's just between us Pat. No one should know.'

***

Brian had called Mellyn Fyfield on Friday to see if he could pop in to see her about something urgent and she had invited him round for a cup of tea on Sunday afternoon. Brian had decided that Mellyn should be told about the situation and how the money the choir had raised for the Hospice in memory of her husband had been taken by Honey.

Helen McNeil went with him as she knew what was going on. She had been watching him very carefully these last few days and was terrified that he would have a recurrence of his bipolar depressions bought on by his stress and anger caused by Honey's actions. Helen was also very aware that David Honey had used Brian's bad spell over Christmas to get some choir bank forms signed. She had no idea what they were or what they meant at the time. Looking back now she could clearly see that the visit just after Christmas from the smarmy man who was about to take over as choir treasurer was a deliberate ploy. That devious odious person knew that her husband was vulnerable and he used that to get access to the choir's money.

***

Mellyn listened carefully as Brian explained what had happened and how Honey had cleared out all the money the choir had. This included the £6,500 that they were going to present the following week to the Hospice. He would contact the Hospice the next day and ask them if they could hold fire on the planned presentation the following Wednesday until after the choir had returned from its Poland tour. Brian had not told the Hospice fundraising manager the real reason but said he would be in touch in June to invite her to a choir rehearsal. Hopefully, he thought, by then Honey will have been caught and the choir would have some money back in its bank account.

Mellyn had not actually met David Honey. Or his wife, come to that. However she was involved in the annual WRVS Christmas Day lunch for the elderly and the Honeys had been helping in the kitchen last December.

'He did seem rather out of place with his blazer, slacks and cravat at the same time wearing a WRVS pinny in the kitchen. His wife did seem very nice and worked hard all day. The husband spent most of his time chatting to the elderly ladies. He was certainly a charmer.'

Mellyn pressed Brian for more information on the real financial situation the choir was now in.

'Len was very much involved, as you may know Brian, in the finances of the choir back in the Isaac days. There were some ups and downs even then but nothing as awful as this. I remember Isaac once booking the Guildhall and a cello soloist for lots of money. He went to the choir committee and told them without any consultation. It was a *fait accompli*. They had no money in those days to even cover the Guildhall cost and no one had heard of the soloist. Isaac was a very headstrong man, that's for sure.'

Leaving Brian and Helen sat in her living room, she went out to the kitchen to freshen up the teapot. When she eventually returned she had a piece of paper in her hand. Giving it to Brian she said, 'I don't want any argument or discussion Brian, but here is a cheque for £8,500. You know how The Verlis Singers played such a part in our marriage. If Len was alive today...' Mellyn paused and went to the window to gather her composure. Quietly she said: 'He would have wanted to help and now we have sorted out all his affairs he left me very comfortable... This cheque is so you can go ahead and pay the Hospice the money you raised as I think people will expect that to happen before you go on tour. The additional £2,000 is to add to your donations to cover the money that evil man stole. I am sure you will get it back and then you can repay me the £6,500. I do not want the £2,000 back, that is a gift from Len.'

**

'I wanted to catch you Rona, before you got glued to the BBC in time for *Songs of Praise*. As you know, confidentiality is very much part of my everyday work, but for once I have made a decision to break a confidence because I feel the circumstances require it.'

Pat had called Rona when he got back home.

'I visited Ron and Peggy at lunchtime today. I am not sure how much you know, Rona, but they are extremely wealthy and I am happy to say that they have donated £25,000 to our fighting fund. I have just chatted to Brian and we now have all the deposits covered, but I will come to that in a minute. They will bring a cheque to choir, but it will be payable to me. I will pay it in first thing Tuesday and do a direct debit to the choir as soon as it clears. I promised Ron and Peggy that no one would know of their generosity. I have not told Brian, although he may guess, BUT I am telling you Rona on the understanding that this is strictly between us. They are not worried about when they would get the money back and I explained that we hoped Honey would be caught before he blew the lot. They paid for Clare as well last year but that's water under the bridge now. I estimate that we now have about £50,000 and I am going to check with Brian on the exact total as soon as I have spoken with you.'

He paused.

'You have been very unkind to Peggy, Rona, on a number of occasions. I cannot understand it but you and some others in the choir were very judgmental when the question of Ron coming on the tour came up.'

Not allowing her to respond, Pat continued.

'We all know of your feelings about committee rules and I am telling you this because I would ask you to be just a bit more pleasant to them in future. Yes they are a bit of a quirky couple but their commitment to the choir and to Gavin is without question. You must not mention any of this to them but I wanted you to know the true facts. I told them that you were personally putting in £5,000 of your own savings and they thought this was very generous of you.'

Rona spoke: 'Gosh, well, I had heard the Lord and Lady Verlis rumours and Elaine told me that her son works at that plush hotel where they charge around £500 for Christmas Day lunch. The Trenholms were there last year. They can't have paid for that from egg sales! They have really got us out of hole, I am glad you told me Pat and it will go no further.'

***

'Fantastic! That means the choir has the money we need to cover the payments next week. The Poland trip is on.' Brian had called Pat as soon as he and Helen got home from seeing Mellyn. It was twenty past four on Sunday afternoon. Pat had told Brian that there was another £25,000 to add.

'I am in a difficult situation, Brian, and I have to really ask for total confidence on this. We have Lord Williton's £10,000, Mellyn Fyfield has given you a cheque for £8,500, Rona has put in £5,000 and the Trenholms have loaned the choir £25,000 and, of course, you have donated £1,500 Brian.'

'Hang on, Pat,' said Brian. 'That amounts to £50,000. You said that we had to pay the Hospice from Mellyn's generosity?'

'Well you have to add to that £10,000 from me, Brian. That gives us the £52,000 we need plus the £6,500 to go to the Hospice.'

Brian replied, 'Bloody hell Pat that is very generous of you; are you sure? You have done enough without dipping in yourself.'

'Don't worry Brian,' responded Pat. 'The next time I defend some fucking evil East End murdering gangster and get him off on some technicality, I will add the ten grand on his fee! Sort of divine justice if you like! One nasty evil shit paying for another conniving crook. Anyway we all have to hope that the Met fraud squad who are now on the case will catch Honey before he syphons it all away.'

In a strange way Pat knew that Rona would keep the confidence of the Trenholm loan. He wished he could be so sure about Brian who could get carried away at times and put his foot well and truly in it. Brian told Pat that he would call Rona and between them all the committee members would be contacted that evening.

'At least everyone will be able to get a decent night's sleep. I will ask Rona to tell everyone that we have the money and the tour will happen and that we will tell the choir tomorrow night the full facts. I will see you at the rehearsal Pat. Thanks again for all you do for the choir, you deserve a bloody knighthood!'

***

Polly and Dominic were having a *Songs of Praise* celebration party. Dom had arrived at 5pm loaded with bottles of Prosecco and pizzas had been ordered. They were sat on the sofa together and as the opening credits started to roll they both started to whoop and cheer.

'Come on the Verlis Singers – knock 'em bandy!' shouted Polly with a mouth full of Pepperoni Festa! 'That dishy Italian cameraman with the ponytail was hot, Dom. Did I tell you that he came back to my flat after the recording?'

'You are a tramp Polly James,' Dominic said. 'Hey we are

about to sing! There's a close-up of you, no doubt thanks to your Italian shag cameraman.'

The programme featured four different choirs from around the UK, each sang two hymns, eight in total. Gavin was interviewed by Aled Jones and at the end of the programme; he said that a BBC CD of all the hymns featured in the three broadcasts would be out in July.

The Verlis Singers sang two hymns with words by Charles Wesley. They were *Jesu Lover of My Soul*, and *O Thou Who Camest from Above*. The interview with Gavin was all about Wesley's influence on Methodism in Cornwall and in the interview Gavin deliberately paid tribute to the contribution of Isaac Grenfell, the founder of The Verlis Singers.

'We were very good Dom, weren't we? I am really quite proud to part of the choir. Okay, we have a few oddballs and people who can be a bit offhand at times, but any organisation is only as good as its leader or boss. You know, I see that so often in the businesses whose accounts I have to oversee. A crap business always has a weak boss. The Verlis Singers has a great conductor. He is so good with the choir and brilliant in front of a camera. Gavin is the star, the choir would be lost if he ever left.'

***

Joan Davies never interfered with choir matters. The couple had sat and watched *Songs of Praise* and the two beautifully sung hymns from The Verlis Singers. They had loved the brief close-ups of the tenor section with Terry looking so handsome.

'Your family will all be watching you Taff Davies, over the bridge. You are the hero of the Valleys!'

Joan knew all about the Poland business and Honey's disappearing act. Terry could not keep a secret and she would not say a word to anyone. When Rona called that evening with the news that they had the necessary money loaned to the choir to make the Poland trip happen, she did not exactly share Terry's excitement and relief.

'Why are you not pleased Joan? Pat and Brian have worked a miracle, that's a serious amount to get in, it seems £25,000 of it is anonymous. God knows who has that sort of money to lend to our choir.'

Joan explained that whilst she was delighted that the money had been raised, he should remember that he was a committee member and it had, one day, to be repaid.

'Have you stopped to think Terry, what will be done if they don't catch David Honey and, if they do, they then discover that all the money has gone? What happens then? You are a committee member, Terry, and does that mean you have a legal responsibility to find the money?'

***

O Thou Who Camest from Above

Hear The Verlis Singers, conducted by Gavin James, singing the hymn.

Recorded in Verlis Cathedral in 2011.

www.verlis-singers.org.uk

Chapter 26

The hugely successful appearance of The Verlis Singers on *Songs of Praise* the previous evening was the talk of the choir as members filed into the rehearsal room. Brian had even brought his wife Helen along with him to the choir practice. Accompanist Sheila Stirton was also there. Becky had been playing at rehearsals for the past month as Gavin was concentrating on the pieces the choir would sing in Poland and Sheila had been coming in to page turn for her.

Sheila Stirton was an accomplished pianist, who in her early life had accompanied many well-known soloists and choirs. Isaac Grenfell had recruited her and they had been firm friends, even if he could exasperate her at times. After retiring as a music and piano teacher 15 years ago, she had continued with The Verlis Singers. Heather Strong had been hard work and very demanding and when Gavin took over Sheila was apprehensive about a younger man with no apparent academic music qualifications.

As the years progressed with Gavin she could see that he did possess an amazing talent for getting a true sound from the choir that reminded her of the days when Isaac Grenfell was at his very best. Gavin resembled Isaac in many ways and could also drive her up the wall with his last minute changes to concert programmes.

As she sat next to Becky Morris these past weeks she could see that this young woman was a remarkably talented pianist. Sheila knew that Gavin wanted her to step down. She was approaching 70 and with her first grandchild due next month had decided that when The Verlis Singers got back from Poland she would talk to Gavin and ask if she could continue, perhaps as a deputy to Becky when she was on holiday or not available.

***

It was generally agreed that the two hymns on *Songs of Praise* had been sung really well and that the camera shots of the choir seemed to feature Polly James quite a lot! One of the hymns, *Oh Thou Who Camest from Above,* had even earned a comment from the presenter Aled Jones who had remarked, "What truly beautiful hymn singing from our Cornish choir, The Verlis Singers."

***

Following the Rotary Carols last December and Gavin's regular appearances as host of the Sunday morning Radio Cornwall show, there had been a number of applications to join The Verlis Singers in recent months. Four new members had passed the audition, but many had not and Gavin had kept contact details for all of them. The workshop on Saturday had given him a long list of names of people who wanted to join a choir.

When he got back from Poland he would turn his attention to whether he should start a new male voice choir In Verlis. He also wondered if there would be sufficient people to support a new mixed voice choir, perhaps one more in the style of a community choir with no auditions and everyone welcome; there was nothing really like that in the Verlis area and he already had over 100 email and postal addresses of prospective members.

Gavin was starting to realise that he could earn his living through music. His retainer with The Verlis Singers and the small fee for the radio show, with more requests coming in, were giving him a regular income. If he were to start a couple of choirs he could manage them himself from his office at home and there could be membership fees to add to his income. Something to ponder, although he knew that some members of The Verlis Singers would NOT be happy.

Two of the new members were former school students of Heather Young. Gayle Bidden was an excellent alto and Amy Thomson a very good second soprano. Gayle had put her name down for the Poland tour, as had Philip Stokes, another quality singer and baritone. The tour had increased to 54 people in total, but was now 52 without David and Laura Honey of course.

However, true to form, Richard Parish had taken up one of the places left by the Honeys at the last minute, which meant that the total number going was now 53. Eight were non-singing partners, Gavin and Becky as accompanist and Brian as choir chairman. The choir was 42 singers with an excellent balance across all of the sections.

It was a near 100% turnout at the rehearsal in response to the phone calls and emails sent out by Rona. Whilst the committee members knew all the facts about what David Honey had done, most were genuinely surprised that the only choir members missing seemed to be David and Laura Honey. Everyone assumed that the call to attend had been because of the choir's successful appearance on national TV and because final details of the tour itinerary were due to be handed out. No one but the committee knew of the bombshell that was about to go off!

***

After the singing of *Deep Harmony*, Gavin complimented the choir on their TV performance. The singing was, he said, 'very moving'. Gavin then told the choir that he was handing over to Brian, the choir chairman, and Pat Nicholls. They had some very important information.

Brian had rehearsed carefully what we had to say to the choir during the day, Helen had made sure of that. Walking to the front, and with notes in his hand to read from, he then told the choir of the goings on of the past few days, starting with the news that David Honey had disappeared with over £80,000, clearing out all the choir bank accounts. On hearing this there were gasps from all of the members, but Brian was quick to point out that with the intervention of Pat, who had spent many hours for the choir over the past few days, the money had been found to pay the required amounts to the tour operator and the Festival organisers in Poland.

'This has been a simply dreadful few days for the choir, but the tour to Poland in two weeks WILL happen and we have many people to thank for that, but I will come back to that later, if I may?'

Brian then told the choir the background to the Honey situation and how he was an ex-convict and a fraudster who had served a long sentence in an East Anglian prison where he had met Laura. She, he informed the choir, had been devastated at what he had done and had returned home to Norfolk to be with her family last Friday. Gavin had visited her and she told him that Honey had also taken all of her money, something around £75,000. He had learned that the fraud squad had been called in from the Metropolitan Police and a number of other misdemeanours from his recent past were coming to light each day.

Brian continued: 'It seems that when they lived in Haverfordwest, prior to Verlis, Honey had conned an elderly lady out of £150,000, all of her savings. Only that day the police had also told Brian that whilst in Wales he had taken £30,000 from a retired Miners' Association account after being appointed as its branch treasurer. He told everyone in Wales that he was Welsh and changed his name. It seems he had a Welsh accent as well, which everyone believed. David Honey is a devious conman and we can only hope that the police will catch him soon.' The Chief Constable himself had assured Brian that there was not a stone in the UK he would able to hide under.

The police were putting out a press release with a picture of David Honey the following day, and so his face would undoubtedly be seen across the national media. They could not hide from the fact that his taking the choir money would be a main part of the story. They could not avoid that.

'The police say that when they show the face of a wanted person on the TV screen and in the national press there are always sightings. Public sympathy will be with the innocent organisations of course and the individuals he has ripped off. This will help in the search to locate him and would certainly increase the chances of getting back everyone's, including the choir's, money. The chances are that all the Cornish papers will feature the story in a big way when they pick it up. You could get calls yourselves as a member of The Verlis Singers. We all know how the press like to get what they see as the local angle. All I can ask is that you are very careful what you say. I don't think Laura should be mentioned, so would ask you please to think carefully about any response you might make. My suggestion is that you direct them to either Rona or Gavin.'

Brian heard a snort come from the alto section and the choir's so-called publicity officer Elaine Bridges. He knew only too well that if she got a call she would wallow in her chance to get her name in the papers! Brian then asked Pat to speak, telling everyone that Pat himself had loaned the choir £10,000. The monies taken by Honey included the £6,500 raised at Len's Memorial Concert and Mellyn Fyfield had lent the choir the £6,500 so that could be paid to the Hospice, plus £2,000, which was a gift to The Verlis Singers.

'The committee has agreed that we will make it a priority to repay the Hospice money to Mellyn first, but the additional £2,000 is a gift to the choir as Mellyn said that this would have been her husband's wish if he had been alive. She was very upset to hear of Honey's actions and told Brian that Len would have wanted to do something to help his friends.'

Pat then told the choir about the loans from Lord David Williton, Brian, Rona, as well as himself.

'I can also tell you that we have received an anonymous donation of £25,000 from a very generous supporter of The Verlis Singers.'

In the front row of the choir, Rona Hancock kept her eyes firmly on Brian, not daring to look across in Peggy's direction. Peggy was sat with her arm around Clare Taylor who had been very shocked to hear what had happened.

At this point, Dick Wilson held his hand up indicating that he wanted to speak. Although Dick was not able to go on the Poland tour he was a good choir member and an excellent bass. Pat said, 'Yes Dick? What would you like to say?'

Dick walked to the front to address the members of The Verlis Singers. Clearing his throat he said: 'What we have heard tonight has been quite earth-shattering and I would like to say that as a choir we are very fortunate to have a man the calibre of Pat Nicholls as a member. But, Mr Chairman, there is a question that has to be asked of the elected committee of this choir.' He paused. 'It's simple really, however did we get to put a man, this ex-convict and crook, in sole control of all our funds? How was he able to whisk away £80,000 from under our noses? How was he allowed to be elected to be the treasurer without any check or character reference? You tell us that he is a convicted fraudster so, I am sorry, but this really HAS to be asked. Why the hell didn't someone take the time to check his background?'

There was silence in the room. Polly looked across and Dominic grimaced.

Dick continued, 'I agree that it is good that the choir will still go on the tour but this does not give answers, it just asks more questions. What if we don't get the money back, if he has spent it or it is hidden away? We, WE, ladies and gentlemen,' he paused, 'have a bill, a loan in fact of £50,000 to repay if I read this correctly. How does the committee that allowed this fiasco to take place, intend to do that if the man is not caught and the money found?'

It was silent in the rehearsal room. Polly James had wanted to ask the same question. Anyone with any accountancy skills, or any business sense come to that, would have said what Dick had just said. Pat started to answer, but Brian stood up and interrupted him. His voice was quiet.

'I am the person to answer you Dick, and the rest of the choir as I owe you all an explanation. For many years I have suffered from bouts of depression and I am sure some of you will have noticed that from time to time I have been absent from the choir.'

He paused and looked across at his wife, who was sat at the back of the room. She smiled at him, tears welling in her eyes.

Brian continued, 'I was diagnosed as having a bipolar depressive condition two years ago and I am sure you will all know that this gives highs and lows which thankfully these days can be kept under control with medication. This is something I have battled with the wonderful support of my wife Helen and I wonder sometimes how she was able to put up with my dreadful mood swings. You will probably remember that last Christmas I was out of the way for quite a long time. The reason was that I had a very low period, which was brought on by some sort of kidney infection. I even missed your Rotary Carols in the Cathedral. It was about that time that David Honey called Helen and said that he needed to pop around to see me. I don't remember too much but I know he got me to sign some forms. I can see now, looking back, that these were some type of bank mandates, which obviously gave him the necessary accreditation to access all the choir monies. I should have known better, I should not have signed anything, but, he was very convincing and I am so very sorry that I allowed him to trick me.'

The rehearsal room full of choir members was quiet. Rona looked up at Brian with affection and sadness in her eyes.

Helen was in tears at the back of the room. She remembered all too well the visit from that smarmy man and how he had just needed 'a couple of signatures' from her husband. He could then 'sort out some choir business so that Brian need not be bothered with it, until he felt better.'

Pat Nicholls stood up. 'Thank you Brian for your honesty with all of us here tonight. I am sure that it was extremely difficult for you to stand in front of us and share such personal information with us. Looking at the faces of the choir members here tonight as you spoke, I am sure we all understand that Honey simply took advantage of you in a truly despicable way. We are dealing here with a man of considerable experience when it comes to manoeuvring people without them knowing it. I know that I speak for the choir when I tell you there is no one here who holds you in any way responsible for this situation. You were vulnerable Brian, and you have explained to us why that was. Honey saw that and used it to his advantage. Words cannot describe how we all feel about him and his actions.'

'Hear hear!' shouted Alan Younger from the tenor section. He started to clap and the whole room responded, the applause went on for a long time, some people even stood up.

Pat held his hand up to continue, he could see that Brian was not in a fit state to lead the meeting until he had regained his composure. Pat said: 'We should also thank you Dick for asking the question of the committee, of which I am a member, and it was I who took over the chair at the start of the year when Brian was absent through illness. None of us had any idea that Honey was setting up the accounts to allow him the launder the money. This was a question, Dick, that needed to be asked and we all share the responsibility of being tricked by a very devious man. As for the recovery of the money and paying back the loans, as explained, Mellyn Fyfield has generously let us have the £6,500 to give to the Hospice and the presentation will go ahead this week. As

Brian told you, the additional £2,000 is a gift on behalf of her and Len, a thank you for the years of pleasure they gained from his membership in the bass section. We will have to repay the Hospice donation to Mellyn when we can, and no time limit has been set on this, as is the case with all of the money loaned. I spoke to Lord Williton this afternoon. He is chairman of the Police Authority and has very generously lent the choir £10,000 and is a personal friend of two of our singers. He also made it very clear to me that through our conductor's connections with the Cornwall Music Festival, of which he is patron, and the tremendous success Gavin has made of the workshop on Saturday, he feels that this choir, and its conductor are a great asset to the musical heritage of this county. I think we should all take pride in the way Gavin is appreciated across Cornwall in musical circles.'

Dominic glanced across at Polly and blew her a kiss.

Pat then explained to the choir that a massive UK-wide hunt was being carried out to find David Honey and bring him to justice. Lord David Williton was in touch with the chief constable of the county and a London-based specialist police fraud team had now been brought in.

'It appears that he is wanted for other fraudulent activities in East Anglia and Wales. Laura Honey told Gavin that he had emptied her bank account of several thousand pounds as well. Fraud is not an area that I deal with in the courts but I have spoken to specialists in my Chambers and they tell me that, in their view, the police have a very good track record in these types of cases. It is a complex area, but in this world of computerised accounts there are actually fewer places where money can be hidden away. The police have called a press conference tomorrow at their headquarters in Verlis. Brian will attend as our chairman to answer any media questions about the choir. As Brian said, you are bound to be asked by the press or your friends and neighbours about this over the next few days as it will no doubt be THE Cornwall news story. I cannot tell you what to say, and wouldn't even try, but

I would suggest,' Pat paused in the hope that Verlis Singers members might take notice, 'that if you do talk to any media you should stress about how convincing David Honey was and how everyone connected to The Verlis Singers is disappointed and devastated by what has happened. Brian will explain at the press conference that the choir is still going to Krakow for the Choral Festival and that there have been generous loans from a number of choir supporters in Cornwall to make this happen. He will also tell the media that the choir will still be making a donation of £6,500 to the Hospice this week as planned. Again, this is through the wonderful support of a choir friend. No names will be divulged of the people who are coming to the rescue of the choir and I would ask you please to treat the information you have heard tonight as confidential. There is supposed to be no such thing as bad publicity, we are told, so we'll have to see. If his devious face is flashed across TV screens and appears in the national press we are told that does vastly increase the chance of someone spotting him and an arrest following. This has to be best for The Verlis Singers and increases the chances of getting our money back. I suggest, Brian and Gavin, that we leave it at that and now hand back over to the conductor. Rona will be sending out the final itineraries this week to those of you who are on the tour. We have two more rehearsals before we set off to Poland. Let's carry the flag for Cornwall and show the people of Poland and the other countries represented what the famous Verlis Singers are made of.'

Gavin then called the break. When the choir returned to their seats and normal rehearsal places, it was obvious that no one really had a great enthusiasm for singing, least of all the conductor. At 9am, 30 minutes before the official end, Gavin said, 'It has been a very difficult evening for all of you, but well done again for representing the West of England so brilliantly last evening on *Songs of Praise*, you were brilliant. Let's call it a night!'

Chapter 27

Rona was working out the final itinerary for the Poland tour at home on her computer. After all the comings and goings of the past few days she had lost much of her enthusiasm for the tour but Monday's rehearsal had put her in a far more positive frame of mind. They were definitely going so she must catch up on the preparations and concentrate on making it a smoothly organised choir visit to Poland.

Dick Wilson had been perfectly right to question the committee, she accepted that, and she was as much to blame as anyone for pushing 'that bloody man' forward as treasurer. Brian's sad admission about his mental health had certainly focused the choir members present on the situation. She did not want to think what would happen if Honey was not found; she had decided in her own mind that the money (or most of it) would be returned to the choir.

She focused on the job in hand, the tour itinerary, meticulous planning and daily schedules, something she was very good at. The final payments had been made and travel schedules, rooming lists, etc., had to be resolved. All of the people had been reminded to take some Polish zloty currency as not all restaurants, it seemed, accepted euros. The accommodation in Krakow was organised by the Krakow Choral Association but the visit to Rzeszon had proved more difficult. Tatania's former choir had not been able to offer hosting to all the Verlis choir party so Rona had booked 12 people into hotels with the help of Tatania's sister who lived in the Polish town. They had found a reasonably priced hotel, but she had to book mostly single rooms as all the doubles in the hotel were not available. Fortunately it was close to the church where they would perform the Sunday evening concert so no coaches were needed to get the hotel people to and from the church; they would be able to walk the short distance.

The appearance of David Honey's smarmy face on National TV News and all across the media had certainly set tongues wagging in Cornwall after it appeared the previous evening. The story was featured heavily on both the regional ITV and BBC TV 6.30pm news and the BBC had even included it in their 6pm national news programme. Sympathy was with the choir he had unscrupulously ripped off, as well as the increasing number of other people and organisations whose names were coming to light. All of them had fallen for his deceit and cunning.

The TV reports told how, in his early 20s, he had worked in the city and conned an international bank out of millions of pounds. It described him as 'one of the first people to discover the black art of hacking into unprotected accounts which held massive amounts of money. He was a brilliant but highly dangerous fraudster.' He preyed on vulnerable people, the report had said. His smiling charming face had been shown, but no reference was made to Laura in any of the reports. Brian, as chairman, had been put forward for interview at a press conference called by the Verlis Police. Pat Nicholls advised Gavin to stay away as he said that the choir chairman should be seen as the face of the choir on this occasion.

Rona had received many calls at home, some from Cornish newspapers and even a couple from the national press. Her response had been very short and sharp, stating that she had nothing to add to the statement of The Verlis Singers chairman Brian McNeil, and that was all she would say. Rona Hancock knew how to be blunt and put people in their place, and even news-hungry national journalists would not, *not* manipulate her!

Brian had come across on TV as a rather sad bumbling figure at the press conference and Rona had realised that Pat and Gavin had deliberately stood back to put the choir chairman in the firing line.

Pat Nicholls had been in the choir for a good number of years but over the last few months his presence had certainly been noticed. Rona had come to realise that he obviously had some considerable influence with the Trenholms and how their wealth was managed. There were also some rumours going around the choir that the little cottage where Gavin now lived was owned by them. She was not entirely happy about the way Pat had taken over the choir rehearsal on Monday and acted as if he were in the high court, leading the choir members like a jury to agree with him.

The Verlis Singers were going through a period of great change. It was not just about the Honey fiasco, but it went far deeper than that. Gavin was starting to become the celebrity conductor and she feared that this would eventually distract from *her* choir, The Verlis Singers. She had been through this before with the founder conductor and to a certain extent that bossy woman, Heather Strong. *Please, not again*, she thought.

Gavin's recent appearances on TV, his Sunday morning radio show on BBC Radio Cornwall (she didn't listen to it as she preferred Radio 4), the clamour of attention by people like Heather Strong, and even Isaac Grenfell's son David all caused her concern.

David Grenfell hated The Verlis Singers. It was he who had demanded that absolutely no mention of the choir would be made at the memorial service of his father a few years back.

Things were not good, Rona knew that there could be change and bad feeling ahead. For now, however, getting the choir to Poland was the project to concentrate her mind and energies on.

Room allocations were first priority. Two weeks ago, putting the names of a certain single brazen soprano and a pretty single tenor together in a shared twin room would have meant a phone call to the chairman and much heated debate.

Rona's dog Duffy had padded into the room, tail wagging and panting; he snuggled down under the desk between her feet in his basket, his favourite position. Rona's sister and daughter Ruthie were coming down to look after him whilst Rona was in Poland. They would stay at her house in Verlis whist she was away.

'Oh sod it,' said Rona out loud, and Duffy's ears twitched on hearing her voice.

She keyed in:

Shared Double Rooms, Olive Hotel Krakow

Dominic Gordon and Polly Jones

***

That afternoon Gavin had the studio booked at the Radio Cornwall office in Verlis; he had already planned the order for his show the following Sunday which would go out pre-recorded on this occasion whilst he was away.

He had received a call on Tuesday morning from Ingrid Steel, the station's news editor, and they had discussed at length how the breaking of the Honey story should be dealt with. Obviously the station had to follow it and it was of major local and national interest. They had recorded an interview with the choir chairman and that went out in the main Tuesday evening drive-time show.

Gavin agreed that he would refer to it during his Sunday show but it would only be a passing comment. It was possible that Honey might be caught whilst he was in Poland and that could affect how the ongoing story would develop over the next few days. Ingrid agreed that she would call Gavin in Poland and would speak to him if there were any developments and they needed to interview someone.

Meanwhile they would follow the story with the Cornwall police press office. She did explain that as Gavin presented their Sunday show that made an obvious link with the listening audience:

'We have to be seen to be treating this and every other story without bias, but I am sure that everyone's sympathy is with you and all the other people this devious man manipulated,' she told Gavin.

***

Lizz and Jenny were meeting for a coffee in the Cathedral restaurant on Wednesday afternoon. The original plan had been to discuss choices of clothing for Krakow, shoe selection and other such vital matters. The revelations of the past few days and Monday's rehearsal had put a far more serious slant on discussions. Jenny had told Lizz that she knew of Honey's disappearance last week, as all the committee had been told by either Gavin, Brian or Rona. They were sworn to secrecy and she hadn't even told her husband.

Now, of course, the truth was out. The whole world seemed to know after the Honey face appeared across the media and the story was national news. Lizz said, 'Olag told me that the choir were the talk of the offices and his colleagues. He couldn't understand how the committee had been tricked. I didn't tell him about Brian's quite moving explanation. He is a tough businessman and certainly would not understand such things as human frailty.'

They both agreed that Laura had been a victim of his evil ways.

'They are a very private couple,' said Jenny. 'When I invited them to dinner I felt that she really wanted to come but refused for some other reason I could not understand at the time.'

Lizz replied, 'Now I think I see it, I guess when you live in a world of lies and deceit, the last thing you want is to be in on an open discussion where people may ask questions that might catch you out.'

Lizz Ozroy was a highly intelligent woman. Jenny had not seen it in that way before. She smiled at her friend.

'Of course Lizz, you are right. Well, we'll be on that coach in a few days. I have been looking at Krakow on the Internet. It is a lovely place, do you know that they have white horse-drawn carriages doing tours around the old town? Shall we splash out and go on one?'

'Let's do that,' replied Lizz. 'It will be my treat.'

'Perhaps a certain choir conductor, one Mr Gavin James, might like to come with us. If you don't mind me playing gooseberry, Jenny?'

Lizz blushed and they both laughed. Lizz reached out and held Jenny's hand.

'I'm so glad I joined the choir and met you, Jenny, you really have become a very special friend. I hope I don't lead you astray.' It was Jenny Dalton's turn to go red. She leaned forward and said quietly: 'There's something else Lizz. I have had a letter from Laura Honey. It arrived yesterday. She says how devastated she is by what happened and is now living with her parents, somewhere near Norwich I think. She is obviously very low and confused and I think I should not tell the choir about the letter. I do think it's better to just keep it to myself, but I wanted to ask your advice. What do you think I should do?'

Lizz thought for a while, taking a sip from the glass of sparkling water she had ordered.

'I agree, Jenny, don't tell anyone. She sent the letter to you at your home. Best to keep it between just you and me. There's enough going on around the Honey name and I don't think it would do any good to give people any more to gossip about.'

'Thanks Lizz,' said Jenny. 'I'll take your wise advice. Now, what clothes are you taking on the trip to Poland? I have looked at the weather forecast for June, it could be really hot!'

Chapter 28

Thursday June 16th

There was a big turnout for the 6.45am departure at Verlis coach park that morning. Wives, families, husbands and dogs were everywhere. Terry Davies' crazy dog Brutus had taken a dislike to Rona's even dafter mongrel Duffy, although Rona's niece Ruthie and Joan Davies did their best to keep the two animals apart.

Accompanist Sheila Stirton had even come in especially to wave the choir off. Her daughter's baby had not yet arrived, although she expected the call any day now. The Verlis Singers were a lovely choir that had played a major part in her life these past years and she really liked the talented Becky Morris. When they came back from Poland she should step aside as accompanist and tell Gavin. It would be wrong to lose the talents of Becky.

***

Richard Parish arrived by taxi at the coach park. He had added his name at the last minute, taking advantage of the vacated places booked by David and Laura Honey. He had even asked Rona if he could get a discount as they had paid for their place. Needless to say he got a blunt response from the honorary secretary!

'They have not PAID for anything, how can you say that after what happened? You will send the full fee Roger, today if you want to come. Gavin seems to think that you are an asset to the bass section and I hope that you know all the pieces we will sing.'

Even more annoyingly, because the Honeys had a double room, the oversized bass was to get a room to himself. Rona had considered rearranging the rooming schedules but, on the advice of Brian, had reluctantly agreed to allocate him the double room previously given to the Honeys.

'Keep it simple Rona,' Brian had told her. 'Don't make any extra work for yourself. If Gavin wants him in the choir as a singer, let's just go with the flow. It's just not worth the hassle, goodness knows we've had enough of that these past couple of weeks.'

***

The last minute arrival of Dominic and Polly at the coach park in a taxi caused quite a stir and disapproving glances from certain members of the tour party. They were both wearing bright yellow T-shirts with the words 'I'm a Verlis Virgin' emblazoned on the back in large black letters. Rona immediately walked over to where Brian was saying his farewells to Helen McNeil. He knew exactly what to expect and didn't give her a chance to start!

'Come on, Rona, we need to have the fun element. OK they are a bit naughty, but those two will keep everyone amused that's for sure. Let it go, there's been enough doom and gloom these past days after all. We need some fun and those two crazy young people will help to provide it, *and* don't overlook the fact that they seem very pally with His Lordship. His £10,000 loan made a big difference, and he is a very good man to have on our side, best not to forget that either. I wonder if, when we get back from Poland, we should invite him to become a Patron of the choir?'

The one thing that a choir conductor soon learns is that when you take your group away from home, they all of a sudden transform to become something rather similar to a class of primary school children on a zoo trip, and very small children at that! Rona Hancock however, was well equipped to take on the role of a bossy teacher, in charge and armed with her clipboard as tour leader. She was back at the coach door ticking names off on her lists from the moment people started to arrive at the coach park.

***

Bristol airport was busy at around 11 o'clock when the members of The Verlis Singers tour party arrived for their Thursday early afternoon flight to Krakow. There had been a short 'comfort-stop' at the Exeter services and the roads had been pretty clear. Stag and hen parties were everywhere in the departure hall, with groups heading off for the weekend to celebrate at various European cities.

As they queued to go through security, Richard Parish whispered in Taff Davies's ear, 'Taff, look over there, I think that's David Honey. The scheming bastard is fleeing the country!'

The man that Richard was pointing to was a very tall man in Muslim Thobe and headscarf, with a very long bushy beard. He was surrounded by Asian children.

'Richard, sod off!' Taff was angry. 'Sometimes your jokes are fucking out of place. Do yourself a favour and keep that man's name OUT of your stupid banter this weekend or you could be in big trouble. People do NOT want to hear it!'

***

Checking in and boarding the early afternoon flight from Bristol to Krakow was fairly stress-free and the Captain even welcomed 'The famous Verlis Singers' to everyone else on the flight. Thankfully he didn't mention to the other passengers the fact that part of the reason they were famous was because their ex-treasurer had ripped them off for 80,000 pounds and had featured all over the national news a couple of weeks previously.

The choir had heard nothing from the police since the TV news story broke. The day before leaving, Pat Nicholls had called Lord David Williton for an update and to see if there were any positive reports to pass on to the choir.

'Nothing to tell you I'm afraid,' Lord Williton had told Pat. 'There were many so-called 'sightings' after his face appeared across the national media and I am told that some of them were quite good leads, especially some in London where he seems to have contacts. All we can do is leave it in the hands of the fraud squad now. One thing is for sure, that devious bastard will have changed his appearance to try and not be caught. The fraud squad know what they are dealing with. I am pretty confident they will find him. I know that Interpol are also involved and all ports and airports are being watched. The boys in blue seem to think he is still in the UK so, from that, I am hoping they really do have a positive lead. If there is any news while you are in Poland I will call you Pat, straight away. You can rest assured of that, meanwhile have a great time and tell that lovely Miss Polly James and her pretty friend to behave themselves, although somehow I doubt they will!'

Pat Nicholls QC and his wife had attended a Masonic highbrow dinner in May. He had been astounded to see the Grand Master, Lord Williton, with the tall, elegantly dressed, long-legged Polly James on his arm. They certainly seemed to be very friendly. Perhaps the rumours that Lord David 'batted for the other team' were not true after all, even if he was old enough to be her father. She had certainly turned a few heads that night and David Wilson seemed very fond of her.

***

Gavin had spent quite a lot of time in the week before the tour researching the other choirs on the Internet that were taking part in the Krakow Choral Festival. He had not been surprised to discover that some of them were good, frighteningly good in fact. One was a University Choir from the Philippines who had won a number of big awards around the world including the National Eisteddfod at Llangollen. They were going to be very special, he suspected.

Verlis were the only English choir; the others were from Germany, Norway, Finland, Sweden, and many from Poland itself. The Verlis Singers had entered one competition class singing sacred songs on the Saturday and would sing at the concerts on Thursday, Friday and Saturday with the other choirs. The programme had been published on the Choral Festival's website the week before.

The Verlis Singers choice of songs was shown with a photograph of the choir in Verlis Cathedral taken the day of the *Songs of Praise* recording when, thankfully, David Honey was not present, although Laura was standing smiling in the front row.

Category A (Sacred Class)

Beati Quorum Via – Charles Villiers Stanford

The Long Day Closes – Sullivan

For the Beauty of the Earth – John Rutter

Dear Lord and Father of Mankind – Bob Chilcott

Category D (Concert Programme)

Linden Lea – Vaughan Williams

My Delight and thy Delight – Hubert Parry

The Londonderry Air – Bob Chilcott

Cantilena – Karl Jenkins

Gavin had to stick to the eight pieces submitted, the Festival had made that very clear in the strict notes that had been sent out to all participating choir conductors. No last-minute changes at the whim of the conductor were allowed!

The Verlis Singers also had set rehearsal schedules. These were at a university, which appeared to be in the centre of the old town of Krakow where the festival took place and within walking distance of their hotel. The instructions also made it clear that rehearsal times must be adhered to.

Reading the programmes chosen by the other choirs Gavin soon twigged that they would all be singing some very complex pieces. Most of the European contemporary composers were unknown to Gavin James, however he felt sure that his choir would hear some pretty spectacular singing in Krakow. He wondered how they would cope with performing alongside choirs who would probably be technically superior to them.

Each choir had its photograph in the programme, from which it was obvious that most comprised younger singers, and, most likely, music students. The standard was going to be extremely high and Gavin wondered if he should have included one more technically demanding piece. But that was not what The Verlis Singers were about. They were a concert choir that entertained audiences and that is what the only English choir in the festival would try to do in Krakow. Anyway it was too late now to change things.

His choice had been UK composers only, in both categories. Gavin knew that The Verlis Singers would not win any awards against what appeared to be a number of highly talented music groups. If they entertained their audiences, that would be an achievement in itself in such company.

The plane from Bristol touched down on time, the sun shining on a beautiful day in Poland. With the advantage of the time zone's hour gain, it was about 3pm in Poland and a sizzling hot summer afternoon. Krakow airport was a bit basic to say the least and they were met on arrival by a smiling young woman from the Choral Festival wearing a green sash saying *Proszł Bardzo,* which Tatania told them was *Most Welcome* in Polish.

Tatania was obviously enjoying speaking to the young woman in her home language. They sat at the front of the coach together after it was loaded up with all the cases and they chatted throughout the 30-minute drive into the town. Tatania was very excited at being back in her home country, with the visit to her hometown of Rzeszon to look forward to on Sunday, where they would be met by her sister Lena and all the family.

The Verlis group were staying at a hotel in the old town called The Olive and many of the choir members were texting home with safe arrival news to loved ones back in the UK.

Hey Joan – the Welsh eagle has landed – coach trip went well and a good flight and we even got a mention over the air – just on the coach to the hotel now and everyone is happy. Lots of singing today TVS will show em .. Give B a kick and remind him he has no balls – bloody 50 next week but with the body of a 30 year old ... you are Mrs Lucky ..luv Tx

They had a rehearsal booked in later that afternoon at 6pm and the concert later in the evening. During the coach journey to the hotel, many of the Verlis choir were planning their Thursday evening, out exploring the town, following the concert sing, with Polly and Dominic as self-appointed guides, assisted by Tatania and Becky Morris who had already bought a city centre map at the airport.

Becky announced on the coach that she and Polly were up for anything that night after the concert when a shout came from the back where the Trenholms were eating a pasty from their food stash.

'Count Ron and me in Becky, Ron wants to try out the Polish beer!'

Before they filed off the coach Gavin went to the front to speak to everyone:

'Well, happy landings folks, can you noisy lot in back hear me? Here we are then and Rona will sign you all in, but I just wanted to remind you that this evening we are singing two of our sacred pieces at a concert in a church which is close to the hotel. It's a tight schedule on our first day but I think that after we have sung we may be able to leave the church. We have a short rehearsal first booked at 6pm and someone from the Festival will meet the choir in the foyer at 5.30 to walk us to the rehearsal room. Please wear your uniforms as we will then go to the church after our rehearsal. Verlis groupies (our non-singers) obviously do not have to come to the rehearsal, although you will be very welcome, and we hope to see you at the concert to cheer us on. It starts at 8pm and I think I am right in saying the there are five choirs singing tonight. We are third on. The church name and details are all in Rona's itinerary, which you all have. Remember please that Rona and my mobile numbers are there just in case you need to need to ask anything. We are doing *Beati Quorum* and the Rutter, *Beauty of the Earth* tonight at the concert so you will play for the Rutter piece Becky. Ok folks, off we get and Rona will sort out your rooms.'

Rona then jumped off the coach and marched in front of the choir members with the guide and Tatania to oversee the distribution of room cards. The men of the choir were supervising the unloading of the cases and bags from the hold of the coach. As the members of The Verlis Singers waited to be called forward by the hon. sec. in the hotel lobby to collect their room cards, Polly whispered in Lizz's ear, 'I have you and Jenny down for the tour of the town later this evening, I'm sure you'll be pleased to know that our conductor is going to join us!'

***

When the choir had originally signed up for the festival, Rona had pencilled in a possible coach tour to the Salt Mines on the Friday morning. After consulting with Brian she had been able to cancel this without losing any money after Honey took all the funds. The choir had also taken their names from the welcome party on Thursday evening. Rona got the feeling that this was over-subscribed as the Festival people did not quibble when asked if they could drop out as they would not arrive in Krakow till mid-afternoon. That saved another £650 from their festival fee as they charged £12.50 per person to attend. These amounts had been included of course in the original charges paid by the choir members, with the subsidy added in. No one had queried this, but Rona knew that when they got back many people in The Verlis Singers would be scrutinising the figures, very carefully!

All of the money loaned had therefore not been used and Rona was dreading the first committee meeting back in Verlis when financial matters would have to be addressed. It was going to be a nightmare to unravel, that was obvious. The payment to the festival was around £3,000 less than originally anticipated and Brian had agreed that this was a very sensible decision and a quick ring around to committee members the week before had confirmed it.

'We get to save a bit of money Rona, and the choir will understand in the circumstances. It was good of the Festival people to allow us to cancel at such short notice.'

Rona said: 'Goodness knows what our finances will look like Brian when we get back. We now have the BBC *Songs of Praise* cheque in plus some spare festival money so that does mean that we have about £4,000 in the new bank account.'

Brian had suggested that Polly James should be asked to join the committee to oversee the finances in the short term.

'You know Rona that she is very well thought of at one the biggest accountants in Cornwall. She has only been there a few months and I understand is about to be promoted. She also happens to be very close to Lord David Williton who lent us the £10,000. According to Pat, Polly goes out to some quite posh functions on the arm of His Lordship these days.'

This suggestion had NOT gone down well with the honorary secretary.

The rehearsal room was at the university, which was close to the hotel, and a smart rather austere lady from the Festival Committee was waiting for them to gather in the hotel foyer at 4.30. Tatania and Rona introduced Gavin to her and she informed them, with Tatania interpreting as she spoke little English, that they had a short walk to their allocated 45-minute rehearsal room. Chairman Brian had decided to join them with Ron Trenholm for their first rehearsal in Poland. The Verlis group didn't know it but their chairman had other plans for the Friday and Saturday.

Gavin had been given the updated concert schedule by the Festival lady and saw that the Philippine student choir were singing before them that evening. A choir from Poland were first out and The Verlis Singers were choir number three. Six choirs would perform at this concert with the twelve other choirs performing at different churches around Krakow.

The choir members had settled into their rooms and tidied up after the journey from Verlis. They were in high spirits and set off from the hotel led by the Festival lady, holding an umbrella aloft so everyone could see her. The streets were very busy with many tourists meandering along and enjoying the beautiful weather. The umbrella prompted a song and dance from Polly and Dominic who were walking arm in arm. Their impromptu rendition of *Singing in the Rain* earned a disapproving frown from the Festival lady and the honorary secretary!

***

As they arrived at the university the rehearsal room was on the first floor and another choir were filing out of the main door. Richard Parish shook hands with them all individually saying '*czesc*', the Polish word for 'hello', loudly. 'Richard!' shouted Tatania from the front of the choir. 'Try Halla!' They are a choir from Sweden. Everyone laughed and Richard started going back through the whole group saying 'Halla' instead.

'Don't get too friendly, Richard, you might have to buy them all a drink later on. Your Cornish fiver will soon run out!' shouted Taff Davies. Everyone laughed as Gavin ushered them into the rehearsal room.

***

After the early start, the coach journey from Verlis, flight and bus into Krakow, the brushed up and showered members of The Verlis Singers understandably were not particularly in the right mood for a choir rehearsal. Becky was sat at a Steinway grand piano in the corner of the rehearsal room and Gavin ran through the opening bars of some of the pieces. Realising that he was not getting the full concentration of the choir, he called a halt after just 30 minutes.

'It's 6.30 now and I suggest we all meet outside the university at 7.30pm to be taken to the church where we sing this evening. I'll see you all later.' Lizz went up to Gavin. 'Come on, Gavin, Jenny and I are going for a drink, come with us. Let's find a nice coffee bar to relax in and enjoy the sun.'

The choir members duly returned to the university entrance where the Festival umbrella lady appeared, to lead them to the nearby St Mary's Basilica, which was very close to the busy main square of the town. As they wandered through the bustling streets to the church some of the choir were making plans to hire one of the many eight-seater tourist golf buggies the next morning, which seemed to be everywhere. Eric Stroman was taking down names for a trip to a Jewish quarter and the Schindler Factory.

On arrival at the church, the brightly coloured young women from the Philippine University Choir were all outside chatting excitedly. They were wearing traditional red long-sleeved dresses with layers of coloured beads. The young men looked equally stunning in blue dress coats and red shirts. 'I hope they don't sing as good as they look,' Jenny Dalton said to Lizz.

The Verlis singers were wearing their choir concert uniforms, the ladies in black dresses with turquoise scarves and the men in dinner suits. Most men had by now taken off their jackets during the walk from the hotel and the rehearsal room, as the temperature was well into the 30s that afternoon.

Gavin and Rona went ahead into the church with the umbrella lady to sign The Verlis Singers in. Taff Davies meanwhile, was testing his chatting up skills on some of the giggling Philippine young girls. 'Try some Welsh Taff, you might have more success,' hollered Richard Parish across from the other side of the steps outside the church as Rona appeared at the entrance and called them all to come in.

The concert was to start at 8pm and Verlis were third on. It was a massive high ceiling, a beautiful gothic styled building and at the far end in front of the magnificent wooden altarpiece, a stage had been erected. The Verlis group trooped in and were shown seats at the back, they were followed in by the Philippine University Choir. The church seemed full of mostly singers, with just a handful of supporters or tourists who had wandered in to get into the shade and away from the searing heat outside.

The first choir out were a jazz-styled group of around 50 young people led by a dynamic young female conductor. They were amazing and The Verlis Singers sat agog as they performed two unaccompanied pieces, which included a highly complicated arrangement of the Beatles song *Eleanor Rigby*, brilliantly delivered.

If the jazz choir were very good the Philippine University Choir who sang next were in an entirely different league altogether. For their first song the young women sat in a semi-circle with the men standing behind them. The piece was called *Hallelujah*. Gavin had never heard such a beautiful singing in all of his life. The richness of the young bass voices sent shivers down his spine. The freshness of the soprano voices was staggering as they soared effortlessly around top As and even B flat. This was choral singing in an entirely different league, and next out, following them would be, The Verlis Singers from Cornwall.

Gavin had chosen to start with the lovely Stanford *Beati Quorum Via*, an unaccompanied piece that they had sung many times before. It was a total disaster. The sopranos have the opening first lines with the altos complementing them. After only eight bars the alto line had dragged down the pitch. Gavin was lost; his choir was out of control. Thankfully Dominic was standing by Philip Stokes who was also singing tenor. They were both such good musicians and they knew that the pitch was sliding and tried gallantly to push the chording back into some form of harmony.

Gavin was sweating profusely as he desperately tried to keep his choir together. He even fancied he heard sniggers from the student German choir who were sitting in the front church pews just behind them waiting to sing next. Gavin slowed the choir down and concentrated on the top line of sopranos. Thankfully, Clare and Claire also responded, but by the time they had reached the final phrase they had dropped almost a full tone, a fact that 99% of the audience sat behind him in the pews and the other choirs would all be aware of. The applause was sympathetic and Gavin tried to smile at his choir to give them some confidence. Peggy Trenholm beamed back. She thought that they had sung perfectly.

The second piece was John Rutter's *For the Beauty of the Earth,* which was accompanied with an 8-bar piano introduction. Surely this couldn't go wrong? Becky Morris was a brilliant accompanist who never made a mistake, that is until playing the introduction to the well-known John Rutter anthem at the Krakow Choral Festival on Friday June 16, 2011. Gavin could not believe his ears and his face clearly showed his amazement when Becky played a very obvious wrong note on bar six. Her friend Claire looked as if she would burst into tears but thankfully Clare, Jenny, Polly and the other sopranos sang out strongly and the choir managed (just) to get to the end of the piece without too many more disasters.

Gavin could see that Becky had gone ashen white at the end of the piece and she seemed in a trance sat at the piano. Rushing over to her, he put his hand on her shoulder. 'Come on Becky, I'm taking you and the rest of the girls for a drink. Forget what happened, let's look forward to tomorrow and doing better when we've all had a good night's sleep and a Friday morning to relax.'

***

Lizz went across to Gavin after they had left the stage to sympathetic applause and smirks from some of the young singers from competing choirs who were in the audience.

'Hey Gavin, come on, we will all do much better tomorrow for you, I promise. Come on let's go and find a bar and have a drink. It's my treat, you deserve it.'

Lizz leaned forward and kissed him gently on the cheek, saying quietly, 'Please don't show the rest of the choir how disappointed you are, Gavin. Now's the time to be our leader, our very special man. We all love you. Don't go back to the church to hear the rest of the choirs. Pack away your music in your briefcase and come with the rest of us. The social side of the choir being away together is so important after the horrendous last few weeks, you know that Gavin, don't you?'

None of The Verlis Singers were going to stay in the church to hear the next three choirs. Enough was certainly enough for one day and as they gathered outside the despondency and low spirits were obvious. Most of the members of The Verlis Singers realised how badly they had performed and also how amazingly good the other two choirs before them had sung.

***

Peggy had her arms around Becky who was crying uncontrollably. 'Hey, hey Becky my love,' said Peggy. 'Come here and have a good old cry. You'll feel better. That Dominic and Polly and the rest of the young ones are going out for a few drinks I think. If you want, come back to the hotel with Ron and me. He's determined to try all of the Polish beers on the way back. I might need you to help me carry him back to the hotel.'

Even Brian the chairman, who had sat through the experience in the audience, realised that actually The Verlis Singers from Cornwall were not the best choir at the Festival. But they certainly knew how to enjoy themselves and let their hair down. And, after all, he had a very special breakfast meeting to look forward to the next day.

After such a depressing performance, a few of the group seemed keen to join Polly and Dominic on their pub crawl. Phillip Stokes, Gayle Bidden and Tatania were determined to drown their sorrows with the crazy couple out in front and they set off in the direction of the bustling town square. June and Alan Younger and Tony Bridges took charge of steering Clare, the Trenholms and the rest of the choir in the right direction of the hotel. Jenny, Lizz and Gavin were towards the rear of the group and as they strolled along, Lizz slipped her arm through Gavin's.

Walking behind them were Eric and Karen Stroman with Taff Davies. All three of them observed the arm linking. 'There's something definitely going on with those two,' Karen said. The two tenors for once chose not to comment.

'I'm going to text Mrs Davies when we get back to the hotel,' said Terry. 'I bet Brutus is missing the master of the house.'

When they got back Lizz and Jenny opted for an early night. Pat Hardwick, Brian and Gavin decided that a nightcap was required at the hotel bar. Peggy and Ron Trenholm tottered in with Becky a little later who looked very drunk.

'Had a good night folks?' asked Gavin.

They all beamed back at the Verlis conductor and Ron replied, red-faced and slightly slurred, 'Brilliant, Gavin! This Polish beer puts hairs on your chest. It's almost as good as my home brew and I tell you what, young Becky almost drank me under the table! Come on bird, let's get off to that big double bed.' Gavin smiled, all that unpleasantness about Ron not joining the tour had been ridiculous. They were obviously having a happy time and they deserved it for many reasons.

Chapter 29

Gavin had got up very early and gone for a wander into the town. It was another beautiful clear morning in Krakow and the street cleaners were out preparing the city for the tourists. He needed to clear his head and concentrate on pulling the Verlis Singers back together. Perhaps he should have worked the choir harder at the rehearsal and not let them all go off having fun. From today he would give more thought to the rehearsals and make best use of the time.

He had never visited Poland before, but even after one day realised what a beautiful place Krakow was. The cobbled street and white horse-drawn carriages with their top-hatted girl drivers in their black tailcoats and white jodhpurs perched out the front, the bars and restaurants, and the fact that everything was so inexpensive. He'd like to come back to Krakow one day, perhaps a weekend away with someone special?

When he walked back into the breakfast area at the hotel, Taff Davies was sat on his own at one of the tables. It was 7am and there were no other Verlis folk in sight, all still tucked up in their beds, thought Gavin.

'Come and join me Gavin,' shouted Taff. Gavin smiled and went to the breakfast bar to stock up on cereal and yoghurt and sat down with him.

'A bit of a cock up last night, Gavin, we really let you down in the tenors. He's a big girl's blouse that Dominic, but he is also a brilliant singer and an asset to the choir. We all know that Gavin. I knew that he and young Phil were working hard to get us back in tune, that's the real musicians for you. The rest of us just do our best, you know that.'

Gavin smiled. 'Terry, last night is history. Everyone was very tired after the day's travelling, we really should not have sung last night. But it's easy being wise in hindsight isn't it? Anyway how do you like Krakow? And I bet the lovely Mrs Davies is at home getting everything ready for your big weekend coming up. Thanks for asking me to the big party on Saturday by the way, and I'm looking forward to it. I was going to bring Georgina but decided against it.' He paused.

Terry Davies, never known to be the soul of tact and discretion, jumped straight in:

'You are becoming very fond of Lizz, aren't you Gavin? We can all see it, it's pretty obvious when the two of you are together, the way she looks at you Gavin, she obviously adores you Boyo, we can all see it!'

This was bloke talk, man to man. Up till now, Gavin had not really discussed his feelings with anyone, except perhaps Suzy, his future sister-in-law.

'When Georgina buggered off, Taff, I was pretty shattered you know, and it left me wondering what life was all about. That wasn't helped of course by the shop going tits up but, looking back, I can now see how I let things slide. Well anyway, as I'm sure you know, Georgina has come back into my life and whilst I knew that Lizz was very special, her being married and all that, I just tried to keep my feelings for her bottled up. But I've told Georgina that we are finished Taff, whatever happens between Lizz and me. Being here with her has, sort of, opened the floodgates and now I'm not really sure what to do. You have a lovely wife Terry, you are so happy together and I just envy you that. You and Joan are meant to be and here I am now falling for a married lady, it's all a bit of a mess. I know one thing though Terry, I can't wait to see her walk through that door and come in for breakfast. This conductor is totally smitten Taff.'

Taff smiled; yes he was lucky to have his Joan who had been his lover and pal from the first day they met at school and sat together. Only this morning, she had sent him a text to tell him that everything was going to plan for the next weekend. It seemed that Daniel's parents might also be coming. First chance to meet the new in laws. 'You'll have to be *exceptionally* nice to them Tom Jones or your marital rights will be permanently withdrawn!!!'

Taff looked at the tousle-haired Gavin James, sat eating his yoghurt. 'Well, Gav, I'm not really the wisest person to give you any guidance, but I can see how much you care for each other. It's so bloody obvious. You won't be able to stop that you know. She is an adult, you are an adult, and if she is anything like my Joan she will have already worked out what is going on and will be two steps ahead of you Boyo! But be careful not to get hurt again, won't you?'

***

Members of the Verlis party were starting to arrive and were stacking up their plates at the breakfast bar and chatting away to each other. Richard Parish had befriended an elderly American couple and was telling them jokes. The American lady was roaring with laughter. Taff said to Gavin, 'Parish is onto someone who will buy him drinks all night, did you see them at the bar last night. I bet that famous £5 note hasn't been out of his wallet yet!'

Richard looked across at Taff and Gavin sat together and boomed out to his new bar sponsors, 'That's our conductor over there Mildred, do you know that he's the finest ever conductor in The Verlis Singers all the way from Cornwall?'

Mildred and Henry Talbot Jnr, gun shop proprietors from Ohio, waved across to Gavin James who waved back.

'Big daft bugger,' muttered Taff, and blew Mildred an eggy kiss across the room.

***

Many of the Verlis group were going on a tourist excursion of the town that Friday morning. Eric Stroman had negotiated a deal and four of the eight-seater golf buggies had been booked to arrive at the hotel reception for 11am. Lizz and Jenny had appeared and had joined Taff and Gavin at their breakfast table. Loud laughter continued as the Richard Parish entertainment continued, much to the obvious enjoyment of his new equally large American chums. Peggy and Ron were sat with Pat Nicholls and a rather hung over Becky Morris with Ron in full flow, obviously not at all affected after his introduction to Polish beer. Polly was sat with Clare and Claire as Dominic had not yet surfaced.

'He's still asleep in bed,' said Polly. 'I don't know what time he eventually got in. He started chatting to some young guys and girls in the square who I think were from a German choir. Dom speaks good German and he was definitely getting on rather well with their sexy conductor. I've no idea what time he eventually got in, but it was long after me. I do remember him coming in as I was dozing. He ruffled my hair and pecked me on the cheek and said night, night, I do remember that. He's such a lovely friend. I'm sure he'll appear at breakfast soon.'

***

Brian was sat with Elaine and Tony Bridges. He had asked Tatania to join them for some unknown reason. He had also kept an empty chair at their table, the reason why soon became clear. The Verlis Singers it seemed had acquired a new follower in Krakow. A middle-aged attractive Polish lady had appeared and, spotting Brian, rushed across to embrace the choir chairman. All of the choir turned to stare as Brian and, the lady hugged each other. Rona was sat with Eric and Karen Stroman; the glances exchanged were self-evident.

A gay tenor on the loose and man-hunting long-legged soprano was one thing. Add to that, the blatant developing relationship and frisson between Lizz and Gavin, that was enough in itself. Now the choir chairman was being hugged by a very striking silver-haired elderly Polish woman in full view of the members of The Verlis Singers. Elaine and Tony Bridges were breakfasting with Alan and June Younger.

'I'll bet Helen McNeil is not aware of this,' said Elaine loudly so everyone around her could hear.

'It's like those singles holidays for old farts you read about,' said husband Tony.

'We'll all be getting our car keys out soon and throwing them on the table next,' said Alan.

Tony and Alan sniggered. Elaine and June were not amused.

***

The Verlis Singers gathered on Friday afternoon for their rehearsal.

'There's no point in beating about the bush, we were pretty awful last night,' said Gavin. 'You don't need me to tell you and I suggest that we all put this behind us. We've had a night's sleep, a morning off and a good breakfast so let's look forward. Becky, a chord please?'

Becky smiled across at Gavin and hit the opening notes for *Deep Harmony*. The members of The Verlis Singers all stood up and started to sing.

Sweet is the work, My God, My King... even Pat Nicholls gave of his best.

Gavin worked the choir hard at the rehearsal, going through all of the pieces they were going to perform. He deliberately avoided singing *Beati Quorum Via* until the end of their allotted time.

'Now we will sing *Beati Quorum*, because we have to sing it again tomorrow at the sacred class of the competition. Listen to each other and do not be overawed by the other choirs. Concentrate solely on OUR sound, OUR choir, watch me and imagine you are back home singing it in Verlis Cathedral.' The previous evening the performance of the lovely Stanford motet had been a disaster. Fourteen hours later, in the university rehearsal room, they sang it perfectly.

'Wonderful,' Gavin told them. 'The Verlis Singers have arrived in Krakow. I will see you all later at 6.30pm at the St Mark's Church to sing our concert four pieces.

***

The choir members had free time following the afternoon rehearsal and Polly, Dominic, Becky, Clare, Claire, Phillip Stokes, Phil Hardwick and Gayle Bidden, with Tatania as guide, had all linked arms and were setting off in a long line from the church in the direction of the market square.

'There's Phil with all his grandchildren, how sweet,' Richard Parish said to Pat Nicholls.

'Fancy a beer?' Pat asked Richard.

'I'm very sorry, I can't,' replied a rather hot and sweaty Richard Parish as they stood on the steps outside the church with the afternoon sun beating down on them. 'I'm meeting Henry Jnr and the delightful Mildred at an exclusive restaurant they found yesterday, just off the market square. They want to show me true Ohio hospitality, so I couldn't really refuse could I Pat?'

Pat Nicholls chuckled; Roger Parish was a one-off and a pain in the arse most of the time, but he was a fine bass and, if you sat next to him at rehearsals or concerts, he was one of the mainstays of the bass section. He remembered Len Fyfield once saying to him, 'You know, Pat, Richard Parish would be all at sea without The Verlis Singers. Yes, he's a big buffoon, but underneath all that bluster, he's really a lost little boy who needs the choir in his life. Apart from all that, he has one of the best and richest bass voices that has ever graced The Verlis Singers during my time, and that includes the days when Isaac was conductor.'

***

Gavin didn't recognise the names of three of the other choirs who were taking part in the Friday evening concert but the Philippine students were again due to sing before Verlis, who were number four in the performance order.

Brian and his Polish friend had arrived at the church of St Mark's for the evening concert. Spotting Gavin and Pat together outside, Brian wandered across.

'Barbara, this is our famous conductor Gavin James and our equally celebrated Pat Nicholls, who is a member of the choir and a leading barrister and *great* asset to The Verlis Singers in so many ways. When I worked for Target Printing, I used to come over to Poland regularly to meet our clients. Barbara was the head of marketing and sales at one of our main Polish customers so we became very good friends over the years.'

Barbara smiled and shook hands with Gavin and Pat. In perfect English, she explained that she had relations who live near Krakow and had arranged to stay with them so she could catch up with Brian and all his news.

'I have booked into your hotel this evening and tomorrow night as it is quite a long drive to Kallowice where my sister and her husband live. I am looking forward to hearing your choir sing now and also tomorrow.'

Bloody hell, thought Pat, as he smiled at the very strikingly elegant Polish lady with her silver hair, standing next to the choir chairman who looked rather like the cat who had got the cream. What goes on tour, stays on tour. He hoped all of the Verlis singers knew that unspoken rule!

The choirs were grouped in a massive hall alongside the church of St Mark, waiting to be called to sing. The first choir were a Polish children's group, followed by an elderly choir from Hungary. It was a beautiful afternoon and he gathered the choir around him in the hall as the Philippine students filed into the church to sing their four concert pieces. One thing was for sure, they were going to be amazing and as much as Gavin would have liked to hear them sing, his place was with his choir.

'OK everyone, no nerves, let's go and sing our four pieces as well as we can. This is what we do best, entertain concert audiences. Line up please in your singing positions so we are ready to walk in looking as if we want to sing. Let's sing *and* smile!'

Twenty minutes later, The Verlis Singers trooped in; the Philippine students walked past them back into the hall. The audience applause was deafening, they had obviously been incredibly good. Many of the people in the audience were standing and cheering.

'Bugger me, we've got to follow them,' whispered Taff Davies to Alan Younger.

Dominic heard him. 'Come on Terry, let's show them we have the finest tenor section out of all the choirs. You get your big chance to shine in *Linden Lea!*'

Linden Lea was the first piece and unaccompanied. The Verlis Singers sang it with great enthusiasm and Gavin almost had a tear in his eye as the tenors sang the verse when they took over the solo line. They were brilliant, full of confidence and the rest of the choir knew it. Gavin looked at Lizz in the front row of the altos as they ended the piece to rather loud audience applause and even some cheers from the back of the church where some of the young German choir were sat in the pews to listen.

The Long Day Closes was the next item and Gavin by now was in total command, using the soft passages to great effect. The pitch was good and the toning spot on. Becky sat at the piano and was listening intently. This was really good unaccompanied singing; he knew that the dreadful opening performance the previous evening was forgotten. Verlis were certainly not the best choir technically at the Festival, but at least they were together as a unit and Gavin was in control.

Lizz smiled at the delighted Gavin as they ended, the final phrases so softly sung the audience had to strain to hear them. The applause was even louder, more of the German choir had arrived and were cheering Dominic. The young conductor of the choir looked particularly pleased to see his new tenor friend Dominic singing on the stage with his choir from Cornwall, wherever that was in England.

The final two pieces were accompanied by Becky Morris and were again sung beautifully. As The Verlis Singers ended the Karl Jenkins TV ad arrangement of *Cantilena*, the audience cheered and clapped and the Germans whooped. A success; four songs from UK composers, performed very well to an audience of Polish tourists, supporters from the other choirs and many of the singers from the competing groups.

The concert had gone on till about 10.30 and Brian and his lady friend rushed over to Gavin on the church steps as they all walked out.

'You were wonderful, Mr James, no wonder Brian is proud to be your chairman. I loved all the songs you sang.' Barbara was ecstatic as the choir members all dispersed.

'That's the best I have ever heard you sing Gavin,' said Ron Trenholm. 'I was proud to be Cornish in there. Are you coming back to the hotel as we'd love to buy you a beer, wouldn't we bird?' he said, turning to Peggy.

Gavin said he would as he was desperate to change out of the dress suit he had been wearing since the afternoon rehearsal.

'Great idea Ron; I'll just go and see if Lizz and Jenny want to come back with us.'

As Gavin disappeared to find them, Peggy smiled sweetly and whispered in her husband's ear. 'Oh Ron, he's falling in love with that Lizz. It's so obvious. I do hope she doesn't break his heart.'

***

The Long Day Closes

The Verlis Singers conducted by Gavin James, sing the Sullivan choral classic –recorded in Verlis Methodist Chapel in April 2011.

www.verlis-singers.co.uk

Chapter 30

Saturday June 18th

Gavin had been right, the university choir from the Philippines were spectacular. When The Verlis Singers arrived by coach at the university campus venue for the Saturday competitive sections, they had to rehearse in the same room following the university choir who had left the double doors open so they could be seen and heard. As the Cornish group gathered in the entrance hall, they could hear them practising. To add to their performance, they were now wearing different highly colourful Philippine costumes. They looked absolutely amazing, they sang like no other choir Gavin had ever heard before, and someone in the choir had been told that they had come top in a Worldwide Choir Competition in Scandinavia just a few weeks before. If any member of The Verlis Singers had any doubt about the quality of the competition before, after the past two days in Poland, they did now!

Peggy Trenholm was chatting to Gavin, Terry Davies and Richard Parish. 'Tell you what, Gavin, we ought to get some uniforms like that. I'd love to wear a grass skirt and a flower garland!'

Terry, Pat and Gavin fell apart laughing, good old Peggy.

'Tell you what Peggy, throw your plastic Santa suit and go Hawaiian, that will get English audiences all fired up,' said Richard. Pat's sides were aching. He hadn't laughed so much for years.

Brian McNeil had brought his Polish lady friend along on

341

Saturday and was introducing her to a rather disgruntled-looking Rona. Brian was explaining that he would not be attending the performances that morning but would certainly be at the final concert at the St Catherine Church at 7pm that evening. Watching them from the other side of the hall as they waited to go into the rehearsal room, Polly and Dominic had joined Richard Parish and Pat Nicholls.

Richard said, 'Well the Cornish invaders are certainly doing their bit to extend the hand of friendship as they say in Ireland, some of our team are deffo up for the Krack...ow!'

Dominic Gordon giggled uncontrollably and Polly poked him in the ribs.

***

All of the choirs were taking part in the Saturday morning and afternoon competitive class. It was another searing hot day with temperatures in the mid-30s, far too hot for wearing choir uniforms and singing. There were classes for mixed choirs, male and female groups, children's choirs, and chamber choirs. Everything was supervised by the numerous officials from the festival committee who seemed to be buzzing around everywhere.

As Pat Hardwick observed to Alan Younger, 'They do take this rather too seriously. I'm pretty sure most of our lot would rather be out doing the tourist bit and enjoying the wonderful weather, but we are here to sing so let's bloody well show these European choirs what we are made of.'

The performances were in a huge concert hall with space for a large audience. The Verlis Singers were to follow a choir of rather elderly people from Hungary. Appearances were deceptive and they delivered four beautifully sung rather complex pieces, the final one the haunting *Cantemus* by Lajos Bardos.

The Verlis Singers were to sing all of their sacred pieces, starting with the now rather infamous *Beati Quorum*, the 'disaster piece' from the Thursday evening's concert. Standing in front of them, Gavin James gave them all a huge smile as Becky gave them the opening notes. The choir were now relaxed. They had all had an enjoyable Friday, a good rehearsal and a good evening concert. They were back at their best, a choir that loved to entertain.

They sang the Stanford and Rutter pieces superbly with the lightness of touch Gavin had asked for. The toning was perfect, every member of The Verlis Singers absolutely determined to make Gavin proud of their performance. As they ended their fourth piece, the Bob Chilcott arrangement of the hymn *Dear Lord and Father,* the audience of about 500, including many of the other choirs gave The Verlis Singers enthusiastic applause. Some of the German young men who had befriended Dominic even stood up and whooped, as did a rather distinguished elderly bass from Sweden who had also made the 'acquaintance' of Dominic the previous evening.

The Philippine choir were sat together. They all stood to applaud the English choir. The Verlis Singers from Cornwall had certainly arrived at the Krakow Choral Festival. During the final break, Gavin and Lizz had gone for a snack together, urged on by Jenny.

'Oh go on Lizz, take him off. I don't mind as Peggy and Ron want me to go with them for a meal. Ron likes his food as you know but I doubt that we'll find a pasty and chips shop here in Poland.'

The conductor and the alto found a park nearby and wandered through it. Lizz slipped her arm through Gavin's and when Becky and Clare appeared and walked past them giggling, Lizz made no attempt to take it away.

Gavin was in high spirits; his choir had come alive and sang as well as he had ever heard them. Whether it was as good as the other choirs really didn't matter. Here he was now with a lady who he knew he was falling in love with. Yes, she was married, yes he still had Georgina texting him every day, but this was where he wanted to be and he was with the person he wanted to be with.

The couple had not embraced since the day before Christmas all those months ago in his car after the hotel sing. Gavin stopped and turned to Lizz, the sun was shining through the trees. He didn't care if all of the Verlis Singers were wandering past. He pulled her gently towards him, and they kissed each other lovingly. Polly Jones had walked into the park with Dominic and the two saw what was happening. Polly turned to Dominic and buried her head in his shoulder.

'There, there Poll,' said Dominic. 'You can't ignore true love when it stares you in the face can you? You will find your man one day, sweety, just wait and see. Meanwhile, you'll just have to put up with me.'

***

In the final festival concert that Saturday evening The Verlis Singers gave their best, with all of the four pieces Gavin had chosen included. Brian and his Polish lady friend were in the audience at St Catherine's Church, which was pretty well packed.

Terry Davies had sent his wife a raunchy text that afternoon, as he was feeling much better after the dismal showing on Thursday night. He would wait until he got back before he told the full story to Joan. Looking ahead, his birthday and wedding anniversary celebrations were all planned for the following weekend. Verlis and Cornwall seemed a long way from where they were, here in the heat of Krakow.

Before The Verlis Singers went onto the stage Gavin spoke to the choir:

'Go out and do what you do best folks, watch me carefully, and let's ENTERTAIN the audience. Enjoy yourselves and after the concert, we'll go out for a drink or two. I hope everyone will come along. I suggest that we all go back to the hotel bar first as some of you will want to freshen up after another day in the sun. There's a big bar area and we do have to be away early tomorrow morning, on the next stage of our tour!'

The Verlis Singers were fourth in a list of six choirs that were to perform. Gavin, Lizz and Jenny decided that they would listen to the choirs before them.

The St Catherine Church was another massive old Catholic building with an amazing acoustic. It would have been difficult for any choir to sing badly in such surroundings. The second choir were the young German group Dominic had befriended. Yes, they were very good, but all of their pieces somehow sounded the same. Gavin wondered if they should have included a lighter piece. This was something the audience wanted to hear. Next came the elderly choir from Hungary who they had heard that morning, about 18 ladies and only 6 men. Gavin smiled when the conductor walked out and they all opened their music folders and most put on their reading glasses. He had heard choirs of older people in England, the vibrato of the sopranos and wobbly aged tenor voices. Gavin shut his eyes when they were singing. They sounded more like a younger choir, it was quite extraordinary. When he got back he was going to find out more European choirs and play them on his Sunday morning radio show. He would make a regular feature of it. UK choirs thought they were all so wonderful. The fact was, however, that the European choirs he had heard over the past two days were far, far superior.

**

Sunday June 19th

The members of The Verlis Singers tour party were all drifting into the hotel reception, ready to sign out and get off to the airport and the next leg of their tour, the concert and the final overnight stay in Rzeszon. Everyone had ended up in the hotel bar the previous evening for a Cornwall celebration. There was a piano, and tenor Alan Younger led the singing. He was one of those people who could sit at the piano and play just about anything in a singalong style. People started to drift away around midnight and Gavin said goodnight to the hangers on. Lizz and Jenny had disappeared at about 11.30pm and it was only a handful of hardy drinkers left. Richard Parish amazed everyone by offering to buy a round and then let it be known that he only had the equivalent of £10 in Polish currency left!

'Never mind,' shouted Pat Nicholls. 'We know you are a tight sod. I'll get the round in as you did sing well tonight Richard. Dear old Len would have been very proud of you.'

***

It was only a short flight from Krakow to Rzeszon and thankfully the temperature had dropped to something more acceptable to a group of overheated Cornish visitors. Seats were not allocated on the flight, it was a free for all and The Verlis Singers virtually filled the whole plane. Rona had always been concerned about the flight plans for this part of the trip, but everything went smoothly.

Tatania was particularly excited as her sister, her parents, and the entire Bakowski clan would be meeting them when they arrived at Rzeszon. She had not seen them all for a couple of years and her sister now had a baby, whom she would see and cuddle for the first time.

They had to fly out from the internal terminal at Krakow airport, which was even more basic than the international shed. If Krakow airport resembled an aircraft hangar, then Jasionka airport on the outskirts of Rzeszon was even more spartan on arrival. When the plane landed after the short flight the choir had to walk to the main block where grumpy-looking security police checked their passports.

As they entered the main hall a young woman shrieked out and came running forward to embrace Tatania. Lena, Tatania's sister, it seemed had brought along all of the Bakowski family, plus half of the members of her ladies' choir. They started to sing a welcome folk song and at the end all of the Verlis party clapped in appreciation at their memorable Polish welcome.

Two rickety old coaches were waiting to take them back to a church hall outside the town where the Polish host families would collect their overnight guests. Cold drinks were served as the choir members set off to their respective homes. The twelve who would stay in the hotel included Gavin and Terry Davies, Richard Parish, Elaine and Terry Bridges, Eric and Karen Stroman, Polly and Dominic as well as Lizz, Jenny and Becky Morris.

It was a tight schedule. They had landed at Rzeszon at midday and the concert was due to start at 7.30 that evening at the main church in the town centre, with a short rehearsal planned for The Verlis Singers in the church at around 6pm. Gavin was looking forward to doing a 'proper concert' that evening, as the choir members set off with suitcases being taken by car to the homes of their Polish hosts. Rona had entrusted Eric Stroman to take charge of the group who had a coach organised to get them to their hotel, which was just off the market square.

Later that afternoon the choir members started to arrive at the Church of Holy Cross in the centre of Rzeszon close to the market square. Polly Jones was in very high spirits. She had received an email from her boss John Stroman. On Tuesday of last week she had attended a review meeting with the partners of the accountancy practice. It had gone very well, amazingly well, as she had been told that her work was 'outstanding' and that the main board were going to make her a junior partner. The email confirmed that to be the case. Polly had told Dominic of the interview and when they met in the reception of the rather shabby hotel to walk to the church she threw her arms around him.

'I've got promotion, Dom, bloody hell I am going to be a junior partner, how about that? Let's have a celebration after the concert tonight. Tonight's the night Dom. I'm gonna get fucking legless!'

***

The ladies' choir were so welcoming to their visitors from England it was almost embarrassing. Nothing was too much trouble and the massive church was packed to capacity for the visit of the famous Cornish guests.

Brian asked Gavin if he could speak to the choir before they sang as he had some news for them. Taff Davies overheard and flippantly wondered if the choir chairman had decided to stay on in Poland and start a new life with his mystery friend from the past.

'I just wanted to have a quick chat with you all before your concert, whilst you are all together. I had a call earlier this afternoon from Lord David Williton and thought I should pass this on to you. As you know there have been several so-called sightings of David Honey after the TV and newspapers reports on his disappearance. It seems that he is in London somewhere, where the Metropolitan Police fraud squad have been investigating a number of, what they refer to as "very strong leads". Although they have not actually discovered where he is yet, the fact that he is still in the UK is a good thing it seems. It's not the best news I know, but David Wilson felt you should all be updated on the latest information. Let's hope for positive information when we get back to the UK and Lord Williton asked me to pass on his congratulations to a certain young lady, on her promotion. I presume you know all about that Polly?'

Polly grinned from the back of the group. That explained why the partners at Stroman Maycroft Accountants had quizzed her about her friendship with Lord Williton during the interview. Being his chum and occasional escort to snooty

Cornish functions was brilliant. Life was good with her brilliant job and great boss, lovely gay Dominic and Moira back in touch, and her cuddly 'old queen', his lordship, David. Yes life was good, even though seeing Gavin and Lizz kiss each other so lovingly had tugged at her heartstrings, for reasons she really didn't quite understand.

***

After the rather strange musical experience and the ups and downs of Krakow, it was good to get back to performing at a good old-fashioned concert. Gavin could actually talk to the audience with Tatania acting as his interpreter. They even managed to get the audience laughing as she struggled with some of his phrases.

The Verlis Singers were back in good voice and, after the final encores, flowers (and tears) from Tatania's family, the hosted choir members were taken off to their Polish homes for the night. The non-hosted people had a short walk back to the small, rather scruffy hotel where they would stay the night, led by an excited Polly Jones.

Everyone was shattered after such a long and tiring day. Richard Parish, Terry Davies and Polly stayed at the bar for a celebration beer and even Dominic headed for his single room shouting across to Polly, 'Hey sexy legs, don't go knocking me up tonight Poll, I've got a bloody headache!'

'I won't be doing that, Dom, you are quite safe tonight,' she replied.

***

Gavin was sitting up in bed reading a book Pat Nicholls had loaned him for the flight tomorrow. He thought it would help him to get to sleep and drive the sound of singing out of his head. He heard a knock at his door. Who would that be at this time of night? Lizz was standing there.

'Hi Gavin. I'm in a single room tonight but I want to be with you on our last evening, can I come in?'

Further down the corridor there was another knock on another door. Single room occupant Taff Davies opened his door to find Polly Jones in just a dressing gown, hair wet and looking as if she had just jumped out of the shower.

'Terry Davies, what is now about to happen is for one night only, never to be told to anyone!'

She pushed past him and shut the door. Putting her arms round him, she let the dressing gown drop off to the floor and kissed him violently and felt his response. 'Turn the light out, we are going to bed, I have something to celebrate,' she said, 'whether you like it or not!'

Chapter 31

Monday June 20th

The tall, well-dressed, dark-haired man was ordering coffee at the busy snack bar in Fishguard. The Saturday morning early Stena Line ferry to Rosslare was due to leave in about 20 minutes. The place was seething with people. Families heading off to Ireland on holiday, a large group of English golfers wearing Pringle jumpers and about a dozen young girls already slightly worse for wear and setting off on a hen party trip dressed up as nuns. One of them was wearing a large red letter 'L' tied around her neck and a giant pink blow-up penis.

The man had chatted to one of the 'nuns' at the counter as she ordered a coffee.

'I'm sure you'll have a wonderful time in Ireland Sister, when is your friend getting married?' he asked with a grin.

'Oh, not until the end of June, we're on a pilgrimage to ravage a few Irish hunks, that's an Irish accent isn't it you have? Where do you come from?'

The man replied that his hometown was Limerick and picked up his tray to return to the table.

As he sat down he saw two men walk into the coffee bar, he felt the hairs on the back of his neck tingle and buried his face in the Ferry glossy magazine on the table. The two men were now standing next to him, one each side. The youngest one spoke:

'Mr David Honey, or Michael Kerry, or even Sebastian

Carter, we would like you to come with us to the police station. You are wanted for questioning on fraud and embezzlement charges. I am Inspector Steve Cox from the fraud squad and this is my Sergeant, Guy Douglas. You have led us quite a dance, Mr Honey, these past weeks, but as the well-worn phrase goes, the game is up! Please come with us now to the station. We would prefer not to handcuff you here in front of all these people, as we don't believe you to be a runner. My Sergeant here has eight London Marathons to his credit so it's highly unlikely you could shake him off! You will see there are also two uniformed officers also standing in the corner, just in case you do fancy a sprint for the door. Stand up now and come with us please,' he ordered.

'And you as well madam!' He spoke to the smartly dressed attractive woman with the short stylish blonde hair and fake tan. 'Mrs Honey, I believe?'

David looked across at Laura Honey and smiled. In his new soft Irish accent he said, 'Ah well sweetheart, it was good while it lasted.'

Chapter 32

The members of the Verlis party were all starting to arrive at Rzeszon airport. Most had been brought by car by their host families and there was another full turnout of Tatania's relatives. The 7am flight was the only one to Krakow that morning, which enabled the Verlis group to get their connecting flight back home from Krakow to Bristol. The choir members staying in the hotel had been brought in by a small bus. Everyone looked pretty jaded and the long journey home with two flights and then the coach back from Bristol beckoned. Arriving back home at Verlis coach park seemed a long time ahead.

Becky Morris was one of the more upbeat members of the group that Monday morning. She had been very upset at the Thursday concert, after fluffing the introduction to the Rutter piece. She knew that she was surrounded by some very talented musicians from the other choirs and some had made it very obvious that her playing was pretty crap that night. For most of the Krakow performance she just had to give Gavin the opening notes as the choir sang unaccompanied. She had perfect pitch and had also had to suffer as she heard the famous Verlis Singers go badly flat at that first performance, just three bars into their first piece.

However she had got to play on the Saturday evening concert in Krakow and last night she knew she was at her best. More importantly, Gavin knew it, and at the end of the concert he presented her with a T-shirt he had bought for her in Krakow. She felt very pleased that he had made an effort for her and he also presented Rona with a glass memento of Krakow, again a surprise gift. The choir members were all impressed by his thoughtfulness. Becky Morris really wanted to be the full-time accompanist to The Verlis Singers, not just a choir tour stand-in.

Pat Nicholls had received a call on his mobile the previous evening. Lord David Williton had some news about David Honey to pass on. The police had told him that Honey had served time with an expert forger who had been released many years ago and was now going straight. The man had not like David Honey whilst they were in prison together and had called the Met Fraud Squad to report that Honey had contacted him as he wanted a new passport.

'I thought you should know, Pat. It's not exactly good news but it does show that the police are closing the net on him.'

Pat Nicholls had decided to keep this to himself for the time being. He'd chat to the chairman later that day when they were back in the UK.

As the tour members started to file onto the plane, Terry Davies chose a seat by the window. He was surprised when a voice said, 'Move over Mr Davies, I'm sitting with you. Were you up with the lark this morning?'

Polly Jones was wearing her yellow Verlis Virgin T-shirt for the trip home. She sat next to Terry and shouted out to Dominic who was sat with Becky Morris a few seats in front.

'Hey Dom, that was a nice old gent you were chatting to after the concert last night. Did he tuck you up in bed before you went to sleep with your mug of Horlicks?'

Dominic ignored his friend and stuck up two fingers in her direction.

There was just one air hostess on the short flight to Krakow and take-off time was crucial to ensure they caught the Bristol connecting flight. Farewells made and tearful moments from the Bakowski family members, everyone was on board and slotted in to their seats. Bang on time, the plane taxied out to the runway. Terry had not spoken to Polly. He had no words to say to her.

The plane took off at just after 7am and started to turn. Terry Davies looked out of the window at the sleepy town of Rzeszon below. For the first, the only time in his life, he had been unfaithful to the lovely Joan Davies. *Christ Terry,* he thought, *what have you done?* As he looked out of the window he saw another plane coming directly at them in the air. It seemed so close, too fucking close. He automatically reached over and instinctively grabbed Polly Jones's arm very tightly.

His mind was racing. *Joan, Joan my lovely Joan what have I done…?*

A piercing scream came from somewhere behind them.

Chapter 33

It was 8am in Cornwall and Mrs Joan Davies was showering on Monday morning. She was excited and joyfully singing out loud, something she rarely did. It had been a late night as she was up till 2am making the table decorations for the very special Davies weekend coming up. She had heard from Jenny, her daughter, the day before that Daniel's parents were flying over from their home in Spain to attend. It would be the first time that Terry and Joan would meet the parents of their son-in-law to be. Joan hoped that Terry would behave himself and would make an extra effort to be nice to her mother!

After the weekend away with the choir, she knew that her husband would be pleased to be back home with her and Brutus. He'd surely be on his best behaviour for their wedding anniversary celebration and his 50th birthday. For some reason the tenor solo her husband Terry had sung at the Christmas concert back in December, the third verse of *In the Bleak Midwinter* was in her head. She sang to herself – '*If I were a wise man I would do my part.*' Terry had spent hours upon hours going over it before the concert at home, so no wonder really that Joan also knew it back to front.

She had got up early and couldn't wait to see her husband again. She loved the Welshman deeply, even though his ridiculous attempts sometimes to be (and sound) more Welsh than he actually was, and his numerous annoying traits, drove her up the wall, he was her man. When she met Terry first when they were at school, he didn't have a Welsh accent, it had sort of 'developed' over the past 25 years. Terry had spent quite a lot of time discovering and researching his ancestry and that had somehow influenced his 'Welshness'. Joan didn't object. He was Terry, her special man.

***

Various lady bodily attentions had been made before and during showering. She would be at her very best for Terry in every way when she welcomed him off the coach later that evening. Joan laughed out loud as she towelled herself dry. Very soon she would be reunited with Mervyn, the 'Mighty Welsh Weapon'. Terry's name for his willy. Joan had only ever seen one willy in her life – Terry's of course, and had never had any interest in any other man, well, not counting Colin Firth (dripping wet) as Mr Darcy of course!

She once enquired why Terry referred to his mighty weapon as Mervyn and was told, 'Mervyn was a Welsh rugby international who stood head and shoulders above everyone and with a majestic head on him. Just like my cock really.'

The last few days had been lonely at night in bed and the truth was that whilst macho-man Taff Davies might LIKE everyone to think he was a super stud this was far from the truth. In recent years it was Joan who had got bored with sex. She had read books and started to lead Terry into a far more sensual and experimental love life. At first, he had been almost prudish about it but she was slowly but surely winning him over.

She had gone out over the weekend and bought herself some very tight jeans, a really nice top and a sexy bra. Yes, Terry Davies was in for some hot loving on return to his wife in Verlis.

Joan had even battled with bathing Brutus the daft dog in preparation for the return of the master! Brutus had been sulking and missing Terry. Even out on walks, Joan had to drag him along. Daft as he was, he loved, and pined for Terry's return. Brutus washing and scrubbing was a job usually left to Terry but she had booked the dog in for a grooming and, after the battle of the bathtub, even Mr Brutus was looking, and smelling, tip top.

The choir had a long journey home today from Bristol Airport and would eventually get back to Verlis late that evening. She would of course be there (with Brutus) to welcome him home to Cornwall. Her sister Sally had visited from Essex for three days and they had enjoyed each other's company. The weather had been fine and they been out on sunny shopping trips all week, and enjoyed a visit to the Eden Project, as well as some coastal walking. Joan had also discussed with Sally the big event of the year coming next week, the joint wedding and 50th birthday celebration. Both agreed that success hinged on keeping their mother and Terry well away from each other.

All preparations were in place. All Terry had to do was get home, throw himself into the party atmosphere, and be extra nice to her mother. There had been numerous text messages and even a phone call early on Saturday morning just before they left for a rehearsal at some church or other in Krakow. She had not heard from him at the other town they were visiting, as the choir had been told that mobile reception there might not be good.

She had bumped into Helen McNeil, wife of the choir chairman in town who had said that she had spoken to Brian who seemed to be having 'a whale of a time'.

The latest text received two evenings ago, however, had been 100% Taff Davies!

Hey gorgeous wife, Tom Jones wants me for a duet,
told him to sod off – see you on Tuesday – any chance
Thursday afty could move forward to Tuesday afternoon
??????? yours hopefully – Mr Darcy (Mervyn)

***

With the noise of the shower, and Mary's singing, she had not noticed that her mobile had been constantly ringing as well as the downstairs phone. As she stepped out of the bathroom she heard both phones. Picking up the mobile, which was closest and in the bedroom, she pressed receive. It was her daughter Jenny. Something was wrong, very wrong, Jenny was screaming down the phone at her mother.

'Mum where the bloody hell have you been, why haven't you answered?'

Joan, all of a sudden, was overcome by a horrible feeling of dread. Her daughter was now crying in a way Joan had never heard before. A young man's voice was now speaking; it was Daniel, her daughter's fiancé.

Joan thought she heard someone banging at her front door. Who could that be at 7.15pm in the morning? Brutus was starting to bark loudly and chase around downstairs. Her world was starting to turn upside down.

'Mrs Davies,' said Daniel. 'Have you not heard the news? It's the choir.' His voice was faltering.

'No, no, WHAT *is* it Daniel?'

'There has been a terrible plane crash in Poland... a collision in the air and the plane with the choir was hit. Mrs Davies... they... they say that many of the passengers have lost their lives! Mrs Davies... they say there may not be any survivors.'

***

Deep Harmony – *Sweet is the work my God, my King*

The VERLIS SINGERS sing their choir 'anthem' in Verlis
Cathedral conducted by Gavin James – March 2011. The verse two
solo is sung by tenor Terry Davies.

www.verlis-singers.org.uk